RAVE REVIEWS FOR GAIL LINK:

"Gail Link was born to write romance!"
—Jayne Ann Krentz

"*All I Ask Of You* is a poignant love story that is destined to touch readers."
—*Romantic Times*

"*All I Ask Of You* is a book to cherish, filled with passion, poignancy, and a marvelous cast of characters sure to win readers' hearts!"
—Raine Cantrell

"*All I Ask Of You* is a well-drawn and scintillating story populated with empathetic characters!"
—*Affaire de Coeur*

"*Never Call It Loving* is a gift to the senses....A provocative read!"
—Kasey Michaels

"*Encantadora* is a sweet battle-of-wills romance with a charming cast of characters!"
—*Romantic Times*

"*Embrace* began at a fast pace and kept it up!"
—Shirl Henke

A LOVE THROUGH TIME

Rachel forgot propriety as she closed the distance between them. "Matthew!" she exclaimed, rushing into his open arms.

His arms closed about her, holding her as close as was possible. Matt breathed in the sweet scent of her hair, the subtle traces of the perfume she favored. How good it felt to feel the solid warmth of her skin through the thin fabric she wore.

"I saw you standing there on the gallery," he said, one hand tangled in the mass of her golden-blonde hair, stroking it until he entwined a fistful around his hand. "I debated with myself about coming to you now, so late at night." Matthew put a few inches between their bodies, tilting his head down to look at her. "I know that I shouldn't be here, that I shouldn't be with you," he stated with a groan, "but, God, I couldn't stay away. It was as if you were somehow calling to me inside my mind, Rachel, asking, no pleading with me to come."

"I was," she revealed shyly, a sweetly serene smile on her face.

"You beckoned me like an angel," he insisted, "promising heaven, and I couldn't resist."

Other *Leisure* and *Love Spell* Books by Gail Link:
ALL I ASK OF YOU
NEVER CALL IT LOVING
ENCANTADORA
WOLF'S EMBRACE

There Never Was A Time

GAIL LINK

LOVE SPELL NEW YORK CITY

To Kasey Michaels:
For being there before and after.
For sharing all the eccentricities of the craft.
For listening.
For the music—we've dreamed the dream;
now may all our fantasies unwind.
Thanks!

LOVE SPELL®

May 1995

Published by

Dorchester Publishing Co., Inc.
276 Fifth Avenue
New York, NY 10001

Printed in the United States of America.

ACKNOWLEDGMENTS

To Suzanne Coleburn—aka "my publicist." You're a special person. Thanks for being in my corner.

To Marti Robb—out of the clouds and into the sun. May your garden always produce bestsellers!

To Susan Scott—thanks for never being more than a phone call away.

To some very special booksellers—to Barbara Cournoyer; to Trish McNeil; to Donita Lawrence; to Donna Young and Bobbie McLane. Thanks for supporting my work!

And to the talented cast of my favorite soap—*Another World*. You guys are the best! Class and sophistication, heart and soul.

Prologue:
Call Back Yesterday

Louisiana, 1864

The woman stood alone before the huge stone monument, which lay nestled under a massive oak tree dripping with Spanish moss.

She was dressed in black, from the lace veil that covered her fashionable black hat to the slippers that covered her feet. Trickles of perspiration ran between her full breasts. It was late September, and the hot, humid weather gathered around her like another layer of clothing. Even now, with evening fast approaching, the sultry temperatures gave no sign of abating.

Gently, she knelt upon the ground, the black silk of her skirt spreading out around her, and

11

placed the bouquet of white roses against the carved stone front. She reached out a black gloved hand and traced the letters in the name so handsomely carved into the marble—*Matthew Justin Devereaux*. Beneath that was the inscription: *And flights of angels sing thee to thy rest.* Then she shyly touched the relief sculpture of an angel above his name.

Before folding her hands in prayer, she made the sign of the cross. She bowed her head, the mother-of-pearl rosary in her hands gleaming richly against her black lace gloves.

Oh Matthew, she thought, tears coursing down her pale cheeks, we had so little time together. It isn't fair.

Do you know what I regret most, my love? she asked silently, lifting her head and staring at the marble. That I never knew the joy of waking up in your arms, of having you hold me so close to your body that our flesh was one.

I can feel no shame, she confessed to herself honestly, for having these thoughts, my love. My only shame is that I never gave in to the depth of my feelings for you. How I wish that I had. Perhaps then I would have memories to cherish rather than an aching, empty heart. Or I could possibly have had your child. Your son or daughter would have been such a comfort to me, something of you to hold and keep. For that, I would have risked any shame, any scandal.

But forgive me, I did not realize that then, my love, she thought. I believed that I could hold

12

myself above the wants of the flesh. I believed that we had all the time in the world for the promise of tomorrow. And I believed you when you told me that you would come back. I trusted you, Matthew! Bitterness at the cruel twists of fate rose within her. You said that not even the war could keep us apart. That we were meant to be together—forever.

She looked down at the rosary in her hands, tears stinging her eyes. It was torn in two, the silver links rent.

Like her heart, it was irretrievably broken.

She lifted her veil, kissing the crucifix before she wrapped it slowly around the roses. One last token, she thought. One last remembrance. He'd given her the rosary, an heirloom from an ancestor.

She touched her gold initialed locket, which gleamed against the dark material of her bodice, her fingers clenching it tightly. Matthew had given that to her also, just before he'd gone away. Their portraits were inside.

Moving closer to the stone, she placed her lips against the surface of the marble, tears spilling freely.

Farewell, my love.

I shall never, ever forget you.

She stood up, walking away from the past, yet knowing that she would always carry it within her heart.

As she moved slowly toward her waiting carriage, she couldn't resist turning her head and giving one last glance at the stone sepulcher.

Someday, somewhere, somehow, Matthew, she vowed silently, we will be together again. If there is justice for lovers, it must be so.

PART ONE:
ONCE UPON A DREAM

Chapter One

"Savannah, you can't marry my brother!" the man shouted, bursting into the wedding chapel just as the minister had asked the question, "Is there anyone here who knows just cause?"

"Joshua," the petite brunette sighed, dropping her small bouquet of wedding flowers as she watched the tall man stride down the aisle. Tears welled in her eyes. "Oh my God, it can't be you," she said, her face blanching from the shock of seeing her supposedly dead husband come back to life. Two years. Two long years. If this was a dream she didn't want to wake up. She couldn't possibly go through this once again. Losing him had been too painful.

The man standing beside the woman watched as his brother rejoined the living. Damn! Jack

Benson thought. Just a few minutes more and Savannah, the woman he'd loved so deeply for years, would have been his. He'd finally persuaded her that it was time to start living again, and the best way to do that would be to marry him. And now Joshua, his bastard half brother, had risen from the grave. He should have known—Joshua had always had a flair for the dramatic.

Joshua, his white teeth flashing in an engaging grin, reached out his tanned hand and caressed the woman's soft cheek. "It's me, darlin'," he said and bent his head, capturing the woman's mouth with his, kissing her passionately.

Savannah Creed nearly swooned with delight to be back in her beloved Joshua's strong arms again. No one kissed her quite like Josh—so savagely tender. She would know the feel of his mouth. No one could fake that. Wasn't that how she'd exposed the man who'd pretended last year that he was Josh, albeit with a surgically altered face? One taste of the impostor's lips and she'd known that it was a setup, that someone was trying to get control of Josh's enormous fortune.

"Oh, baby," he said, his warm baritone delivering the lines in a husky tone, "I missed you so much. Dreaming of you is what kept me alive all that time in the jungle."

Savannah, tears flowing even more freely, slowly pulled the engagement ring, an overly large diamond, from her finger and handed it to Jack. "I'm sorry, Jack, but I can't marry you. I know you understand. I could never love anyone the way I love your brother." She kissed Jack's cheek fondly and turned her attention back to the long-haired, jean-clad man before her. "If you hadn't stopped this, I would have made such a mistake, Josh," she said softly.

Josh smiled again. "I told you, darlin'," he explained, his large hands cupping her gamine face, "no matter what, that I would always come back to you. Nothing, and no one, could ever keep me from you." He drew her to him for another deep kiss.

"Camera two, close-up," the director called out in the control booth. "Hold it just a moment longer. Terrific! Cue theme music." He ground out his stub of a cigarette. "Okay, that's a wrap. Great job, everyone."

The actors relaxed as the cameras went dark. The taping was complete and another episode of the award-winning, number-one soap "Tomorrow's Promise" was history.

The stage manager, Bob, checked a few last-minute details with the director via his mike linkup and smiled broadly.

The cast and crew gathered around the set. Instead of the actors moving toward their assorted dressing rooms to change to their street clothes, and the crew seeing to their duties before everyone called it a night, they all remained where they were, joined by others from nearby sets and the personnel from the control booth.

19

One actress adjusted the terry bathrobe she'd donned to cover up the skimpy teddy she wore beneath, her feet in thick, knee-high socks, as she entered, followed by her TV lover, who wore jogging shorts and a well-worn T-shirt that hugged his massive chest.

The actress playing the role of Savannah Creed burst out laughing. "What a fashion statement, Meg," she said, giggling.

Meg shrugged her shoulders, replying with a wicked grin, "Gee, I thought so." She grabbed for the baseball cap her TV brother wore and plunked it upon her strawberry curls. "Now where's that photographer?" she called out.

"Right here, Miss Carmichael," the thin man said, emerging from the shadows, camera ready, snapping a photo of the actress, who jumped into the arms of another male costar, a venerable older man who played her father. She kicked one leg in the air and waved.

"Well, that ought to get you a feature, at least," stated the smiling, tall blonde who walked onto the set.

"Hell," Meg crowed, "I was hoping for the cover," she responded as she was passed to the brawny arms of her love-scene partner.

The blonde chuckled. Rebecca Gallagher Fraser's rich, warm laugh and good looks could have made her a star on daytime dramas, if she'd chosen. She'd been a fan of soaps since she was a teenager, but for her, the lure had been writing for soaps, not acting in them. That had been her ultimate goal, and through hard work and talent she'd achieved the position of head writer on "Tomorrow's Promise" just a little over 18 months earlier. She'd taken the soap from near the bottom of the daytime ratings to the number-one show for the last four months. Rebecca was damned proud of what she'd accomplished, and she had expected to be with the show for a few more years, at least.

That had been the plan, until the network approached her with a job offer she couldn't refuse two months ago. She would be given her own show to develop to replace an hour's worth of unworkable talk shows currently clogging the network's daytime arteries. Today was her last official day on the set of her soap.

So, in recognition, the cast and crew were throwing her a farewell party, complete with photographers from the leading soap publications to record the event.

A huge cake was wheeled in, with a congratulatory message and a slightly risque couple pictured in frosting. The assembled crowd broke out into wild guffaws at the confectionary treat.

"Somehow, I don't think you'd better get a close-up of the cake, fellas," Rebecca said to the photographers, "at least not for publication. But," she added dryly, "I'd like one for my scrapbook."

Champagne corks popped and glasses were passed around so that all could join in the toast.

"At least it's finally the real thing." Ally James sighed as the bubbly was poured into her fluted glass. "If I had to drink one more glass of sparkling cider I was gonna puke, I swear it," she grumbled good-naturedly. She was truly sorry to see Rebecca go—for many reasons. It had been Rebecca, while she was an associate writer, who'd created the character Savannah Creed. That part had garnered Ally a Daytime Emmy, several best-actress awards from the major soap-opera publications, and bags of fan mail. It had provided her with a role she relished playing, a hefty income, and the man she was engaged to marry, Rebecca's former husband, Ben Tyler.

Rebecca cut the cake. "Chocolate?" she said with an ingenuous look on her face. "How did you ever guess?"

That broke everyone up. Everybody who knew Rebecca knew of her weakness for anything chocolate. Caffeine and chocolate were in abundant supply in her office. They were the two things that she swore got her through a day—especially on a day when her office was the scene of an actor demanding to know, "Why am I being put on the back burner, storywise?" Or another saying, "Rebecca, I've got a surprise for you. I just found out that I'm pregnant. Can you write that into the script?" And there were always the actors who came to her with the ever popular: "I loathe the fill-in-the-blank I'm doing a love scene with. Please can't you help me?"

She'd grown fond of her group, with all their various idiosyncrasies, but the challenge of creating her own soap from scratch was much too good to pass up. She would have six months to come up with the concept and see to the rest of the details.

"Congratulations, Rebecca."

She turned around to see a man standing there, a wide smile on his pleasant face. "Ben," she said, taking his outstretched hands in hers and leaning over to give him a friendly kiss on the cheek. "How great of you to stop by."

"Well, I certainly couldn't miss your last day at the factory, now could I?" he asked, raising one thick blond eyebrow.

Rebecca grinned at his use of her favorite term regarding work—the factory. It was one of their personal jokes. She stepped back and gave her ex-husband the once-over. Ben looked healthy and happy, and every inch the successful corporate lawyer that he was. His endearingly boyish face often fooled opponents into thinking him less experienced than he was, often to his, and his clients', benefit. "You look terrific," she stated.

"So do you, my dear." Ben slipped his arm about Rebecca's waist, enjoying the feel of the silk blouse that she wore. "Now," he asked, "is there a new man in your life?"

Rebecca groaned. "Oh, Ben, not you too?"

He smiled. "Don't give me that, Rebecca." He leveled his tawny-brown gaze at her through his

23

thin wire frames. "I only want you to be happy."

She hugged him. "I know you do, Ben."

"Then tell me. What gives? Are you at least dating someone?"

"No," she admitted, giving a small shake of her head.

"I have a friend—"

Rebecca rolled her blue eyes. "Oh my God, Ben. Spare me. My ex trying to fix me up?"

Ben gave her a fixed stare. "What's wrong with that? You did the same for me, if you'll recall?" he prodded.

"That was different," she protested.

"Bullshit," he shot back, taking the edge off his word with a smile. "You know I still care about you, Rebecca. There's nothing wrong in my wanting to see you taken care of."

"You're sweet, Ben, really you are, and I appreciate your concern," she said with a smile, "but I'm okay."

"Just okay, 'Becca?"

"Please," she responded, "don't get overly distraught about my love life, or lack of one. Right now I have my work, and that's enough."

"I certainly hope that you're not trying to convince me of that fact, my dear, because it won't work. Remember, I'm the man you were married to." He squeezed her hand, a touch of regret in his voice for the past. "I just wish that I could have been what you were looking for, Rebecca. I really do."

Rebecca returned the squeeze. "Maybe I don't

know what I'm looking for," she said with a graceful shrug of her shoulders.

"Oh, but you do, my dear," Ben assured her in a smooth tone. "You most certainly do."

Rebecca was left pondering Ben's remark while he went to find his fiancee, who dashed into his arms, kissing him wildly before all. Rebecca was glad that Ben had apparently found what he was looking for—the right wife for him. A woman who had no problem with passion or showing it. She'd be willing to bet that Ally had no problem with surrendering herself to Ben's lovemaking.

Rebecca's lips curled into an ironic smile. Passion was a part of her business, the lifeblood of the storyline. She wrote love scenes that were erotically charged; she wrote of passion denied, of passion quenched; she crafted dialogue of high drama, ringing every ounce of emotion she could from her actors and the audience.

But Rebecca felt no such great passion in her life, except for her work. Even lovemaking had only been, at best, a merely pleasant experience. She'd admit that she had little real knowledge, having only had one lover, Ben. And she couldn't fault Ben. He'd done his damnedest to elicit some kind of deep response from his wife.

Had she desired further practical lessons in sex, she could have very well taken several of the actors who worked for her, or whom she'd met at various functions, up on their offers. Handsome, virile men were abundant in her business. And some of them Rebecca had found extremely attractive. However, Rebecca wasn't interested in a mere sharing of bodies for a few hours or a few days or even a few months. She couldn't imagine being intimate with anyone she didn't truly care about. A fantasy was one thing; cold reality was another.

Just once in her life, though, Rebecca had wanted to feel the longing, the completeness of total oneness with another person.

In the back of her mind she wondered: Was there someone just for her, waiting, searching, somehow, for her?

When she was younger, she'd thought that person was Ben. But she'd been wrong, mistaking friendship and caring for the soul-shattering dream of love she'd harbored deep in her heart.

When she unlocked her spacious apartment on New York's West Side, Rebecca collapsed back against the door, thankful that her last day on "Tomorrow's Promise" was finally over. After the cake and champagne had come the presents. Some were gag gifts; others were expensive tokens; a few were chosen with care, the givers knowing Rebecca's taste.

Rebecca placed two large fancy gift bags on the floor and sorted through her mail. Nothing that couldn't wait till later. She noticed that the red light on her answering machine was blinking like a warning beacon, and she pressed the button to retrieve her messages.

She began to laugh at the number of calls she was getting from actors—or their eager agents—wanting a chance to be in her new show. Since the announcement had been made, Rebecca had been flooded, both at the office and at home, with tapes of actors, male and female, asking to be considered for a role in her new soap.

Oh, God, she groaned, how long would this keep up? She listened to the calls as she stepped out of her flat brown leather shoes, wiggling her toes. How was she even to begin to think about actors when she still didn't have a notion of where she was going with the storyline? she wondered as she moved toward the spacious kitchen and put on her coffeepot. Several ideas had been perking in her brain, and yet none hit her with the resounding force that would make her say, "Yes, this is it." She wanted something that was different, something that would grab an audience right away, something that had a feel, not only of the present, but of the past. Timeless. Solid. Connected.

Leaving the kitchen, she made her way down the hall into her bedroom. Rebecca heaved a sigh. This was her sanctuary. Like all the rooms in her apartment, it had a high ceiling, giving the feeling of space. A massive queen-size sleigh bed, piled high with an eclectic assortment of pillows in all shapes, sizes, and fabrics, dominated the room. To the right was a TV set and a collection of videotapes in several piles on the bare floor. Rebecca favored the romantic movies of the past, mostly what were then labeled the women's movies—pictures that ranged from screwball comedies to high drama, from Westerns to sophisticated mysteries and rousing swashbuckling adventure. On the opposite wall was an old framed movie poster of *The Mark Of Zorro* with Tyrone Power and Linda Darnell. Next to it was a smaller one of *Casablanca*. She smiled when she thought of the new addition that Meg had given her today—*Robin Hood* with Errol Flynn.

Rebecca removed the hunter-green tailored trousers she wore and the cream silk blouse, anxious to get into relaxing clothes, hoping that the change would somehow ease the tension she felt.

That accomplished, she went back to her kitchen, popping a frozen pizza into the microwave and pouring herself a generous mug of coffee. She sprinkled a little dash of cinnamon into the rich brew and added cream.

Perhaps she should have taken Ben and Ally up on their idea to go out to dinner?

Rebecca shook her head. No, she decided, that really wouldn't have been a very smart idea. To be out with her ex and his soon-to-be bride was asking for trouble, especially with the mood she was in.

And just what the hell kind of mood was that? Rebecca pondered as she removed the pizza-for-one from the microwave, cutting a slice and devouring the pepperoni and sausage.

Unsettled was the closest word she could come up with.

Chapter Two

Now, Rebecca thought as she fixed herself a cup of coffee the next morning, just what was it that she had to feel unsettled about?

She heard the sharp ring of the phone and let the machine pick it up as she walked into her living room. She was glad that she had. It was only another agent calling for two of his clients, promising that tapes of them would be sent to her by messenger later that day.

Rebecca sipped her coffee. Was this what she had to look forward to for the next six months?

She curled up on her sofa, listening to the sound of the rain as it beat upon the leaded glass windows. It felt so strange not to be at work, having staff meetings, reading some of the viewer mail, going over changes that had to be made, or just watching the taping.

Restless, she returned to the kitchen for another cup of coffee, and the phone rang again. As soon as she heard the voice of her doorman, she picked up the receiver.

"Another package?" she said with a weary shrug of her shoulders. "Just bring it up, if you wouldn't mind."

Rebecca walked to the door and heard the old-fashioned elevator make its way up. She stood there, a bright smile on her face for the doorman. He was a retired cop in his late fifties, and his presence made the tenants of the building feel all that much more secure.

"Thanks, Mr. Slovak. I appreciate your doing this."

The big man, standing over six feet two inches, gave her a wide grin. "Happy to do it for you, Miss Rebecca," he said, his voice betraying his Bronx upbringing.

She took the large envelope and felt its weight. Another video cassette. "I have a feeling that you're gonna find that I'll be getting a few more of these kinds of packages today," she told him. "If I do, just keep them downstairs and I'll get them later. Believe me, there's no big rush on these things," she said.

"Okay," he said, going back to his duties as Rebecca added the newest envelope to the pile on her hall sideboard.

She looked at the growing collection, blankly

staring at them for a minute until a quick flash of an idea hit her.

Rebecca dashed into her bedroom and went straight to her closet, pulling out one of her suitcases. She quickly opened drawers, flinging clothes into the case, along with a few paperbacks from the nightstand. She added several pairs of jeans, some thick sweaters, and a couple of practical shirts to the mix.

She'd be damned if she was going to stay cooped up in here with the incessant ring of the phone and the constant stream of video cassettes and faxes arriving. She'd never get any serious work done that way.

What she needed was a change of scene, someplace where she could be alone to think and work away from this maddening crowd, and she knew just where to go.

A late-spring snow blotted the landscape white as Rebecca pulled up into the driveway of her family home in Stowe, Vermont, later that day. A large, sprawling stone farmhouse stood bathed in the light of the moon and snow combined, giving it a glowing presence. Smoke curled from the main chimney.

Rebecca smiled as she parked the car in the large garage that was separate from the house, added only about 40 years ago. Several lights were on, giving a welcoming feel to the place. When Rebecca had stopped for a late lunch, she'd called her neighbors, the Robertsons, and asked if they would light a fire in the largest of the fireplaces, the one in the living room, and turn on some lights.

She fit her key into the lock, pushing her suitcase inside, and went back out to fetch her laptop computer. Shutting the door, Rebecca breathed a deep, contented sigh. Here she had no doubt she would find peace.

Rebecca loved this house. It was where she'd grown up, and it had been in her family since the early 1800s. It was hers now, her parents having deeded it to her when they decided to retire to the sun of New Mexico a few years earlier. She used it infrequently of late, since she usually remained in New York due to her heavy and hectic workload.

But now she could relax and appreciate it. Time was finally on her side.

The smell of something aromatic cooking drew her into the kitchen. The floor was brick, with a large bird's-eye maple table centered there. Several braided rugs were scattered throughout the room, giving it a homey touch. A deep green Crockpot was plugged in on the counter. Rebecca lifted the glass lid and sniffed the contents. Fresh chicken and rice soup, with hearty chunks of vegetables, simmered inside.

It was then that she saw the handwritten note next to the Crockpot. Removing her coat and hanging it over the back of one of the chairs, she picked up the slip of paper and read:

Dear Rebecca:
I thought that you'd probably be hungry when you got home and in no mood to fix a proper meal, so here's a little something for you. There are corn muffins in the basket and I stocked the fridge also.
If you need anything else, don't hesitate to call. When you get settled in, come on over for lunch or dinner—that's up to you.

Rebecca saw the small basket decorated with ivy leaves and covered with a lace cloth. Nicole Robertson was an artist, whether it was doing her own line of recycled, hand-painted stationery—the piece Rebecca held had a small red squirrel at the top—or fixing a basket so that something plain was made delightful or making a delicious home-cooked meal. Rebecca envied her the last skill, as her own repertoire in the kitchen was severely limited.

Since it was after nine in the evening, and the drive in from New York had been a long one, Rebecca wanted only to get out of her clothes, curl up in front of the fireplace, relax, have a bowl—or two—of the soup, and crash.

She did just that.

"I will come back for you."

Rebecca awoke quickly, looking around. Had she really heard that masculine voice? Or had it been a dream? She shivered with apprehension. It had sounded so real, as if whispered fervently into her ear.

She shifted slightly, listening for any noises.

God, she was getting paranoid. It was just a dream, for heaven's sake. If it were an intruder, she doubted seriously that he would announce himself to her.

But the voice had been so clear, so distinct—a deep voice with traces of an accent. Rebecca's brow wrinkled in concentration. It had been a smooth Southern accent, slow and melodious. And the speaker had been vehement, as if he'd been making an impassioned promise, a solemn pledge.

The rest of the dream had been vague. She could only recall warmth and the intoxicating smell of jasmine.

Rebecca stood, stretching to ease her cramped muscles. It was definitely time for bed, she decided, taking care of the fire in the hearth. Casting a glance at the empty soup bowl and the half-finished bottle of white zinfandel, she concluded that it must have been her imagination working overtime.

Gathering up the tray, she carried it back to the kitchen. The clock on the wall read one A.M.

When she finished tidying up, Rebecca made her way up the stairs. Entering her bedroom, she saw that the bed was unmade. She'd completely forgotten to check before she'd eaten.

Rebecca didn't really feel like going to the trouble of making it up just then, being far too tired. All she really needed was one of her mother's many antique quilts, collected over the years and stored in the third-floor loft, to throw over herself. Rebecca recalled that, when she was younger, she'd loved exploring up there, selecting the treasured pieces of work that they would use for the bedrooms and for decorating the various sofas.

One of Rebecca's favorites was a very old quilt that had been sewn by her great-great-grandmother in tribute to her homeland of Ireland. It was a special piece of work done in shades of white and green with embroidered roses. It was that quilt she had to have tonight.

Climbing the short flight of stairs, Rebecca flicked on the light and walked into the room. She located the cedar-lined mahogany armoire that stood against one wall. Here her mother stored all the precious linens and quilts.

Running her palm against the wood, as if absorbing the memories stored there, Rebecca finally opened one of the doors, comforted by the smell of cedar, fresh and crisp inside. This armoire was an antique also, the property of her great-great-grandmother, Rachel. The name of the maker was still visible inside—P. Mallard, New Orleans—etched on a brass plate.

She went through the stack of quilts, locating the one she wanted on the very bottom of the pile. When she slipped her hand inside to pull that one out, Rebecca felt another small object. Her fingers touched a piece of metal, and she drew it out along with the quilt.

It was a key on a slim velvet ribbon.

Curious, Rebecca examined the key and wondered what it was for and why it was hidden. She couldn't remember her mother saying anything about a key before.

Yawning, Rebecca knew she was too tired to search the room for whatever it was that the key would unlock.

She shrugged her shoulders. There was always tomorrow. There wasn't any particular reason why she should be in a hurry. Better to explore this room in the daylight when she could give it her full, wide-awake attention.

She placed the key upon the top quilt and, on a whim, opened one of the bottom drawers. Inside, wrapped in tissue paper, were several nightgowns, all made of cotton and lace. Rebecca smelled a hint of jasmine as she lifted one from the drawer. Jasmine—the fragrance in her dream. She held the nightdress up; it was delicate and very simple with a square neck and hem edged in a small band of lace.

Why not wear it tonight? she asked herself.

Because I'll probably freeze my butt off, she responded.

The garment was made for a hot, sultry night, guaranteed to raise the temperature of any man privileged to see the woman in it. Not because it was overt; rather, Rebecca judged, because it was a nightgown suited to the tempting innocence of a bygone era. It revealed while it concealed, wrapping the wearer in seductive modesty.

Perhaps some other time, Rebecca promised herself. But not in mid-April in Vermont. That wouldn't be a very wise move.

She returned the nightgown to the drawer and scooped up the quilt. Stifling another yawn, she reluctantly closed the door to the loft.

Tomorrow would suffice for explorations.

The next morning Rebecca awoke late. She turned over and picked up her watch from the bedside table, noting the time. It was after eleven o'clock. Rebecca couldn't recall the last time she'd slept past seven. One night here had already altered her usual frantic pace. She felt refreshed, revitalized. She had energy to burn.

After having a long, hot shower, Rebecca dressed and made her way downstairs for a late breakfast. The wide windows in the kitchen provided a spectacular view of the Green Mountains. She could see the sheen of snow covering Mt Mansfield and imagined a few die-hard skiers were enjoying the spring bounty. Her hometown made a lot of its collective living on servicing the ski trade. Mike, Nicole's husband, had a superb French restaurant nestled in the woods. During ski season, it was staffed by men and women drawn to the superb conditions that the mountains offered.

Rebecca picked up the phone and dialed the country restaurant, thinking that Nicole might be there. She was proved right when her friend picked up on the second ring.

"Hello," Rebecca said, pouring a large mug of freshly brewed coffee and adding cream. "Glad I found you there. I wanted to thank you for the care package last night. That soup really hit the spot." Rebecca took a sip while Nicole talked.

"I'm glad. So what brings you up here now?" Nicole asked, knowing that Rebecca's normally busy schedule didn't leave much time for visits back home.

Pride threaded through Rebecca's voice. "I got a fantastic job offer," she said. "I get to create a new daytime drama for the network."

"Oh, Rebecca," her friend responded enthusiastically, "I know how much that must mean to you. To be able to do what you want, how you want."

"Yes," Rebecca said, "I'm a very happy camper."

Nicole considered the situation. "Then why aren't you holed up in New York working your buns off?"

"Because I got so damned tired of my phone ringing nonstop with agents and actors calling and wanting to be considered for the new show. And," Rebecca said, then paused to take another sip of her coffee, "I needed a respite from all the audition videos arriving at my door. My apartment was beginning to get swamped with the stuff. I left word that anything else was to be put in storage and I'll see to it later.

"Hell," she said with a sigh, "I don't even know what I want to do with this hour yet. How am I gonna tell who would be right for what if I don't have a clue yet myself?"

Nicole laughed softly. "Oh, yes, I guess it must be so"—she drawled that word out—"tough to sit down and view those hunky dudes all day long. Gee," she said with an exaggerated sigh, "if you need any help forming an opinion, please don't hesitate to call."

"As if you'd ever look at any man other than Mike," Rebecca teased.

"Hey there, friend, I'm married, not dead," Nicole said emphatically with a hearty laugh. "No harm in looking." Her mouth curved into a smile. "Besides, you know the only man who could really tempt me would be Frank Langella waltzing into either my shop or this restaurant. Other than him, old Mike is pretty safe." Nicole, seven years older than Rebecca, had seen the actor give his mesmerizing performance on Broadway in *Dracula*, and ever since then, she'd harbored a very soft spot for the handsome, sensual actor. "Now," Nicole said, "if you could find an actor who looked like him and cast him in the soap in a prominent role, that would be a real treat."

Rebecca laughed. "I promise that, should I find anyone who even remotely resembles him, I'll give you a copy of the tape."

"You'd better," her friend insisted. "So are

you free for lunch?" Nicole asked, switching topics.

"I only got up an hour ago," Rebecca confessed, "and I'm just having breakfast now."

"Okay," Nicole responded, "how about coming over for dinner this evening?"

"That sounds great," Rebecca said. "I want to get things together here, and by the time I'm finished, a meal out will be most welcome." Rebecca didn't mention that she was planning on scouring the attic to find whatever it was the key unlocked.

"Shall I arrange to have an extra man at the table?" Nicole asked.

Rebecca shook her head and stifled a groan. Another matchmaker. "That won't be necessary," Rebecca said, her tone of voice conveying to her friend just what she thought of that idea.

"I get the message, Rebecca. I promise, no surprises," Nicole stated. "Is eight okay for you?"

"Yes, that should be fine," Rebecca agreed.

"See you then."

Rebecca poured herself a refill and headed back up the staircase, eager to explore. When she entered the attic loft again, she pulled the key from the pocket of her jeans. Just why finding what the key fit was so important to her, she couldn't fathom. It simply was.

Rebecca looked around the room for something the key might open, poking her head around boxes, shifting a large trunk, but with no luck.

In the corner was a white iron daybed piled with accent pillows. Rebecca knew her mother had often put things either underneath or behind the daybed, out of the way. She walked to it and checked, bending down and looking underneath, smiling when she discovered a small wooden chest hidden behind it. She reached for the chest and drew it out.

Sitting on the daybed, Rebecca tried the key in the lock. It was a perfect fit. She opened the lid and a delighted gasp of surprise burst from her lips. Inside the cedar box were several notebooks. Rebecca opened one and saw the date, 1860, and the place, New Orleans, written inside, along with the name of the writer—Rachel Gallagher. A bundle of letters, the faded ink almost indecipherable, was wrapped in a lilac velvet ribbon that matched the ribbon that held the key. Several scraps of material also filled the crowded treasure box. Picking up one, a midnight-blue silk, she found it protected a single photograph. Stamped on the back was the name E. Jacobs.

Rebecca turned it over. She was riveted by the handsome face that stared back at her, a hint of a smile on his mouth. It was the eyes that captured Rebecca's attention most, though. She couldn't tell what color they were, of course, but for some reason she presumed that they were a shade of blue. They were pen-

etrating, seductive eyes, set in a most haunt-
ingly masculine face, with a wide, high
forehead and thick, slashing dark brows and
curling dark hair. Altogether, a man most
women would stop and give a second glance to
and, she suspected, a third look as well.

Several minutes ticked by before Rebecca
could tear herself away from the photograph
and the vague sensation that the man wasn't a
stranger to her.

And that, of course, was ridiculous. He was
long since dead and gone, judging by the
clothes that he wore, and the date beneath the
photographer's name, 1861.

But who was he?

Rebecca knew that it wasn't her great-great-
grandfather. She'd seen an old photograph of
Barrett Fraser and his wife, Rachel, and he
looked nothing like the man in this picture.

Finally tearing her gaze away from the picture, Rebecca explored further, finding a delicate lace-edged handkerchief with a butterfly
motif embroidered on the material. Inside was
a locket of gold on a slender chain. It was a marvelous piece of jewelry, with a filigreed set of
initials intertwined: *R* and *M*. Rebecca pressed
the snap and it opened, revealing two miniature
portraits—a man and a woman.

Rebecca recognized the woman—it was her
great-great-grandmother, Rachel—and the
man was the one in the photograph.

Rebecca shivered. The artist had captured a

color so richly blue that even after all these years, the man's eyes were still riveting. And Rachel's hair was the same shade of natural golden blonde that Rebecca possessed.

Unable to resist, Rebecca picked up the locket and placed it over her head, letting it nestle in the hollow between her breasts. She closed the snap with a soft click.

She picked up one of the leather-bound diaries and momentarily debated whether or not she should read it. Would she be invading her ancestor's privacy?

Well, yes, technically, she mentally answered.

But, Rebecca reasoned, if Rachel hadn't wanted them to be read, she could have destroyed them.

Maybe Rachel wanted them to be found eventually. Perhaps her writings contained some hint as to the identity of the man in the portrait and the photograph. The man Rachel hadn't wed.

She must have loved him very much, Rebecca thought. Or maybe I'm just being fanciful, seeing something with my writer's imagination that isn't really there at all.

But Rebecca knew that she was right. She felt it, deep in her heart. Rachel had loved this man enough that she never forgot him, even though she wed another.

Rebecca envied that kind of love.

She made herself comfortable on the iron daybed and began to read:

Today I met the man whom I want to be my husband. Oh, faith—I know that sounds foolish—I've just laid eyes on him, but 'tis true. Nothing will ever be the same for me again.

How can that be? My heart has met its keeper. . . .

Chapter Three

Louisiana, 1860

Rachel Gallagher watched the man ride across the lush grass on the back of a spirited stallion. It was one of her papa's best horses, she thought proudly, and a perfect match for the rider. They moved as one. She stood there, under the shade of a live oak dripping with Spanish moss, the warmth of the day wafting around her, along with the scent of the jasmine that grew nearby.

The masculine rider put the animal through its paces, discovering what the horse could handle. Rachel's breath caught in her throat as she watched the man move the big red horse toward the three large stone jumps, each one successively higher than the previous. Horse and rider took each one cleanly, sailing over the obstacles with a minimum of fuss, to the cheering of the spectators, both black and white, who had gathered around the whitewashed fence.

"Faith," boomed the big voice of Connor Gallagher, Rachel's father, "I knew the lad could handle that bloody stubborn horse. See, me darlin'," he said to his daughter, pointing to the rider as the man took the mount over the jumps again, this time at a gallop. Vicarious pride rang in his voice.

Rachel's white-gloved hands were clenched at her sides in fear. *He* was taking too great a risk. What if the animal balked? He could be hurt or, worse, killed. Even as fear gripped her, Rachel couldn't look away. Her unblinking eyes followed the man and the horse until they'd cleared the last hurdle, again to overwhelming approval from the assembled crowd.

She blinked then and let out the breath that she'd been holding. Her papa was right, as he usually was in matters pertaining to horses: the rider was magnificent.

"Would *mademoiselle* care for some refreshment?" a smooth-as-honey feminine voice asked.

Rachel turned and stared at one of the most beautiful women she'd ever seen. Tall, with a turban of cherry red wrapped around her head, she had skin the color of *cafe au lait* and eyes of deepest gold.

"Why, yes, I would, thank you," Rachel murmured, accepting the tall glass filled with crushed ice and lemonade. Ice was a precious—and expensive—commodity in the South. It was shipped down the Mississippi and carefully stored so that the rich planters could make use of it in their households, especially on days like that day.

Rachel sipped the drink, enjoying the sweetly tart taste on her tongue. For a girl who before had drunk only milk or tea, each new beverage she'd sampled since her arrival in New Orleans only six months before was a delight to be savored. The rich taste of the coffee found at the Cafe du Monde had quickly seduced Rachel; now she insisted on drinking it upon waking each morning.

Almost everything about this section of Louisiana, and New Orleans especially, was fascinating to Rachel. Life here was so different from what she was used to at the boarding school she'd attended in her native Ireland. There, she'd belonged in a very feminine world, with little or no contact with the masculine sex, save for the occassional farm boy or village elder.

Here too the men were different—excitingly so. Gallant. Willing, if this man were any indication, to take a dare or challenge. They were, she'd observed, both courtly and charming.

"Name your price."

At the sound of a rich, masculine voice, Rachel raised her head and looked up into the face

49

of the man on the horse.

What she saw there was her destiny. She knew it as she knew her own name. In that instant, everything changed in her life. Love had accomplished that transformation. Swift, sudden, and sure.

With that man, there would be no boundaries, no even keel. It would be all or nothing.

"Five thousand, just as we agreed," Connor Gallagher replied, pleased that the horse and man suited each other so well.

"I would have paid twice that amount," the man stated honestly, dismounting, one of his hands stroking the stallion's neck and cream-colored mane.

Rachel was fascinated by his large, tanned hands and long, slender, strong fingers. She could well imagine such hands wielding a fencing weapon with great skill, lifting a delicate wineglass, dealing a deck of cards, or holding a woman close as they danced beneath a sultry Louisiana sky.

" 'Tis well aware I am that you would have, lad, but when Connor Gallagher gives his word on something, that's as it shall be."

"Done then," came the tall man's reply as he extended his hand toward Connor.

They shook, and it was then that the man saw Rachel standing there. He smiled, revealing even white teeth against his tanned face. It was a generous smile, lighting up his very blue eyes.

"May I present my daughter, Rachel, *mon-*

sieur," Connor Gallagher said, his face glowing with pride as he introduced his offspring. "Rachel, this is Matthew Devereaux."

Rachel wet her dry lips with a quick flick of her tongue. She had heard his name before; he was the scion of one of Louisiana's first families. A wealthy young Creole-American of impeccable lineage who was first in the hearts of the marrying mamas. She could scarcely believe that this man actually existed, so legendary was his prowess. He could dance longer, ride faster, shoot straighter, and hold his liquor better than any ten men in any parish in Louisiana. Whispers of his skill with an épée abounded, as did rumours of a beautiful quadroon mistress in Rampart Street. All this and more Rachel had gleaned from some of the younger American female residents of the Garden District, who couldn't resist the stories connected with and about a Devereaux.

"*Enchanté*, Miss Gallagher," Matthew Devereaux said, taking her gloved hand and bringing it to his lips.

Rachel trembled, even though his mouth hadn't actually made contact with her bare flesh. She was afraid that she was blushing, so warm did she feel.

"I am ever so pleased to make your acquaintance, Mr. Devereaux," she responded, giving him a tender smile.

"Won't you both stay and join me for luncheon?" Matthew asked.

Connor hastily glanced in his daughter's direction before answering. "Be happy to, my boy," he said in his direct manner.

"Good." Matthew Devereaux turned and called to a lanky lad of about 14. "Jason, come here."

The boy did his bidding quickly, a wide smile on his dark face.

"So what are you to be naming this fine beauty, Mr. Devereaux?" Connor inquired.

Matthew regarded the big red stallion with a thoughtful gaze. He considered for a moment before he spoke. When he did, his blue eyes gleamed with a devilish light. "Would you care to do the honors, Miss Gallagher?"

Rachel raised her gaze to Matthew's, heat suffusing her face. "If you wish," she said.

"I would be most pleased," he responded warmly.

Rachel thought for a moment, giving her attention to the proud-looking animal. "Cimarron," she said.

Matthew Devereaux gave Rachel a rakish smile, showing his approval of her choice. She'd come up with the Spanish word for wild, untamed. A clever name for this animal, he thought. He gave her a small nod of his head, thick black waves of hair curling about his face. "*Merci trés bien*, Miss Gallagher, for your most inspired choice."

"Take Cimarron to the stables, Jason," Matthew said, giving the reins to the young groom,

"and see that he has an extra treat in his feed."
He smoothed his hand along the big stallion's
flank. "Give him special attention with the cur-
rycomb too."

"Yes, sir," Jason responded, leading the horse
away, speaking softly in a soothing patois to the
large animal as he did so.

"If I may?" Matthew asked, holding out his
arm so that he could escort Rachel.

She looked toward her father for permission.
When Connor nodded with pleasure, Rachel
placed her arm atop Matthew's and they made
their way to the plantation house. She was conscious of the fact that he shortened his long
strides to hers and of the warmth that emanated
from him. Beneath the fabric of his pale gray
frock coat, Rachel could feel the rippling play
of muscles in his arm.

As they sauntered along the path, Rachel
sensed that there was something wild and untamed, much like the stallion, about this very
picture of Southern manhood.

The house itself was bigger than anything Rachel had ever seen since coming to this country.
It was a grand home, with stately moss-covered
oaks flanking each side, like guardian sentinels.
Massive columns held up the roof of the second
floor; a long balcony with grilled black ironwork surrounded the upper level on three sides.
This provided shade for the first floor, where
red bricks also ran the length of the house on
the three sides. French doors adorned both lev-

els, several open now to catch the languid breeze, white lace curtains fluttering gently. Sunlight dappled the lush grass as they approached. A large dog stood to one side of the house, warily watching before he sprang toward them.

Rachel halted, her eyes wide as she watched the huge beast race the few feet that separated them from the porch. The dog stopped and barked in recognition, pushing its head toward his master's hand.

"What is it?" she asked, standing still, her eyes never leaving the beast.

Matthew laughed. "A little bit of this and that," he said. "I won him in a card game two years ago."

"You gambled for a dog?" she asked incredulously.

"On this occasion, yes, I did. The dog had been mistreated and I wagered the owner five double eagles for the animal."

At Rachel's curious look, Matthew said, "A double eagle is a twenty-dollar gold piece, Miss Gallagher."

Rachel was impressed. "You were willing to risk losing that sum to save the dog?"

Matt shrugged his broad shoulders. He didn't elaborate on the story.

What a strange, interesting man, Rachel thought as he ushered her into the cool depths of the house.

"Angelique," Matt called softly, and the red-turbaned woman came gliding into the room.

"*Oui*, monsieur," she asked, her voice a sooth-ing balm.

"Take Miss Gallagher to one of the upstairs bedrooms so that she may freshen up before luncheon. Are Mama and Marguerite within the house?"

Angelique gave Matthew a knowing smile. "The mistress is with your papa in their room, and your sister is playing with her dolls."

Matt chuckled. "*Eh, bien*, Angelique." He re-linquished Rachel's arm and tilted his head to-ward Connor Gallagher. "Mr. Gallagher, can I interest you in a glass of wine while we con-clude our business?"

"You may indeed, my boy," he answered, giv-ing his daughter's gloved hand a reassuring pat as she ascended the huge winding stairway to the second floor.

Rachel's gaze lingered on the portraits of Matthew Devereaux's ancestors that lined the walls. One woman in particular caught her eye. The painting depicted a handsome woman in her later years, stiffly proud, yet with a glimmer of humor in her blue eyes and a touch of wick-edness to her mouth.

Angelique paused, watching. "That was mon-sieur's great-grandmother, Baroness Made-leine-Anneé de Chartier. She was a great beauty and much loved by her family."

Rachel could detect the family resemblance between the baroness and Matthew Devereaux.

Each seemed blessed by the ability to draw people toward them, to intrigue with the merest hint of a smile.

They continued their way to the top of the stairs, where Angelique showed Rachel into a large, comfortably appointed room, with a massive canopied bed of walnut dominating one wall. Sheer white bed curtains, which were used at night to protect the sleeper from mosquitoes, were pulled back with a thin gold-braided chain of silk and tied loosely to the carved bedposts. Marble-topped night tables stood at each side, a silver branch of candles atop each. An armoire stood at one side of the capacious room, and a tufted aubergine velvet chaise on the other.

"Faith!" Rachel exclaimed, marveling at the loveliness of the bedchamber. Her room in the boarding school had been plain and utilitarian. There, excessive frills were discouraged in favor of practicality. This, Rachel thought, was absolutely luxurious.

"I shall return with water for your toilette, mademoiselle," Angelique said, a warm smile on her face.

Rachel blinked. "Yes, thank you, Angelique. I would appreciate that," she said, feeling almost overwhelmed by the room.

With the door shut, Rachel cautiously explored the room, not wanting to disturb anything. Her mama would love this room, Rachel reflected. It was the pampered domain of a woman who loved beauty. Removing her gloves, she trailed her fingers along the sheer bed curtains—soft, so very soft. She adjusted her wide skirt and sat carefully upon a small sofa at the end of the bed piled with petit-point pillows. She examined the embroidery and smiled in appreciation of the skill of the worker. A spaniel decorated one pillow; another held a forest-glade scene of a doe and fawn.

A soft knock sounded at the door and Angelique reentered. She carried a copper pail of water and poured it into a porcelain washbasin. She removed a small bottle of purple-colored glass from the deep pocket of her skirt and uncapped it. "Essence of violets, mademoiselle. Do you have any objections?"

"None," Rachel responded.

Angelique poured a small amount of the scent into the warm water. She gave a delicate sniff and was satisfied with the results.

"Do you have need of anything else, mademoiselle?"

Rachel couldn't think of anything and said so, removing her bonnet and placing it upon the vacated sofa.

"I shall leave you then and come back within a half hour. The family will be down then for their midday meal."

"Thank you so much, Angelique."

Another warm smile was Angelique's response to Rachel's words of praise.

Rachel made her brief ablutions and felt refreshed. As she buttoned her bodice, her thoughts drifted once again to the man known as Matthew Devereaux. Her pulse quickened with the memory of his face, with the thought of his deep, intensely seductive blue eyes.

Fortune's wheel had turned, and he was the one: her own Prince Charming, her brave knight, her heart's true measure. Without warning, he'd captured her love, for now and, she knew, for all time.

Rachel's generous mouth curved into a secret smile. He might not know it yet, but that was of no consequence. She did.

"So you've only recently come to America, Miss Gallagher?"

"Aye, that's correct," Rachel answered Matthew's mother, taking another spoonful of the delicious cream soup thick with chunks of crawfish, onions, and potatoes. "I was in boarding school whilst my parents came to America; then I stayed on to help with some of the younger girls."

"You enjoyed teaching?" Frances Devereaux asked.

"Very much so, madame," Rachel responded enthusiastically, her blue eyes alight with satisfaction. "It was a great pleasure for me to help prepare them. I looked upon it as a grand opportunity to see to it that they were given a chance to experience more of the world than could be found in their villages."

"However did you manage that?" Matt asked. He'd been unable to take his eyes off her since she entered the room, or, truth be told, since he'd first caught sight of her standing beneath the oak. It was more than mere loveliness, for Matthew had met other women far more sophisticated and beautiful than Miss Gallagher. Just what it was he wasn't really certain. If he'd believed in magic, he would have thought himself caught in a sorceress's enchanted spell.

Rachel found herself staring momentarily at Matthew before she broke free of his captivating glance.

"By giving them the gift of reading, monsieur. With that, they can go anywhere, live other lives, see other things. Knowledge, I believe, is the best foundation for life."

"Gets that from her mother, she does," Connor Gallagher interjected with a fond twinkle in his eye for his daughter. "Her mama's quality, and she instructed our girl well. Me, well"—he shrugged his big shoulders—"I never had much time for book learning."

Rachel returned her father's loving glance with one of her own. "What my papa is trying to say is that in some circles in Ireland, an education was considered a waste for a young Catholic man."

"Yet what of your mama?" asked Frances.

"She was one of the English gentry, madame, and therefore," Rachel pointed out, "she was availed of a suitable education befitting her status."

" 'Tis another reason why I came to this country," Connor pronounced. "Here a man's a man and bother about religion. In my country, 'tis sad that you are your faith first before all else." Connor picked up his wine goblet and drained the contents.

It was the first time Rachel had ever heard her father make a comment laced with such bitterness about his homeland.

"We have some pressing problems in our own country, Mr. Gallagher," Matthew stated. "If they are not addressed soon, we shall be forced, I'm afraid, to 'Cry havoc! and let slip the dogs of war.' "

"I don't think that your mother wants her table troubled with talk of that sort just now, Matthew," the senior M. Devereaux said.

Frances Devereaux gave a fond glance toward the other end of the table at her husband of 27 years, Eduoard, who reciprocated the gesture.

"We must have your mama for a visit soon," she insisted, speaking to Rachel.

"She would love that, madame." Rachel knew that Kathleen Ainsley Gallagher had given up much to wed her poor Irishman, least of which was acceptance by her peers. A chance to get to know someone like Frances Devereaux and visit a house like this would do her mother a world of good. Rachel had the feeling that her warm-hearted mother and Matthew's would get along famously.

"Excellent," Frances said, "then it shall be soon." She looked across the table at her son, whose eyes were on their lovely guest. "Yes, very soon, I think."

Rachel flushed, her gaze meeting that of Matthew. It was she who dropped her glance first, concentrating once more on her soup. Surreptitiously, she lifted her lids and sneaked a look at him, at the way he curled his lean fingers around the stem of his crystal wine goblet. On his left hand she noted that he wore a small gold and topaz ring on his little finger. The stone shone brightly, like a drop of burnished gold frozen in time. It suited him, she decided, more so than a fancier stone would have. This was something different, something that said he made his own rules rather than following society's, which might have dictated another, more expensive stone, a diamond, for instance, a sapphire, or a ruby.

Servants removed the soup and returned with a selection of cold meats and cheeses, and fresh loaves of still-warm bread.

Rachel indulged her appetite, constantly aware of the man who sat across the table from her. She listened as he spoke of horses to her father and his. She was sure that he could have been quoting the price of fish in the marketplace and she would have thought his voice wonderful to hear. There was such joy in the way he used words, much like the Irish, she thought.

"Do you ride, Miss Gallagher?" Matthew asked after luncheon as they strolled across the grounds, leaving his parents and her father on the veranda sipping their cool drinks.

Rachel slid a sideways glance up at him. "A little," she replied, knowing that riding a very placid little mare was hardly in the category of what she'd seen him do earlier.

"Then would you consider riding with me one afternoon soon?" he inquired, stopping beneath a large oak.

Rachel answered quickly, without hesitation. "I would be most happy to do so, sir."

"Matthew, please," he coaxed.

Rachel felt her pulse quicken, wondering if he felt the same way. Or was it mere foolishness? "Matthew," she repeated, the name coming out in a husky whisper.

"And may I call you Rachel?"

She granted him permission with alacrity.

"Rachel," he said. "What a lovely name."

"It was my grandmother's."

He laughed. "That's something we have in common then," he said, his blue eyes alight with humor. "I was named for my mother's father, one Matthew Allencourt of Philadelphia."

"Your mama is from the North?" she asked, her curiosity aroused. Even with the little time she had spent in New Orleans, Rachel was aware that there were deep differences between those who lived here in the South and were natives, and those whom she'd heard called "Yankees." She lived in the American section of the city, after all, and it was there that she met the families that had come to New Orleans from elsewhere. In the house next to her papa's resided the Chandlers. Mr. Chandler was an officer of the Bank of New York, and his wife had become very friendly with Rachel's mother, as she had become friendly with the eldest of the three Chandler daughters.

"From a fine old Philadelphia family. I just returned from a visit there two months ago. My uncle runs the family business, and I've lots of cousins. It was a family wedding, and we were all supposed to attend," he explained, "but my sister had just recovered from a severe case of pneumonia and it was thought wise not to subject her to a long trip."

"She has fully recovered?"

Matthew smiled. "Thank *le bon Dieu*, she has," he said gratefully, "though Marguerite does tire easily. And now that her governess has had to leave our house to care for her own sister who is in a delicate way, Marguerite has become bored as well."

Rachel was pleased that he spoke so kindly of his sibling. The love he felt for his younger sister was much evident in the way Matthew Devereaux talked about Marguerite. "Can I be of some help then?" she volunteered without thinking of the consequences.

"You wish to surrender some of your own time to tutor my sister?"

"I believe," Rachel proposed, "that I can spare a few hours a week if that would meet with your parents' approval?"

"I think that they would be most appreciative. Matthew took hold of her ungloved hand, carrying it to his warm lips. "I know that I would be most pleased," he said, his voice a husky caress.

"Rachel!" Connor Gallagher called. " 'Tis time we were leaving, me darlin'."

Rachel's heart skipped a beat with the touch of Matthew's mouth on her flesh.

What had she let herself in for?

Chapter Four

Not a day has passed these past two weeks that I have not thought of Matthew Devereaux. Each morning brings me some new awareness of him, and how important he is to my life.

We have twice gone riding along the magnificent River Road. It is there, exploring the land with Matthew as my guide, that I find myself falling deeper and deeper under his spell.

Is love, I wonder, so much like a sorcerer's charm that each exposure is sure to intensify the feeling? 'Tis almost like one of the fairy folk had sprinkled some powerful enchanted dust over me whilst I slept. If 'tis indeed magic, I wish never to break the spell.

Rachel closed the cover of her diary, her thoughts far away from her house in New Orleans. Her right hand propped up one side of her face as she stared out the window of her bedroom; so deep in thought was she that she didn't even notice the antics of a songbird perched in the tree right outside, singing merrily.

Kathleen Ainsley Gallagher stepped into her daughter's bedroom, carrying a large cut-glass vase filled with fresh flowers.

"Aren't they ever so lovely?" Kathleen Gallagher asked, setting the vase down on the low table. "I couldn't resist when I saw a flower merchant in the marketplace. The old woman had some excellent choices, and"—she bent down to take another sniff of the bouquet—"I've added some from our own garden."

Rachel turned when she heard her mother's voice. She knew her mother was happiest working in her own small garden, tending to the arrangement of colors and the varieties of her plants.

Rachel herself was an indifferent gardener, lacking the proper focus, though she appreciated the results. She would rather take her watercolors and attempt to paint what her mother had skillfully created.

"I've asked Liselle to serve our tea in here, if you don't mind, my dear," Kathleen said.

"I should like that, Mama," Rachel responded, slipping the diary into the drawer of her secretary and locking it with a tiny key.

That action did not go unnoticed by her mother, who chose not to say anything on the matter until after their tea had been served.

Liselle, a free woman of color, entered carrying a silver tray laden with a round teapot and tea service; each bone china item bore the same design, a sprig of blue wisteria in the shape of an A against a white background. As soon as she relinquished the tea tray, Liselle withdrew a thick cream-colored envelope from the pocket of her white apron.

"For you, mademoiselle," she announced, handing the envelope to Rachel. "It was delivered several minutes ago by one of the Devereaux servants." Liselle's tone indicated that she was impressed by her mistress's connection to one of the most respected families in New Orleans. She smiled her congratulations as she left the room.

Kathleen poured her daughter a cup of the strong brew, then added milk and sugar. She watched as Rachel broke the wax seal and opened the envelope.

"From Mr. Matthew Devereaux, I presume?" Kathleen asked with a delicately raised brow.

Rachel shook her head, her gaze still focused on the graceful, feminine handwriting. "No, Mama, his mother."

Kathleen observed the flags of color in her daughter's cheeks. It was clear to her that Matthew Devereaux was more than just a passing fancy in her daughter's life. Something was there in her child's face that wasn't there before. "Your tea, Rachel."

Rachel accepted the cup from her mother's hand, giving Kathleen a small smile. She took a sip of the beverage, her thoughts once again with the note. It was an invitation, asking Rachel and her parents to a dinner party that Mrs. Devereaux was giving the following week at their house in the city. "Our family has been asked to attend a dinner at the Devereauxs' home here in New Orleans."

"May I see that?" Kathleen Gallagher asked politely.

"Of course, Mama," Rachel agreed, handing over the note. While she drank her tea, she watched as her mother quickly scanned the handwritten note. She waited impatiently while Kathleen pondered quietly for a few moments.

Finally, unable to stand the wondering any longer, Rachel asked, "Well, may we attend, Mama?"

"It would please you, dearest?" Kathleen was sure she already possessed the answer to the question.

Rachel nodded. "Yes, it would, Mama," she admitted freely, "very much."

Kathleen leaned across the low table and grasped her daughter's hand. She was exceedingly proud of her child, happy with the young woman Rachel had become. It had been so hard for her to leave her daughter to the care of the private school, but she and Connor had agreed that he must make his way first in this new country before they could send for their girl. And Kathleen had secured a promise from her estranged parents that should anything happen to them, they would see to their granddaughter's care.

"Then I think we must go," she said softly. "I shall send 'round a reply to Mrs. Devereaux, thanking her for her gracious invitation and conveying our acceptance." Her hand still holding her daughter's, Kathleen asked, "Do you have a *tendre* for the Devereaux son?"

Rachel raised her blue eyes to her mother's, which were a soft shade of gray. She knew that she couldn't lie to her mother, not about something as important as what she felt for Matthew.

"I love him," she admitted without preamble.

A deep sigh left Kathleen Gallagher's lungs. "Does he return your feelings?"

Rachel shrugged. "I truly do not know, Mama." She pulled her hand from her mother's and stood up, walking just a few feet away. "I've never told Matthew how I feel."

"You're but eighteen, Rachel. Could it be mere infatuation?" she suggested.

Rachel turned and fixed her mother with a sharp look. "You were seventeen when you fell in love with my father, were you not?"

Kathleen smiled ruefully. She was caught in the net of her own past. "That's true," she admitted. "I met your father and from that moment on, there was no one else for me."

"That is how I feel about Matthew," Rachel acknowledged. "From that first meeting, Mama, when Papa asked me to accompany him when delivering the horse to Belle Chanson, I knew Matthew was the man I wanted for my husband."

Kathleen prodded, "Suppose he does not want you for a wife? Have you given thought to that?"

"I do not believe that he is indifferent to me," Rachel admitted.

"Has he compromised you?" Kathleen demanded.

"Oh no, Mama." Rachel quickly rose to Matthew's defense. "He has been the soul of propriety. Even when we go riding, there is always a groom with us. Nothing untoward has happened between us, I promise. You may have my word of honor."

Kathleen heaved another sigh. "Thank the good Lord for that."

Rachel added earnestly, "Though he has said nothing, 'tis something that I can sense in my heart."

Kathleen rose and stood behind her daughter, one hand lightly stroking Rachel's unbound long golden-blonde hair. "You are so young, my dearest, and he is a man, and a wordly man at that, used to having what he wants."

"So," Rachel asked, turning to face her

mother, "you've heard the same rumors as I have?"

"Mrs. Chandler informed me of Matthew Devereaux's reputation, if that is what you're asking," Kathleen responded, "and I am most grateful for her doing so."

Rachel could tell that her mother was holding something back. She thought about it for a moment before asking, her tongue reaching out to wet her lips, "Did she also tell you about the house in Rampart Street?"

It was Kathleen Ainsley Gallagher's turn to blush. "Yes," she replied.

"I don't care, Mama," Rachel stated adamantly. "That is the past."

"If he still provides for her, then 'tis very much the present," Kathleen pointed out. "He is, from all accounts, a very virile man, my dearest, and men have a fondness for their pleasures."

"I would not deny Matthew the company he needs for now, Mama, nor begrudge that part of him that this nameless woman has had," Rachel said ingenuously, believing it to be true, "for at this time, I have no real claim on his affections."

"But you want to." It was a simple statement.

"With all my heart," Rachel admitted.

That thought was put to the test less than three days later when Rachel, accompanied by her friend Carolyn Chandler, entered Madame

71

de la Poeur's exclusive dress shop in the Vieux Carré. The modiste had been recommended by Carolyn's mother as the best in all New Orleans, and worth every penny she charged, for her handiwork was exquisite, worthy of Paris or London.

As the two girls browsed among the assorted bolts of rich fabrics stored to one side of the shop, Madame herself came to attend them.

"Bonjour, mesdemoiselles," she said in a soft, Louisiana-accented voice. "May I be of some service today?"

"My friend is going to a very special dinner party, madame," Carolyn explained, "and we thought that you could make something memorable for her."

"*Oui, quelque chose incroyable, n'est-ce pas?*" Madame de la Poeur shrewdly assessed Rachel's figure. She produced a tape measure, a short stub of a pencil, and a slender notebook from her apron pocket and began to make a series of notes, calling on one of her assistants to bring some bolts of cloth from another room.

Rachel stood still, her arms held out, as the modiste draped different fabrics about her still-clothed body. The woman discarded several immediately, then found two to her liking.

"The rose silk and the deep blue velvet will be best," madame proclaimed, a shrewd smile on her face. She handed the bolts back to her assistant, and asked that Rachel take a seat while she fetched her sketchbook.

While Rachel and Carolyn did just that, a servant entered the room and gave each of them a fluted glass of champagne.

As they sipped, another customer entered the main room and checked the fit of her ball gown in the triple mahogany mirror.

Rachel thought the young woman, whom she guessed was about her own age, to be one of the most beautiful, graceful women she'd ever seen. The gown of deep gold complemented her golden skin and artfully curled light brown hair.

The woman twirled about, then came to an abrupt stop when she saw the other two young women sitting to one side. "Oh, *pardonnez-moi*," she said, a sweet grin on her face. "I did not know that madame had other customers. You must excuse me," she begged.

"Whatever for?" Rachel demanded, noting how well the dress flattered the girl. If Madame de la Poeur could do as well for her, she would have Matthew's full attention the night of the dinner party.

The girl stepped closer to them. "Do you like it?" she asked in a somewhat anxious voice, her wide, hazel eyes focused on them.

"It is very beautiful, mademoiselle," Rachel answered, adding, "as are you."

"*Merci*, mademoiselle," the other customer replied.

"No need for thanks," Rachel admonished, "since I am merely stating the obvious."

"Still, it is most kind of you." The young

73

woman preened before the triple mirror once more, satisfied with her choice.

Madame de la Poeur came back into the room carrying a few thick books that contained heavy sheets of paper filled with finished designs. "Here are some ideas, mademoiselle. Feel free to look, see if you find something you like."

"Actually, I do," Rachel replied right away. "The design of that dress is most pleasing to me." Rachel indicated what the other girl was wearing.

"Mademoiselle has good taste," madame responded, "though perhaps not quite so low in the neckline for you?"

Rachel looked at the golden dress once more, noticing that the other girl was a bit more slender than she in the chest. "No, I think that would suit me just fine the way it is," she declared. It was time to come out of the schoolroom, she'd decided, and this dinner party would be just the thing to announce it in a rather unmistakable form.

"Rachel, are you certain?" Carolyn asked. "Your mother may object."

"It's what I want," Rachel insisted.

"As you wish, Mlle Gallagher," madame replied with an eye to pleasing her customer. "I shall get to work on them *immédiatement* and I shall expect you to return in two days' time for a fitting."

"Very well, madame," Rachel agreed. "I shall return in two days."

Their business concluded, Rachel and Carolyn made their way toward the door as one of madame's assistants came back into the room, carrying her sewing basket.

"So," the modiste posed the question to the other customer, "you are satisfied, Mlle Du Lac?"

The young woman gave the modiste a huge smile. "I am very, very pleased with this gown, madame, and I think that Matthieu will be also."

At the sound of that name, which she knew was *Matthew* in French, Rachel halted at the door.

"What's wrong, Rachel?" Carolyn asked, her hand upon the door.

"Sssh," she hissed under her breath to her friend, her attention focused on the other woman. Rachel's heart beat quickly as she waited to hear more of the conversation.

"Shall I place the dress on M. Devereaux's account?" the assistant inquired as she opened the account ledger.

"*Mais, oui*," the customer replied, returning to her changing room.

Matthew Devereaux's account.

Rachel felt the breath leave her body momentarily. That beautiful young woman was undoubtedly Matthew's mistress, his *fille de joie*.

"Devereaux," Carolyn said in a low voice filled with surprise. "Did you hear that, Rachel?"

Rachel cast her a slightly quelling look. "Yes,"

she said softly, making her way outside. On the banquette she took a deep breath of air while she composed herself. Running away wasn't an option, much as she would have liked to have done just that at that moment, pretending that she hadn't heard what she had.

That woman, that beautiful young woman, shared a bed with Matthew, Rachel thought. He paid for her clothes, her house, and anything else she wanted in exchange for having exclusive rights to her favors.

"Rachel?"

She heard her name called and snapped out of her lethargy. Carolyn was at her side, an anxious look in her bright sky-blue eyes.

"I'm all right, Carolyn," she assured her friend with a tiny smile.

"Are you sure?" Carolyn asked. "It can't have been easy to have heard what you did."

Rachel sighed. " 'Tis not as though I had no inkling he kept a woman," she murmured.

"But you hadn't met her," Carolyn pointed out.

Rachel gave her friend a sharp look. "You're right." She turned her head and gazed at the door to the establishment.

"Come along," Carolyn urged, taking Rachel's arm and walking a few paces to where the Chandler carriage waited for them. As they made their way into the carriage, something made Rachel pause and take another glance toward the dress shop. She saw a curricle pulled by two striking matched bay horses stop, and the driver, a tall, lean man, get out and assist the customer from the shop into his rig.

At that moment, the man turned his head also and stared directly at Rachel.

Matthew's eyes widened in shock for the merest instant before he responded to his companion's question in the same flawless French that she used, getting back into the vehicle and flicking the reins, setting the pair off.

Rachel sank into the plush interior of the Chandler carriage and closed her eyes. "Would you mind if we didn't stop at Coleburn's today?" she asked Carolyn. "Suddenly I'm rather tired."

"We can visit the bookshop tomorrow if you want," her friend agreed.

They journeyed in silence until they reached their destination. Having emerged from the carriage, the young women stood on the brick banquette outside their respective houses.

"If you want to talk later . . ." Carolyn offered.

Rachel shook her head. "Thank you anyway, but no. There really is nothing to say, is there?"

"Still . . ."

Rachel lifted the latch of the wrought-iron gate that led to her front door. Unlike the Creoles who built with the back of their houses to the street, the Americans, and others who built in this section of the city, faced theirs to the thoroughfare. A large pecan tree and magnolias flanked the walkway.

"I appreciate your concern, really I do," Rachel insisted, "but there's no need. I just want to be alone."

"As you wish," Carolyn conceded. She gave Rachel a warm hug and proceeded to make her way onto her own property.

Rachel turned the glass knob and walked into the cool hallway. She sank back against the door, as if gathering strength, until Liselle emerged from one of the back rooms.

"Is something wrong, Miss Rachel?" she asked, hurrying forward to help the younger woman remove the *pardessus*-styled jacket from her outfit.

Rachel pulled at the strings of her bonnet, wetting her lips. "I'm a trifle warm, that's all," she said in explanation as she shrugged out of the taffeta jacket. "Could I possibly have some of your refreshing lemonade?"

"Of course, Miss Rachel. Shall I send it to your room?"

Rachel considered for a moment. "Is Mama at home?"

"She and your papa went for a drive since it was such a beautiful afternoon. They left soon after you did."

"Then," Rachel instructed their housekeeper, "the library will do."

"As you wish," Liselle responded, taking the dangling silk bonnet from Rachel's fingers.

Rachel slowly made her way down the hall and entered the room kept as a library. Originally it had been an extra parlor, but Kathleen changed that as soon as they moved in. Books were everywhere, along with flowers in assorted vases and several paintings of horses. It wasn't like the more formal libraries that were found in the great houses; rather, it was simple and well used. The volumes, belonging mainly to Rachel and her mother, were well read and consisted predominantly of poetry and novels. Since coming to America, Rachel had taken an interest in the literature of her adopted country, and several of the novels were recent purchases from Coleburn's bookshop. An embroidered satin bookmark rested atop the novel she'd just finished: Nathaniel Hawthorne's *The Scarlet Letter*.

A scarlet letter of shame.

And what of the scarlet woman? Did she feel shame?

Mlle Du Lac exhibited no such sentiment. Instead, she'd looked happy and assured.

Rachel sank down onto the horsehair sofa, undoing the top few buttons of her muslin blouse. Did Matthew love this woman? That thought caused a deep inner pain to tear at her belly. Fingers locked into fists, Rachel sat there, just thinking, until Liselle entered with her cool drink.

"Are you sure that there is nothing more I can do for you, Miss Rachel?" Liselle asked anxiously.

Rachel gave her a wan smile. "No, I've got a bit of the headache, 'tis all." She reached down and picked up the cool glass. She sipped it and sighed with a geniality she was far from feeling. "This is wonderful, and just what I needed."

A distant rumble of thunder was heard from the open window. Rachel stood up and investigated. "It appears we shall have a storm soon," she said to the departing Liselle, watching as the sky began to darken. In Ireland, she had loved the magnificent fury of a storm, often sneaking out whenever she could to be a part of it. The crack of lightning and the roar of thunder stimulated something wild and abandoned within Rachel's soul. Here, the air was thicker, hotter, more oppressive as the storm front moved in.

The changing weather matched her mood.

She was caught up in her own storm, tossed about by her feelings for Matthew. It was one thing to know the man one loved had a mistress; it was another to actually meet her face-to-face.

And how would she react when next she saw Matthew? Should she pretend that the incident had never happened? That she was totally ignorant of the fact that he kept a woman? Ladies weren't supposed to know about those things, and if they did, it wasn't expected that they would ever talk about them to the man involved.

She recalled the words she had so blithely uttered to her mother just days ago. How foolishly naive she felt now as strands of jealousy wrapped themselves about her unprotected heart.

Rachel lost track of the amount of time that she stood there, gazing out into the ever-darkening sky. Several times she blinked as jagged bolts of lightning illuminated the gloom. The splash of raindrops fell like tiny, angry darts. This was no fine, soft Irish mist, but a full-fledged, fast-moving tempest.

She heard vague sounds coming from the front hall, raised voices, and thought that her parents had made it home in time to avoid the worst of the storm.

The door to the library swung open and Rachel spun around, one of her hands going to her mouth to cover an "*O*" of surprise.

Chapter Five

Whomever else I had expected to see standing there, it was never Matthew Devereaux. That came as such a complete surprise that I almost dropped the glass of lemonade I'd been holding.

Yet, as taken aback as I was, I could not control the leap of my pulse when he entered the room so abruptly.

Rachel uttered his name on a gasp of amazement, nearly letting go of the heavy leaded glass in her hand. She recovered in time and her fingers gripped the piece tightly, the pattern leaving visible imprints on her palm.

"Matthew." His name was uttered whisper-soft.

"I'm sorry, Miss Rachel," Liselle apologized, arriving right behind the tall man and standing in the entranceway, "but M. Devereaux"—and with that Liselle cast him a heavy look for this breach of etiquette—"insisted on seeing you before I could find out if you were receiving."

Rachel found her voice. " 'Tis all right, Liselle," she said, gathering her wits about her and moving from the window. "I shall see M. Devereaux." She placed the glass down upon a small, marble-topped table, her hand shaking slightly.

"But, Miss Rachel . . ." Liselle began.

Rachel had a good idea what the housekeeper was about to say. She was alone with a man in her house; what was more, a man with a decidedly rakish reputation. Obviously not quite the done thing.

Rachel realized the implication—she should have refused him entrance and made it quite clear that she was not at home to guests.

But Rachel couldn't refuse Matthew, she realized. Not now. Not ever.

"I wish only to talk to Mlle Gallagher on a matter of some importance," Matthew stressed, removing his low-crowned, wide-brimmed cream felt hat and tossing it carelessly onto the stack of books that rested on another nearby table.

Liselle hovered in the doorway, waiting for her cue.

"I will hear what M. Devereaux has come to

say, Liselle," Rachel stated, seating herself on one of the comfortable padded chairs, hands folded primly in her lap to keep them from betraying the utter nervousness she felt with Matthew looming so large in the room. He dominated the space, she thought, like a big, sleek black cat. And he made her nervous.

Liselle, a careful, considering look on her face, nodded her head. "I shall be near should you have need of anything, Miss Rachel," she said, casting another swift glance in Matthew's direction. With that pronouncement, she shut the library door and left them alone.

"I had to see you," he said.

Rachel lifted her head and watched him. He stood but a few feet from her, his lean frame dressed in a cream-colored frock coat and matching trousers. A waistcoat of deep bronze silk, along with a matching cravat, completed the ensemble. A topaz stickpin, which matched his ring, caught Rachel's eye. She fastened her gaze there, thinking it safer than looking him directly in the eyes.

Matthew, however, would have none of that. "Look at me," he commanded gently in his deep, drawling voice.

Rachel did so, unable to ignore the summons of his softly accented tones.

"That's better," he commented with a wry smile. "I want to explain about this afternoon, and why I did not formally acknowledge your presence."

Rachel interjected, "There was no need. I think that I know all that I need to know about Mlle Du Lac."

If he was surprised that she knew his mistress's identity, Matthew hid it well. "No," he said, "I don't think you do."

"I know that she . . . that you . . ." Rachel's voice trailed off as embarrassment flooded her at the subject, highlighting her cheeks with rosy color.

Matthew, who rarely gave a damn what anyone thought about his actions, and who almost never explained his motives, found himself needing to tell Rachel that what she had seen had nothing to do with them. And he truly believed that it didn't. But how could he clarify the situation between himself and Mlle Du Lac to a demure woman of gentle breeding?

"Do you deny that she is your mistress?" Rachel found the courage to ask.

Matthew moved closer to Rachel, taking a seat across from her. "No, I cannot deny that," he stated honestly, his gaze falling momentarily to the green-and-gold patterned carpet before he returned it to Rachel. "To do so would be to insult both you and Dominique."

"Dominique," Rachel said. "That is her name?"

"Yes," he responded. "She's our housekeeper's half sister."

Rachel's eyes widened in surprise. "Angelique?"

86

"Yes."

Rachel visibly shrank back in her seat. She found herself stating the obvious. "Mlle Du Lac is very beautiful, and," she added with a touch of asperity, "very young."

"Dominique is three and twenty."

"I thought her younger," Rachel murmured, surprised at that fact. Dominique looked as if she had recently emerged from the schoolroom. Rachel wondered, then, just how long this other woman had been sharing Matthew's affections.

"How young?" Matthew asked, fixing Rachel with a deep, hungry look. "As young as yourself?"

Rachel stiffened slightly. "I am eighteen," she announced in her most prim voice.

"It is you who are so very young, Miss Gallagher," Matthew observed.

"Not so young that I am not aware of the particular custom hereabouts," Rachel pointed out, "of buying women of color for a man's personal use. I may be new to your country, but I have read and seen things since arriving here that fill me with sadness and loathing."

Now it was Matthew who stiffened. "I did not buy Dominique, Rachel. She came to me of her own free will."

"How much free will does a slave have?" The trade in human flesh that Rachel had observed since coming to Louisiana sickened her; it was something she could never reconcile herself to.

"She and Angelique are not slaves, Rachel,"

Matthew said quietly. "They are free women of color, like your Liselle, I would assume?" he asked, one black brow raised.

"Aye, that she is," Rachel responded.

"As are they. Free to make their own choices."

"And it was Dominique's choice to become your mistress?"

"Yes," Matthew answered truthfully. "It's what . . ." He muttered a dark curse in French under his breath, frustration taking hold. "Oh, how can I explain this?" he asked, his patience wearing thin.

A loud crack of thunder shook the French windows and the rain came down even harder.

Matthew narrowed his gaze and looked sharply at the young woman sitting there. How could he describe to an innocent the custom of Creole men for more years than he could count of taking unto themselves mistresses from among the many lovely women of mixed race? He could simply state that that was the way it was and be done with it, but somehow, he knew that Rachel needed more. She needed the truth.

Rachel sat quietly, her thoughts and emotions jumbled.

"We have a custom here in New Orleans, long established," Matthew began, "which consists of young men selecting a partner from the ranks of women eager to be chosen for this arrangement. Women, I might add, who have been trained since birth in the gentler arts of taking very good care of a man. These are most certainly not women who seek favor with just anyone. A certain level of income and breeding is expected of the man who seeks an alliance. He must be willing to accept responsibility for this woman, to give her his assurance that she has his full protection, and to be most generous to her and whatever children result from this union.

"Years ago, in my papa's time, there were regular Quadroon Balls held so that the young men of Louisiana could meet the ladies. More often than not, the *placées* are quadroons, or octaroons, who are carefully guarded and reared by their mothers for just such a life."

"Their own mamas are part of this bargaining?" Rachel asked incredulously.

Matthew smiled wryly. "Indeed. This system worked well enough for them, so why wouldn't they want it for their daughters?"

"What about marriage? Respectability?"

Matthew shrugged his broad shoulders. "Marriage is not a consideration in the negotiations."

"No exceptions?"

"I have known of only one man who married his *femme de couleur*," Matthew stated solemnly. "They were not received here in New Orleans after that event, so eventually they left and journeyed to France, and settled there."

Rachel's face softened with that revelation. "He must have loved her very much to have given up his country and all he had known for her."

"*Oui*, he did indeed," Matthew commented.

"You knew him personally?" Rachel questioned, something in the tone of Matthew's voice sparking her curiosity.

"He was my uncle, my father's younger brother, Etienne."

Rachel was surprised, and quite pleased, that Matthew had admitted that to her. "They are accepted there?"

"Yes," he said, "and their children have made advantageous marriages, giving Uncle Etienne and Aunt Jeanette many fine grandchildren.

"Set your mind at ease, Rachel," Matthew assured her, "there are no slaves at Belle Chanson."

"Really?" she asked, her tone slightly skeptical.

"You have my word, the word of a Devereaux, on that," Matthew insisted.

"When Papa took me to your plantation, I saw many dark-skinned people, some working inside your house and others in the fields."

"That's true," he admitted. "We employ many laborers on our plantation. Besides growing sugar, we have horses and cedar, pecans and fruit trees. All must be carefully maintained or the plantation loses money."

"And they aren't slaves?"

"Some were at one time," Matthew conceded. "My father bought many who live there now at the auctions in New Orleans."

Rachel shuddered. She couldn't imagine how humiliating and degrading it must feel to be treated as a piece of property—to be bought and sold at another's whim.

"But they are slaves no longer?"

Matthew shook his head. "They haven't been since the day my father married my mother," he explained. "Remember, I told you that my mama was from Philadelphia? Well, the idea of owning human property was abhorrent to her, and she insisted that she would accept my father's proposal only on the condition that he manumitted his slaves."

"Oh, how delightful!" Rachel exclaimed. "That he loved her enough to do that for her, and that your mother was willing to risk her happiness in order to uphold her principles."

"*Oui*, my father loved my mother very much. And for that," Matthew pointed out, "my father took much grievance from his friends, who couldn't understand how he allowed himself to be so persuaded. It went against the society that he'd been brought up in."

"Then I applaud your papa most heartily," Rachel said with a broad smile, "for his courage. To risk censure for love is a very brave thing, as I well know. My own parents risked so very much to be together, eventually giving up their birth land so that they could have a future without people saying them nay."

"Then we have something very much in common," Matthew said, reaching out his large hand and clasping her much smaller one. Her milky-white flesh contrasted with Matthew's much darker, tanned skin.

Another loud crack of thunder exploded outside and Rachel tugged on his hand and pulled him up with her as she went back to the French window. She turned the brass handle and opened it, breathing in the humid air, watching the rain splash against the stones of the small courtyard.

Matthew stood behind her, so close, despite the wide hoops of her skirt, that Rachel could feel the heat of his body enveloping hers. She was surrounded by warmth.

Matthew trailed his hand along the slope of her shoulder, downward, his fingers skating delicately across the soft fabric of her blouse and down her arm until they reached her hand. He lifted it to his mouth, caressing it with his lips.

Rachel shivered, trembling with sensation. No one had ever touched her like this, so intimately. It was gentle, like the touch of a feather gliding across her skin.

"Rachel." He groaned her name against her ear, turning her to face him.

Matthew bent his head and captured her mouth with his own, slowly at first, letting Rachel accept him. When she willingly gave him her lips, he proceeded further, coaxing her lips apart and deepening the kiss, his arms pulling her tighter to his already aroused body.

Rachel felt her head swimming with delight as various sensations swept through her body like wildfire. Her eyes drifted closed as she let herself go with the tide, drowning in the unexpected and overwhelming feelings of the moment. Like nothing she had ever experienced before, Matthew's mouth did strange things to her, removing her from her surroundings and carrying her along on a voyage of discovery.

Her hands crept slowly up the length of his broad back, clinging to the material of his frock coat in an attempt to pull him closer to her. That accomplished, she inched one hand higher along the nape of his neck, threading her fingers through his glossy black hair. It felt like heavy silk, thick and luxurious.

Matthew removed his mouth from hers, placing soft kisses along her neck, exposed by the loosened buttons of her blouse. One arm wrapped securely around her slender waist, he brought the other to her head, anchoring it there, her long tumbled ringlets swaying back and forth across his hand.

"Oh, *ma belle*," Matthew breathed huskily in her ear; the sound was like the deep, contented purr of a well-fed cat. "*Tu es charmante, ravissante*," he whispered, falling back on his father's tongue. "*Je te désire, ma bien-aimée*."

Rachel's mind drifted out of the fog that Matthew's lovemaking had led it into. When she heard his huskily uttered words in French, the cold slap of reality set in. Were these the same words he murmured at night to his mistress, Dominique?

Upset, she pushed at the solid wall of his chest, eager to break free, embarrassed that she had relinquished control of herself to that extent. What had come over her? And worse, what did he think of her now?

Matthew, sensing her sudden resistance to their embrace, let her go. "What's wrong, *ma belle*?" His voice was husky.

Rachel, her pulse racing, her breathing somewhat constricted, forced herself to regain her calm. "English, if you please," she insisted, her voice quavering slightly. "Or have you forgotten that I am not your *belle amie*?" She returned to her chair, deciding to keep some small distance between them.

Matthew took a deep, steadying breath himself. "I never imagined you were, *cherie*." He closed the French doors and followed her back into the room.

"How long have you kep—been with her?" Rachel asked, still trembling from Matthew's potent, intoxicating kisses. He was like a swift, sharp taste of her papa's Irish whiskey—it went right to your head if you weren't used to it.

"Since her seventeenth birthday."

The color drained from Rachel's face. Six years, she thought. Matthew had been with her for six years.

She fell silent, too stunned to talk.

"Have you nothing else to say?" Matthew inquired.

Rachel raised her eyes to his. "What can I say?" she asked. " 'Twould appear as if I am the interloper here."

"No," Matthew denied. "That's not true."

"Do you have . . ." She paused, taking another deep breath, "has she borne you any children?" Her heart prayed he would respond in the negative.

"There are no children, Rachel," he answered her.

She breathed a sigh of relief.

"Do you love her?" Rachel feared his reply, but she had to know; especially now, more than ever, with his kisses still burning fervently in her memory. Could her heart have been so wrong about this being the man for her? Her one true and forever love?

Matthew considered his answer. "Yes and no."

Rachel's face wore a puzzled look. "What does that mean?" she demanded.

"It means that yes, I do love Dominique. I care for her deeply," he explained. "She has been a very dear friend to me; a confidant of sorts, if you will." Matthew came closer to Rachel, bending down on one knee before her seated figure. "It also means that no, I am not in love with her.

"Nor," he declared, "is she with me."

"Are you certain?"

"As much as I can be," he assured her.

The tempo of the storm outside changed, becoming softer, quieter; the rain eased its fierce beat, falling in a gentler rhythm. The stifling heat had lowered several degrees, though the air retained its sticky quality.

Several seconds of silence ended when Matthew at last spoke. "I shall end it with Dominique," he promised.

Rachel couldn't believe her ears. "You will?"

He nodded.

"Why?" She waited for his answer, her heart beating a crazy tattoo in her chest.

"Because I must." Matthew rose, moving away from her, his back to Rachel for a moment before he turned and faced her. "I think I knew that when first I laid eyes on you," he confessed, his blue eyes blazing with a deep, intense flame.

Rachel felt the heat of his gaze from across the width of the library. That he was willing to give up this other woman for her meant the world to Rachel. For as deeply as she loved him, she knew now that her words to her mother were false—she could no more share Matthew with another woman than she could cease breathing. Rachel wanted his whole heart, and would settle for nothing less.

"Do you believe me?" he asked.

Rachel smiled. "If you tell me it is so, I will always believe you, Matthew." And she knew instinctively that that was true. Whatever Matthew told her she would trust, for she had faith in him, and in his pledges. She couldn't question what made her so certain—she just was.

"Then shall we still expect you and your family to dinner? I know my mother is looking forward to it."

"As am I," she responded.

"I think my mother has something to ask you, also," he added, "something that I hope you will consider, for it will give us a chance to see more of one another." He bent and retrieved his hat. "You'd like that, wouldn't you, Rachel?"

Like it? Rachel thought. By the holy cross of St. Patrick, she'd be overjoyed. It would be a dream come true. "I do believe I could bear it," she said in as calm a tone as she could manage.

"May I call on you tomorrow?"

As if she could refuse him.

"I will look forward to it."

Matthew put on his hat and made to leave. As he got to the door of the library, he stopped and spun around, glancing at Rachel sitting so quietly in her chair. He came back and lifted her out of the tufted apple-green velvet seat, his arms on hers holding her upright as he kissed her.

Rachel sank back to the chair, one hand moving automatically to her lips, still warm and tingling from the imprint of his.

She was still sitting there minutes later when Liselle walked in.

"Miss Rachel," she inquired, "are you all right?"

Rachel took a deep, steadying breath, rising from her seat. "Indeed, I am fine," she insisted. She selected a slim leather volume of Shakespeare's sonnets from one of the bookshelves, something to occupy her trembling hands. "Quite fine, actually."

Liselle took note of the flushed color in Rachel's cheeks, the sparkle in her eyes, and the contented, dreamy expression of her face, and deduced that M. Devereaux had had quite an effect on the young Irish girl.

"I think I'd best change before dinner," Rachel said, the book in one hand. "Have my parents returned yet?"

"No, Miss Rachel."

"I'm sure that they stopped to find shelter from the storm and will be home soon," she told the housekeeper. "What have you fixed for this evening?"

"One of your papa's favorites. Chicken with dumplings. And, for dessert, my pecan pie."

"I think I shall have to loosen my stays before I eat that," Rachel said with a laugh.

Rachel's mood abruptly became more serious. "Liselle, I must ask you something, if you don't mind."

"If I can be of help, you have but to ask," replied the housekeeper.

"You were born here in New Orleans, am I correct?"

"*Oui*, Miss Rachel, that is so."

"Then you must be familiar with the Creole

custom of"—Rachel blushed—"keeping a woman?"

Liselle gave Rachel a curious look. "Why do you ask?"

"Do you think that some of the women fall in love with the men who . . . protect them?" she asked.

The housekeeper shrugged her shoulders. "I would imagine that is a possibility."

"Oh," was Rachel's soft reply.

"For some, it is a business arrangement only, an investment in one's future. A matter of practicality," Liselle said. "There are others, and I have met a few, for whom it is an *affaire d'amour*. They love the men who have chosen them."

"I see." Rachel cast a speculative look at her housekeeper. Liselle was a striking woman with amber skin and hair.

"You are wondering, are you not, Miss Rachel, if perhaps a Creole gentleman has offered for me?"

Rachel flushed. "I would not pry, Liselle."

Liselle shrugged. "I will be happy to tell you. *Oui*, a fine gentleman came to see my mama and wanted to make me his *belle amie*. He was a good friend of my papa and owned a small plantation not far outside of New Orleans. I would have had a very comfortable life if I had agreed to his plans."

"But you refused?"

"*Oui*," Liselle replied. "My *grandmère* was

taken without her consent by the man who owned her; my mother was my father's woman since she was fourteen, and yet he did not free her. When she died, she was still a slave. He only freed me when she begged him, threatening to kill herself.

"I am a free woman, Miss Rachel," Liselle stated proudly. "I make my own way. That means more to me than a life as any gentleman's pampered mistress, no matter how comfortable. To agree to such an arrangement would make me a slave once again. And that I will never be," she insisted adamantly.

Rachel and the housekeeper exchanged understanding looks, Rachel mentally applauding her housekeeper's stand.

Liselle smiled. "Now, I had best return to the kitchen and see about supper."

"I appreciate your frankness with me, Liselle," Rachel said, "and you can be assured that what we have spoken of here today will remain between us."

"I know it will," the housekeeper said.

Later, as Rachel lay in her bed, having decided to take a short nap before the evening meal, she thought about all that Liselle had said, and most especially about the chance that Dominique was in love with Matthew.

Rachel wondered about the other woman. She knew firsthand how deeply and completely one could fall in love with Matthew Devereaux.

Just the thought of losing him could summon depths of pain heretofore unimagined within her heart.

She hugged one of the fluffy feather pillows to her breast. How complicated this was becoming. She hadn't wanted to cause another woman pain so that she could enjoy love, but Rachel was unable to stop herself from wanting Matthew as her own, or from believing that they were meant to be together.

Chapter Six

Time has slipped slowly by, and yet I can still feel the captivating magic of Matthew's mouth on mine whenever I close my eyes.

Like a recurring dream that grows stonger and more vivid with each repetition, that kiss lives on in my mind. 'Tis as if I were some touch-me-not fairy-tale princess from long ago who'd been trapped in a secluded tower until Matthew's kiss woke me to the world around me.

Rachel reread the words that she'd written earlier that day in her diary. A bemused smile curved her mouth. A fairy-tale princess indeed, she mused, a dreamy smile on her face. She rather felt that way, what with her gown lying

across the chaise, waiting to transform her into
the belle of the ball, or at the very least, the belle
of the Devereaux dinner party.

She'd not seen Matthew since that rainy afternoon. He'd sent a note to her house the next
day explaining that he'd been unexpectedly
called out of town on important business and
wouldn't be returning until the night of his
mother's soiree. He'd hinted that he would have
something important to discuss with her upon
his return.

Rachel unlocked the drawer to her secretary,
pulling out the letter from Matthew as she
slipped in the journal. Her index finger traced
the bold dark script that spelled out her name.
Opening the thick cream envelope, she withdrew the matching sheet of vellum with the dis-
tinctively Gothic *D* printed on the top.

> Ma Chère *Rachel*,
> *Business forces me to leave when I would*
> *so much rather stay. To part from you now*
> *is to leave behind some measure of myself.*

A bemused smile crossed Rachel's mouth
upon rereading that statement. Matthew had a
poetic way with words.

> *You must know that what transpired be-*
> *tween us today was not taken lightly by me.*
> *What we shared has meant more to me than*
> *you could ever know, especially now.*

There Never Was A Time

*Please, as a sign of my deep regard for you,
I would have you accept this small token
and beg you keep me in your thoughts, as
you are constantly in mine.*
                    Matthew Devereaux

Rachel was extremely touched by the gift
Matthew had given her. It had come separate
from the note, wrapped in a small square of
white lace, with a card tucked inside. On the
card was written: *This belonged to my great-
grandmother. Now it is yours.*

She loved the gift and vowed to keep it with
her always. Tonight, it would be carried in her
reticule so that she could show Matthew how
much she appreciated this wonderful treasure.
Unwrapping the lace, Rachel gently picked up
the rosary. Silver links held together the ellip-
tical mother-of-pearl beads. It was delicate and
beautiful, made for a lady.

Since receiving it, she'd kept it a secret, showing no one. Selfishly, Rachel wanted to keep it
to herself, afraid to break the connection to
Matthew that it represented. She regarded it as
much too personal to share with anyone else,
too much a part of Matthew. And, although she
had been brought up in the Anglican faith of her
mother, Rachel was well aware of what significance this object held for Catholics, her father
having shared his religion with her.

It was, she knew, a gift of respect and affection—and, dared she hope, love?

Rachel returned the letter to the drawer and locked it. She stood up, wandering to the long cheval glass, regarding herself there. Could she make him forget there was ever anyone else in his life before her? Matthew was a sophisticated man, and she was still so much a girl, a girl not far removed from the sheltered milieu of the boarding school.

Still, he hadn't kissed her like a child. He'd taken her in his arms and kissed her with true passion; she was sure of that in her heart.

She picked up the dress and held it up to her body, smiling at her reflection. She even practiced a curtsy.

"I knocked, my dear, but you obviously didn't hear me," Kathleen Gallagher stated, coming into her daughter's bedroom with a velvet box in her hand. She smiled at the picture Rachel made, delighted that her daughter had grown into such a fine beauty. To mark this very special occasion, Kathleen had decided to offer Rachel a surprise.

"I'd like you to wear these tonight, my dearest," Kathleen said, proffering the box to Rachel.

Rachel laid the dress back down on the chaise and took the black velvet heart-shaped box from her mother's outstretched hand. Opening the lid, she raised her eyes to her mother's face. "Your pearls, Mama," she said in surprise.

"Yes, I thought tonight called for them." Kathleen removed them from their bed of soft velvet and placed the necklace around her daughter's slender throat. The three strands of cream-colored pearls glowed against the equally creamy skin of Rachel's neck. Next, Kathleen fixed the earbobs into her daughter's ears and stepped back a pace to observe her handiwork. "They look superb on you, dearest," she pronounced.

Rachel spun back toward the mirror, her hand skimming over the texture of the pearls, admiring their glow. "Oh, Mama, they're so beautiful," Rachel said.

Kathleen hugged her child. "No, 'tis you who are beautiful, my dearest," she countered. "The pearls reflect your loveliness."

"But don't you want to wear them tonight?"

Kathleen shook her head. "Tonight they belong to you, Rachel. With your new gown, they will make a certain Mr. Devereaux unable to take his eyes off you."

"Do you really think so?" Rachel asked.

"Without a doubt." Kathleen picked up her daughter's dress. "Now, shall I play your lady's maid and help you get into this?"

"Please," Rachel responded, "but first, I want to add another petticoat." She walked to her armoire and pulled out a petticoat of white lace to add to the two she already had covering her crinoline. She tied the tapes around her waist and then slithered into the ball gown, her mother adjusting the fancy silk-covered buttons in the back.

107

Rachel stepped in front of the cheval glass and smiled deeply, giving herself a silent nod of approval for how well the dress and her mother's pearls looked. The cut of the gown, coupled with the corset she wore underneath, emphasized the smallness of her waist and the fullness of her bosom.

The mantel clock chimed the hour of seven.

"I must go and get dressed," Kathleen said, giving her daughter a warm, swift hug. "I feel that tonight will be somehow fortunate for you," she murmured approvingly.

Only an hour remained before she would know how Matthew would react upon seeing her. Making a minor adjustment to the bodice, Rachel prayed that her mother was right, that tonight would indeed be a night most felicitous for her. For, should Matthew not love her as she loved him, then she didn't know how she would react. How could she bear the pain?

"My dear, you look beautiful," exclaimed Frances Devereaux when a servant helped Rachel remove the blue cloak that matched Rachel's dress. She turned to her husband, who stood next to her as they greeted their guests. "Doesn't she, Eduoard?"

The elder M. Devereaux bent and kissed Rachel's hand in his most suave manner. "*Très belle, vraiment*," he said, echoing his wife's words.

Rachel blushed, accepting Mme Devereaux's

words as she introduced her mother to the couple, her eyes searching the hallway for Matthew's tall form.

Frances Devereaux interpreted Rachel's hurried glance. "Matthew will be joining us in a few minutes, my dear," she said for Rachel's ears alone. "He only just returned from his trip and is upstairs changing." Frances smiled in the direction of the Gallaghers. "Now, shall we adjourn upstairs to the salon to await the arrival of my son and our other guests?"

Connor stepped forward, offering his arm to Matthew's mother as Eduoard proffered his to Kathleen. Rachel followed behind, her mind racing with thoughts of Matthew, practically oblivious to the elegant surroundings of the house. Nerves beset her, making her stomach feel slightly queasy with the anticipation of seeing him after this temporary absence. Could she believe in that old saying that absence did indeed make the heart grow fonder? How could she love him any more than she already did? That, she believed, was impossible.

Minutes dragged slowly by, as if held back by an invisible hand. Rachel sipped at the cool rum punch provided by one of the Devereauxs' smiling servants, listening politely to the comments made around her, adding her own brief responses when called upon. She met the other guests; Eduoard Devereaux's cousin and his wife and Dr. Gervais Mallorin, whom Rachel judged to be somewhere between her father's and Eduoard Devereaux's ages.

Talk was mostly polite chitchat about safe topics that kept the conversation from veering into dangerous waters during this convivial time. All the while, Rachel waited with as much patience as she could muster for Matthew's arrival.

Finally, she was rewarded.

Without turning her head, she knew when he entered the room. It was as if an invisible string connected them, and all he had to do was touch it lightly to send the vibration to her. She could feel it to the soles of her feet.

"Matthew!" his mother exclaimed in her most welcoming voice.

He strode into the room and went directly to his mother's side and bent, kissing her cheek. He said all the right things in greeting Rachel's parents, in welcoming the doctor and his relatives; then it was time to address her. "Miss Gallagher," he said in a tone just short of formal.

It was the look in his eyes that warmed Rachel's heart. Though Matthew appeared tired, his face drawn and paler than normal, his eyes told a different story. They proclaimed that the sight of her was like a tonic to his weary body.

Rachel's mouth curved into a felicitous smile. "Matthew," she murmured in a slightly husky tone, uncaring if the depth of her feeling for this man was apparent to all assembled in the room.

At that moment, the Devereauxs' butler, Jean-Marc, a tall black man with a head of close-cropped white hair, entered the salon, his West Indian–accented voice giving a musical flavor to his announcement that dinner was served.

Matthew extended his hand and helped Rachel arise from her seat, lingering an extra minute while the others left the room. "Come, *chérie*," he drawled, linking their arms together and escorting her to the magnificent dining room.

Rachel's eyes opened wider at the richness of the decor and the table in the family dining room. The walls were painted a pale lemon yellow with sage-colored silk drapes covering the long French windows. Instead of silver, the flatware was made of highly polished gold, gleaming in the light of the beeswax tapers set into golden candelabrum. Gold trimmed the exclusive dinner service also.

Rachel sat down, picking up her napkin ring and noting that it, too, was made of a band of gold, with a flower design—roses, she judged—carved into the surface.

Above the walnut sideboard hung a painting that Rachel was sure she'd read about once, an elegant Renaissance piece that was an allegorical tale using classical motifs.

Her parents sat opposite her, with Connor seated at Frances's left hand, and Kathleen at Eduoard's right hand; the young couple were seated between the Gallaghers and Dr. Mallorin next to Rachel.

The meal was a tempting assortment of

dishes that featured the seafood the area was noted for: some hot, some cold, and all very Creole. Rachel decided that she could indeed get used to the spicier fare that the cooks in Louisiana made, tasting each new dish placed before her with a sense of adventure. It was worlds away from the steady diet of potatoes, mutton, and oatmeal she had eaten at boarding school.

As she sipped her wine, Rachel listened to the change in the conversation that flowed around her. It seemed as though the earlier restriction on talk about the growing conflict between the northern and southern states was now lifted. Rachel sensed, in fact, that talk of this subject was almost inevitable. It was a topic hotly debated wherever she went, and featured in whatever newspapers she chanced to read.

"If we could only settle this like gentlemen," Dr. Mallorin proposed, "each side could keep its pride without forcing the other to grovel."

"We Southerners will never bow down to the Yankees," Alain Delacourt, Eduoard's cousin, argued. "Never!" he repeated. "It's folly for them to think that they can force their attitudes on us." He looked toward his cousin Eduoard for confirmation of his position.

Eduoard Devereaux was the cynosure of all eyes at the table. He breathed a heavy sigh before replying to his cousin. "Whether it be folly or not is immaterial now, Alain. The die has been cast and I fear that it is too late to stop what is to come."

"Which is?" Gervais Mallorin asked.

"A destruction of all that I hold dear, my good fellow," Eduoard said sadly. He waved his hand in the air; his gesture encompassed all who sat at his table. "We shall be called upon to make a choice, I fear, and tested to the breaking point."

"I think that perhaps you exaggerate just the smallest bit, my friend," the doctor insisted.

"My father is right," Matthew put in, the deep red of his wine glowing an intense ruby shade in his sparkling crystal goblet. "Like the color of this wine, I think the country will run red with blood before this situation comes to its sad conclusion."

"Pshaw," Alain Delacourt murmured in a dismissive tone. "The Yankees don't possess the will to fight, Matthew," he said with smug satisfaction. "They will turn tail and run, mark my words."

"And that is where you are wrong," Matthew insisted in a firm voice.

"I'll match any of our fine young men against one of the Kaintucks," Alain said with a slightly condescending tone.

"We are not talking about personal bravery here, Alain, but sheer numbers," Matthew pointed out. "The North has more men than the South; it has more industrial capabilities to produce weapons of war. Manufacturing will be a key factor if it comes to sustained action. Even James De Bow in his *Review* advocates that the South develop more manufacturing. He recognizes the economic need for it."

"We're gentlemen, Matthew, not money-grubbing Yankees," Alain protested, "and one Louisiana gentleman is worth ten Northeners."

"And it will be ten to one, don't you see?" Matthew asked, exasperation lacing his words.

Alain shrugged his shoulders. "So what?"

Rachel watched Matthew's face darken with frustrated anger at his relative's cavalier attitude.

"Our land must bend before it is broken," Matthew said wearily.

Alain and Gervais turned their shocked gazes to him. It was Matthew's cousin who spoke first. "I cannot believe you think our cause lost before it has begun." He gave a haughty sigh. "You know if it comes to war, Matthew, that you will be given a command. How can you lead our men into battle with such defeatist talk?"

Rachel's breath grew tight in her throat. Such talk brought home the truth about war—that someone's beloved could be susceptible to harm. Her mind reeled with the thought of Matthew involved in a war, with the possibility of his getting hurt, or worse.

Oh God, she prayed quickly and silently, please no, not after we've just found each other.

In a cool, clear voice Matthew responded to his relative's question. "I can't. I won't fight for the Southern cause."

"What?" That query was echoed by the doctor and Alain; even Alain's timid wife let that query escape her shocked lips.

"You heard what I said."

"Impossible," Alain remarked, shaking his head. He protested in an amazed tone, "You cannot mean that! You would fight against your own state, against your own family and friends if it comes to war?"

Matthew responded, "I cannot fight against my own *country*."

"How dare you turn your back on Louisiana?" Alain thundered. "Are you a fool?"

Rachel gasped at the blatant insult.

Matthew fixed Alain with a cold stare. "Are you impugning my honor?" he demanded in a voice Rachel had never heard him use. It was soft, and yet deadly.

Alain, who was well aware of his relative's skill with a sword and pistol, began to shrink back in his seat. He swallowed nervously, but he was too agitated to back down. "If you feel that way, then perhaps—"

"Enough," stated Eduoard, not giving his cousin a chance to finish his rash statement. "I will not have my wife's table the setting for an ugly family scene," he warned.

Alain looked shamefaced. "You are quite right, Eduoard." He turned and addressed Frances at the other end of the table. "Please forgive me, cousin Frances."

"Of course," she replied, glad that her husband had seen fit to enter the fray before it became uglier.

The doctor focused his attention on Eduoard. "Do you support your son's decision?"

Rachel wanted desperately to slip her hand over Matthew's as it lay upon the polished table and link their fingers in a gesture of support. She could well imagine how much it cost him to say what he did. Had she only a short while ago wondered if she could love him any more? She knew the answer to that. Yes, it was indeed possible, for she loved him now with a great welling of respect for his stand.

"Yes, I do," Eduoard said, his voice reflecting the pride he felt in his son's words. "The Devereauxs have been citizens of this nation since the time of my great-grandfather, who came to this country with his good friend, the Marquis de Lafayette, to fight for freedom," he stated. "My own father fought with Gen. Jackson in the Battle for New Orleans against the British when we were in danger of losing the very thing we'd won once before from them. I myself," he said in a somewhat casual manner, as if downplaying his own role, "went to Mexico with the army when my country needed me. Along with many other men, both Southern and Northern alike." Eduoard paused, as if recalling faces long gone. He added in a somber tone, "Some of whom never came home.

"The Devereauxs have fought and bled for these United States. Can I expect my son to do any less?"

The idea of Matthew bleeding somewhere,

hurt and perhaps dying, caused Rachel to freeze, her fingers loosening on her wine goblet. It dropped from her nerveless fingers and hit the carpet underneath with a thud, shattering.

"I'm so sorry!" she exclaimed in an embarrassed rush, realizing what had happened.

"No, don't try to pick it up," Matthew cautioned, his hand staying her arm.

A servant, summoned by the alert Jean-Marc, appeared with a dustpan and quickly removed the debris.

"I think—" Frances gave the guests at her table an encompassing glance—"that that is enough of this talk about war. The Gallaghers are new to our land, and when I offered them our hospitality, I did not think it would include a heated debate on the probability of armed conflict."

"You're quite right, Mme Devereaux," Dr. Mallorin said with a slight lift of his mouth. "We have almost ruined a lovely meal with our boorish behavior. I beg forgiveness."

"Granted," she replied. She signaled to Jean-Marc to bring in the dessert. With its appearance, conversation resumed in a less combative form. It was then that she faced her son and the woman sitting by his side. "I would ask a favor of you, Miss Gallagher."

"If it is in my power to grant it, I shall, Mme Devereaux," Rachel remarked with a smile as she put her spoon into the mixture of fresh cream and thick, juicy strawberry slices, served

117

over a sponge cake soaked in brandy.

"You told me some weeks ago that you had experience in tutoring."

"I have."

"Then would you consider coming to stay at Belle Chanson for a short while to help my daughter Marguerite?"

"Matthew has explained something of your situation to me, madame, and if my parents have no objections, I would love to be of assistance."

"By all means, you must talk it over with your parents, my dear. I would have you do nothing without their consent." Frances Devereaux threw a fond look in her son's direction. She couldn't help but be aware of the secret glances exchanged between her eldest child and the girl at his side. "And you must assure your dear mama that all will be circumspect. Matthew will, of course, move to one of the *garçonnières*.

Rachel was intrigued by the word. "What is that, madame?" she asked.

"Sometimes I forget that, like you, I was once new to this place," she said with a tinkling laugh. "It's a sort of small house that is used by bachelors of the family. For their own privacy, when unmarried female guests are within the main house, or it can be used as a place to entertain friends."

"I shall send my answer 'round on the morrow, madame," Rachel replied.

"And I shall hope that it is favorable. My daughter needs just a few lessons to refresh her memory until a new governess can be found." Frances looked around the table and said, "Ladies, I think it is time to leave the gentlemen to their brandy and cigars." She rose, and as if on cue, so did everyone else.

Rachel slipped away from her mother and Mme Devereaux, choosing instead to take a walk into the garden. She left through the open French doors which led onto a gallery and then down the stairs to the courtyard below. There, she dipped her hand in the splashing fountain, trailing her fingers through the cool water, inhaling the scented breezes of the night. She strolled to a wrought-iron bench and carefully sat down.

It was like a private, miniature Eden.

And as in Eden, forbidden temptation was a silent urge echoing through the corridors of her mind. It whispered in silky, cajoling tones, "Matthew." It slithered along her nerves, making her ache in unfamiliar places.

And then, beside her, out of her wandering fantasies, emerged the man she most wanted to see.

Rachel sat still, only her hands betraying the trembling sensation that she was feeling within herself. It curled inside her stomach, sent flutterings along her sensitized nerves. Her tongue flicked out to wet her suddenly dry lips.

Matthew stood there for a moment, just look-

119

ing at her. Rachel flushed under his intense regard. The sun had long since set and the moon was rising high in the sky. Lanterns set a few feet apart bathed the garden in a pale, flickering light. A fat tabby cat lay curled up upon a large piece of flagstone, asleep just inches from the wrought-iron bench where Rachel sat. The smell of flowers mixed, providing the night with a strong scent of gardenia and jasmine floating around them.

Matthew approached her, seating himself next to her. "God, *chérie*, how I've missed you," he said without preamble. He took her cool hand in his. "What about you, Rachel? Tell me," he asked, his voice a husky drawl, "have you given some scant thought to me while I've been gone?"

Rachel lifted her free hand and stroked his face, her fingertips lightly skimming his temple, his cheekbone, his rugged jaw. She was so close she could smell the scent of the soap he used; she couldn't identify the fragrance, but it was definitely masculine and well suited to him. She could also see the thick black lashes that framed his blue eyes.

Rachel answered him truthfully, for she knew that there was nothing to be gained by putting on a false front of coyness. She didn't think she was capable of that even if she had wanted to. "Without you, I thought the days were endless. One piled upon another, with no real purpose."

Matthew smiled with satisfaction at her honest words. "I found myself thinking about you at odd moments," he confessed, "when my mind should have been on the business at hand. Yet there you were, invading my thoughts without so much as a by-your-leave."

"I'm glad," Rachel added with a smile. And she was. To know that Matthew carried memories of her inside him that came out at odd times thrilled her. She was inside his heart as he was in hers. It was, she decided, another sign that this was meant to be. He was—she searched for the word to describe what she felt—her soul mate, the man fated for her.

Yes, she liked that word. Matthew was her gift from God. While in Ireland, she had prayed for a man she could love with her whole heart. She wanted a love that could bind her as completely to another person as her parents were bound to one another. Deep, tender, true, and forever. God had seen fit in His infinite wisdom to answer her prayers better than she could have imagined.

Matthew's large hand gently cupped her chin, holding her still for his kiss. It was a soft salute; nothing like the storm-inspired hungry exploration of weeks ago. This was simple and short, a way to communicate a sort of harmony between them.

Rachel could well understand Matthew's need for circumspection; after all, they were sitting in the garden of his parents' home, and she

121

was a guest. But oh, she secretly longed for a taste just once again of the passion that they had shared that afternoon.

As if reading her mind, Matt lifted her hand from her lap and brought it to his lips.

Expecting a chaste kiss, Rachel was surprised when his mouth lingered on the pulse beating in her wrist, when his warm breath fanned the fire rising within her, when his tongue slowly traced the path of one of the lines of her palm, lingering on the pad of soft flesh between her middle and ring finger.

Rachel moaned low in her throat, a catlike, contented sound.

"I haven't forgotten," he reminded her, as if reading her thoughts.

"Nor have I," Rachel answered.

She heard the sound of voices from the open doorway above. A heavy disappointment came over her. It was then she recalled that she hadn't told him about her happiness with his present.

"Matthew, I want to thank you so very much for the lovely gift you gave me," she said. "I shall cherish it always."

"I want it to be the first of many gifts you receive from me, *chérie*," he reponded. "Each one will show you in what regard I hold you. But come," he said in a coaxing tone, "we must rejoin the others before I damage your reputation."

He helped her up. "A walk in the garden is

one thing, a moonlight tryst another."

His next words were uttered in a darker, more seductive tone. "And we shall have that tryst one day, *chérie*, I promise you."

Chapter Seven

Since coming to Belle Chanson, some three months have flown by so quickly I scarce have time to write in this diary.

As I suspected they would, my parents gave their permission for me to move here temporarily so that I might tutor Matthew's younger sister. Marguerite is a joy, and so eager to absorb knowledge. My special nickname for her is "little sponge." She's a good-natured child, and on occasion, her brother joins us for lessons. With Matthew's help, I've had a chance to take her outside the confines of a classroom, and it has provided me with a chance to also spend more time with him, especially as he's called away more and more frequently on business, leav-

ing the plantation for weeks at a time.

Sometimes I let my mind drift and think of how Matthew would be as a father: then I realize that I may be putting the cart before the horse as he has been a perfect gentleman whenever we're together. No mention has passed his lips of making me his wife, nor of the kisses we have shared. Our time has been very circumspect. Yet still, the mere touch of his hands on mine sends such a frisson of sensation through me that I think that I may swoon.

Rachel yawned as she finished her entry. She missed Matthew. This last time he'd been gone for over three weeks. She'd once asked him where he went on his business trips and a blank look had come over Matthew's face as he told her that it wasn't important. Rachel believed otherwise, for Matthew always returned exhausted, and with a new look in his eyes, hard and dangerous, but she didn't press the issue. The worry that grew deeper each time he left she learned to keep to herself, not wanting to bother him with her concerns.

Christmas was but a few days away. She'd helped in decorating the rooms of the plantation house with religious symbols, and delighted in the wonderfully carved creches that represented the Nativity. She would leave on the morrow to spend the holiday with her parents in New Orleans, and she wished that Matthew were here so that she could give him the gift she'd recently purchased for him. It was wrapped in plain brown paper, with a length of red satin ribbon, and stood in one corner of her room.

Rachel rose from her desk chair and sauntered over to where it rested. It was a painting she'd commissioned of Matthew's horse Cimarron. She smiled when she recalled the big red stallion's frisky reaction to an artist sketching him. As if the animal knew what was taking place, he'd posed with the grace of any artist's model, lording it over the other horses in the paddock. When that was done, he then gobbled up the special treats Rachel provided him. Bribery to be sure, but the results were worth it, Rachel thought.

The night air was only slightly cool. It blew in the white muslin curtains that surrounded the long windows that opened onto the gallery.

Not really ready for sleep, Rachel moved to the window and pushed back the curtain, walking outside. Her slippered feet made no sound as she took a few steps toward the railing. She breathed the fresh air. It gently ruffled the rose silk cloak she'd thrown over her camisole and single petticoat, and stirred her hair, left unbound and waving to her waist. It was a time of day she found she enjoyed here on the plantation. It was quiet, with only the familiar sounds and smells of the night. So different from the city.

In the distance, she could see lights in the *garconnière*. That could only mean that Matthew had returned.

She longed to run to him, if only to reassure herself that he was well. Her gaze fixed on the small house, wishing that she could force him to come to a window and look out. Only a glimpse. That was all she wanted, needed.

Just then she saw a figure in the upstairs window. Rachel lifted her hand and waved, hoping he would see.

She stood there for what seemed an eternity, waiting for a response. When none came after a few minutes, she decided that it had probably been too dark for him to see her, and that she should go to bed.

However, she stood there, immobile, unable to tear her eyes away from the little cottage across the lawn.

Finally, one by one, all the lights went out in the *garconnière*, plunging it into the surrounding darkness.

Rachel realized that her vigil wasn't coming to the conclusion that she'd hoped, so she gave up and returned to her room, saddened that she hadn't had the chance to see Matthew. No doubt he would be too exhausted to rise early on the morrow and she'd be gone before he came to the house.

With a sigh, Rachel touched her two fingers

to her lips and blew a kiss in his direction. "Sleep well, my love, and may God hold you close in his hand."

She went back into her room, extinguishing all the lamps except for the one at her bedside. Slowly, she removed the cloak and placed it back in the armoire that held her dresses and fancier clothes. A matching chest of drawers on the other side of the room held her nightwear and underthings. Both were lined with cedar, giving off a distinctive scent whenever a drawer or door was opened.

She was standing there, her hand on the brass knob of the armoire door, when she heard a deep, husky voice behind her call out her name softly. "Rachel."

Startled, she spun around and saw Matthew standing there, on the threshold of her room. Rachel blinked, focusing on his appearance as he slowly moved closer. Instead of the immaculate grooming that was his hallmark, he seemed slightly disheveled, with traces of stubble darkening his jaw; his once-white shirt was unbuttoned halfway down his chest, exposing the whorls of dark hair there, and there was a stark white bandage wrapped around his lower right arm where his shirtsleeve had been rolled up.

Rachel forgot propriety as she closed the distance between them. "Matthew!" she exclaimed, rushing into his open arms.

His arms closed about her, holding her as

129

close as was possible. Matt breathed in the sweet scent of her hair, the subtle traces of the perfume she favored. How good it was to feel the solid warmth of her skin through the thin fabric she wore.

"I saw you standing there on the gallery," he said, one hand tangled in the mass of her golden-blonde hair, stroking it until he entwined a fistful around his hand. "I debated with myself about coming to you now, so late at night." Matthew put a few inches between their bodies, tilting his head down to look at her. "I know that I shouldn't be here, that I shouldn't be with you," he stated with a groan, "but God, I couldn't stay away. It was as if you were somehow calling to me inside my mind, Rachel, asking—no, pleading with me to come."

"I was," she revealed shyly, a sweetly serene smile on her face.

"You beckoned me like an angel," he insisted, "promising heaven, and I couldn't resist." Matthew placed one hand beneath her chin and lifted her face up, placing his mouth on hers.

Rachel surrendered instantly to the pressure of his lips, returning the kiss. It was wild and abandoned, pushing aside her defenses. Her mind swirled, caught up in the heady power of sensual delight. She gladly opened her mouth to him, permitting the entrance of his tongue. It stroked and teased, and she followed his lead, returning the same, delighting in the sensations this form of kissing could engender.

Held so close to his male body, Rachel could feel the strength of Matthew's lean, muscled flesh. In response, her own body altered: her nipples tightened against the sheer lawn of her camisole, rubbing against his chest. A sweet, languorous feeling stole over her, making her feel as if she were ready to faint.

Breaking the kiss, Matthew swung her up into his embrace.

"Your arm," she managed to say as he carried her to the low mahogany bed that was placed at the foot of her great bed. Originally used as a birthing bed, called a *lit d'accouchement*, it now served a different purpose.

"Damn my arm," he ground out, lowering her to the comfort of the small down-filled mattress, following her body with his own.

They were so close Rachel could see the fine lines around Matthew's blue eyes, eyes that were so focused on her she couldn't help but stare back until he shifted his weight, sitting up, his body slanted across the structure and over hers. It was too short for a man of his height to lie full-length, so he moderated his position.

Rachel lay there, her heart beating furiously, her breath coming in short gasps, her breasts moving beneath the material, waiting for whatever came next.

She didn't have long to contemplate Matthew's next move, for his arm, the bandage white against his tanned flesh, lifted. He brought his hand down upon her neck, fingers skirting the pulse that beat there. He followed that with his mouth, lightly nipping.

Trembling, Rachel managed to ask, "How did you injure your arm?"

"An accident," he murmured dismissively, raising his head. "It's of no consequence."

Matthew then lowered his gaze to the thrust of her bosom. His hand went likewise, long, slender fingers gently touching, stroking, cupping, until he finally held the weight of her flesh in his palm.

Rachel closed her eyes on a deep sigh, a quick shot of heat flaring to life in her lower body.

Her eyes flew open when she felt the moist tip of his tongue as it laved the fine lawn, which damply outlined her puckered nipple. Once more, exquisite pleasure knifed through Rachel's body; from her throat, small whimpering, moaning sounds erupted. Like lightning, Matthew's touch electrified her, causing shocks to dart haphazardly throughout her system.

Rachel watched as Matthew raised his head, a deep smile on his mouth. He proceeded to slowly unbutton the camisole, spreading it aside so that he would have nothing between his hand and her breast. He cupped her flesh again, his thumb tracing circles around the crest. All the while he kept his eyes riveted to hers, to the rise of color in her cheeks, to Rachel's sharp inhalations of breath.

Each new touch took Rachel farther and farther along this dark and sensual highway. Her head swam from Matthew's ministrations. Yet even though she was falling deeper and deeper under this erotic enchantment, some rational part of her brain was telling her that this wasn't right for her. Moral lessons from her childhood came flooding back, like an oft-repeated catechism, sounding louder with each passing second, warning her that she would soon pass the point of no return.

When Matthew dipped his head to experience her naked flesh, Rachel raised her formerly languid arms and pushed at his chest, her fingertips sliding through the dark chest hair. "Please," she pleaded in a strained voice, "release me."

Matthew, taken aback by the vehemence of her demand, did as Rachel requested. Seeing the slightly panicked look in her eyes, he rose and stood with his back to her, getting his ragged breathing under control and giving her time to compose herself.

Shame flushed her skin pink as Rachel redid the buttons of her camisole with shaking fingers, watching the rise and fall of Matthew's shoulders beneath the white shirt. How could she have let this happen? She'd behaved like a wanton, allowing Matthew to touch her so intimately, reveling in the way his skin had felt so warm under her fingers. She'd even enjoyed the crisp feel of the hair that furred his chest.

"Forgive me, Rachel," Matthew said in a raspy tone, turning to face her again.

Grabbing the counterpane off the nearby bed, Rachel clutched it to her bosom, wrapping it around her body, her legs drawn up under her. She huddled there on the small bed like a frightened child.

And she was afraid—afraid of how Matthew made her feel, as if her own will was suddenly negated; afraid that she would beg him to continue his heart-stirring lovemaking no matter what her protestations; afraid that she would somehow lose him if she withheld herself from him. Her gaze dropped and she could see the evidence of his powerful arousal jutting against his trousers. Her face flamed once again.

Running the tip of her tongue across her kiss-swollen lips, she said, "As you must forgive me," trying to accept some portion of the blame for allowing this wild situation to happen. She should have begged him to leave her room when he first appeared. Instead, she had welcomed him with open arms, pouring out her happiness and concern upon seeing him.

"For being what?" Matthew mocked. "An innocent? You are, Rachel, and I damn near seduced you into betraying what you hold most dear, your honor."

He swore crudely and effectively in French. "If anyone else had attempted to do this to you I would call him out without hesitation. But—" he shrugged his broad shoulders—"I can't very well challenge myself to a duel, now can I?" A bittersweet smile curved his mouth.

"I've disgraced my family and dishonored our hospitality. You must believe me when I tell you that it wasn't planned, *chérie*."

Rachel heard the remorse in Matthew's voice and loved him all the more for it. He wanted to shoulder the burden of this illicit encounter, thereby sparing her feelings. But she couldn't allow him to do that. He hadn't forced her. "Of course I believe you, Matthew," she said. "You'd never do anything to hurt me, I know that."

Matthew closed his eyes for a moment. "Never willingly, my love." He started to make a movement toward her, then abruptly changed his mind. "It's just that when I looked out my window and saw you standing there, I knew I had to see you tonight, devil take the risk," he admitted. "I wanted to ask you something."

"What?" she inquired.

"It will wait till morning."

"I'm returning to New Orleans in the morning, Matthew," Rachel said.

"When?"

"I had hoped to leave after breakfast. I only stayed this long because I was afraid that I wouldn't see you before I left," she confessed.

"You musn't leave until we've talked."

"About what?"

"Not now," he said in a controlled voice. "It can wait till after you've eaten in the morning." He fixed her with a sharp look. "Promise me that you won't leave until we've had a chance to talk."

135

"I promise."

Matthew was gone. Just like that.

Tears clouded Rachel's eyes as she quickly glanced about the room, now empty of his presence. She swung her legs to the floor, sitting up and staring at the curtains as they moved in the soft breeze of the night.

She fought the urge to call him back, to beg him to stay, whatever the consequences. That would be folly, she knew; ah, but what sweet irrationality!

Did Dominique feel this same sense of loss now that Matthew had forsaken her bed? Rachel wondered how any woman having once known love in Matthew's arms could ever willingly give him up. Once or twice she was tempted to ask Angelique how her sister was faring, but wisely, she refrained from so indelicate a topic with the housekeeper.

At that moment, Rachel felt very close to Dominique, for they shared something precious between them. It was a womanly bond that would forever link them, a debt owed for a happiness taken.

One day, Rachel vowed, she would find a way to make it up to the other woman, no matter how long it took.

Matthew made his way back to the lonely enclave of the *garconnière*. As soon as he stepped through the front door, his dog greeted him, pressing his nose against Matthew's hand. A lamp broke the spell of darkness. It was his manservant, Achille.

"Get me a drink," Matthew said in a tone that clearly showed his frustration, both with himself and with circumstances.

Damn! he swore to himself as he bounded up the stairs two at a time until he reached his bedroom, the dog at his heels. He pulled off his shirt, scattering the buttons, and threw it against the wall.

Next he went to the washbasin and splashed the tepid water that was there on his face. It dripped down his neck and torso, yet it did not cool his ardor, or his anger.

Matthew couldn't believe that he'd almost lost his ability to reason when he started to make love to Rachel. He was a man who prided himself on maintaining control of a situation; but with Rachel, he'd come close to losing it, to abandoning his sense of decorum. He could have very well taken her innocence had she not pulled back, so enraptured was he.

The realization that he wanted this Irish girl as he'd never wanted any woman in his life shocked him. He knew it was foolish to have gone to her room like that. Yet he couldn't have stopped himself.

Achille entered the room with a mahogany tray that contained a bottle of brandy and a snifter. He set it down on a marble-topped bedside table and poured a more than generous amount of the expensive French liqueur into the glass, giving Matthew a swift, appraising look, and taking note of the abandoned shirt that lay rumpled in the corner and the sloshed water on the carpet.

Matthew grabbed the glass and tossed the smooth brandy down his throat. "Another," he demanded, slumping into a nearby chair, his dog curling up at his feet.

"Aren't you going to say anything?"

Achille pondered the question for a moment before answering. "What would you have me say?"

"How the hell should I know?" Matthew muttered darkly, taking the glass from the other man's hand.

"I've never seen you like this," Achille finally observed.

"I've never been in love before," Matthew replied, taking a smaller amount of brandy this time.

Matthew raked one hand through his thick hair. In love. He was well and truly in love with Rachel, and there was no getting past that.

Oh God, he thought, what a time to fall in love. What with the war brewing and his work for the government, work that must, because of its nature, take priority over his personal feelings.

"Do you want anything else?" Achille asked.

"No, this will be fine." Matthew closed his eyes and rested his head against the back of the chair.

Several minutes later his lips curved into a smile. He knew what he had to do, grateful that it was also what he wanted to do.

Rachel sat in the smaller family dining room with Matthew's mother, finishing her share of the huge breakfast that was served each morning at the plantation. Eduoard Devereaux had already left the table ten minutes earlier to see to Rachel's carriage for the trip back to New Orleans.

"I've so enjoyed your company, my dear," Frances Devereaux remarked. "It was like having an older daughter at long last." She nodded to a waiting servant to pour her another cup of strong coffee, which she liberally laced with steaming milk. "Between Matthew and Marguerite, I lost several children," she confided. "Two boys and a daughter. Had my Libby lived, she would have been about your age now."

"I'm so sorry," Rachel responded. She thought about how much it must hurt to lose a child, and said a hasty prayer for the departed souls of the Devereaux children. She knew that her own mother had lost a child before its birth, and what emotional turmoil it had caused her parents.

Frances gave her a sad smile. "It was a long time ago, but I still remember them in my heart, and shall till the day I die. But I didn't bring up old memories to darken your joy, my dear, only to pay you my highest compliment."

She reached out her hand and gave Rachel's a squeeze. "You're a part of our lives now and I shall miss you."

"And I you, madame," Rachel responded in earnest. "You've made me feel as if I were a member of your family rather than just a guest, or even a temporary employee."

"Oh, never that, I assure you, Rachel," Frances said. "You're a very special young woman, and your influence on Marguerite is commendable. She can be a hoyden when she wants to be, and I'm afraid that we all spoil her dreadfully, especially Matthew, and most especially since her recent illness."

"Talking about me again, Mama?" Matthew asked, a rakish grin on his face this morning as he sauntered into the room. He stooped and gave his mother a kiss. This day he was freshly shaved, his clothes flawless as usual. There was no visible evidence of last night's worn and weary man.

"When did you get back?" his mother asked, touching his arm.

When Rachel saw the wince of pain that crossed Matthew's face, she was going to mention his wound until she caught the look in his eyes. He shook his head, silently asking her not to.

Respecting his wishes, Rachel reluctantly agreed. She watched as the servant poured a hot cup of fresh coffee for him.

Matthew glanced in Rachel's direction as he

swallowed the beverage. With a smile, he recited a Creole saying for her:

"Noir comme le diable.
Chaud comme l'enfer.
Pur comme une ange.
Doux comme l'amour."

Frances laughed. "I think that you should repeat the words for Rachel in English," she suggested, mirth evident in her eyes.

Rachel was tempted to remind both of the Devereauxs that she did understand basic French; however, if she did so, then she wouldn't have the distinct pleasure of listening to Matthew's voice recite the words. She chose silence.

"With pleasure, Mama," Matthew responded. He gazed deeply into Rachel's eyes and began in his deep, drawling voice:

Black as the devil.

Hot as hell.

Pure as an angel.

Sweet as love.

Each line was spoken slowly and deliberately, with just the right amount of emphasis.

Rachel thought that only Matthew could make a maxim about coffee sound like a love poem. She realized then that she longed to hear that exquisite voice reading sonnets to her. Or, she mused with a smile, even the *Daily Crescent*, so long as she could listen.

141

Matthew finished his coffee and motioned the servant back when he would have refilled his cup. "Perhaps later," he said. "Mama, if you will excuse us, I would have a private word with Rachel."

Frances cast a curious look in her son's direction. "Private? Must it be so?" she gently demanded with a sharp look at her son. "She is to leave for New Orleans soon."

Matthew knew how his mother felt about observing the proprieties. "I will not keep her long, but it is a matter of vital importance, I assure you."

"Very well," Frances conceded. "You may have use of the music room."

"Thank you, Mama," Matthew said and rose, taking Rachel's arm in his and leading her down the long hallway to another elegantly furnished room that contained a grand piano, a tall harp, and an assortment of tufted rose satin brocade chairs and couches by Belter, all arranged for optimum listening.

Matthew escorted her to one of the sofas, while he remained standing. Several seconds ticked by as Rachel waited for him to speak. She did feel a trifle awkward in his presence after last evening's encounter. How was one supposed to feel after almost making love with a man? Was he going to apologize once more for the indiscretion?

"Rachel," he said finally, "I'd like you to do me the great honor of becoming my wife.

Will you marry me?"

Rachel's face reflected her surprise. "Wife?" she asked in a small voice, tears of joy forming in her eyes.

A self-satisfied grin tilted the corners of Matthew's expressive mouth. "Yes, *chérie*, my wife."

" 'Tis not because you feel that you have to, is it?" she inquired. She wanted this desperately—but only for the right reasons.

Matthew came to her and bent one knee, enfolding her smaller hand in his. "Trust me, Rachel, it's not because I feel some sense of guilt or shame for what happened last night. What we shared was beautiful, and I shall cherish those memories," he explained. "I had planned on asking you some time in the New Year, but certain events are unfolding that force me to alter my plans somewhat. Before things get out of control, I want to know that we are promised to one another."

"What events?" The passionate conviction of Matthew's voice had removed her earlier doubts, yet she began to worry about what he intimated in his last sentence.

Matthew took a deep breath. "The coming war. South Carolina has already voted to dissolve ties with the Union, and I would imagine that other states will quickly follow."

"Are you certain that there will be war?"

"Without a doubt," he answered. "President Lincoln will not let the Union falter. I wish to God that I was wrong, Rachel, but too many things have happened to change my mind."

"And what will you do?" Fear for him started to run riot through her system.

Matthew rose and seated himself next to her. "I must do what my conscience advises me to do."

"Then you will join the Union army, won't you?"

"I already have," he admitted.

"That's why you've suddenly been taking so many business trips? It's not plantation concerns, is it?"

He nodded his head. "I volunteered to do some work for Union intelligence, and because of that, I must keep my work secret. Not even my family knows this, though I suspect my father has figured it out."

"Your secret is safe with me," Rachel vowed.

"I knew it would be, my love." Matthew leaned over and lightly pressed his lips to hers in a swift, soft kiss. He drew back, a smile on his mouth. "God, how I want to do more than merely kiss you," he whispered in a husky voice, "but I dare not. Any moment now I expect my mother or a servant to come and tell us that the carriage is ready for you. Oh Rachel, you're such a beguiling, tempting woman, my love, and when we are finally together as man and wife, I want time to enjoy what we have to share. If I kiss you again, I don't know if I could stop from throwing caution to the winds."

He pulled the topaz ring from his little finger.

144

"I haven't had an opportunity to get you a proper ring yet, so will you wear this instead until I can?"

"I'd be honored, Matthew."

He slipped the ring on her slender finger. It was loose.

"I'll wrap a ribbon around it," Rachel said, touching it. She lifted her hand to her lips and kissed the stone. Rachel felt the warmth of the gold band heat her own skin.

"I love you, Rachel," Matthew declared. "Someday soon I'll show the entire world just how much when we marry. I can only hope that this war won't last very long.

"Now," he said reluctantly, "I'd best get you downstairs before a search party is sent for you."

"Will you tell your parents?" She hoped that he would say yes, for she wanted to tell her own parents the happy news as soon as she arrived back in New Orleans.

"Yes," he answered. "I want them to know that when you return to Belle Chanson, you do so as their future daughter-in-law."

They walked hand in hand down the wide steps and out into the sun. The fancy Devereaux carriage was waiting to convey Rachel back to her family's house in the Garden District.

Matthew handed her up into the conveyance, tucking the material that surrounded her wide hoop skirt into the carriage. He was soon joined by his parents and his sister. They all said their good-byes to Rachel.

"I've left a present for you in my room," Rachel said, leaning out the window, remembering the plain paper–wrapped package. "I didn't know if you'd make it back before I left."

Matthew reached out his hand, his long fingertips touching her gloved palm. "Whatever it is, I'm sure I shall love it," he said.

The horses moved and the driver pulled back on the reins.

"I think it best if you let Rachel go now, son," Eduoard Devereaux advised.

The driver flicked his whip and as the carriage pulled away, their hands slowly drew apart as his fingers slid across her palm and down her fingertips until there was no contact.

"*Au revoir, chérie,*" he called after her.

Rachel hugged Matthew's last words to herself later that night when she was curled up in her own bed. She'd related the events of that morning to her parents and they were thrilled for her.

Her papa had even bragged, "Just like us, Kathleen. Knew that the very minute I saw that boy look upon our girl. As smitten as I was the first morn I laid my eyes on you and thought that the blessed saints were after giving me all the wonders of heaven itself."

Connor had addressed his next comment to his daughter. "If you're half as happy with him as I've been with my Kathleen, then you'll be one lucky lass."

One lucky lass indeed, Rachel thought, fingering the ring once again. This time she'd wound a piece of satin ribbon around it so that it fit snugly on her finger. Rachel was of half a mind not to give it back to Matthew after he gave her a new ring. She wanted to keep this as a cherished memento, a ring she would never remove. It was something of Matthew that belonged to her now, as Matthew would soon belong to her. It symbolized his pledge and their love.

And for that reason, Rachel vowed to wear it forever, no matter what.

Chapter Eight

Matthew was right. The war is now upon us. Louisiana has declared that it is no longer a part of the Union.

I've observed how very much this has changed people hereabouts. Friends and families are torn asunder as members must choose sides.

It was only after the vehement protestations of my mama and myself that my father changed his mind about enlisting in the Union army; he has, instead, taken on a job to help provide horses to the army. Papa believes in the Union cause, as does Matthew.

While my head agrees with them, my heart is torn. So much blood and pain may come from this conflict, and all I wish is *that we could leave, go somewhere else, anywhere else so as to avoid what is to follow.*

But I know that is foolish. I could never leave New Orleans without Matthew. My life is with him. So here I will remain, until the happy day when this conflict is ended and Matthew comes home to me. Our wedding has been postponed, and while I wish that I was his wife now, I know Matthew wants us to have a wedding we can both look back upon, something to tell our grandchildren about when we're both old.

Just the thought of spending the rest of my life with him is enough to get me through this lonely time. Children . . . grandchildren. What a happy thought amidst this chaos.

Come home soon, my love.

Rachel sipped her coffee, studying the words she had written. She dipped her pen in the inkwell and scratched out a phrase, writing another above it, satisfied at last with this draft. She was working on an article that she was planning to send to a school friend of hers in Ireland whose father published a newspaper in Dublin. Matthew had mentioned that British sentiment was weighted more in favor of the Southern states, and Rachel, who had recently sold several pieces to women's magazines, most notably *Lady's Book* and *Peterson's Ladies' National Magazine*, decided that perhaps this was something that she could do to help Matthew and the cause that he was fighting for.

Writing was a way for Rachel to make pin money, and it gave her a chance to exercise her ability with words. She'd always enjoyed essays in school, and now she'd discovered that she could make money from her observations and thoughts. At first, they were reviews about books she'd read, then recipes she'd gathered since coming to New Orleans, and finally, her impressions of Creole society. As an outlander, her views were fresh and untainted by cultural prejudice.

She smiled with delight when she glanced at the box that sat upon her desk. It held the ring she'd bought for Matthew with her own money, a band of gold with the initials *M* and *R* intertwined in script. It was a replacement for the topaz signet ring of his that she now wore to mark their engagement.

Rachel planned on giving it to Matthew when next he was home. Each day without him seemed like a form of punishment, a penal sentence that she was forced to endure.

So far, he'd managed to get two hastily written letters to her, and she'd read, and reread, the notes carefully, memorizing each word. They were short and to the point, without the frills she knew Matthew was capable of using to embellish his work. Yet that didn't matter, for they were from Matthew, and therefore to be cherished.

She'd been back to Belle Chanson several times since his departure at the request of his parents, who were overjoyed at the announcement of Rachel's engagement to their son. Frances Devereaux promised that as soon as this ghastly war was over, she would host an engagement ball such as Louisiana had never seen, and then as a wedding present, she and Eduoard would give them a honeymoon on the continent, including London, Paris, Rome, and Vienna.

Rachel was thrilled at the generosity of her future in-laws, and prayed that it wouldn't be long before this conflict came to its conclusion. Already, she heard gossip in the market regarding the stand that Matthew had taken. Ugly whispers of resentment, and harsh words of "traitor," and "turncoat," were bandied about. One afternoon recently, while taking lunch at Antoines with Carolyn, she had overheard a man, well into his cups as indicated by his slurred words, sneer, "Matthew Devereaux is a rotten scoundrel, a traitor to Louisiana who isn't fit to breathe the same air as decent folks. He's a nigger-loving Yankee, just like his mama."

At that, her teeth clamped together to still her rising rage, Rachel stood up and told Carolyn that she was leaving the restauarant, but that she had something to take care of first.

Her friend nodded and waited with a wary look on her face.

Rachel rose and picked up her water goblet. She approached the man and said with a tight smile on her face, "You, sir, are an ignorant jackass," and then proceeded to fling the contents of the goblet into his pasty face. "Matthew Devereaux is a man of honor; a word with which you obviously have no familiarity."

The man sputtered and his companion, noting Rachel's Irish accent, scoffed in a cold, haughty voice, "What would a vulgar Irish slattern know about honor?"

Rachel paused and held her head high, a contemptuous stare in her eyes. "More, I'm thinking, than you could ever possibly hope to understand, madam. I would rather be considered a common street girl than a coward's companion." And with that sally, Rachel left the restaurant.

It still made Rachel angry to think about that incident, that some fool could judge her Matthew a traitor for fighting for his beliefs. He was a hero in her eyes, a man of courage who could fly in the face of the world in which he'd grown up.

Kathleen Gallagher joined her daughter in the room Rachel used as her study cum office. It was originally a tiny nursery that Rachel had converted to a place for her to work, with just a simple oak desk and a chair. A pile of loose paper lay to one side, along with an extra inkwell, a copy of the *Daily Crescent*, and the newest *Lady's Book*, which contained Rachel's first article for them.

"There's someone waiting below to see you, Rachel," her mother announced.

Rachel lifted her head. "Who?"

Kathleen shrugged her shoulders. "I don't know," she confessed. "'Tis some Negro boy who said that he must speak to only you."

Rachel rose hurriedly. "Perhaps he's come from Matthew," she said as she dashed past her mother and made her way quickly down the stairs.

In the hallway stood a boy whom she recognized as Jason, the young groom she'd met that first day at Belle Chanson.

Rachel gave him a friendly smile as she advanced toward him. "What brings you here, Jason?" she asked.

"I was told to bring you this here letter, Miss Rachel," he said, "and I was to deliver it to nobody but you." Jason reached into his pants and dug out a mud-spattered envelope.

Rachel recognized the masculine hand when she took hold of the envelope. It was from Matthew.

"Is he here?" she asked, eager for news.

Jason shook his head, a forlorn look on his face. "That there letter was given to me by Mr. Matthew's father," the boy explained. "It came by a rider last night. He rode in after dark to Belle Chanson and gave the master a leather pouch. Then he took off again real quick, like demons was after him."

"Then I thank you, Jason, for delivering it to me so quickly." Rachel hugged the boy.

Surprise at her gesture widened the young groom's brown eyes.

"Now, you go into the kitchen," Rachel instructed, giving him directions, "follow the hall there, and tell Liselle that I said to fix you something before you return to Belle Chanson."

Rachel stood up and saw the hesitation in the boy's face. "Go ahead now, my fine lad. Off you go, scoot," she admonished, and the boy darted down the hall.

Rachel rushed into the library to read the letter, shutting the door so that she could be alone.

Ma Chère *Rachel:*

I miss you so much, my love, and wish that I didn't have to be so far away from you, but duty does demand its sacrifices.

I cannot tell you where I am, or where I will be, so communication between us will have to remain as haphazard as it is now. I know that this must be intolerable for you, but you know the reason. Fate has twisted us from the path that we were meant to walk, but I know that one day we shall be together.

I would to God that I could see your face right now, hear your laughter, feel the touch of your hand. My comfort during this sep-

aration comes from vivid memories of you, of each day of our time spent with each other. It is for that reason that I write to you the words that another man saw fit to have inscribed on the tomb of his beloved. Do you remember the story I told you about the owner-manager of the New Orleans Theatre and the lady he loved, but could not marry, the actress Jane Placide? Well, I recalled those words and now present them to you as a token of my love, for they speak true of what is in my heart:

"There's not an hour of day or dreaming night but I am with thee;

There's not a breeze but whispers of thy name.

And not a flower that sleeps beneath the moon

But its fragrance tells a tale of thee."

Matthew

Rachel wiped the tears from her eyes with the tips of her fingers. "Oh my love," she whispered, "know that wherever you are, I am with you, for now and for always."

Many more lonely months passed for Rachel before she had physical contact with Matthew again. Brief messages sometimes appeared inside a parcel that she picked up at the market, or were delivered within a bouquet of fresh-picked flowers. No name and nothing to indicate who or where they were from. Just a hastily scribbled note that said, "Pray, love, remember."

As if she could ever forget this love she bore for him. Never, she vowed. It was as fresh this day as it had been on that very first day. Only now it was stronger, deeper, more sure of itself.

One afternoon in late fall, Rachel was shopping in the marketplace with Liselle, selecting some foodstuffs for that evening's dinner. Staples were beginning to be hard to come by, for people were afraid that the war would mean many hardships, and consequently, those that could, stocked up on goods, leaving a scant supply for others. Sugar, always a precious commodity, became more so. Some foodmongers began to inch their prices upward, while others resisted as long as they could.

She left Liselle, who was busy haggling with a fisherman over the catch of the day, and walked just a few feet away to examine some of the wares of a dark-skinned woman who was selling ribbons and threads, along with all manner of interesting gewgaws, just down the street.

"What you lookin' for?" the older woman asked.

Rachel shrugged her shoulders. "I'm not sure," she responded. "Do you mind if I just have a look?"

The old woman grinned, revealing some

missing teeth. "I knows just what you need," she said with a sly wink.

Rachel laughed, thinking that all the world over, whether in Ireland or here in America, merchants were just the same.

She selected a length of dark wine-colored velvet ribbon, her mind going over which of her outfits this trimming could enhance.

"Good choice," the woman said as Rachel picked up another velvet ribbon, this time in a lovely violet shade. She liked it so much she bought several more lengths of the same ribbon, and another for her mother.

"How much for all these?" Rachel asked.

The vendor named her price and although Rachel thought it was ridiculously low, she couldn't ignore the bargain. She pulled out the sum of money in coin from her reticule as the woman placed her wares in a paper wrapper.

She handed the package to Rachel, along with another. Knowing the delightful custom of Creole merchants giving their customers a gift, called a lagniappe, which could be anything from a piece of candy to a flower, Rachel smiled her thanks.

"You be sure to see what *Tante* Germaine done give you, chile," the old woman said with a hearty laugh. "You gonna love it, you hear?" And with that she walked away, singing softly to herself.

Whatever could that woman mean? Rachel wondered as she put the packages in her basket.

Walking only a few feet back to where Liselle waited with a broad smile on her face, indicating that it was she who had won her battle with the fishmonger, Rachel felt her curiosity growing, making her want to rip open the little gift to see what it contained.

While Liselle stepped across the street to get something from the spice merchant, Rachel decided that she'd waited long enough and proceeded to tear open the paper.

What it contained was a miniature portrait of Matthew Devereaux, and a message, written on the inside of the brown paper. "Meet me. River Road. Come as soon as you can."

Rachel gasped in delighted surprise. She couldn't ignore this summons. "Matthew," she said softly. At long last. Her heart beat faster with excitement.

She hurried across the street. "Come, Liselle, we have to return home."

"Why are you in such a hurry, Miss Rachel?" the housekeeper asked, adding the packet of filè she'd just purchased to her basket. "I thought we were going to visit that sick friend of your mama's and meet Miss Kathleen there?"

"I can't explain, but I have to get home now," Rachel said, already walking toward the open carriage. "It's very important, Liselle," she said as the housekeeper quickened her steps to keep up with Rachel.

Rachel decided to stretch the truth just a bit. "There is another appointment that I completely forgot and it is too important to miss."

Liselle leveled a glance at Rachel, heaving a deep sigh. "If that's what you want, then it's fine with me," she said matter-of-factly, "but it is sure gonna disappoint your mama."

"I know," Rachel conceded, getting into the carriage, "but it just cannot be helped."

The journey back to her house in the Garden District was completed as quickly as possible, Rachel verbally urging her driver to "hurry along."

As soon as the carriage came to a stop, Rachel was out of the conveyance and winging her way to the door. Once inside, she hurried up the steps to her room. Pausing at the landing, she called down to Liselle, who'd just entered the hallway. "Oh, Liselle, would you mind telling Sean"—their driver was an Irish lad newly arrived in the city, a boy Connor had found in the "Irish Channel" district of New Orleans near the waterfront—"that I will need my mare saddled and ready for me within the half hour."

Rachel saw the puzzled look Liselle wore when she opened Rachel's bedroom door a few minutes later after seeing to the food. The housekeeper cast another glance at the scattered mound of clothes that lay heaped upon the floor: the petticoats, crinoline, stockings, jacket, skirt, and blouse. It was as if one of the fierce gulf storms had blown through the room, whipping the contents to and fro.

"You're in one powerful hurry, Miss Rachel,"

Liselle observed in her drawling voice as the young Irishwoman removed her sapphire-blue riding habit from the armoire while she tried to restore some order to the clothes tossed aside.

"Leave them," Rachel instructed as she slipped the white lace petticoat around her waist, and then buttoned the batiste blouse. "I shall attend to them later," she promised.

"It's no bother, Miss Rachel," Liselle assured her.

"Where are my boots?" Rachel asked as she fastened the silk taffeta skirt. Standing before the cheval glass, Rachel examined herself as she put on the jacket that completed this stylish ensemble. The jacket's bell sleeves were cut back and notched to let the fuller sleeves of the white blouse show through.

"Here they are," Liselle said, "along with your hat."

Moments later Rachel was outside, stepping onto the stone block so that she could mount her horse.

"Will you be needin' me ta come with ya, Miss Rachel?" Sean asked as he held the bridle of the mare.

"That won't be necessary, young Sean," Rachel insisted, taking the reins. She could hardly go to a rendezvous with her beloved with a chaperon in tow.

"I don't think your da will be liking this," the lad said, venturing his opinion, "what with any kind of ruffian lurking about, and you being a lass and all."

"Let me worry about my da," Rachel insisted, adjusting her leg on the sidesaddle. "As for myself, well, I'll be fine." Especially, she added mentally, as soon as I'm with my darling Matthew. And with that, Rachel tapped the horse's flank with her riding crop, and off it went, galloping down the tree-lined street.

Rachel made her way down River Road, her eyes scanning the roadside, looking for Matthew. She slowed her mare to a comfortable pace, wondering if perhaps she'd gotten the note too late.

Another thought struck her suddenly. Maybe something had happened to Matthew? She knew that he was considered a traitor by those loyal to the Confederate states. Supposing someone had seen him and reported him to the local militia? He could be, at this very moment, a prisoner.

And all because he was risking everything to see her.

Rachel shuddered at the thought. "Oh, my love," she whispered, as if the wind could carry her heartfelt message to her beloved Matthew, "do take care."

Hoofbeats sounded on the road behind her and Rachel turned her head, the long veil of her hat floating about her neck as a dapple-gray horse approached.

She recognized the rider. It was Matthew's trusted servant, Achille, Jean-Marc's eldest son.

Rachel pulled back on the reins and halted her horse. "Achille," she said, her eyes filled with happiness. "Where is Matthew?"

"I was sent to bring you to him, Miss Rachel," he answered, a wide smile on his striking face.

"Then let's not waste time," she insisted.

Achille nodded and said, "Follow me."

Rachel did as she was bidden, setting her mare to follow Achille. They rode through a stand of huge oak trees, across a well-worn path overgrown with neglect, and finally, after several miles, arrived at a small cottage nestled among a copse of trees and wild shrubs.

The house had long since been abandoned; its exterior showed signs of having withstood some of the major storms that preyed upon the area, with shingles torn off the roof, and window shutters hanging by sheer will alone. One of the front doors was missing. Several species of birds made their nests on the second-story gallery. Cobwebs hung across some of the windows and on what was left of the railings.

All in all, Rachel thought it a poor sight, like a once rich and elegant lady who, through no fault of her own, had been buffeted badly by dame fortune and was now forced to beg for scraps.

Yet it wasn't the abandoned house that drew her deepest interest as Rachel rode her mare to the front entrance. Her eyes searched the surrounding area for Matthew, and she was rewarded when a man emerged from the interior, a gun in his hand.

As soon as she saw him she cried, "Matthew!" She didn't wait for Achille to help her from the horse. Rachel leapt from the animal, running to her fiance.

Matthew held her close, as if drawing strength from her love. How he'd needed this. Through all the long, lonely nights . . . nights when he ached for her, and not just physically. He ached to hear her laugh, to see her smile, to listen to her observations. Anything to do with Rachel fascinated him, and would always do so. She was a part of him, like his very blood and bones.

Achille took the horses around to the back of the house, leaving the couple alone.

"Come inside," Matthew said, his voice a husky caress to her ears.

He led her through the dark interior to the room he'd been using. It had been cleared of some debris, but it was a ghostly shade of its former self. A bedroll and blanket were on the bare wooden floor, along with a canteen and a bulging pillowcase.

Rachel took all this in. This was a man raised to expect the best out of life—the finest wines, the softest beds, the grandest meals that expert chefs could provide, the most elegant clothes that could be purchased. And here he was, scion of a wealthy, powerful family, living like a hunted outlaw.

"I should have brought you some food," Rachel said apologetically, her arm about his waist, noting that he'd lost a few pounds.

"No need," Matthew assured her with a ready smile. "Achille managed to smuggle some food for me from Belle Chanson without anyone being the wiser." He indicated the lumpy embroidered white pillowcase.

"Why didn't I meet you there?"

"Too risky," Matthew explained. "I can't put my family, or you, in any more danger. I'm sure if I went there now word would somehow leak out."

"Not from your own people," Rachel protested. "They're completely loyal."

Matthew smiled. "I know that, and I'm grateful. No," he said, "it would be from neighbors determined to keep an eye on the comings and goings at the plantation. People who won't forgive me for what they see as a betrayal. I've never made a secret of where my loyalties lie, Rachel, you know that, but I cannot willingly place you or my family in harm's way. Not for me," he stated. "So, that ruled out my home, or yours. It had to be where no one would suspect." Matthew ushered her to a seat on the blanket. "I'm sorry that I can't offer you better, but this was my only option."

"I don't care a fig where we are, Matthew," Rachel said. "So long as we're together, it will

165

be a palace to me." With that pronouncement, Rachel pulled off her hat and placed it gently on the floor. Next, she unfastened the three buttons that held her jacket together. Matthew helped her to remove it, folding it carefully and placing it next to her hat.

He drank in the sight of her, her breasts gently rising and falling with every breath she took. He longed to pull the hairpins from her carefully secured chignon, letting her long blonde hair tumble in casual abandon about her shoulders as it had that night in her room back at Belle Chanson, but he dared not. There wasn't time enough for that.

He reached out his hand, cupping her cheek.

Rachel turned her head and met his palm with her mouth. "Kiss me, Matthew," she implored in a husky murmur. "Please."

He complied.

Like a fierce, swelling gulf storm, the kiss took on a life of its own, building in intensity, sweeping them along in its torrential path. Their mouths mated instinctively, each in turn offering and taking.

Soon they were lying on the thin blanket, Matthew's body fitting itself to Rachel's curves. She could feel the tightening swell of flesh against his buckskin pants. It rose potently against the cradle of her thighs as Matthew moved even closer to her prone body.

Rachel hugged his broad back tightly, her nails digging into the chambray shirt he wore as if she would never let go. This was her reality, right here and now, with Matthew's kisses sending her reeling with pleasure, with his lean body atop hers. Through the material of her skirt and the thin muslin petticoat, she could feel the hard force of his sex as it pushed against her aching lower body.

Matthew altered the tempo of the kiss, softening it, weaving a soothing spell. It was deep, slow, and languorous, giving them both time to adjust. He realized just how far out of control the situation was going and he quickly decided that he must defuse some of the tension between them.

God, he breathed, when they eventually made love, it would be worth the wait, for between them, it would be complete passion, an explosion and blending of the flesh and soul.

Now was not the time, nor the place.

But someday, the time would be right for them, and he knew it would shatter whatever he thought he'd experienced before.

But that was in the future, and this was the here and now. This was all that he could have and he would make the best of it.

Rachel snuggled against Matthew's lean frame, content to be in his arms even in such a dismal place, and they lay quietly together for some time. These moments were doubly precious to her, for she was certain it would be some time before she saw him again. She mentally took inventory of all the changes in him since their last meeting. He was some few pounds thinner; his skin was tanned even darker than previously; he had the makings of a mustache growing. And he carried a gun.

"When it grows dark, I must be going," he murmured softly against her ear.

Rachel moved out of his loose hold, sitting up. "I thought as much."

"I know it's not much. . . . "

"It's better than having not seen you at all, my love," she responded, putting a smile on her face for Matthew so that he wouldn't see the acute heartache she felt at knowing that their time was so short. "Being here with you is an unexpected blessing that I shall cherish."

"As will I," he promised. Each time it was harder and harder to leave her, to ride away and not look back. If he didn't believe that he was truly helping to end this war sooner, if he didn't hold true to the cause for which he was fighting, he would be tempted to throw it all away and leave here with her now, to find another place and start fresh, make new traditions, new promises.

But he couldn't. And wouldn't. Trouble was, he believed equally as strongly in his love for Rachel as in his love for the Union. If he were to give up his love for his country, then his life, and his love for Rachel, would be a lie.

"Matthew?" Rachel felt him slipping away from her.

"I'm sorry," he said, rising and helping her up.

He gave her a wry smile. "Woolgathering, I suppose you'd call it."

"Where will you go?"

Matthew walked to what was left of one parlor window. He watched as the sun began its descent in the sky. "North," he said.

Rachel breathed a sigh of relief. "Philadelphia?"

Matthew shook his head. "Farther north," he responded.

Rachel chose not to press him for further details. It was enough to know that he was probably safer up there than being with the Union Army, which was hoping to make further inroads into the heart of the South.

He turned around. "When this war is over, I've decided that I don't want to take the grand tour for our wedding trip," he stated.

"Have you thought of somewhere else you'd like to go?" she asked, astonished that he would want to give up such a lavish trip. It made little difference to her where they went, as long as she was with him.

"I have," he answered her, his eyes lighting up with an unexpected flash of interest. "California."

"California?" she repeated.

"Actually, northern California," he amended. "I was there recently and I found it incredibly beautiful." Matthew pulled her gently back into the circle of his arms. "I want to show you the mountains, the beaches, and the water. The Pacific is magnificent, so many shades of blue swirled together, like God's paintbox." He lifted her chin up and stared into the depths of her eyes. "In fact," he teased, "I found the exact shade of blue that matches your eyes. A sort of lapis; so deep you could drown in the color."

"Then we'll go there when this is over," she promised with a fond smile, keeping back the tears.

"Perhaps you should go there now," he said with a sober inflection.

Rachel stiffened. "Why?"

"You and your parents will be safer there," he insisted. "I don't think that California will see any real part of this war, and I can't say the same for Louisiana."

"Is your family leaving?"

"No," he said. "They won't even consider it. Not that I really expected them to," he admitted.

"This is your home, Matthew. I can't leave it, or you," Rachel said.

"Then you must know that should the rest of New Orleans discover that you are engaged to me, you could be harassed."

"I'm not some fragile flower that will wilt under a few nasty words, my love," she said staunchly. "We Irish are made of sterner stuff than that, I can assure you."

"Still," he added, "if wearing my ring brings you any ill will, don't think I'll be hurt should you feel the need to remove it."

"How dare you, Matthew Devereaux?" Rachel

asked, her voice rising in indignation.

"I was only thinking about—"

"I don't give a tinker's damn what you were thinking about," she scolded. "I'll not have you believing that I'm some sort of coward."

"Now, you know I couldn't ever think that of you," he insisted.

"Well, you'd better not," she stated defiantly. "I'm proud to love you and wear this ring, and," she said, "I don't care a fig who knows it." She placed her hands on his broad shoulders. "If you want, I'll be happy to say it out loud in the Vieux Carré and in every *faubourg* in New Orleans."

"No need to go that far, *chérie*," he responded. He kissed her lips quickly. "How did I ever get so lucky?"

" 'Tis I who am the fortunate one, my love," she said, resting her head against his chest.

"I must go now," he said in a heavy voice.

"So soon?"

"Yes."

They walked, their arms linked about each other's waists, as Achille stood waiting for them, the horses tethered to a tree.

"Would you fetch the things that I left inside, Achille?" Matthew asked.

Achille gave a nod of his head and went into the house.

Matthew and Rachel stood there, the night falling fast around them.

"We seem to be always saying good-bye,

171

chérie," he said in a teasing tone.

Rachel allowed herself one moment of despair. " 'Tisn't fair."

"You'll get no argument from me about that," Matthew replied. He kissed her then, deep and full, for only a moment. "But mark my words, *chérie*. I will come back to you. Never doubt that. No matter what happens—no matter how long it takes. I will come back to you. I swear it."

Achille came out and handed the food-stuffed pillowcase and blanket, along with the canteen, to Matthew, who loaded them into his saddlebags. Achille whispered something to Matthew, who nodded his head.

"Achille, see Rachel back safely to New Orleans," he instructed. "Then you'd better plan on spending the night at the house there so that you won't make a tempting target for the local militia." Matthew mounted his big red stallion, taking one last look at his fiancee. "I love you, Rachel. Don't ever forget that, because nothing can ever change that fact."

With those words still ringing in her ears, Rachel watched Matthew as he rode out of sight. Now that he was gone, she lost the brave fight she'd put up to keep the tears at bay and she sank to the dilapidated steps, sobbing.

Rachel remained there like that for a few minutes before she heard Achille's voice.

"We'd better be leaving too, Miss Rachel."

She brushed the heels of her hands across her

eyes. "I left my jacket and hat inside," she said. "I'll just be a minute."

Her items restored, Rachel returned and accepted Achille's help in remounting her mare.

As they rode away from the cottage, a deep sense of loss assailed Rachel, almost making her dizzy. It stayed with her throughout the long ride back to the city, at times crushing in its intensity.

When at last she fell into her own bed, having brushed off her parents' queries when she entered the house as to where she'd been, Rachel cried again, deep, racking sobs that shook her body. "Oh, Matthew," she prayed, "don't ever forget your promise to me, for I never shall."

Chapter Nine

I've always held that if you wanted something strongly enough, if you prayed hard, if you believed, that you would eventually be rewarded.

Now I find that doubt has crept in, crushing down upon the buds of hope. This war has dragged on into another year, and it seems as though all those people who declared that the war wouldn't last more than a few months, that it would just be a temporary measure, have been proved sadly wrong.

New Orleans has surrendered to the Union army, and the blue-uniformed Yankee troops are everywhere. Opinions about Gen. Butler are mixed: some judge him by the

*nickname they have given him—"Beast";
others view him as a man who will bring
order. Already General Butler has commanded that the gutters be cleaned so as not
to allow the spread of disease. But, also, on
the heels of the army, come the profiteers
who seek to make money from a city's mis-
ery. The docks have been empty for so long,
and food scarce.*

*Our neighbors, the Chandlers, have been
gone some four months already, having returned to New York. I miss talking to Carolyn, for I've confided in her my feelings for
Matthew, and my engagement to him. We
exchange letters, yet that isn't quite the same
as having her nearby to talk to.*

*Through all this, I have yet to hear again
from Matthew. The pain and the constant
wondering and worrying are slowly sapping
my spirit. All the uncertainties about this
war and his part in it are constantly occu-
pying my mind. There is never a day that
passes that I don't think of him and long for
his return.*

Rachel knelt at the prie-dieu and bowed her
head, the beads of the rosary that Matthew had
given her clutched in her left hand. As was her
custom these past few months, she came to this
little church to pray for Matthew's health and
safe return. Its welcoming interior, so much
like the medieval chapel in her village in Ire-

land, offered comfort. Here she felt closer to God, to some sort of peace in a world gone mad. And she liked talking with the priest, Father Donovan, who, like herself, was from the old country.

Rachel raised her head and saw a woman genuflecting in the aisle before she turned and made her way to the back of the small church. She thought that there was something familiar about the woman, though she couldn't place her. The woman's face was hidden, the veil of her hat pulled low so that it covered her chin.

Rachel watched as the woman glided across the way and stopped at the marble lavabo. She lifted her veil and dipped her fingers in the water and brought them to her face, blessing herself.

It was then that Rachel knew who it was. Dominique Du Lac. Matthew's erstwhile mistress.

How odd that she should see her now. Had Dominique come to light a candle for her former lover?

Unable to ignore an urge to follow the other woman, Rachel slipped the rosary into her reticule and pulled tight on the strings of her purse. She had to know if Dominique had heard from him.

The bright glare of sunlight hit Rachel's eyes as she walked out the door. It took her a moment to focus and when she did, she was horrified by the sight she witnessed.

Dominique Du Lac stood on the sidewalk, surrounded by grinning, leering Union soldiers. There were five men who'd formed a circle around the woman, effectively trapping her within.

Rachel heard Dominique's softly accented French voice asking them to move aside. "Please, messieurs, I beg you, let me pass."

"Hey, boys, we got us one of them there Frenchie gals." The speaker leaned closer, putting a beefy hand on Dominique's shoulder. She shrugged it off, stepping backward, only to come up against another soldier, who slipped his arm about her waist.

"I think it's one of them 'roons that these Frenchies are always talking about, Sergeant," said the man who held Dominique.

"Them's whores, ain't they?" asked another, licking his fleshy lips.

Rachel could see the terror in the other woman's face when Dominique looked her way. Her eyes were wide and frozen. Someone had obviously pulled off her hat, for it lay on the ground, trampled.

"Let her go." Rachel's voice was sharp and insistent.

The sergeant looked toward where Rachel stood on the steps of the church.

"Mind your own business, missie," he hissed. He gave her a surly look. "Lessen you'd like to join in the fun," he warned her.

Rachel gave him a cold and withering stare

178

in return. "You stupid oaf. How dare you accost this woman?"

"Hey, Sarge," another man spoke up, "is she talking disrespectful to you? 'Cause if'n she is, then we got rights to treat her like a woman of the street, right?"

Rachel's nostrils flared at that remark. She was well aware of the infamous directive of Gen. Butler's that any woman of New Orleans who showed contempt of a soldier was to be considered plying her trade.

Rachel was afraid that she couldn't control the contempt she felt for these bullies. There was no use reasoning with them and at that moment she wished that she had listened to her father's advice and taken the derringer he'd given her. It remained in the drawer of her desk, securely locked away, for Rachel had thought that she could never use it against another person. Right now, she knew that she could, if only to threaten this abominable pig into letting the other woman go.

It was then that recognition flared in Dominique's face.

Rachel saw it and gave the woman a look of support. But what could she do? She was alone, and fear began to seep into her bones at the look on the faces of the men. It was a look of the brute intent on getting his own loutish way.

She shivered.

"I says we take 'em both and show them how women hereabouts should properly welcome their betters," the sergeant said with a smile that revealed his stained teeth.

Two of the men made a grab for Rachel while the sergeant and the two others closed about Dominique. "I got me a taste for some dark meat first, boys," he said with a lascivious grin. "You take this here uppity bitch for yourselves."

Rachel screamed at the top of her lungs, and bit the hand of one man, kicking at the other.

"The crazy bitch bit me," the one man said, holding his injured hand and letting Rachel go.

She broke into a run, determined to find help.

"Hey, you fools," snarled the sergeant, "go get her, 'fore she tells anyone." He grabbed Dominique and hauled her into the church.

Rachel had made it only a few feet when she felt an arm snake around her and pull her to a halt. She fought as best as she could, but the other man, whom she'd kicked, smacked her in the face. She reeled backward from the blow.

The sound of swift hoofbeats echoed in the street.

Rachel, blood dripping from the cut on her lip, saw two men on horseback approaching her. Blue uniforms. Union soldiers.

Oh, God, she prayed, let them be help.

"Corporal," one man snapped the word, "what's going on here? Unhand that woman," he ordered.

The men flushed under the scrutiny of the captain and his lieutenant.

"We wasn't meaning no harm, sir," he said,

his eyes downcast as he poured out his lie. "We was just havin' some fun and this here wench was calling us names and treating us bad like. So we was just following the general's orders regardin' that."

"I think you're lying, Corporal." The officer dismounted and gave the two men a cold, hard stare. "It would give me great pleasure to publicly horsewhip you right here in the street if I were so permitted, but since I'm not, consider yourself under arrest."

"What?"

"You heard me," he said. "I will see you both court-martialed for this."

"Over a whore?" the formerly silent one asked.

Rachel gasped.

The officer stared at her. "Consider yourself lucky at that." He stepped up to Rachel and proffered a clean linen handkerchief. "I'm so sorry, miss," he said. "Please don't judge us all by these scum."

Rachel took a deep breath. "I assure you, Captain," she replied, recognizing his rank by the gold bars on the shoulder straps of his uniform, "that I don't. But you must help me," she pleaded. "Several other of your soldiers," and with that she fairly spat out the word, "have taken a woman hostage." She half turned and pointed to the church. "I think they dragged her in there."

The officer rapped out an order to his lieutenant to stay there while he went to investigate, his firearm pulled from its holster.

Several long minutes passed as Rachel stood on the sidewalk, trembling with fear at what the captain might find. She hoped that she'd been in time to spare Dominique any further injury.

The captain returned with the men at gunpoint, his free arm supporting Mlle Du Lac.

Rachel, her torpor broken, rushed to the other woman's side. "Mlle Du Lac, are you all right?"

Dominique's hazel eyes blinked a few times, as if to reassure herself that she was now safe. "*Oui,* mademoiselle, I am fine, thanks to you." She almost reached out to Rachel to embrace her, and then thought better of it. "You have great courage," she stated in a shaky voice. "No wonder Matthieu loves you so much."

Rachel smiled.

"Lieutenant," the captain commanded, "I want you to ride back to headquarters and get some men to escort these prisoners to the stockade."

"Yes sir," the lieutenant said with a smart salute to his superior officer, wheeling his mount around.

"Ladies, if you will tarry but a little longer, I will see that you are both escorted home." He gave a disgusted look in the general direction of his prisoners. "I apologize again for the behavior of these men, and especially to you, miss," he said, addressing Dominique.

"*Merci, monsieur le capitain*," she responded, her voice still quavering with leftover fright.

Rachel added her own words of gratitude to the Yankee captain. "Yes, Captain, 'tis lucky we were that you happened by, and may I thank you most humbly."

Her words brought a glow of color to the captain's pale cheeks. That blush endeared itself to Rachel.

Within 20 minutes, the lieutenant had returned with a detachment of men, who took the prisoners to the stockade per the captain's orders.

"Now, ladies," he said, "I would see you safely home, and beg you to not let this incident cloud your judgment of all our troops. Unfortunately, in wartime, one does not always have the best and the bravest."

"If all the Yankees were like you, Captain . . . ?" Dominique asked politely.

"Excuse me, miss," he said, "I've forgotten my manners. Capt. Fraser, *mesdemoiselles*. Capt. Barrett Jefferson Fraser." And with a gesture toward his lieutenant, he also introduced him. "My lieutenant, Adam Anderson."

"*Enchanté*, Cap. Fraser," Dominique replied, smiling; then she turned her gaze upon the blond young man who sat upon his horse, "and you, too, monsieur."

"Lieutenant, would you see that Mlle Du Lac is taken home? I will escort mademoiselle.

That is"—he paused— "if that meets with your approval, ladies?"

"My house is not far, Lt. Anderson," Dominique said. "It is within walking distance."

"My pleasure, ma'am," the rather somber young man replied, dismounting and leading his horse behind him as he prepared to walk with her.

Dominique paused and addressed Rachel. "*Merci*, once more, mademoiselle," she said, her voice conveying her gratitude. "You have done me a great favor. I shall never be able to repay you."

Rachel gave the other woman a smile, the cut on her lip aching with the effort. "You already have," she acknowledged.

With a shrug of her elegant shoulders, Dominique returned the smile. "As you wish. *Au'v-oir*," she said softly, making her way with the help of the good lieutenant's arm.

"Now, Miss Gallagher, which way?"

"I, too, walked here, Captain," she said. "My house is a mile or so away from here."

"A brisk walk never hurt anyone, Miss Gallagher, so lead on," he said enthusiastically. "That is, unless you want me to secure you a carriage of some kind?"

Rachel sent him a sly glance. "If you think that a short walk like that will wilt me, sir, then you don't know much about Irish women."

* * *

"Would you like to stay for some refreshment, Capt. Fraser?" Rachel politely inquired after he'd accompanied her to her house. She stood inside the hallway, Liselle fussing over her injury and the state of her clothes, which were rent in some spots.

"Perhaps it would be best for me to go and let you get some rest, Miss Gallagher," he offered. "This cannot have been an easy day for you, and I wouldn't want to add to any distress you might be feeling."

"How very kind of you to be so concerned, Captain," she remarked as Liselle handed her a cool, damp cloth to put over the swelling cut on her mouth.

"It's no trouble, Miss Gallagher," he asserted, giving her a slightly formal nod of his head.

"But you will return and let me repay you in my own small way?"

"If you wish."

"Yes, I do," she stated, extending her hand.

In a correctly formal gesture, he brought her gloved hand to his mouth, fleetingly touching her knuckles with his lips. "Tomorrow, then."

"I shall expect your call, Captain." Rachel stood in the doorway as he made his way down the flagstone path. He waved to her as he mounted, then rode away.

"What happened?" Liselle asked.

Rachel explained the situation to her and endured the scolding she received from her housekeeper.

185

"You should have gone with your parents, Miss Rachel," she said.

"I couldn't leave New Orleans, Liselle, and well you know the reason why," Rachel stated. "Besides, Papa only left to see that Mama was safe in Philadelphia with Mme Devereaux's family. As soon as he has accomplished that, he will return."

"Mr. Matthew wouldn't have wanted you to put your life in danger, though."

"What happened today was an aberration, nothing more," Rachel insisted.

Liselle was skeptical. "Such incidents are occurring more and more frequently, I fear. I've heard some things in the market."

"I cannot leave," she reiterated. "Now, I think I should like to have a bath. Those men were so beastly, Liselle. Just the way they looked at Mlle Du Lac and me made me feel unclean." Rachel shuddered. "Thank the saints that all men are not like that, for then no woman would go willingly to her marriage."

"Or," Liselle added, with a sobering glance, "to her marriage bed."

When he called late the next afternoon, Capt. Barrett Fraser proved to be a most interesting man. Rachel had asked Liselle to serve them some lemonade as they sat in the garden, a plate of small iced cakes between them.

"So, Captain," Rachel inquired, biting into one of the tiny treats, savoring the hint of or-ange and spices, "what did you do before this sad war erupted?"

The captain relaxed his somewhat formal manner, taking in his beautiful surroundings with an encompassing glance. "I was a teacher, Miss Gallagher, at a private boys' school in Vermont."

"Really?" she queried, reaching her hand out to take the glass pitcher; she poured him another glass of the tartly sweet lemonade. "What subject?"

"Mathematics." He shrugged his thick shoulders. "Not an especially enchanting subject, but a much-needed one."

Rachel smiled at him. Barrett Fraser was, she thought, a nice-looking man, just about medium height, with a solid, muscular build. He had a pleasant face, with twinkling dark brown eyes and a thatch of wheat-blond hair.

It was, she mused, too bad that Carolyn had departed New Orleans, for Rachel thought that this man and her friend would have suited each other.

Rachel leaned forward, her blue eyes focused on him. "And just what is your Vermont like, Captain?"

He chuckled. "The exact opposite of this place, I can assure you." Barrett finished the glass of lemonade, a trickle of sweat rolling down the side of his face. "A land of beauty, to be sure, but harsh in winter. Forces a body to be strong, though." He gave a quick look at the many plants growing in the garden, at their bright colors. "Delicate hothouse flowers wouldn't survive there," he observed matter-of-factly. "One has to learn to adapt to our weather." A quiet, faraway look came into his eyes. "Best time to see it, though, is the fall. When the leaves have turned, it's at its loveliest. The mountains are splashed with color that can fairly take your breath away."

"You love it, don't you?"

"Indeed I do, Miss Gallagher," he readily admitted. "My family's lived there for several generations."

"I've found that there are so many different types of beauty when it comes to a geographical place, Captain," Rachel theorized. "There are times when I do so miss the gentle rain and the eternal green of Ireland; then, having lived here for a time, I find I like the sunshine and the warm climate. I think I would, however"—Rachel steepled her fingers in front of her face—"like to see for myself, someday, your Vermont."

"And I would be happy to show you," he offered.

Rachel realized then that she hadn't mentioned something important to this man. It was an oversight she hastened to correct.

"I would have to ask my betrothed if that fits in with his plans for our future," she declared softly.

Barrett's eyebrows rose just a fraction. "You

are affianced?" He managed to keep his tone casual.

Rachel held out her hand and proudly displayed her ring. "Yes."

He stared at the token of a pledge. "He is a most lucky man, then."

" 'Tis I who am fortunate, Captain, I can assure you." Rachel smiled. "My intended is a brave soldier like yourself."

"A Reb?" he asked.

She shook her head. "No," she informed him with a proud smile, "he's a Yankee officer."

"From where?"

"Right here in New Orleans."

"A Union officer from here?" Fraser asked incredulously.

"As loyal to these United States as you are, sir," Rachel insisted. "Matthew quite agreed with the late Mr. Stephen Douglas that in this war, 'there can be no neutrals.' "

"That's quite a surprise, Miss Gallagher." Barrett Fraser let out a puff of breath. "Imagine that."

"I think that the two of you would get along famously," Rachel stated.

"What unit is he assigned to?"

Rachel lowered her glance and took a sip of her drink, which was rapidly warming in the hot sun. "I don't know." She couldn't reveal to this man that Matthew wasn't in a regular army unit, but part of a special force that worked under the direction of a high government official to put an end to Confederate spying and sabatoge.

"What's his name?"

"Matthew Devereaux."

"Devereaux." Capt. Fraser considered for a moment. "Does his family own a large plantation outside of New Orleans?"

"Why yes, they do," Rachel responded.

"I thought I heard the name before. I believe that a man with that last name was given a trade permit because he signed a loyalty oath to the Union." He shrugged, and added skeptically, "Not that I think that every man that signs such a document truly means it."

"Eduoard Devereaux does," Rachel stated emphatically. "You may trust in that, Capt. Fraser. He is as loyal as his son."

Barrett rose. "I'm afraid," he said, looking at his plain pocket watch, "that I must take my leave. I have enjoyed this afternoon. Do I have your permission to call upon you again, seeing as you are now one of the few people I know in New Orleans?" He gave her a rueful smile. "This uniform isn't quite so welcome, I'm afraid, in the majority of houses here."

"Yes, by all means, Captain," Rachel declared wholeheartedly. "I would be pleased if you came again."

After he left, Rachel went upstairs to rest. She decided that she very much enjoyed the captain's company and looked forward to having him as a friend. She missed her parents and

Carolyn Chandler, and Capt. Barrett Fraser was polite, well mannered, and easy to talk to. There was something solid about the man, dependable.

In a world gone upside down with war, there was a comfort to be found in the dependable.

Chapter Ten

Papa has become very fond of Capt. Fraser these past few weeks. He is often, when his duty permits, a guest at our dinner table. And Capt. Fraser has become almost a member of our family. His manner is calm and easy, with little rancor about the war that has changed his life, or the citizens that detest his uniform and his presence in their city.

I've found him to be a good friend, one whom I can talk to about most anything. I think, perhaps, that he is as lonely as I. I so miss Mama and my beloved Matthew.

Yesterday, I received a note from Mlle Du Lac. She has invited me to her home in the Faubourg Marigny, on the Rue Burgundy. I wasn't certain what to make of this, but I've decided that I will go, if only to satisfy my curiosity. It has been months since I've heard from Matthew, and some small part of me wonders if she is still privy to his confidences. And, though it is a strange notion, I have the feeling that, somehow, being with her will make me feel closer to Matthew.

Her carriage stopped in front of the small Creole cottage-style house, and Rachel sat inside for a moment, still pondering her decision to come. What if this was a colossal mistake?

She was half tempted to tell Sean that she'd changed her mind, that he should turn the horses around and return to her own home.

While she hesitated, her young driver leapt from his perch and opened the carriage door, waiting to help her out.

Rachel took a deep breath and stepped down, standing in front of Dominique's house. It was a comfortable-looking dwelling; "modest" was the word she would have used to describe it. Certainly not the overripe, gaudy house of a woman of pleasure, or the secluded, pampered cage of a soiled dove. This was, she judged, a woman's home.

She walked up the brick pathway, and just as she got to the door, it opened slowly, revealing a smiling Dominique.

"Mlle Gallagher, how kind of you to come."

Rachel smiled and followed the other woman

inside. Dominique ushered her into a salon just off the main hallway. A tiny black woman entered the room bearing a silver pot and small china cups on a wooden tray. She placed it down on a low table and left the room without a sound.

Dominique and Rachel sat on the walnut daybed that doubled as a sofa.

"I thought that you might like some chocolate as a change from our fine New Orleans coffee," Dominique suggested as she poured a steaming cup, added a froth of cream, and sprinkled a small spoonful of cinnamon over the top. She handed the cup to Rachel, who tasted the beverage.

"Wonderful," she pronounced.

Dominique smiled in return, sharing a confidence. "I love this, even—dare I admit—more than coffee." She laughed. "Though it has become terribly difficult to obtain since the start of the war.

Rachel relaxed. Perhaps this visit wouldn't be as difficult as she feared.

Dominique drank her chocolate before she asked, "You must be wondering why I asked you here."

"The thought has indeed crossed my mind," Rachel replied.

"For a few reasons," Dominique responded. She set her cup and saucer back onto the table, then linked her hands together in her lap. "First, to say again *merci* for your help that day." There was no need to elaborate on just which day she was referring to—both women knew.

A delicate shudder fluttered through Dominique. "Without your concern, I might not be here." She dropped her eyes to the polished wooden floor. "Also," she remarked, "because I wanted to meet the woman whom Matthew loves so much." She raised her glance to Rachel. "And he does love you, you know. More than anything."

"Just as I love him," Rachel confessed. She finished her drink and put it down.

"Do you believe in fate?" Dominique asked, her tone serious.

Rachel considered the question for a moment. "Yes, I suppose I do."

Dominique nodded. "As do I. Fate led us both to Matthew Devereaux, and then decreed that our paths should cross."

Rachel considered this, then asked, "Do you resent that?"

"Because he fell in love with you?" Dominique shrugged. "That was as it was decreed."

"Yet, still it must have been a surprise?"

"I knew that it would happen eventually, Rachel, if I may presume to call you that?" At Rachel's nod, Dominique continued. "Matthew and I both knew, I think, that we were not the forever love for the other. Ours was an arrangement that was mutually beneficial to us." Dominique smoothed an imaginary wrinkle from the silk of her dress. "That is sometimes hard for someone not of our world to fully understand."

Rachel gave the other woman a direct glance. "Matthew explained all this to me," she said.

"*Eh, bien,*" Dominique replied. "Matthew was, and is a most generous man. He gave me this house. Through his kindness, I have enough money so that I need never depend on another man again, should I choose not to. I can travel if I want, marry when and if I wish. All that is because of Matthew."

In another woman, those words could have been dipped in poison, calculated to wound, or uttered with deliberate smugness; coming from Dominique's mouth, Rachel knew them to be simple honesty.

"You love him, don't you?"

"*Oui,*" Dominique responded. "If I did not, I could never have shared his bed for these six years past." She poured herself another cup of chocolate. "He is, after all, a most exquisite lover," she avowed, "as you will discover."

At that remark, Rachel blushed.

"I was a virgin when I first came to Matthew," Dominique explained, "and he was careful and considerate, teaching me pleasure. He will," she observed, "be the same for you. It is not in his nature to be selfish in bed."

Dominique smiled as the color deepened in Rachel's cheeks. "*Excusez-moi,*" she replied. "I sometimes forget that you are not used to such frank talk, mademoiselle. Pleasure is not the exclusive domain of men, nor should it be," she said with a gleam in her eyes. "Creoles are hot-blooded, and Creole men are especially proud of their lovemaking skills. You will not be disappointed, Rachel. Matthew is very much a man."

"Could we change the subject?" Rachel asked with a nervous cough.

Dominique gave a throaty chuckle. "*Oui*, but of course. I did not mean to offend," she insisted. "All I wanted to do was reassure you that on your wedding night, you have nothing to fear."

"I trust Matthew," Rachel replied.

"As you should," the older woman said.

Rachel decided that since they were being open with one another, she would venture the question uppermost in her mind. "Have you heard from Matthew since he's been gone?"

"Not recently, I'm afraid," Dominique answered. "I did have a letter from him late last year." She reached out her hand and placed it on Rachel's. "He spoke of you throughout it," she assured Rachel. "He told me how very much he loved you and that he was looking forward to starting a new life with you when this war is over."

"He did?"

"*Oui*, you've made him a very happy man, Rachel."

"I want to, for the rest of our lives."

"And you shall, I know it," Dominique stated.

"As I said before, it is your fate to love Matthew."

Rachel thought about Dominique's words when she was back in her own home later that day. Fate. Destiny. Choices. Written in the stars. Whatever, she thought. It was all the same. It all came down to the fact that Matthew was her one true love, and nothing could keep them apart.

Nothing.

Except death.

Only death could sever all the hopes and dreams of the future. Only death could rip apart the seemingly strong fabric of belief and replace it with the ragged cloth of despair.

"Matthew."

Rachel awoke with his name on her lips. She lay in her bed, pillows piled around her, the lace curtains on her windows blowing in the humid breeze.

She tossed back the thin sheet of bleached white cotton that covered her. Rachel sat on the side of her bed, listening to the sound of the birds happily chirping outside her bedroom. It was a day ripe with promise. She wiggled her toes, imagining what it would be like to awake with Matthew beside her.

Rachel turned and cast a dreamy look at the rumpled bed. She half-closed her eyes and envisioned Matthew there, his tanned skin and black hair such a contrast to her white bed linen. Smiling, she stretched out her hand and smoothed the bottom sheet, pretending that as she did, she could feel the texture of his warm flesh, feel the silky whorls of hair that covered the uppermost part of his wide chest and then feathered downward.

By all the saints, how wanton her thoughts were turning.

And did she care? she asked herself.

Not a whit.

All she truly wanted was for this war to be over soon and for Matthew to come home to her. Or, if that were not possible, she wished at least to hear some news from him. It had been so long. Just something. Anything.

She stretched, then walked to her long cheval glass. She stood there, staring into the mirror. Rachel tossed back the tangled mass of her sunny-blonde hair, her arms at her sides. Through the thin cotton of her nightgown, she could see hints of her shape beneath. Lifting one hand, she placed it against the flat contour of her stomach. One day she would carry Matthew's baby beneath her heart, a child created from their love. Her belly would swell with new life. Rachel wanted that, she realized, more so than she could have ever thought possible.

That same hand rose and grasped the gold locket that hung around her throat. It was a match to the signet ring that she'd given him, with their initials entwined. Inside, there were miniature portraits of the two of them. That was the way it should be, and would always be—the two of them, together, forever.

Rachel sat at her desk, scribbling some notes for another article that she wanted to do. Her mother had *just* recently returned from Philadelphia, contradicting her husband's wishes that she stay out of harm's way in the North. And with Kathleen's return came news of the North. The news she imparted provided Rachel with another angle on this bitter conflict—the effect it had on the women who waited, on both sides.

Rachel knew from listening to the women who remained behind in a city now under Union control what it was to be considered the enemy, to be perceived as a possible threat. Or, in her own case, to be considered untrustworthy because of her father, her betrothed, and the fact that a prominent Yankee officer was often seen in her company.

Rachel had watched as the women of New Orleans went about their lives as best they could. They waited for news of their men, took care of the wounded who made it home, tended the needy when they could, and read the papers, searching for news of a loved one; they carried on as best they could with the circumstances they were dealt.

It was the women who bore the brunt of the "glorious adventure," Rachel thought. They remained at home, keeping up the pretense that their lives were the same, and that everything would be as it was again, that somehow their lives would return to normal.

Dipping her pen in the crystal inkwell, Rachel was about to begin another sentence when Liselle walked in through the open door.

"Excuse me, Miss Rachel, but your mama wants you to come downstairs right away."

At the strange tone in her housekeeper's voice, Rachel raised her head. "What's wrong, Liselle?"

"You have a guest."

Rachel glanced at the cherrywood clock on her desk. Since it was only a few minutes past nine, she was surprised that she had a caller this early in the day.

"Who?"

"The Yankee captain," Liselle informed her.

"Barrett?" Rachel laid down her silver pen and smiled. "Whatever can he want at this hour?" She pushed back her chair with a scrape. "Please tell Mama that I shall be right down."

Standing, Rachel glanced at her informal attire as Liselle did as she requested. She wore a simple pale blue dress with a plain bodice and skirt, without an elaborate hoop beneath. It was comfortable, easy to work in, and soft from so many washings. She debated as to whether or not she should change to something more suited to receiving callers, but decided not to postpone this meeting. It wasn't as if Barrett Fraser was a strictly formal man who would be shocked to see that occasionally she didn't wear elaborate clothes.

Perhaps he was here to ask her to accompany him on a ride, she thought as she walked down the hallway to the stairs. They met at least once a week, if possible, to do just that, but because of his increasingly busy schedule, they'd had to forgo that pleasure this week.

But that didn't explain the odd tone in Liselle's voice. That nagged at the back of Rachel's mind.

Rachel entered the small salon on the main floor, struck immediately by the quiet in the room, the somber look on Barrett's face, and her mother, sitting in a chair, her hands working a lined handkerchief back and forth, her features drawn tightly.

"By all the holy saints, what's wrong?" Rachel demanded, moving further into the room. "Papa?" The question came out of her throat in a choked cry. She knew her father was on another horse expedition for the military, this time in Confederate-held Texas.

"As far as I know, Mr. Gallagher is quite fine," Capt. Fraser replied crisply.

Rachel shot her mother another quick look.

With that, Kathleen Gallagher was out of her seat and at her daughter's side in a few seconds.

Rachel could read the sympathy in her mother's eyes and felt panic invade her blood. "Not

Matthew?" she asked in dawning horror.

At the stark look on Barrett Fraser's face, Rachel gasped. "It's a lie!"

"Dearest . . ." her mother began.

"I would know if something had happened to him," Rachel cried. "Don't you understand?" she demanded angrily. "I would know." She looked wildly about her at the two other occupants of the room. "There has to be some mistake."

Barrett Fraser walked closer to Rachel. "I wish that were true, Miss Gallagher," he uttered in a solicitous tone.

When he offered her his hand, Rachel pushed it away.

In a cold voice, she said, "You're a liar."

"Rachel!" Kathleen Gallagher admonished her daughter, trying to calm her. "I know, dearest, that you're upset, but don't—"

"Don't what, Mother?" Rachel asked, interrupting her mother's words. "Challenge this lie? And that's what it is. A monstrous mistake on someone's part," she said. "Matthew is alive. He promised me that he was coming back to me. So you see," she insisted, "there's nothing wrong."

"I wish that I could tell you that was true, Rachel," Barrett Fraser explained, "but it isn't. Capt. Matthew Devereaux was executed as a spy in New York State."

"Get out of my house," Rachel stated coldly,

backing away from him. "And take your filthy lies with you."

"Please, Rachel," Kathleen begged. "Listen to the captain."

Rachel pulled away from the comforting hand that her mother laid on her arm. "How can you believe this?" she demanded. "It's nothing but a horrible lie. Matthew's not dead, I tell you," she declared.

"Rachel," Capt. Fraser said in a soothing tone, "I know that this must be difficult to hear."

"Difficult?" Rachel snapped. "What would you know about that?" She strode to the other side of the room, distancing herself from the people who refused to acknowledge the truth as she saw it. "I loved him."

Rachel took a deep, steadying breath. "Correction. I love him. We're going to be married when this war is over. Or sooner, if I can get my way. He's alive and coming back to me."

"Then how do you explain this?" Fraser asked, hating to have to hurt her further. He pulled something from the pocket of his uniform jacket. In his wide hand he held out a ring toward Rachel.

The glint of gold shimmered in the bright early morning sun.

A deep pain clutched Rachel's stomach. She took a few tentative steps, faltering slightly. "Where did you get that?" she asked in a suddenly weak voice. It was the ring that she'd had made for Matthew to match the locket she wore.

"It was sent, along with other things, papers mostly, by a Southern major whom we suspect is the ringleader of a band of spies who work behind Union lines and who have infiltrated the North."

"But how did he get Matthew's ring?"

Barrett fisted the hand holding the ring. "He said that he was sending the ring as proof that he'd dispatched a traitor to the Southern states. He said that he wanted it known that a man who would turn his back on his own kind deserved what he got."

"No." This word slipped out of Rachel's mouth, accompanied by a low moaning sound. Everything started to grow dark around her, and she longed, then, for the blackness. It was safe and comforting.

When she came to, Rachel was in her own bed, her bodice undone, her mother sitting in a chair pulled up close. A basin of water and a cloth rested on the night table. Kathleen dipped the cloth into the water and wrung it out, placing it on her daughter's temple.

"Mama?"

Kathleen stroked her child's cheek, a gesture of comfort and shared understanding. "I'm here, my dearest," she responded.

Rachel turned her head away, gazing toward the windows, to the brightness of the day, to the sweet smell of flowers, to the excited chirping of the songbirds. Everything was warm and alive outside. Why? When she felt so cold and dead inside. Her spirit was crushed by the news, for she was still in shock.

"Would you like some tea?" Kathleen inquired.

"No," Rachel replied in a flat monotone, her head still turned aside.

"Coffee?"

Rachel made no response, hoping that her mother would take the hint and just leave her alone.

Kathleen tried again. "Do you want to talk about it?"

"What is there to discuss, Mama?" Rachel faced her mother, and Kathleen read the bleakness in her daughter's eyes.

"What do you want to do?"

"Do?" Rachel repeated dully. "If Matthew is truly dead, then I think I want to die too."

"Rachel, you musn't talk like that," Kathleen begged her. A dawning look of fear appeared on Kathleen's features. "You wouldn't consider doing something foolish, would you?"

Rachel understood the question her mother was posing. "No, Mama, I shan't kill myself, if that's what you're asking."

"Thank God for that."

"If you want." Rachel shrugged her shoulders.

Kathleen tenderly squeezed Rachel's cold hand. "He was a very brave man, dearest."

Gail Link

"What good does that bravery do me?" Rachel asked bitterly. "It won't bring back the man I love."

"Matthew was a man of honor."

"Oh yes, Mama, he was. And what did that accomplish?" she asked. "Nothing." Rachel's tone was weary, as if the act of talking itself was a great strain. "Honor. How I shall hate that word for the rest of my life. 'Tis an empty sound coined by men to bolster their pride and maintain their illusions. What has honor given me? An empty future without the man I love, the man whose children I wanted to have, the man with whom I wanted to grow old.

"Damn honor." Rachel turned her head aside and stared out the window.

Minutes moved slowly by until she realized that she was alone.

A short bitter laugh escaped Rachel's mouth. Alone.

Without Matthew she would be forever alone, doomed to wander this earth without her other half. A soul lost in limbo.

Chapter Eleven

I haven't been able to cry.

*It's not that I don't want to cry—my God,
I want to scream and rant over the injustice
of the loss of Matthew, yet somehow I feel
so empty inside, as if there are no tears that
can equal the pain that I'm feeling.*

*Or not feeling—perhaps that's closer to
the truth. I am numb. Each day is a constant reminder that my beloved is gone from
me—and that promises aren't always kept.*

*This afternoon there is a memorial cere-
mony scheduled at Belle Chanson. God
grant me the strength to get through this day
and every other that follows.*

The sky was overcast, the air thick with humidity. Rachel stood alone outside on the veranda, gazing toward the paddock, watching the big red stallion as it pranced back and forth, as if looking for its master.

The memorial ceremony had been brief, with the entire Devereaux clan and their servants crowding into the local church. It was private, with the only other guests being Rachel and her parents, who'd already returned to New Orleans.

Rachel, dressed completely in black silk, moved through the day like an automaton, managing to respond when someone talked to her, to make all the correct gestures; but inside, her heart was frozen. Frances and Eduoard Devereaux had been towers of strength. Rachel could see how much it was costing them to maintain that pose—their faces bore the emotional marks of their devastation. Marguerite was refreshingly honest, crying nonstop for her beloved older brother.

Now that it was over, Eduoard had retired to his study, ordering that a bottle of brandy be sent to him posthaste. Marguerite had been given a dose of laudanum to quiet her down. Frances was resting in her room.

Or so Rachel thought until she heard a sound behind her, and turning, she saw Matthew's mother, looking older than before. A thick, jagged streak of white had recently appeared in

Frances Devereaux's brown hair, as if painted by an unsteady hand.

"I thought that you were upstairs," Rachel remarked.

"I was," Frances responded, slipping her arm about Rachel's slim waist and drawing the younger woman closer, sharing their respective grief, "but I couldn't rest."

"I know what you mean."

"He loved you so much, you know," Frances said, tears clouding her eyes. "You gave my son a very special gift, Rachel, and I shall always think of you as my daughter."

"Thank you," she responded politely.

"No, thank *you*," Frances insisted. "You made Matthew very happy, my dear. With you he was alive in a way that I'd never seen him before." She sniffed delicately, holding back the tears that threatened to spill from her eyes.

"He was everything to me," Rachel confessed.

Frances swallowed, knowing that what she had to say was difficult, for both of them, but necessary nonetheless. "I know my son, Rachel. He wouldn't have wanted you to mourn the rest of your life for him. You're young, and someday will love again."

"No!" Rachel denied. "I won't."

Frances gave Rachel a sympathetic glance. "I know how deep your pain is now, but it will lessen with time," she counseled, struck by the younger woman's tightly held emotions. "Then you can start to rebuild your life."

"The life I wanted was taken from me," Rachel said, bitterness lacing her tone. "And how can you say that I shall forget the pain of his loss? You're his mother. Will you?"

Frances shook her head. "Never. I will have an empty place in my heart forever, but I will survive. I must, for my family's sake. And for my son's memory."

"Then how can you think that I will forget him?" Rachel accused her.

"I don't think that, my dear," she explained. "It's not what I meant at all. Matthew would be a very difficult man to forget, even if he were not my flesh and blood. But you will learn to cherish the memories and go on."

Rachel pulled away from the other woman's embrace. She took a few steps along the worn bricks, her eyes focusing on the *garconnière*. She could hear the plaintive barking of Matthew's dog, Wager. It was as if the animal understood that his master was gone and would never return. Rachel realized that it should be she who was giving comfort to Matthew's mother, instead of the other way around.

However, Rachel found that there was no comfort to be found in her soul. She ached from missing Matthew, from wanting him, from needing him. She mentally damned the war and all foolish politicians who needlessly wasted human life. And she damned Matthew for leaving her alone. She felt like an empty shell, a husk of her former self, buffeted by the cruel winds of fate which had given her a glimpse of the true depth of love, only to snatch it from her grasp before she could barely realize it.

Yes, she would cherish the memories of Matthew and go on with the emptiness of her life. She had no other recourse. Although what kind of a life could it be without the man she still desperately longed for?

"Would you mind if I spent some time in the *garconnière* by myself?" Rachel asked, turning her head to look back at Frances.

"Of course I don't, my dear. Feel free to go and do whatever you want," Frances replied. She cast a glance in that direction herself. "I'm going back to my room. Suddenly I feel very tired."

Rachel walked across the lawn, her back stiff and straight, her head held high as she made her way to the door of the small house. Wager, Matthew's dog, lay on the ground, his head on his large paws, a mournful look in his eyes. He raised his head when Rachel approached.

She bent down in front of the massive animal. "You miss him too, don't you, boy?" she asked softly, holding out her hand to the animal and rubbing his head. "So do I."

Wager gave a yelp and rose, butting his head against Rachel. She stood and ran her hand over the animal's coat, stroking him. "Come with me," she said to the dog, who gratefully followed her into the house.

It was a smaller version of the main house,

furnished with care, and distinctly masculine.
Air circulated from the open windows, and the
house was kept as if Matthew would return at
any moment. A copy of the daily paper was laid
out on his desk when she peered into the room
he must have used as his study. Rachel had
never been inside the confines of this house,
having observed the custom of separateness
that was required, so now she took her time and
savored this exploration.

Walking into the room with the dog at her
side, Rachel moved to the wide mahogany desk.
She pulled back the chair Matthew would have
sat in and traced one hand over the soft leather.
She seated herself, running her gaze over the
expanse of wood before her. A small brass clock
stood to one side, as did an inkwell and a set of
pens. A polished wooden tray held a neat stack
of vellum, each sheet carrying the Devereaux *D*
emblazoned in fancy Gothic script on it. To the
other side of the desk was a cigar box made of
mahogany also. Rachel raised the lid and removed one of the slim cigars that Matthew had
smoked, imported from the island of Cuba.

She brought the cigar to her nose, inhaling
the fragrance of the tobacco. She remembered
how much he liked to smoke a cigar after dinner, or while playing cards. Or while they
walked the grounds of the plantation.

"Who's there?" a man's voice called out.

Rachel accidentally snapped the cigar in two
when she heard the question. For a moment,

she foolishly imagined that it was Matthew, come to make a mockery of this memorial service by proving he was very much alive.

Disappointment rose within her when the man entered the room. It was only Achille.

"Pardon me, mademoiselle," he apologized. "I heard a noise and thought. . . . " His voice trailed off.

Rachel wondered if perhaps he too was having the same fantasy.

"I only wanted to see where he lived," she explained.

"Then I shall leave you, mademoiselle." Achille started to leave and then abruptly spun around. "We all feel the loss deeply, Miss Rachel."

He stepped closer to her and Rachel could see the sheen of unshed tears in the warm, chocolate eyes. "*Peut-etre*, if I'd been with him, he might still be alive," he said sadly.

"You could not have prevented it, Achille," she responded. "Matthew was a very determined man, and someone made him pay the ultimate price for that determination." Rachel picked up the sterling silver paper knife that lay on the desk, staring at the object as it lay in her palm. "If I could find the people responsible, I wouldn't hesitate to make them feel some measure of the pain that we are experiencing. By all the saints," she said with determination, her voice cold, "I would gladly make them suffer for what they did to him."

Achille nodded his head in agreement. "As would I, Miss Rachel."

She replaced the paper knife on the desk, re-assuring Achille, "I shan't disturb anything, I promise you."

"I understand," he said and gave her a slight inclination of his head. He left her alone with her thoughts, and the dog.

Rachel sat there, just looking for a few more minutes before rising.

Slowly, she examined each room of the downstairs, discovering more of Matthew's things. His polished riding boots, his books, his carved chess set, still just as he'd left it, waiting for the next move in the ongoing game.

"Come, Wager, let's go upstairs."

She found his bedroom and paused at the door. It was closed, with a key in the brass lock. Wager sniffed and pawed at the door, making low sounds in his throat.

Taking a deep breath, Rachel turned the heavy key and crossed the threshold.

It was a room that was potent with Matthew's aura. It was all around her, enveloping her in its welcoming embrace. The dog felt it too, she could tell, for it immediately curled up beside the leather chair as if waiting for its master to make an appearance.

Rachel examined every nook and cranny, from the tortoiseshell comb and brush set that lay atop his dresser, to the shaving mug and ivory-handled razor. She picked up the hairbrush and ran her palm over the soft bristles, relishing the texture.

Next she found the armoire that held his clothes. Opening the door, she ran her hands over the shirts and jackets that hung there. Cedar aroma permeated the space inside.

Closing the door, she walked slowly about the room, eager to glean whatever she could from its contents. On the far wall hung the painting of Cimarron that she had given him for Christmas the past year. Grouped around it were smaller hunting prints, mostly English.

How she wished that Matthew were here with her, now. Rachel wanted his strength; she wanted to lean on him. She yearned for the ready smile and reckless look in his dark blue eyes. She craved the warm feel of his arms drawing her closer to the lean hardness of his body.

She wanted . . . forever.

But that wasn't possible. It would never be possible now.

She cast her gaze toward the big, solid-looking mahogany bed with its elaborate carved headboard and netting. In that bed, or one like it, she could have crossed the bridge of innocence and found the road to experience with Matthew as her guide.

Rachel raised her hands before her face and linked her fingers slowly, folding them, resting them against her mouth as she continued to stare longingly at the bed, her mind imagining

217

him lying there with naught but a devilish grin as he waited for her to join him.

She took a few steps forward, as if lured by the bed itself. Across the expanse was thrown a man's dressing gown of golden-brown silk. Picking it up, Rachel drew it to her face, inhaling the scent of him that still clung to it. It had recently been hung out to air, for she could smell the fresh, clean aroma of sunshine that mixed with Matthew's own unique fragrance.

Wager raised his head and began to whine. He got up and trotted over to Rachel, butting his head into the fabric. His plaintive doggie cries tore at Rachel's heart.

Sinking to her knees, Rachel began to sob. Not delicate, ladylike weeping, but hard, hot tears that scalded her face and made her moan as if in excruciating pain. And she was. Finally, the dam that had held back her sorrow broke and the flood of tears tore at her, ripping apart her carefully held defenses.

"Matthew," she cried to the empty room.

The dog, hearing her torment, joined in with howls of his own, until the bedroom was filled with the combined sounds of pain and anguish, both human and animal.

Rachel remained there, in Matthew's bedroom, for almost an hour. When she left it, she carried his robe in her hands, the dog close by her side. Her eyes were red-rimmed, evidence of the copious tears she'd shed for the loss of the man she loved above all others.

She moved slowly down the stairs and along the hallway, giving one last look at the interior before she closed the door behind her. This chapter of her life was over now, and she had to face that fact, no matter how distressing.

As she walked back to the main house, Rachel cast a glance at the large oak tree near the paddock. It was there that the Devereaux family planned to erect a stone monument to their son. Since there was no body, he could not be buried in the family mausoleum.

Rachel took the side stairs to her bedroom, climbing them mechanically, her thoughts still on Matthew. She'd left the signet ring Barrett had given her as proof of his death on his dresser, wrapped in one of her handkerchiefs. It belonged there, among his things.

Until she entered her bedroom, Rachel wasn't even aware that the dog had followed her up the stairs. He made himself comfortable on the floor, his eyes on her as she folded the robe and put it into her capacious traveling bag. She was sure that his mother wouldn't mind.

Rachel had originally planned to spend the night and return to New Orleans on the morrow. But she couldn't do that now, for there was something else that she had to do, and it simply couldn't wait.

She summoned a servant and asked that the Devereauxs' brougham be brought around to the front, as she wanted to go back to New Orleans as soon as possible.

The servant hurried away to see to her request, and Rachel gathered the rest of her things together, the dog watching her intently.

She sat down at the secretary and wrote a note to Matthew's parents, explaining her reasons for leaving so abruptly. She promised them that she would return for a visit within a few weeks and left the note where she knew it would be found.

Picking up her bag, Rachel gave the huge dog one fond glance. "Good-bye, Wager." With that, she turned and exited through the open doors to the outside stairs.

When she arrived below, the carriage was waiting for her and the groom helped her with her bag. As she stepped into the small conveyance, Rachel heard the dog's bark. She turned to see Wager bounding into the coach, intent on leaving with her.

The driver tried to pull the animal from the brougham but the dog wouldn't budge. Instead, Wager growled menacingly and bared his fangs. The driver backed away.

Rachel laid her hand on the dog's head. "All right," she murmured soothingly to the beast. "You can come with me."

"You be wantin' to bring that big devil with you, Miss Rachel?" the driver asked, giving the huge dog a sharp, wary look.

"Yes, I do," she answered him with a sadly sweet smile. It would seem as though Matthew's dog had adopted her, and short of restraining the animal, he wouldn't leave her side. Well, she decided, that was fine by her. Wager was Matthew's dog, and she was Matthew's lady. They belonged together.

She fondled the dog's ears as the vehicle made its way along the path that led to River Road, blinking back the fresh tears that threatened to spill once more from her blue eyes.

"Please, if you would wait here for me, I shan't be very long," Rachel requested of the driver.

"Yes,'m, Miss Rachel," he responded, helping her alight from the vehicle.

When the dog made to leave, Rachel put out her hand and said simply, "Stay," and Wager settled back down to wait.

Clouds gathered in the sky. A storm would soon be upon the city; the air was even more oppressive than usual. Rachel longed for a cool bath and a nap, but this couldn't wait.

She knocked upon the door of Dominique Du Lac's cottage.

The female servant whom Rachel had met before answered the door. She invited Rachel inside, telling her that Mlle Du Lac would be back soon. She'd gone to church to pray for M. Matthew's soul.

Showing Rachel to the salon, the servant left her there while she fetched a glass of something for Rachel to drink. She returned less than five minutes later with a tall glass that she handed to Rachel.

"Thank you," Rachel said as she took the drink, sampling the beverage cautiously. "Mmm, 'tis very good," Rachel murmured. "What is it?"

"A mint julep." The older woman gave Rachel a lopsided smile. "I gots to get back to ma kitchen now, 'cause I got a big pot of gumbo cooking in there."

Rachel sat quietly, sipping the drink. She'd already removed a small token from Matthew's room and placed it inside her reticule for Dominique. It was a man's handkerchief. Of white linen, it was embroidered with Matthew's initials, *MJD*. When she was rummaging about in his room, Rachel found some in a drawer, and thought that perhaps it might mean something to Dominique to have some last remembrance of her former lover.

The front door opened and Rachel rose from her seat on the daybed, putting her drink on the table in front of her.

"Dominique," she called out.

Scarcely a moment later Dominique appeared in the archway.

"Miss Gallagher," she said, removing her bonnet. It was black, as were her clothes.

"My name is Rachel, remember?" Rachel gently reminded her, and then acted on impulse, putting her arms about the other woman.

Dominique, surprised at first, found herself

responding to Rachel's gesture of shared grief.

"The family held a memorial service early this morning for Matthew and I was shocked to see that you were not there," Rachel said.

Dominique took a deep breath and joined Rachel in sitting down on the makeshift sofa. "Come now, Miss Rachel, you must know that it wouldn't have been wise, or right, for me to have shown up there today. Especially," she added, "as I wasn't invited or expected."

"But you were close to Matthew," Rachel argued. "You shared a life with him." As much as it hurt her to admit that, Rachel couldn't deny or ignore the truth.

"With him, yes," Dominique agreed, "but not with his family."

Rachel detected the pain in the other woman's voice. "I'm sorry."

Dominique smiled. "There is no need for you to be sorry, Rachel; life is as it is here in New Orleans. I was the shadow woman for Matthieu," she said, using the French pronunciation of his name, "and proud to be so. I know what that means; what's permitted and what's not," she said with a fatalistic shrug of her slim shoulders.

"Still . . ."

"There is no *still*, Rachel," Dominique addressed her. "I knew what I was doing when I entered into my agreement with Matthieu," she said.

"I have something here that I thought you'd

like to have," Rachel said, opening up the small handbag and extracting the piece of linen.

"It's Matthieu's," Dominique replied, clutching the handkerchief.

Rachel nodded her head in agreement. "I took it from his bedroom in the *garconnière* this morning." Her voice trembled slightly as she related the story. "I thought that you should have something personal, in case you hadn't something already."

"When we parted, I had only my memories left."

"That's what I have now," Rachel said. "Memories." She touched her locket. "And several things that I shall cherish for as long as I live. Yet I'd trade them all for one more day with him," she said vehemently, tears streaming unchecked down her pale cheeks.

It was then that Dominique gathered the other woman into her arms and offered comfort, as her tears also fell freely in sad remembrance of the man they both had loved.

For Dominique it was the love and loss of a dear friend; for Rachel it was the love and loss of a lifetime.

Later that evening, Rachel remained alone in her bedroom, refusing any human offer of companionship. Her parents had been surprised when she showed up, especially when she arrived with the huge dog in tow. The fierce-looking creature was as mild-mannered as a pup around Rachel, who insisted that the dog now belonged to her.

She'd closeted herself in her room since her return, spurning the meals Liselle tried to foist upon her. She wanted nothing so much as to be left alone. Alone with her memories and with thoughts of what could have been; what should have been.

The storm had begun. Rain poured forth and lightning lit up the sky with its jagged bursts. She stood by the open window, feeling the heavy air and rain all around her.

Earlier, when she'd come home, Rachel had ordered a bath and then attempted to rest, but found that impossible. Rising, she went to her traveling bag and removed Matthew's silk dressing gown. Unbuttoning her night rail, she let it fall to the floor in a white heap about her feet. Rachel stood there, naked, and drew on Matthew's robe, wrapping the too-large garment about her slender waist. The silk felt cool and sensuous against her bare skin. The robe trailed on the floor, and the sleeves hid her hands. She didn't care. It was as if some part of Matthew wrapped around her, providing a form of comfort.

Rachel watched as the storm intensified. How could she ever truly say good-bye to him? He was still there, inside her heart, as alive as ever.

Oh Matthew, how do I do it? she silently asked, her eyes gazing upward to the sky. How do I stop thinking, wanting, feeling? How do I go on as if there is a tomorrow for me without you? What do I do? Where do I go?

Rachel's hands formed tight fists, her nails biting deeply into her palms. Damn you! she silently cried. By all the saints, damn you, Matthew, for dying and leaving me alone.

Chapter Twelve

Almost a year has passed since Matthew's death, and still I miss him. Nothing, and no one, has filled the void. Each day I still ache for his loss.

Without the support of my parents and friends I don't know how I would have endured. Dominique and I have become quite close. She's very happy now that there is a new man in her life, a free man of color who is partners with another man in a shipping venture. Commerce has slowly come back to New Orleans. I still spend time at Belle Chanson with the Devereaux family when I can. Things have changed there—a somber mood prevails. Marguerite, once a happy, loving child, has turned sullen and with-

drawn since Matthew's death. Six months ago she was sent to live temporarily with relatives in Philadelphia. The joy has left the faces of the Devereauxs. They've lost their son and exiled their daughter, albeit for her own protection.

By all the saints—how much more will this war take from those I love? It continues to drag on. So much killing, so many lost or destroyed lives. Life here goes on—but at what price? All civility has gone, replaced by a sense of doom and weariness. Each reported battle brings with it the hope that this is the last, that somehow reason will finally prevail and the endless slaughter will cease.

Papa is talking seriously about moving to California, to the city of San Francisco. He and Mama are quite fond of that location, and Papa is afraid that the war has so devastated this part of the country that the only place to go to escape the bitterness is the West. How long ago it seems that Matthew and I discussed honeymooning in the northern part of California.

Now I face another choice. Do I go with them? Leave New Orleans and my last links to Matthew? Do I try to forge a new life for myself away from the ties that bind me here?

I don't know what to do.

"You said that your parents are planning to leave New Orleans soon?" Capt. Barrett Fraser asked Rachel over dinner one evening. He'd brought her to one of the better restaurants in the city, telling her that he had something to celebrate.

"Yes," she said, spearing another fat, succulent shrimp from the many on her plate. She washed it down with the champagne that the Union captain had ordered. Tonight Rachel felt happy. Not overjoyed, not ecstatic—merely happy. And it felt good.

"Will you go with them?" he inquired, trying to keep his voice from betraying the anxiety he felt at losing her company.

Rachel shrugged. "I truly don't know. They want me to come with them." She waited as Barrett refilled their glasses. She took a sip and a sad look crossed her face. "Matthew was planning on taking me there for our wedding trip."

"Matthew," Barrett muttered beneath his breath.

"Pardon?"

"Nothing," he lied.

"I suppose that I should go," she said, "but I'm just not sure that I want to."

"What do you want, Rachel?" he asked, one brow raised, his hand sneaking across the table to take hold of hers.

"For Matthew to walk in that door right now and tell me that this has all been a very bad dream. That he is alive and well, and come back to me."

Barrett heaved a deep sigh. "That's not going to happen."

Rachel gave the captain a bittersweet smile. "You didn't ask if I thought that that was going to happen, only what I wanted to happen," she explained.

"Don't you think," he asked, "that one day you'd like to get married? Have a home of your own? Children?"

Pain pinched her face. "I planned that kind of life with Matthew," she responded.

"You could still have it," he insisted.

"That's something I don't even think about, Barrett."

"You should," he asserted. "You're a young woman, Rachel, with a lot to offer a man."

"What man would honestly want to wed a woman whose heart is forever given to a dead man?"

He replied, "I would."

Barrett Fraser's words hung in the air between them like a challenge.

Rachel blinked in surprise.

He gave her an earnest smile. "I love you, Rachel, and I think that I could make you happy." He leveled his gaze at her. "If you'd just give me the chance, I know we'd suit."

Rachel lowered her lids. She'd never suspected that the captain's feelings for her had gone beyond friendship. "I don't love you," she said honestly.

"But you like me, don't you?"

"Of course I do," she replied.

"Then that's a start," he said. "I could wait, Rachel. Love will come later, I'm sure of it."

He sounded as if he actually believed that, she thought. And what if he were right? She was fond of him. But there wasn't the soul-deep feeling that Matthew inspired. There was no thrill at his touch, no leap of her pulse at the nearness of him.

Still, he offered her what she had wanted all her life—a home and a family of her own. Except that she'd wanted them with Matthew. It was in Matthew's arms that she wanted to discover her deepest passions; it was in his house that she wanted to raise a family; it was in his life that she wanted to have an influence; it was in his world that she wanted to belong.

"Think about it," he suggested. "Am I such a horrible alternative to remaining a spinster the rest of your days?" he teased, trying to get the conversation back on a lighter note.

"When would you need your answer?"

"Soon," he replied. "I don't mean to rush you, but with your folks thinking about moving to California, and what with the leave I've got coming to me, I thought that we could get married and then I could take you back to Vermont. You'd really love it there, Rachel. It's so beautiful. Very different from here, I can assure you."

Rachel had no doubt about that. Everything would be different. She would wear his wedding band. She would sleep in his bed. She would bear his children.

At the thought of children a stabbing ache hit Rachel deep in the pit of her belly. It should have been Matthew's children she carried. His bed she conceived them in. A son and a daughter, each resembling him. That was what she'd wanted. Children of her own.

"I'll think about it," she promised.

Barrett was happy that she hadn't refused him outright. There was still hope. He licked his dry lips. "I know I'm not the grand love of your life, Rachel, but I would be a good husband to you, and a good father to our children. You've my word on that."

"I believe you would be," she said. "Now, tell me more about your farm." While he did so, she gave his proposal consideration, mulling over in her mind her response. He was a good man, kind and gentle. While it was true that no raging sparks flew between them, there was a companionship that had deep roots. He had a good sense of humor, and she liked hearing him laugh. He was caring and courteous. She doubted that he had a mean bone in his body. And he would be patient. He didn't expect that she would declare her undying love to him. His love didn't demand her whole heart as had Matthew's. Barrett was willing to accept what she gave.

". . . so that's why I'm celebrating," he said.

"I'm sorry, Barrett. My mind was elsewhere.

Woolgathering, I guess," she admitted. "What did you say?"

"That today's my thirtieth birthday."

"How lovely," Rachel exclaimed, then frowned. "Why didn't you tell me?" she demanded. "I would have gotten you something."

He shrugged. "No matter. I just wanted you to have dinner with me. That's gift enough."

The waiter returned to clear away their dishes, asking if mademoiselle and monsieur were finished, or if they would like some dessert.

"I would like to go home now, Barrett," Rachel announced.

"As you wish, my dear."

Barrett hailed a hack and gave the driver Rachel's address. He joined her in the coach as they made their way in silence to her house.

When they reached there and Barrett stepped out to help her from the conveyance, she whispered, "Send it along and come inside."

He paid the driver and escorted her into the house, where Wager greeted them as they entered. The lights were dimmed.

"I think Mama and Papa are in bed," she said in a low voice, laying her hand on the dog's head.

"Then I should leave," he insisted.

Rachel put her other hand on his arm. "Come with me," she said.

Barrett followed her into her father's study. Wager remained outside. Rachel lit the lamp on his desk and the room was bathed in a soft glow. There was a decanter and several glasses on the desk. "Irish whiskey?" she offered, her hand poised to pour.

"All right," he said, accepting the drink.

"I believe that I shall have one too," she decided.

Barrett raised his brows. He'd never seen a lady drink hard spirits before. She clinked her small tumbler against his and downed the tiny amount that she'd poured into her glass.

"I think the occasion demands something more but I know Papa doesn't keep any champagne in the house," she said.

Barrett questioned her. "What occasion?"

Rachel wet her lips and put down her glass. "I accept your proposal, Capt. Fraser."

He appeared dumbfounded. "Pardon?"

She smiled. "I will marry you, Barrett."

"Oh my God," he said, his jaw going slack.

She took the glass from his hands and walked closer to him, raising her head.

"May I?" he asked.

"Yes," she responded.

He kissed her. An easy, polite salute. Just the gentle touching of his lips to hers. No stars bursting. No quivering, intense heat that soared through her body. Just the sweet, quiet sense of comfort.

She prayed that she'd made the right decision for both of them.

* * *

"It isn't too late to change your mind, my dearest," Kathleen Gallagher said in a quiet voice as she helped her daughter adjust her wedding dress. Since Rachel still considered herself in mourning for Matthew, she wore a two-piece dress of dark gray satin instead of a gown of white. It had originally been trimmed with black lace; last night she'd removed it in deference to Barrett.

Within the hour Rachel would make her solemn wedding vows to a man other than Matthew. A sharp sense of betrayal ran through her. Her mother was right. It wasn't too late. She could cancel now before she took the final, irrevocable step that would link her forever to Barrett. She could tell him that she'd made a mistake. That she couldn't go through with this. That she'd been far too hasty.

She could—but she wouldn't.

Rachel cared about Barrett. And she would keep her vow to be a good wife to him. It wasn't his fault that he wasn't Matthew.

She'd said her good-byes to Matthew yesterday. Of course they weren't final good-byes— that would only come when she too lay in her grave. If she closed her eyes she could still see him. But that was an image, a memory. After this ceremony she would lock him forever in her heart and keep him to herself. Her husband deserved something of her, and if she couldn't give him the depth of love that he wanted, then she could at least give him her attention and affection.

"I don't want to change my mind, Mama," she replied. "I know what I'm doing."

"Marriage is forever."

Rachel gave her mother an understanding smile. She knew that this contract she was entering into couldn't be broken. It didn't matter. Only one flesh-and-blood man could have ever seduced her away from the man she was about to marry, and that man was dead. So she was safe.

Besides, the only thing that she believed was forever was her love for Matthew.

"I'm ready," she announced, accepting the floral bouquet that was handed to her.

The excited bark of a dog split the air.

"I really can't imagine why you wanted to have that big brute at your wedding ceremony, Rachel," Kathleen said as they entered the church from a side room. Connor waited for them, a wide grin on his face, to escort his little girl to her waiting fiance.

The bride-to-be insisted, "Wager belongs here."

"He belongs," her mother added sotto voce, "at home."

"Are you ready, me darlin'?" Connor asked, giving Rachel a kiss.

"Yes, Papa, I am," she responded, watching as her mother quickly walked to her seat in the front of the chapel. They took the short walk and from the corner of her eye, Rachel saw a woman sitting in the last pew in the back, who gave Rachel a nod beneath the black-veiled hat she wore over a dress of gold.

Dominique had come to her wedding to wish her well. Early this morning she had received a telegram from Carolyn congratulating her on her marriage and inviting Rachel and Barrett to pay a visit to her New York home on their way to Vermont.

Rachel felt that these were good omens.

Barrett stood waiting for her, looking quite handsome in his dress uniform, Lt. Anderson, his best man, at his side. Several of his fellow officers also attended, for Barrett Fraser was a popular man. His wide smile welcomed her as Connor placed her hand in Barrett's.

"You look beautiful, Rachel," he whispered.

She gave him a shy smile in return. From this day on Rachel would count on that love to support her.

They exchanged their vows and Barrett placed the slim gold band on her finger, sealing their troth.

"You may kiss your bride," the minister, a tall thin man with thick glasses, intoned.

Barrett smiled. "With pleasure." He drew Rachel into his arms and kissed her, a pledge of his faith in their marriage; then he lifted her hand and kissed the ring that he'd placed there. "I love you, Rachel Fraser. As God is my everlasting judge, I love you."

* * *

In her cabin later than night, Rachel drew on the silky golden-brown robe. Since she'd claimed it for her own, she'd made alterations so that it fit her.

They were on their way upriver, enjoying a comfortable room on a huge steamboat. Later in the journey, they would disembark and take a train to New York City, there to be Carolyn's guests.

Rachel gazed out the small porthole, watching the moon. It silvered the Mississippi, giving it a serene quality.

That was how she felt. Calm. Serene.

Rachel glanced back fondly at her sleeping husband. He looked so much like a little boy, happy and content; although he'd been anything but boyish some hours earlier when he'd made love to her.

Alternately dreading the experience and yet wishing to get it over with, Rachel had been anxiously awaiting the moment when Barrett would make her his wife in deed as well as name. His gentle care and concern alleviated her fears and won her trust. He took his time, making sure that Rachel was a partner in the act.

For that she was grateful, though it was gratitude mixed with sadness.

Barrett would never know that she'd closed her eyes and pretended that it was Matthew who kissed her, Matthew who caressed her, Matthew who ultimately possessed her.

"I'm sorry that we missed most of the leaves turning," Barrett said as the private coach he'd hired carried them toward his farm.

Rachel couldn't help constantly scanning the landscape, seeing the last glory of red and gold as the trees that surrounded the area began to fade. So many shades of autumn dotted the Green Mountains. The air was crisp, fresh-smelling.

"Next year," he promised her, patting her arm, which was drawn through his. "When you see the colors as they peak, you'll know why I think that this is the most beautiful spot on earth."

Rachel snuggled closer to Barrett's warm body. A chilly breeze filtered around them through the open windows. The weather here was so different from the often sweltering temperatures of New Orleans. Tonight they might even have need of a fire.

Soon the driver pulled up to a large farmhouse made of stone, surrounded by a grove of maple trees, giving Rachel her first glimpse of her new abode. She saw an elderly couple standing in the wide doorway, relief and joy at having their son back again on their faces.

"We're home, darling," Barrett proudly announced as he helped the driver unload their bags.

Rachel mentally corrected her husband. They were here in Stowe. Matthew was her home—this was merely the place where she would live from now on.

Rachel got along well with Barrett's parents, and with his older sister and her husband. She was immediately welcomed into the bosom of the Fraser family, and found out that by marriage she was an aunt seven times over, soon to be followed by an eighth niece or nephew.

Within a year of her wedding, Rachel had given Barrett a son. He'd returned to the war, and was wounded in the final campaign.

"I'm so glad that you're home to stay, my darling," Rachel commented one evening as they watched their son sleeping, with Wager curled up next to the cradle. The big dog had taken an instant liking to Rachel's child and had become the boy's personal watchdog.

It was an Indian summer night, and the sky was crowded with stars. Rachel had hovered over Barrett these past weeks, making sure that he was comfortable, fussing over his meals. Thankful that the war hadn't stolen another man from her, she lavished her attention on her husband. Afraid that somehow, because she loved Barrett—though she knew deep inside that it wasn't the same way she loved Matthew—he, too, would be taken from her. When she'd heard he was wounded, she was frantic with worry. Discovering that his wound wasn't life-threatening, she eventually relaxed. Now he was safe. Safe and with her, having recovered from his injuries.

Rachel had seen the look in his eyes; Barrett wanted her. Now. Tonight. His parents had gone to visit his sister and her family in Montpelier, so they were alone. She enjoyed the closeness she and Barrett shared while they were in bed even more than the actual physical act. She'd missed that closeness when he was away, and looked forward to reestablishing that special bond this evening.

He'd just lit a fire in the massive stone fireplace while she moved into the farmhouse's large kitchen, removing a jug of buttermilk from the icebox so that she could make biscuits for their supper. She had a chicken stewing in a pot with fresh vegetables, and a blueberry pie for their dessert.

He stood in the doorway, watching her.

Rachel sensed him behind her and greeted him with a warm smile. "Supper will be ready in half an hour," she told him, going back to her mixture.

When she didn't hear him move, she looked up. Barrett was still standing there. "Is something wrong?" she asked.

"I was just looking over the mail that arrived today," he said. "It would appear that you have a letter from New Orleans. From your friend Dominique."

"How lovely," she murmured, beating the batter for her biscuits. "Put it on the table, would you?" she requested. "I'll be reading it when I've set these in the oven."

Barrett did as she asked, then took the few extra steps that would bring him to her, stopping to lift her chin with his hand. "I love you, Rachel." He bent and kissed her mouth. "More than I ever thought possible. God," he groaned, "when that bullet hit me, I figured I was done for. I felt myself sinking into some black hole and I prayed so hard then that God would give me more time," he whispered with a hungry urgency, "time for you. To be with you, to love you.

"When I woke up in that miserable tent that passed as a surgeons ward, my first thoughts were of you. What a good wife you've made me, and how lucky I am to be your husband. I never want to lose you."

Rachel smiled. "And you never will," she assured him.

He walked back into the other room, leaving her to finish her preparations. When she'd put her biscuits into the oven and washed her hands, removing the last traces of flour, she sat down to read her letter. Funny, she mused, she'd just written to Dominique a little over two weeks ago, catching her up on all her news. Perhaps Dominique was writing to tell her that she and Adam, her husband, were expecting a baby.

Rachel paused at that thought. She would like another child. A little girl, if possible.

Maybe tonight they could start.

She picked up a knife and slit the envelope. A folded piece of newspaper fell into her lap. She picked it up and placed it on the table while she read the note inside.

> *Dear Rachel*:
> *The most extrordinary thing has happened. A miracle. The man we believed lost to us has come home. Alive.*

Upon reading these words Rachel's heart began to pound.

> *I have sent you the article from today's* Daily Crescent.
> *No doubt Matthew will contact you soon. Isn't this wonderful news?*

Rachel noted the date on Dominique's letter. It was written almost three weeks ago.

Taking a deep breath, Rachel unfolded the newspaper.

DEVEREAUX HEIR RETURNS
FROM THE DEAD

In a surprising bit of good fortune, Matthew Devereaux, scion of the Louisiana Devereaux family, was found to be alive. In a bizarre twist of fate, the former Union Army captain was reported to have been executed as a spy over two years ago.

It would seem that Devereaux was actually a prisoner of war, languishing in a private jail compound on the island of Bermuda before being transferred to Andersonville Prison in Georgia, where he spent the last two months of the war.

Matthew was alive!

Rachel groaned, pain knifing through her entire body. The article slid through her nerveless fingers. She sat there, stunned.

Matthew had returned—and she was another man's wife.

Barrett came back into the kitchen when he smelled the biscuits burning. He saw his wife sitting at the table, her face pale, her eyes staring straight ahead. He rushed to grab the food from the oven, taking a towel and wrapping it around his hand as he removed the blackened lumps and dumped them into the sink.

"Rachel," he asked, "what's wrong?" He knelt in front of her, noticing the scrap of newspaper on the brick floor.

When she didn't respond, Barrett cast a quick glance at the paper. He quickly scanned the contents and realized what had happened. He swallowed the fear he felt and said softly, "What wonderful news."

Rachel blinked in confusion. "He's alive." Tears began to pour from her eyes. "It's true, Barrett. Matthew's alive and come home." Her left hand, with his gold ring on her finger, raised to her trembling lips.

Barrett gathered his wife into his arms while she cried for the return of her first love. Selfishly, he wished that Matthew Devereaux had stayed dead. Sharing her with a ghost was one thing—with a man who lived once more was impossible.

Rachel waited.
Weeks passed.
Months passed.
And still no word from Matthew.
Finally, she received an envelope from New Orleans. It was from Matthew.
She hastily ripped it open. A single sheet of stationery was inside, with a brief message written upon it.

Rachel:
Congratulations on your marriage. My parents assured me that the man you wed was a fine, decent person, and that you were very happy.

I understand that you and he have a son. That's an important bond between a husband and wife.

I wish that things could have turned out differently, but we must all live with the consequences of our actions.

I remain your humble servant,
Matthew Justin Devereaux.

Rachel acknowledged just what the letter meant—Matthew wouldn't be keeping his promise.

James banged one of his wooden toys against his crib, drawing Rachel's attention. She went to her son, who was teething, and soothed the child, holding him close to her and crooning an old Irish tune to him as she rocked back and forth, a solitary tear wet on her cheek.

That was the last word I ever had from Matthew himself. Occasionally I heard from his mother or his sister throughout the years, but never again from him directly. He later married, and sired a family of his own.

Do you ever think about the promise you made me, Matthew? Do you ever lie awake at night, as I sometimes do, and think how very different our lives would be if you had only kept that promise to come back for me? Do you cheat your wife by imagining it is me to whom you make love? Do you bear the burden of guilt that I do?

Or have you forgotten the words you said to me? It would have been so much easier for me if I had forgotten them. I have a husband and family that I hold dear, yet still I cannot help but wonder what choice I would have made had you come.

But you never did, nor shall you ever. I know that in my heart, though still I wait.

If there never was a time for us in this life,

then there has to be in another. I will hold that thought with me always.

Chapter Thirteen

He never came.

Rebecca closed the last diary after reading the final entry, clasping the leather book to her breast, tears streaming down her cheeks. She reached for a tissue and wiped them away, reflecting on just how sad her ancestor's story was. To have loved so deeply, so completely, and to have lost the one person you felt so connected to.

"So much for soul mates and fate," Rebecca said aloud to the empty house as she rose from her reclining position on the couch. Once she'd started reading the diaries, she'd been unable to put them down, finding the story so compelling that she'd begged off her friend's invitation to dinner so that she could continue reading them.

What would it feel like to love so intensely? So passionately? To know a love so strong that it overshadowed one's life forever?

That was the kind of love that had been missing in her first marriage. As much as Rebecca loved Ben, and she did, it had been the love of a good friend, like a comfortable shoe that fit well and was easy to slip on and off. Never the deep, sharp love that wouldn't let go, that demanded the most that one person had to give.

That dark, profound love was what was missing in her life. Ben had hit the nail on the head when he said that she did know what she was looking for. Rebecca had been unintentionally blind to the truth—she'd been searching for a love of her own. A love that would last, that would make her feel as alive as was humanly possible. The kind of love that she had created for her popular soap characters. Timeless. A love that conquered the odds. Unique and everlasting. A love that wouldn't accept defeat.

But her great-great-grandmother had had that and where did it get her? Rebecca wondered. Rachel had waited her whole life for the man she loved to keep his promise.

And he hadn't.

Her ancestor had been trapped in a prison of sorts—her heart given to one man while her body was given to another.

Rebecca added another log to the small fire. She stood gazing into the flames. Had Rachel ever regretted loving Matthew Devereaux?

She closed the glass doors and paced about the room. Why had Rachel kept the diaries? Why risk someone, her husband perhaps, finding them? Wouldn't it have been better to have destroyed damning evidence of loving someone else? Shouldn't Rachel have hidden them more carefully? Or had they been meant to be found and shared?

And what about Matthew Devereaux? The picture of a dashing, handsome, blue-eyed man flashed into Rebecca's mind. Had he ever regretted not claiming Rachel, even though she was another man's wife? Had he wanted to keep his promise, or had his love for her great-great-grandmother faded during the time that they'd spent apart? Had he too given his body to one person while reserving his heart for another? Or had he merely moved on with his life without caring how Rachel fared?

So many unanswered questions.

Rebecca walked into the well-lit kitchen and made a fresh pot of coffee, her hands mechanically performing the task while her mind continued to speculate on the answers.

A light snow began to fall, and Rebecca stood in the kitchen and watched the huge flakes as they coated the landscape once again. What would the weather be like in New Orleans now, she wondered? Hot, sultry, steamy?

It was then that the germ of an idea hit her. She went into the other room and located her portable laptop and returned to the kitchen, machine in hand. She set it down on the expanse of kitchen table and plugged it in. Rebecca slipped in a disk and began to type quickly.

Several hours—and two pots of coffee—later, she'd produced the outline of her new show. It would be set in and around New Orleans, with a female lawyer from New England marrying a businessman from the South. She carefully read over the pages she'd written: the groundwork was laid for the series, and she knew where she wanted it to go. Character studies abounded, with her notes for the three main families, two white and one black, completed. This would be a blending of the Old and New South, with a dash of Yankee pragmatism tossed into the gumbo pot.

Deciding that she deserved a reward, Rachel took out a pint of Ben & Jerry's Rainforest Crunch ice cream from the freezer and began to eat it right out of the container, thinking that perhaps it would be a good idea to go to New Orleans herself to get more of a feel for the setting. Her ancestor's diaries had helped, sparking the creative process, but maybe a trip would give her a different perspective.

And, she wondered, what if there was still something left of Belle Chanson?

Rebecca picked up the phone book and dialed the local travel agent after glancing at the kitchen clock; there was still some time left in this business day and she didn't want to wait till tomorrow.

"Can you tell me if there are any bed-and-breakfasts located outside of the city?" she queried the agent. While the woman checked, Rebecca got excited just thinking about making this trip. Her excitement increased dramatically when the agent informed her that there were several places that would suit her needs, but that the best was a restored antebellum mansion that was still in the hands of the original owners, and was also famous for being the home of a very popular author of historical fiction.

"What's the name of this place?" Rebecca asked.

When Rebecca heard the travel agent's crisp tones utter the name Belle Chanson, the theme from the old "Twilight Zone" TV series started to play in her head.

The Devereaux plantation.

It was then that Rebecca grabbed a chair and sat down. "You said that it's been in the same family?" she demanded in a soft voice. "Who would that be?"

The travel agent told her that the house was owned by Morgan Devereaux, and that his cousin and her husband ran the inn for him. The plantation house had been restored to its former glory within the last ten years, and had been operating as a first-class bed-and-breakfast for about four years. Did Rebecca want her to make a reservation?

"Yes, I do," Rebecca responded, still in a state of shock. She couldn't believe her luck—that she would be staying in the house that had played so prominent a part in her ancestor's life. And imagine that a Devereaux heir still lived there!

What was he like?

"You can get me a room? Good," she murmured. "I also want you to make arrangements for me to get a flight leaving Burlington Friday morning, if possible, for New Orleans," Rebecca instructed the agent, "and as for the room, I want it for at least a week, maybe longer."

She gave the agent her credit card number for payment and sat back down again, the ice cream melting unforgotten in the container on the table.

Belle Chanson. What ghosts awaited her there?

Having made her decision to go to New Orleans, and having had a long, refreshing sleep the night before, Rebecca wanted to see if she could find one of Morgan Devereaux's books. She wanted a clue as to his character, and she believed that she could find at least one in his own work.

The local bookstore in Stowe, located on the main street in a renovated building that also housed several other shops, had several of Morgan Devereaux's paperback novels. Each, Rebecca discovered, had made the nation's top best-seller lists, according to the blurb on the back cover, and one was being made into a TV miniseries for a major network.

Rebecca selected a novel that was set in the South during the American Revolution and paid for her purchase. Instead of rushing home, she chose to have lunch in the hotel next door to the shop. While she waited for the young waitress to bring her order of the hotel's famous potato-spinach soup, she sipped her coffee and opened the book. Her seat next to the window provided enough sunlight to read by. She was going to skim the first few pages just to give herself an idea of how he wrote.

Rebecca was hooked from the very first page. Morgan Devereaux's prose was rich and evocative, drawing the reader into his world. The novel skillfully wove politics with an intense love triangle: two best friends, each on opposite sides of the American Revolution, both in love with the daughter of a rich English merchant.

She refused to put the book down while she ate, so she held it with one hand while she dipped her spoon into the soup with the other, mechanically eating. It had been so long since a book held her interest as this one did. Rebecca rarely had the time to devote to a book. If she could spare an hour or two, she preferred to read a short contemporary romance novel. This was over 500 pages.

" 'Becca?"

Rebecca looked up from the book and saw Nicole Robertson standing there, a large shopping bag in her hand.

"I thought that was you," Nicole said, sitting down opposite Rebecca. "I was in the craft shop picking up an order of mine, and on my way to my car I saw you through the window." Nicole picked up the book that Rebecca had set down, a paper napkin marking her place. "I didn't know you read those big historical novels." Nicole examined the front and back covers, flipping to the teaser page and reading it quickly.

"Normally I don't," Rebecca admitted, "but I had to buy this."

"Why?" Nicole asked with a puzzled frown, replacing the book and mouthing the word "tea" to the waitress.

Rebecca gave her friend a smile. "Because the author's ancestor and mine were romantically linked."

Nicole's eyes grew wide. "Say what?" This was uttered in a voice that rose in an excited semisqueak, causing several other patrons of the restaurant to pause in the midst of their afternoon tea and stare at the table.

Rebecca grinned. "You heard me," she said. "I found my great-great-grandmother's diaries and it was all in there. She was in love with a man named Matthew Devereaux."

"And you're sure that this man was related to the author?"

Rebecca nodded her head. "Without a doubt."

"Wow," Nicole said, pouring the small pot of tea into her cup, adding a slice of lemon and two lumps of sugar. "How interesting."

"More than you can imagine," Rebecca assured her cryptically. She signaled the waitress for a fresh pot of coffee.

It was then that Nicole noticed the gold locket that hung about Rebecca's neck. It stood out against the hunter-green sweater that her friend wore. "Where did you get that locket?" she asked. "Is it new?"

Rebecca smiled. "Sort of. It belonged to my great-great-grandmother. I found it among her things." Rebecca leaned over and held out the locket so that Nicole could see it. "Isn't that work lovely?" she asked, referring to the detailed interlocking initials. "*M* and *R* for Matthew and Rachel." She snapped the lock and revealed the miniature portraits inside.

Nicole gasped. "She looks like you."

Rebecca asked, "Do you think so?"

Nicole nodded. "Very much so," she remarked. She took a closer look at the man's face in the locket. "He's a very handsome man." Nicole took a sip of her tea, her face wearing a speculative look. "Now wouldn't it be funny if this Morgan Devereaux"—and with that she tapped her left index finger on the book—"looked just like his ancestor?"

At that thought, Rebecca paled slightly. Suppose he did? she wondered. Would it matter?

No, of course not, she assured herself. It would mean nothing to her. It would be a co-incidence. Besides, Morgan Devereaux was probably an older man who was tweedy, bald-ing, and had a paunch. Hardly the stuff of ro-mantic fantasies.

"She loved him very much," Rebecca as-serted.

"Yet they didn't marry?"

"Rachel thought he was dead," Rebecca ex-plained. "It happened during the Civil War and he was reported as being killed. Eventually, she married someone else, then later found out that Matthew was alive."

"Bummer. What did she do?"

"Waited." Rebecca held the locket in her hand, her fingers rubbing over it. "She waited for him to come back to her."

"And he never did."

Rebecca shook her head. "He eventually wrote to her and wished her well in her mar-riage."

"That's all?"

She nodded. "Exactly." Rebecca shrugged her shoulders. "So much for happy endings, eh?"

Nicole shot her friend a sharp glance. "Now, 'Becca, if you were scripting this, Matthew would have made a miraculous comeback just in the nick of time." Nicole snapped her fingers. "In fact, just like you did in the wedding scene on 'Tomorrow's Promise.' " She tasted her tea.

"You're such a romantic, you wouldn't have been able to resist."

"You really think I'm a romantic?" Rebecca asked, her chin resting on her palm.

Nicole laughed. "Of course I think that, because it's true. Why do you think that soap shot to number one in the ratings when you took over as head writer, my dear girl?" she pointed out. "Granted, you've got some pretty damn good actors on that show, but it's the relationships that you've created, the romances you've crafted, that keep people tuning in. Viewers love your characters, 'Becca. They care about them because you do," she insisted. "Studly hunks without shirts only go so far. It's the romance the viewers crave, and that's what you give them."

Nicole gave a quick glance to her watch. "I gotta go." She swallowed the rest of her tea. "I promised Mike I'd stop and pick up a few jars of honey and some cider from the Stedman farm." She rose. "Now why don't you come to dinner tonight?"

Rebecca thought it over. "Okay. But I can't stay long. I'm leaving day after tomorrow and I have a few things to take care of first."

"Leaving? You just got here."

"I know," Rebecca admitted, "but after reading the diaries I got an incredible idea for my next soap." While she dug out her wallet and placed several bills on the check the waitress had left minutes before, Rebecca quickly outlined the idea to Nicole. "So what do you think?" she asked her friend.

"Sounds great," Nicole agreed. "Different, and yet compelling."

"I thought so," Rebecca said. "Now, if I can successfully pitch it to the daytime brass."

"You shouldn't have a problem," Nicole assured her as they walked outside to the car park. "And who knows," she observed, "you could run into this Morgan Devereaux. Now wouldn't that be a hoot?" Nicole gave Rebecca a questioning look. "Maybe you two could compare notes on your respective ancestors?"

Rebecca shrugged. "Who knows?"

Nicole got into her car, rolling down her window. "Hey, 'who knows' is right." She arched an eyebrow. "It could be fun. See you around seven," she said as she pulled out.

Dinner was pleasant, but Rebecca couldn't wait to get back to her house and dive back into the book. Putting on a classical CD, she settled back on her couch to read, having shed her regular clothes for a far more comfortable pair of sweats.

Time flew by as she became engrossed in the novel, falling in love with Morgan Devereaux's writing style. His words were passionate and sensual, which, she admitted to herself, was a rather interesting surprise. Rebecca was surprised by how deftly he handled the love scenes. Expecting a quick, cursory scene along the lines of wham-bam-thank-you-ma'am, she thrilled to his evocative prose.

She closed the book, slipping in her marker, and lay back, unable to put aside his powerful emotionalism. She was unsettled by Morgan's stunning grasp of a woman's sexual awakening. That this writer, this *man*, could so capture his heroine's psyche, astounded her.

What kind of a man was Morgan Devereaux?

It occurred to her that she wanted to add one more item to her already packed suitcase. Bounding off the couch, Rebecca ran up the stairs, all the way to the loft, where she went directly to the armoire and brought out one of her great-great-grandmother's nightgowns from the drawer.

Rebecca held it up. It was the one she'd selected a few days earlier. Somehow, she thought it would be a perfect complement to the much warmer weather in Louisiana. The row of tiny pearl buttons extended all the way to the waist of the gown.

Suddenly Rebecca shivered. She knew without question that this nightgown was to have been worn by Rachel when she married Matthew—and she also knew that Rachel had never worn it. The hint of jasmine still clung to it, as did the expectations of a woman waiting for her beloved.

Perhaps she shouldn't take it with her.

But she had to.

That feeling was unmistakable—one that she couldn't ignore.

Rebecca located the matching peignoir and withdrew it, placing it atop the nightgown. She'd take both of them with her.

A half hour later, tucked warmly into her bed, the novel at hand, Rebecca drifted off to sleep, once again wondering just what type of man was this Morgan Devereaux?

PART TWO
LOVE,
REMEMBER
ME

Chapter Fourteen

Morgan Devereaux sat in his office, poring over research books. Several were piled up on his desk, and he made notes directly onto his laptop computer, storing the information for reference later. His next book, he'd decided, would finally address the Civil War. So far in his career, he'd avoided dealing with the conflict between the states, but lately it had begun to tickle his creative fancy. And since his was such a rich family history, what with his great-great-grandfather having fought for the Union instead of the Confederacy, Morgan thought that that story alone could prove compelling reading.

His grandfather had saved all of his ancestor's papers and journals, carefully securing them, and before he'd died, he'd given the key to a safe-deposit box in New Orleans to his favorite grandson. Those firsthand accounts would be invaluable to Morgan's research.

Morgan pushed back his desk chair and gazed up at the portrait that hung over his desk; his cousin had found it carefully packed away in the attic of Belle Chanson while the house was being restored. It was of Matthew Devereaux, painted just after the end of the war. The man possessed a certain air of gravity and sadness, Morgan thought. How much his world must have changed during the interim of the war—could that explain the look of grim resolution in his ancestor's blue eyes?

Morgan often found himself wondering about this man. They shared similar features. Sometimes it was like looking into a mirror, distorted by age.

The intercom buzzed on his phone. At Morgan's booted feet, a drowsing black Labrador raised his head. He patted the dog's head fondly.

"Yes?"

The smooth, drawling voice of his secretary answered, "You asked me to remind you that you have an appointment today in the city. The reporter from *Newsweek* called a few minutes ago to say she was looking forward to meeting you."

Morgan groaned. Interviews were a necessary evil in his work. He was an intensely private person, and spoke to the press only when he had to.

Resigned, he checked his watch. "It's for two o'clock, right?"

"Yes," the female voice informed him. "And shall I accept the invitation you just received from . . ."

Morgan listened as his secretary mentioned the name of a small, intimate writer's conference in southeast Texas that he frequented almost every fall. "Tell them I'll be happy to come," he replied, ending the interruption. That was one thing he did enjoy, meeting and discussing the craft of writing with other writers. Generally, he gave a research workshop or participated in a panel. There, talk remained about business, never veering, as reporters were wont to do, toward his personal life.

Morgan smiled wryly at that observation. What personal life? Right now he had none. He was a man in his midthirties without—what was the current term?—a constant companion. And not for lack of offers. He'd had girlfriends, even a fiancee, but nothing permanent had ever come of his relationships. It was as if he were waiting for something—or someone—else.

For what? For whom?

Rebecca had rented a car upon her arrival in New Orleans, and she enjoyed her drive along the famous River Road. She passed several restored plantations, and only the fact that she was tired from her trip—and too excited to get to Belle Chanson—prevented her from stopping to peruse other examples of Louisiana's antebellum past.

Tomorrow, she promised herself. She'd drive out and go exploring after she'd rested. After she'd seen as much as she could of the Devereaux plantation.

She turned her car into the long, oak-lined driveway, through the large brick gates, feeling as if she were driving backward in time. Automatically, one hand searched for and found the gold locket around her neck. She gripped it tightly for a moment, as if drawing strength from her ancestor as she drove her car to the front entrance.

The house was exactly the way Rachel had described it in her diary. Elegant, beautiful, it was the archetypal Southern mansion.

Rebecca got out of her rented vehicle and stood there, drinking in the sights and smells. All this seemed so familiar to her. She immediately put this down to her great-great-grandmother's diaries. Plants bloomed in abundance, and their exotic fragrances wafted about her, sending her a clear welcome.

An older, retired couple lounged on large chairs on the veranda, sipping from glasses of iced tea.

"Hello," Rebecca said.

The older man and woman smiled graciously and repeated Rebecca's greeting. At that moment, the screen door opened and out walked a woman in her late thirties, a beaming smile on her long, thin face.

"Hi there."

Rebecca listened to the smooth accent, so very soft and Southern. She extended her hand and introduced herself. "I'm Rebecca Fraser. I have a reservation."

"You sure do, Miss Fraser," the other woman acknowledged, shaking Rebecca's hand. "Welcome to Belle Chanson. I'm Della Devereaux St. Just, your hostess. We certainly hope you will enjoy your stay with us."

"I'm sure I shall," Rebecca responded.

"This is Mr. and Mrs. Michaels," Della said, introducing the older couple, who shook hands with Rebecca, "from Allentown, Pennsylvania."

"How do you do?" Rebecca asked.

"Very well, young lady," the man said with a smile.

"Now, what about your bags?" Della asked.

Rebecca popped the trunk lid and removed her solitary suitcase and her portable laptop.

"A computer, right?" Della inquired.

"Have laptop, will travel," she answered with a slight laugh.

"Are you by any chance a writer?"

Rebecca nodded.

"Novels?"

"No," Rebecca responded. "Actually, I write for television."

"Really?" Della asked, her curiosity aroused,

her eyes widening. "What show?"

"For daytime TV," Rebecca said. "I'm the former head writer of 'Tomorrow's Promise'."

"Oh no," Della said enthusiastically. "That's my favorite soap. I can't believe it. I never miss an episode."

"Glad to hear it."

"I'll have to introduce you to my cousin, Morgan. He's a writer too," Della said with a sparkle in her brown eyes.

"The historical novelist, right?"

Della smiled proudly. "That's him."

"I've just finished reading *Against The Wind*," Rebecca stated. "He's a very talented writer."

"We all think so," Della said, "but then again, we're family. It's always nice to hear somebody else say so." She rolled her eyes. "Dear me, how I've been going on while you're standing here," she said in an apologetic tone. "Let me show you to your room before you wilt in our heat. Most times the weather's very cooperative at this time of year, but we've hit quite a warm spell just now." She glanced at Rebecca's jeans and long-sleeved shirt. "I sure hope that you brought something cooler to wear?"

Rebecca smiled. "I did," she assured her hostess.

"Good. Then let's get you settled inside so that you can change." She grabbed hold of Rebecca's suitcase and walked through the screen door.

"Nice to have met you," Rebecca called out to the older couple as she followed Della inside.

The interior of the plantation house was magnificent. Rebecca felt as though she had stepped through a portal to the past, so faithfully had the place been restored. Any minute now she thought she would see women in hoop skirts and men in frock coats come down the stairs or through the doors. Scarlett and Rhett would have felt comfortable here.

Della led her up a winding staircase, the walls lined with portraits of the previous Devereauxs, down a long hallway until they reached a large bedroom. A ceiling fan whirled above their heads, providing a breath of relief from the rising heat. "Dinner is served at eight, and we do tea here at four." She opened the French doors to the gallery. "You've got a great view here of the rest of the grounds."

Rebecca joined her, looking toward where the *garçonnière* should have been.

At the puzzled look on her guest's face, Della asked, "Is there something wrong?"

Rebecca shook her head. "No, nothing's wrong. I just thought that these old houses had smaller residences set aside for bachelor sons. For some reason, it just seemed as though there should be one around here." Rebecca didn't want to reveal her connection to the past just yet, so she deliberately kept quiet about her ancestor's link to this house and family. She disliked evading the truth, but she deemed it best.

"Funny you should ask," Della said. "There was a *garçonnière* on the property." She pointed to a wooden gazebo surrounded by rose bushes and assorted flowers. "Right there, in fact. It was destroyed by a fire around the turn of the century."

Della turned around and walked back into the bedroom. She showed Rebecca the connecting bathroom. "Now, can I get you something, or would you like to rest?"

Rebecca yawned. "I think I'm going to take a cool bath and then a nap, if you don't mind."

Della smiled. "This is your vacation, remember? You can do whatever you like."

"Vacation. That's almost a foreign term to me," Rebecca said with an engaging smile. "Yes, there is one thing I would like, if you don't mind. I would dearly love a large glass of the iced tea I saw the Michaelses enjoying. With extra lemon, please."

"I'll leave it on your night table while you bathe," Della said, closing the door behind her.

Rebecca walked back out to the gallery, staring at the gazebo. She couldn't believe that she was finally here. A sense of familiarity washed over her. As if she belonged here. Almost as if this trip were somehow meant to happen.

Ridiculous! she mentally scoffed as she walked back into the bedroom, shedding her pale blue oxford shirt. She was getting too caught up in her ancestor's words, that was all, she thought as she unzipped her jeans and stepped out of them. So many things here had been viewed through Rachel's eyes. That was all it was. It wasn't as if she'd ever been here before.

She padded into the bathroom, turning on the taps and filling the huge claw-footed tub with cool water; then she added a sprinkle of the bath salts that were there. Rebecca sniffed the fragrance. Jasmine.

When she emerged from her long soak, Rebecca saw the glass of iced tea waiting for her. Strolling over, clad in only a short indigo blue terry robe, she noticed a magazine lying on the white counterpane. On it was a Post-It note from Della. *Thought you'd like to read this if you have the time.*

Rebecca picked it up and peeled off the note, staring into the very dark blue eyes of a handsome, familiar stranger.

It was a well-thumbed copy of *People* magazine, dated almost a year ago. The cover picture had the title, "Historical Heartthrob."

So this was Morgan Devereaux.

"Would you please come by for dessert, at least, Morgan?" Della pleaded with her cousin. "I want you to meet the woman who arrived today."

"Is she a reporter?" he asked wearily, one thick black brow raised. "If so, I've done my duty today, thank you."

"No. She's a writer."

"Ah." The word was drawn out, giving it a world of meaning.

Della sighed. "It's not what you think."

"And what do I think?" Morgan asked.

"That she's come here to meet you, specifically." She gave Morgan a measured look. "That she's come to glean pearls of wisdom from you." Della laughed at the expression on Morgan's face. "She's not like that, Morgan."

"You're sure?"

Della nodded. "She's as successful in her field as you are, *mon cher*," she gently chided him.

"Which is?"

"Television," she stated. "She writes daytime dramas."

"Soaps?"

"Yes," Della admitted. " 'Tomorrow's Promise' just won the Daytime Emmy for best show and best writing, not to mention sweeping all the best-actor categories." Della was an avid fan and kept up with who won what, where and when.

"Okay," Morgan said with a grin. "I admit defeat. Besides"—he flashed his cousin a teasing look—"I could never resist your peach cobbler anyway."

"How did you know I made peach cobbler for tonight?"

"Isn't that what you always use to seduce me into showing up? You know I have a weakness for the way you prepare it."

It was Della's turn to grin. "I have a feeling that you won't regret this, Morgan."

* * *

Rebecca was more tired than she realized; she slept through the serving of afternoon tea and awoke just after 7:30 P.M.

She'd perused the article on Morgan, finding it fascinating reading. So much for her theory that he was short, dumpy, and bald. Rebecca was struck by how much he resembled the picture of Matthew Devereaux that was contained within the locket. Eerily so.

She climbed out of the high bed, her feet hitting the cool bare floorboards. Rebecca couldn't resist turning her head and gazing at the magazine where it lay upon the marble-topped night table. In her profession, she'd met her fair share of handsome, attractive men; yet there was something that drew her eyes back to the picture of Morgan Devereaux. It produced a tingle in her tummy, a trembling of her lips, as if she knew exactly how his generous mouth would feel against hers. As if she could recall how his tall body would fit against hers, his lean frame complementing the soft curves of her shape.

It was the atmosphere of this place that was messing with her mind, she thought as she secured the open French doors so that she could change for dinner. She pulled the thin nightshirt over her head, tossing it casually to the foot of the bed. Catching sight of herself in the full-length cheval mirror, Rebecca stared. Her skin was tinged with a slight flush of color, and her breasts were high and full, the nipples puck-

275

ered and pebble-hard. There was no mistaking her figure for the boyish slenderness of the current crop of models. She possessed a woman's body, trim and fit; Rebecca was comfortable with it.

Was it the kind of body that a man like Morgan Devereaux would find attractive?

Where had that thought sprung from?

Rebecca frowned as she mentally dismissed the idea as stupid. Who cared what this man thought? She certainly didn't. He meant nothing to her, except that he was sort of a link to her great-great-grandmother. That was all.

She slipped on her clothes as quickly as possible, opting for a more informal style this night. The article mentioned that Devereaux had a town house in New Orleans. Chances were he lived there as a primary residence, rather than at the plantation. She probably wouldn't even meet him while she stayed here.

And perhaps that was for the best. If a picture could get such an intense reaction from her, she didn't want to push the envelope. It would be safer for her to keep this man at arm's length.

Damn safety.

Those were the first words that popped into Rebecca's head when she was introduced to Morgan Devereaux later that evening.

She was sitting out on the veranda with Della and Della's husband Jack, a retired schoolteacher, enjoying the scented breeze that wafted across the lawn, and the delicious peach cobbler. It was warm and sweet, loaded with peaches that Della had canned herself soaked in brandy. A hint of spices added to the flavor. The Michaelses had driven into New Orleans after dinner to visit some local jazz clubs.

At the bark of a dog, Rebecca turned her head. It was then that she saw a man crossing the grass, his long legs making short work of the distance between a brick building set among a group of moss-covered oaks and the main house.

The black Lab at his side left his owner and quickened his pace. He bounded onto the brick and wagged his tail, his tongue lolling. He hesitated for a few seconds before he made his way to Rebecca, coming to rest at her chair, sitting there, waiting for attention.

Rebecca couldn't ignore the dog's obvious ploy. Laughing lightly, she patted his head. The dog's response was a low growl of contentment as he settled at her feet.

"Jester always knows a soft touch when he sees one," a deeply masculine voice said.

Rebecca raised her head and looked up. An odd tingling rippled through her body, as if the man standing before her had caressed her from head to toe just by one sweeping glance of his eyes. It was instant recognition of the deepest, most powerful, sexual attraction she'd ever felt in her life. Like a bolt of lightning, it infused her with an awareness so acute, Rebecca found the breath catching painfully in her chest.

"Have we met before?" Morgan asked. He knew this woman. Something told him that. As odd as the notion was, he recognized her. Invisible threads of awareness spun between them.

"Of course you haven't," Della interrupted. "Rebecca, this is Morgan Devereaux, my cousin," she said in a cheery tone of voice, completely oblivious to what was happening between the couple. "Morgan, this is Rebecca Fraser."

When their hands connected, both Morgan and Rebecca felt electricity shoot through them. Crackling tension sizzled the air around them, like a sudden summer storm that promises relief, but only succeeds in making things hotter than before.

Morgan took a seat across from Rebecca, unable to take his eyes from her. Like metal to a magnet, he was attracted to her. Under the soft glow of the light provided by the glass-covered wall sconces, Morgan carefully observed her. A delicate peach shaded her cheeks and lips; her golden-blonde hair was warm and natural, with paler and darker strands mixed; her eyes were a rich, welcoming shade of blue, neither light nor dark. The white cotton camp shirt she wore outlined her curvaceous shape, as did her short denim skirt. Her legs were long and bare. Did they feel as smooth as they looked? he wondered. What would they feel like wrapped around his own bare skin?

Rebecca grew hotter under Morgan's blatantly sexual inspection. It wasn't that he was rude, or even crude; she'd experienced her fair share of lewd glances—one couldn't live in New York and entirely escape them. But his regard was sensual, touching her internally, reaching her as no one ever had.

That frightened Rebecca. She'd always had a strong sense of self, of security. Now, five minutes after meeting this man, her world was shaken to the core.

Once again.

She heard the words echo through her mind.

Oh God, what was happening to her?

What was happening to him?

She probably thought he was the rudest man she'd ever met, but Morgan couldn't stop staring at her. It was as if he were seeing someone he'd known before, just slightly altered. Like a memory locked inside his brain trying to get out.

Morgan examined this phenomenon. He was a man used to control, of his life and his work, to keeping his emotions in check. Strong swings of mood weren't the norm for him; yet he felt as though he could sweep this woman out of her seat and carry her off, preferably to his bedroom, and there, lock out the rest of the world.

He ached with wanting her. And, strangely enough, it seemed as though it was a familiar ache. That somewhere, somehow, he'd ached for her before, just as intensely.

What the hell was going on here?

When he finally looked away, Rebecca reached for the china plate that contained the cobbler, grateful to have something on which to focus her attention. She concentrated on the dessert, anxious to get some kind of control back into the evening.

Inconsequential chatter followed, with the loquacious Della leading the conversation, keeping it moving smoothly, while Morgan and Rebecca made occasional comments. They were each well aware of the other, and of the shadowy undercurrent that flowed between them.

"What are your plans, Miss Fraser?" Morgan asked.

"Well," she said, wetting her lips with a quick flick of her tongue, "I want to visit some of the houses on River Road, drive around a bit and scout out places that might be viable for location shooting, and definitely see New Orleans. You know, walk the streets, check out the shops, and see the sights. Very touristy things, but I think I'll be able to get more of a feel for this area that way. It'll be important to making my characters more fully fleshed."

"Would you like a guide?"

Rebecca almost fell out of her chair upon hearing his question. To have his help would be wonderful—and dangerous.

"I hadn't really thought about it, but I suppose that it would be helpful to have someone along who knows the area," she replied.

"Good."

Della's jaw dropped at her cousin's offer. Morgan always guarded his privacy. Now here he was volunteering to take time from his own busy schedule to play personal tour director for this woman. What was going on?

"What time did you have in mind?" he inquired, finishing his glass of iced tea.

Rebecca watched the play of muscles in his throat as he swallowed the drink. "How about nine?"

Morgan rose from his seat, Jester joining him. "Nine it is then," he agreed. "Now, if you'll excuse me, I have some work to do."

"Of course," Rebecca murmured, unable to take her eyes away from his retreating figure. God, what had she consented to?

Morgan was unable to concentrate on his work. Every time he tried to keep his mind focused on the research, his thoughts would take him somewhere else. To the plantation house. To her. Closing his eyes, he conjured her image easily. Soft. Fresh. Exciting.

What was it about her? A sense of the familiar? An encounter with the unknown? No woman he'd ever met had had this kind of impact on him. It was both comforting and unsettling.

He got up and went to the window. He could see a faint light coming from the main house on the upper floor. Was it emanating from her room? Did she suffer from the same restlessness as he? Did desire edge along her veins in the same way as it did in his? Could she feel this same tug of yearning?

Rebecca stood by the open French doors to her room, watching the pale glow of light coming from the bottom floor of the carriage house. Della had told her earlier that Morgan had restored the old building for use as an office and as his residence. The house in New Orleans was for use whenever he was in town. It was in the country where he felt most at home, Della explained. In that respect, he was, his cousin assured her, a true Devereaux.

Had he experienced the same pull of attraction as she had? Was this feeling as puzzling to him as it was to her?

She leaned against the door frame, breathing deeply of the night air. His was the voice of her dreams. She'd recognized it as soon as he spoke. And such a voice, she thought. Warm. Arousing. Powerful. Pitched to seduce.

Softly the breeze caressed her skin. She savored it, along with vague memories of another night like this.

But how could she experience hints of memory? This was the first time she'd been here. It must be fragments of her great-great-grandmother's words that haunted her, scraps of phrases that lingered in her own consciousness like jumbled pieces of fabric, some hers, some Rachel's.

How alive was the past in this place. It surrounded her like a second fragile layer of skin.

Rebecca left the doors open, unable to break the tenuous bond of shared intimacy she imagined existed between this house and his.

She climbed into the mahogany four-poster, snuggling into the sheets, reveling in the slide of the material against her bare legs and arms. She caught a faint hint of jasmine in the percale as she moved her head on the pillow.

What would tomorrow bring?

Chapter Fifteen

Rebecca awoke early the next morning, anxious to get a start on her day. She wanted to see Morgan again, to discover if that deeply felt response was a fluke, a trick of imagination brought on by her ancestor's diaries; or, had she, as Rachel had, fallen completely in love at first sight? And if she had, what was she to do?

She entered the informal dining room, craving her first cup of coffee. Rebecca spied the pot sitting atop a small sideboard and walked over, pouring a fresh, steaming cup. She added cream and drank one cup standing there. Refilling the cup, she sat down at one of the two tables.

Through the etched glass doors that separated the dining room from a smaller sitting room, Della entered. She carried a basket of assorted freshly baked muffins. Placing them on the table in front of Rebecca, she said, "Good morning. I trust that you slept well?"

"Yes, thank you," Rebecca replied, inhaling the warm scent of the muffins. She couldn't resist, picking a large muffin loaded with plump blueberries.

Della inquired with a friendly smile, "What would you like for breakfast?"

"If you don't mind, I think that I'll just sample some of these, and coffee."

"Nothing else?"

"No, really," Rebecca said, "this will be just fine." She buttered the muffin, asking, "Am I the only person up so far?"

"The Michaelses have already left for the day, more sightseeing, I believe, and I'm expecting other guests later in the day."

"How many rooms do you let out?"

"Four," Della replied, taking a seat opposite Rebecca. "I didn't want this to be too much like a hotel, where a guest can get lost in the impersonality of the place. This way I can meet people and get to know them. And guests can mingle with each other. Too much company, I've found, and service gets shunted aside by too many demands. I like people to think that they're visiting friends while staying at Belle Chanson. It's always had a reputation for gracious hospitality, and I'd like to keep it that way. As would Morgan."

"As would Morgan what?" he asked, coming into the room.

He brought with him, Rebecca discovered, a masculine electricity that flipped a switch in Rebecca's body. She quivered in response.

Della rose and greeted her taller cousin with a kiss. "I was explaining to Rebecca the philosophy behind our brand of hospitality here at Belle Chanson."

"You'll find our pace much slower than what you're used to, I'm sure, Miss Fraser," Morgan said, taking the chair his cousin vacated.

"Coffee, Morgan?" Della asked.

"Please," he responded.

If anything, Rebecca thought, she was even more attracted to him this morning. "It's a pleasant change," Rebecca stated, taking another bite out of her muffin.

"Most people find it so," he answered, his eyes meeting and holding hers. "Della," he requested, keeping his gaze on Rebecca, "would you mind fixing me breakfast?"

"You know I don't mind, *cher*," she said happily. "What would you like?"

"Just something simple. Eggs and toast."

"Scrambled?"

"That'll be fine." Returning to his previous comments, Morgan said, "We like to appreciate life here, Miss Fraser, all aspects of life." He shrugged his wide shoulders. "Here we learn at an early age to metaphorically stop and smell the roses. It's an old habit that works well."

Rebecca gave a faint laugh. "I'm from the Puritan work ethic school, myself. I love what I do."

"So do I," he said. "But all work and no play makes—"

"For a very successful career," she interjected.

"Yes, I suppose it would. But," Morgan offered, "at what price? I love what I do, and I've never wanted to be anything other than a writer. Yet as much as I love my work—and I do, believe me—I take pleasure in my life. Shutting yourself off from the world around you does little to improve the quality of the work."

Rebecca listened to his words and reflected on just what he was saying to her. It could be true, she thought. She'd spent so much time on her work that she often neglected to do the things she used to make time for. The theater, the movies, dinner with friends, relaxing weekends away from the city.

"Forgive me," he said in his drawling baritone. "Sometimes I do go on."

"Don't apologize," she insisted. "I think that you could be right. At the very least, you've given me something to think about."

Della entered again, a tray in her hands. She set it down, removing the lid from the plate that held a pile of fluffy, golden scrambled eggs. She also handed her cousin a tiny bottle of hot sauce and the toast holder, each slot filled with thick slices of bread. Della added a crystal jar of strawberry preserves and left the couple alone, smiling to herself.

"Now," Morgan asked, sprinkling some of the hot sauce on his eggs, "where would you like to go today?"

"I think I'll leave that up to you," Rebecca answered.

He flashed her a wide smile. "Good. Then bring a camera if you have one, and be prepared to stay out late."

"Will I have to change?" Rebecca stood up so that Morgan could see what she was wearing.

His blue eyes did a slow tour of her body, frankly relishing the way she wore clothes. Nothing trendy or too tight, this lady had a classic style. She wore another simple camp shirt, this time in a shade he reckoned would be called apricot, and a pair of cuffed walking shorts in white. "Perfect. Don't change a thing," he said.

Rebecca blushed at the compliment and sat back down. She wondered if now was the time to tell him about their connection. The locket remained around her neck, a conscious reminder of Rachel and Matthew. She could tell him what she'd discovered and see if he knew anything more about the couple. Or she could maintain her silence about the subject and see what developed.

Yes, Rebecca decided, spreading the thick preserves on a corn bread muffin, she would keep quiet for now and see what happened between them.

And just what did she want to happen? a voice inside her head asked.

The answer came quickly. She wanted to get closer to Morgan. As close as possible.

They spent the day driving along the river, visiting several of the magnificent plantation homes, including Houmas House, the Tezcuco Plantation, and the San Francisco Plantation house. Morgan was a natural-born storyteller, and he regaled Rebecca with tales of life along the Mississippi: of blood feuds lasting generations; of duels fought for honor and beautiful women; of loves lost and won; of the tragedy and honor found in war.

They walked along a trail and sought out a spot to sit for a few minutes. The day had gone well, with both of them enjoying the warm spring weather and each other's company. Through a grove of live oaks, each tree covered with clingy Spanish moss, they sauntered casually, Rebecca stopping to admire the multi-colored azalea bushes.

She could almost believe, except for their modern dress, that they had gone back through time, so peaceful and magic a spot had they found, far removed from the bustle of life. It was just the two of them, with no tourists, no oil rigs searching for Louisiana's black gold, no fishermen out to harvest the catch of the day.

Just as she was about to plop down on the ground, Morgan took hold of her bare arm. From the pocket of his jeans, he produced a snowy white handkerchief. He opened it up and laid it on the grass. "Now," he said in a teasing tone, "my lady may sit."

Rebecca laughed at this touching gesture of chivalry. She gave him a curtsy and sat down, aware of everything around her. She heard the bees buzzing, watched different species of birds as they flitted from trees to bushes and back again. A resplendent magnolia provided a beautiful complement to the surroundings.

"It's so lovely here. I can't believe that it just grew this way," Rebecca observed.

"It didn't," Morgan confessed. "This is part of an estate that's owned by a cousin of mine."

"Just how big a family do you have?" she asked.

"Enormous," he replied with a laugh. "The original Devereaux clan spawned a lot of branches around here. Even some of the French branch came back here in the late 1880s. Plus, the family occasionally intermarried, so we've plenty of relatives hereabouts."

"What about you? Do you have any brothers or sisters?"

Morgan smiled. "Yes. I have two brothers: one's in college, studying law; the other's a geologist. Both very practical occupations."

"As opposed to what we do?" Rebecca challenged.

"That's right. We get paid to dream, to make up stories."

"It's all I ever wanted to do," she confessed.

"Same here," he admitted. "I loved listening to my grandfather when he told his stories of the family, and I can't remember when I wasn't making up tales in my head." Morgan stretched his tall frame out, not minding lying on the grass.

Rebecca took the opportunity to skim her glance over his body. It was lean and muscled, with a long torso and long legs, legs that the jeans only enhanced. If he removed his black T-shirt, would his chest have a coating of dark hair? And what would it feel like? Smell like? She knew he wore an intoxicating cologne. Subtle, yet extremely masculine.

If she closed her eyes, she could picture him fresh from a shower, with a white towel wrapped around his lean hips. It would be a day much hotter than today, with the sultry heat of Louisiana rising. He'd collapse on top of a pristine white sheet that covered his massive bed, and he'd smile when he saw her, bearing something that would both cool and inflame him. Rebecca would pour the cool water from the pitcher over the ice cubes contained in the porcelain bowl, then wait for a few seconds so that the water would chill slightly, then dip in the thick washcloth. It would be deep green in color, a rich, soothing shade.

Morgan would gasp when the cold wet cloth

trailed across his flesh. He would gasp again when her lips followed the cloth, especially as the towel rubbed against his male nipples, puckering them for her laving tongue. His large hands would grab hold of the sheet, grasping it as he groaned low in his throat when she continued her ministrations, moving steadily lower.

A quick snap of her wrist and the towel would cease hiding all his assets.

Oh God, Rebecca thought, what sort of dangerous fantasy game was she playing? Imagining him thus made her ache to see for herself. It created an intense yearning to experience the touch of flesh against naked flesh, to feel the sharp tang of desire, to ride out the storm on the back of a tiger, thrilling to the chance to go where she'd never gone before.

A savagely sweet craving burned in the depths of her body, warming her skin and heating her blood.

This was what had been missing from her marriage. This was what she and Ben didn't have together. Wild, erotic, and compelling, this sensuality both frightened and fascinated Rebecca.

What lay beneath her shirt and shorts? Morgan wondered, his eyes closed against the increasingly hot sun as he imagined his own scenario.

He would be walking into his house, intent on a quick, cool shower to refresh him, making his way to the circular ironwork staircase that would take him to the upper level and the spacious glass-walled shower, and, just as he was ready to put his foot on the first rung, she would be coming down the stairs, clad only in a mid-calf terry robe. Dark blue; indigo, he fancied. Her blonde hair would be loose, and there would be a soft glow on her face, along with a hint of color in her cheeks.

Slowly, with tender care, as if he were unwrapping a precious gift, he would reach out his hand and untie the knot that held the robe together. Then he would know just what her clothes kept hidden. Morgan could well envision the delights of her body: the swell of her breasts, the color and taste of her nipples; he could touch the curve of her hip, explore the arch of her neck, trace the path from her knee upward, skimming her thigh lightly until his fingers came to rest against the delta of blonde curls that guarded her feminine portal.

She would cry out softly when he slipped one long, lean finger inside her.

Abruptly, Morgan sat up, resting his arms on his knees. The fantasy had galvanized his body, hardening his flesh, pushing it against the fabric of his jeans. What was it about this woman he'd just met? Why did she alone seem to possess the ability to instantly arouse his flesh and to engage his mind all at once? His mind named her a stranger, yet his heart deemed her a woman he'd known for more years than he believed possible.

Could it be that he'd fallen in love with her?

Or was it simply a case of good old-fashioned lust, albeit stronger and more acute than any he'd ever experienced?

Would bedding her rid him of this intractable desire?

And why did he have the feeling that somewhere a clock was ticking down—that he must fight against losing, once more, something precious that he couldn't afford to lose again?

"Since we've skipped lunch, how about an early dinner?" Morgan rose, brushing off the back of his jeans, then held out his hand to help Rebecca up. "I know a great little place not far from here that serves some of the best Cajun-Creole cooking. You'll love it, I promise."

Rebecca considered his offer for about a nanosecond. "I'd love to," she responded softly, her hand still linked with his.

Morgan glanced down at their entwined hands and smiled. He could tell that she trusted him; it was there in that seemingly casual gesture. He hadn't had to utter the words "Trust me." She did so, giving him the responsibility for not disappointing her, or ruining the faith she placed in him.

"You won't regret this, *chérie*."

Rebecca prayed that Morgan was right.

* * *

It was an out-of-the-way place that Morgan took her to. The building looked down on its luck, with two battered pickup trucks parked outside.

Morgan parked his Rover beside the others, and to her surprise, he left it unlocked.

Used to New York, she questioned him about that. "Aren't you going to lock up your car?" She knew that his vehicle was an extremely expensive import; she was certain it was worth a lot of money, either whole or for parts.

He chuckled. "If I were in the city, yes, but not here, *chérie*. Out here things are different. People respect each other's property and businesses."

"Okay," she said, somewhat reluctantly.

"You'll get used to it," he assured her.

Rebecca heard his words and shrugged. Morgan spoke as if he thought she would be around for some time. She was only passing through, gathering research for her series, revisiting some of the places Rachel loved. That was all. When she'd fulfilled her last wish list, she would return to her own home. All this would be something to file away in her mental scrapbook.

They entered the establishment, Morgan holding Rebecca's hand. As soon as they crossed the darkened threshold, cool after the warm sun outside, they were greeted by a tall, heavyset black woman, whom Rebecca guessed to be about fifty or so. It was hard to tell.

"Morgan, *cher*," the woman's voice called out,

"where you been keeping yourself?"

"Busy working, *Tante* Isabeau," he said, hugging the woman close.

"I see you brung one fine-looking woman wit' you this time, eh?" She smiled, revealing one gold tooth. "'Course she needs to get some meat on them bones," she stated after a critical look, "or do you still like 'em skinny, *cher*?"

Rebecca laughed at the exchange, even while her curiosity was piqued by the thought of who else Morgan had brought here. "Excuse me," she interrupted, "but I'm hardly the skin-and-bones type."

"You got some sass, eh girl?" *Tante* Isabeau asked, smiling at Rebecca. She stood back, giving Rebecca another look. "Yes, I see you got something of a figure." She smiled again, as if sharing a valued piece of information. "'Course you know a man likes to have something he can cuddle with, don't you, sugar? No real man wants to share his bed with a bag of bones," she said with a snort. "Why, a man roll over and injure himself bad with that kind. Now me, I gets no complaints." At that remark, she gave a hearty laugh.

Rebecca blushed at *Tante* Isabeau's frank, earthy talk. Why was that? she wondered. She'd heard bluer language, and far more provocative comments made at the studio, or even on the streets, yet somehow, here, with Morgan, she felt as if she were somehow different—as if she were sheltered.

Or was it because *Tante* Isabeau brought up the topic of sharing a bed? Suddenly, a provocative picture of entwined limbs and exhausted bodies floated into Rebecca's brain. The bodies were hers and Morgan's.

"I'll guess you want a table by yourselves," *Tante* Isabeau said with a knowing wink, "eh, *cher*?"

Morgan grinned. "You got that right."

"Then follow me, and I put you somewhere private."

Morgan shifted and placed an arm about Rebecca's shoulders, drawing her closer to his lean body. She liked the sensation of belonging.

Tante Isabeau showed them to a corner of her restaurant. There was a small, circular table, covered in a navy cloth. The lights were low, providing more of an intimate scene. Several circular fans whirred overhead. Morgan held out Rebecca's chair and seated her, taking the chair opposite.

Tante Isabeau stood there, a conspiratorial grin on her face. "So, what you want?"

"Will you let me order for you?" Morgan demanded.

"I'd like that," Rebecca said.

Morgan flashed her a deep smile, which she noted went all the way to his eyes. It was like being pulled in slowly to a deep well, losing oneself happily along the journey.

"To start, some spicy crayfish, I think, along with a couple of beers?" Morgan shot her a look.

At Rebecca's nod, he continued. "Then some of your special jambalaya, and pecan pie for dessert."

"I fix it for you myself," she promised. *Tante* Isabeau left them to see to their order.

"She's a great cook," Morgan said with enthusiasm. "Just wait till you taste her food. You'll swear it's to die for."

"If you say so."

"I do."

"Then," Rebecca answered him, "that's good enough for me." And she knew it was. She trusted him, almost as if they'd known each other for years and were comfortable with the judgment calls each made.

Tante Isabeau returned a few minutes later, bringing with her a big pewter tray containing two very large chilled glasses of beer and two bowls loaded with steaming crayfish. She gave them each a wide napkin. *"Bon appétit,"* she said, making her way back to her kitchen.

"Dig in," Morgan insisted.

Rebecca did, and found herself liking the new experience of eating food with her fingers, relishing the taste. She discovered she had a large appetite, and they shared another small bowl. Eating with gusto, Morgan had said, and he was right. Used to dining in very fancy restaurants for business meals, or grabbing something at her desk, Rebecca found she took pleasure in the simple act of eating.

But it was Morgan who made the difference,

she noted. They never lacked for conversation, ranging from childhood remembrances to work-related information. She could listen to his deep, drawling voice all evening. Nothing was said just to fill up silence. He listened as well, drawing responses from her so honest she wondered if he were a pyschologist on the side.

Morgan adored her openness. Like a child, Rebecca talked straightforwardly, without guile or glibness. He discovered he liked the person she was, more and more. It was exciting to talk shop, as it were, with another writer, to use a writer's version of shorthand when referring to people, places, and things. He had only to mention a quote and she could finish it. She understood his sometimes oblique references.

Was this the start of an affair, destined to run its course while she was here—or something deeper, with the potential for permanence?

"I don't think I should plan on eating anything for the next week or so," Rebecca declared, pushing away the second plate of jambalaya she'd consumed.

"Nonsense. By tomorrow morning you'll feel differently," Morgan assured her.

"I don't know about that."

"I do," he said with confidence. "Before we get dessert, how about a dance to work off some of *Tante* Isabeau's meal?"

"I think to balance out what I ate," she said with a laugh, "I would have to dance *Swan Lake* in its entirety."

"Nothing so strenuous, *chérie*," he said. "Just a couple of turns around the floor should do it."

She gave him a skeptical look.

Morgan stood up, walking a short distance away to an old-fashioned jukebox. Removing several coins from the pocket of his jeans, he popped them into the machine; the neon lights came alive as he made his selections.

He held out his hand to her and Rebecca rose instantly. The music played around them, oldies calculated to bring a couple together on the dance floor. Rebecca leaned against his solid body, swaying to the beat, her head resting upon the wide wall of his chest as they glided across the floor.

Morgan had chosen songs she loved hearing. Sentimental favorites that one listened to over and over. Golden oldies, most from before she was listening to the radio, but songs she'd discovered long after their first airplay. What she'd heard referred to as classic make-out songs. The harmonious strains of the Righteous Brothers filled the corner of the room as they crooned "Unchained Melody," and "You're My Soul and My Inspiration."

Then he'd picked two particular favorites of hers: the first was by Elvis, "Can't Help Falling in Love;" the second, a soul-filled duet that reached into her heart and made it soar, "With You I'm Born Again."

Rebecca was incredibly mellow. All in all, she was having a wonderful time and didn't want it to end. It felt good being in Morgan's arms. As if she belonged. As if she had always belonged there.

She was reluctant to end this day. As if she were holding on to a dream, she clung to him as they danced, afraid to think beyond this moment.

"Shall I have *Tante* Isabeau wrap up our dessert?" he asked. "We can eat it later, back at the plantation."

Was he as sad as she that this day would soon come to a conclusion? Did he want to postpone that as long as possible also?

"Yes, that would be fine," she told him, returning to her chair, watching him stride away from her. She calculated that they would have at least an hour's drive back to Belle Chanson, and then . . .

What?

Where was this all leading?

To its inevitable conclusion, she reckoned. Sooner or later they would make love.

Morgan returned with a large paper bag, and *Tante* Isabeau in tow.

Rebecca rose, a contented smile on her face. "Thank you, *Tante* Isabeau, for the fantastic meal. It's one of the best I've ever eaten."

"I'm glad you liked it, sugar." The restaurateur beamed. "You come back here any ol' time, you hear?"

Rebecca laughed in response. "I hear," she responded, wondering if she would ever be back.

"Good. As for you"—she hugged Morgan, gently admonishing him—"be smart and keep this one, *cher*." She shot a glance at Rebecca. "She's quality.

"And you," she said, referring to Rebecca, "hold on to him, sugar."

Slightly embarrassed, Rebecca's only response was to smile. What could she say?

The moon shone overhead as they left the restaurant, and the night air had overtaken the day's heat.

"There's coffee in the sack too," Morgan said as he slipped on his seat belt. He opened the bag, removing the large plastic containers. "It's New Orleans coffee," he warned her. "Much stronger than what you're used to, I expect."

"I think I can handle it," Rebecca said, taking the cup and sipping tentatively. It was good and strong, laced with thick whipped cream. "Ahhhh," she sighed.

Morgan took a swallow of his. "You adapt well, 'Becca."

Rebecca found she liked the sound of her nickname on his tongue. The intimacy of the gesture stirred something delicious inside her.

"*Tante* Isabeau has sent along slices of her pecan pie and a couple of beignets," he said, "in case you get hungry on the way back."

"Hungry? Is she kidding?" Rebecca relaxed back into the comfortable seat, enjoying the warmth of the coffee. "Perhaps tomorrow with breakfast," she said sleepily, yawning despite the influx of caffeine.

Morgan shot a quick glance in her direction a few minutes later and noticed the fan of her lashes against her skin. He wanted to reach out and stroke the delicate flesh of her cheek with his finger, but he feared waking her. Carefully, he lifted the container of coffee from her hand and brought it to his mouth, putting his lips to where she'd been drinking. Morgan finished the still-hot beverage and set it down, thinking about what he'd just done. He'd never before been one to drink from another's cup or glass; with this he hadn't thought about it, he'd just reacted instinctively.

Rebecca looked so relaxed and carefree, breathing deeply. What would she look like curled up in his bed? In moonlight? In sunlight? On a day soft with rain, or wild with a storm? Through each of the four seasons? A year from now? Ten years from now? Fifty years from now?

He wanted to know.

Morgan pulled into the driveway less than an hour later.

" 'Becca. We're back," he said softly, gently nudging her.

"What?" she asked sleepily, rubbing her cheek against his hand.

"We've come home."

"Home?" Rebecca sat up, blinking. The moon glimmered brightly across the grounds of Belle

Chanson, giving the entire area a magical, mystical look.

Morgan shut off the engine, leaving the car outside on the drive. He got out and by the time he went around to open Rebecca's door, she'd already made her way out of the Rover.

"Do you ride?"

"You mean like horses?"

He laughed softly, sending a shiver of warmth down her spine.

"Like horses," he agreed.

"Years ago I did, when I was small. There's not much call for them in New York nowadays," she pointed out, "unless you're part of the NYPD."

"Think you could handle a mount?"

"If you're not expecting me to race you across the county—oh, excuse me," she said, "parish?"

He took her arm and guided her to the front door, where a light had been left on to welcome her. Morgan took a key from his pocket and fitted it into the lock, turning it and opening up the door.

"No, I'm not expecting you to race me. I thought that a ride would give you another sense of the area."

"If you don't mind a general amateur, then I'd love to give it a go," she said.

"After breakfast?"

"Yes." If Morgan had asked her to ride with him through the bowels of hell, Rebecca thought that she would have accepted just as readily as she did now. She realized that she wasn't in a position to refuse him whatever he wanted of her.

Morgan dipped his head and kissed her lips softly.

Rebecca took a step backward, her hand on the door. "Goodnight, Morgan."

"*Bonsoir, chérie.*"

French. The language of love, she thought. And, of Matthew Devereaux.

Chapter Sixteen

His kiss had been like a breeze, lightly stirring across her mouth, leaving her wanting more.

Rebecca touched her lips with the tip of her index finger. What would it feel like if Morgan were to kiss her, really kiss her?

She pulled on a plain white T-shirt and tucked it into the slim jeans she wore. Fastening the braided brown leather belt, she contemplated how Morgan would kiss. Would he be ruthless or reckless? Powerful or poignant? Or a combination of all of the above?

That was one of the things Rebecca missed most about not being in a relationship. Kisses and cuddling. Ben had been a great kisser; she could never fault him for that. Her problems began when she no longer cared if he went further than that, which hadn't been fair to him.

Rebecca recalled Rachel's words about Matthew's kisses. They'd sent her great-great-grandmother's head spinning. Had Morgan inherited his ancestor's ability? Or had it been merely the powerful chemistry between the two would-be lovers? As great as the sexual attraction was that she felt for Morgan, would his passionate kisses stir something grander and deeper than she'd ever known? Or was she fooling herself?

And who was to say that Morgan wanted her in quite the same way as she wanted him?

Morgan strolled toward the stables, anxious to see to the horses they would be riding this morning. He kept several at the plantation, one for his own personal use, and several more for family, friends, or guests of the house. Jester joined him, eager for an adventure.

As he walked, Morgan thought about his restless night. After he left Rebecca, he'd been unable to sleep, so he'd turned on his laptop and proceeded to work, keeping his mind focused on research for his novel, *A House Divided*. He'd found that impossible for more than a few minutes. Constant thoughts of Rebecca kept creeping in, tempting him away from writing. The touch of her hand, the sound of her laugh, the smile on her face, the light in her eyes. All these things came back to haunt him when he least expected them to.

If she hadn't been so sleepy, he would have kissed her as he wanted to kiss her. He had to know just what her lips would taste like when she gave herself fully aware, not half asleep.

Maybe today.

Morgan hoped so, for he didn't think that he could wait much longer. Like an impatient youth, he was hungry to grab the experience, to savor the moment.

Which surprised him.

From the moment that he'd first laid eyes on her, nothing was the same as it had been before. Meeting Rebecca had changed him, given him a new perspective on love.

This singular woman had the capacity to break his heart.

The stable doors were open, and the young girl who he'd hired last year as a groom was cleaning out an empty stall. "'Morning, Jill," Morgan called out as Jester barked his greeting.

A freckle-faced girl with carrot-colored hair popped up from her chore. "Hi there, Mr. Devereaux."

"Can you throw a saddle onto the Duchess for me while I take care of Shadow?"

"Sure thing, Mr. Devereaux." She hustled out of the stall and went to gather the gear for the pretty bay while Morgan fitted the English riding saddle he used on his gray Andalusian stallion. He loved this horse, and took every opportunity he could to ride. When he was deep into a book, the chances never came as frequently as he liked. Sometimes he wondered if he was a throwback to an earlier time, for as much as he enjoyed driving his car, he still loved the feel of riding a horse more, of being one with the animal.

Today Morgan was determined to make the ride as special as he could. Since Rebecca wasn't a regular rider, he would have to go slower than he might have liked, but that would be fine since it would mean that they would have time to talk while they rode.

Morgan led his horse outside, with his black Lab trailing behind, and was amazed to see that Rebecca had arrived.

"I was going to come and get you," he said, holding on to the stallion's bridle as the animal shook his head.

"What a beautiful creature," Rebecca stated, moving closer. "May I?" she asked, indicating that she wanted to pet the horse.

"Yes," Morgan said, keeping a tight grip on his horse as she did so.

She leaned in and ran her hand lightly across the stallion's muzzle.

Jill led out the bay mare, and the horse whickered softly.

"Is this one for me?" Rebecca asked.

"The Duchess is very gentle," Morgan assured her. He introduced Rebecca to her mount and gave her a hand up into the saddle. He adjusted the stirrups, watching as Rebecca fitted herself into a comfortable position in the saddle. Morgan stopped himself from laying a hand on her thigh, much as he wanted to stroke it, feel the firmness of the jean-clad flesh as it gripped the mare.

Rebecca watched him mount. He swung himself into position with such ease and grace. Morgan was also wearing jeans this morning, which fit his slim hips to perfection, and a black T-shirt, which outlined his broad shoulders. If he had wanted another career, she could easily see him modeling for top designers in male fashion magazines. A camera would love his features, and women would flock to buy the clothes he modeled, hoping that their men would look as well in what they wore as did Morgan Devereaux.

"Ready?"

" 'Lay on, MacDuff,' " she quipped.

"So, did you enjoy your ride?" Della asked as Rebecca walked slowly up to the veranda from the stables.

Rebecca grinned, rubbing her slightly sore posterior. "Let's just say that I don't think that I'll be doing any point-to-point in the near future."

Della grinned as she peeled the apples she'd chosen for the pie she was going to make. "I think that a long soak in a hot tub will ease the pain of your first riding lesson."

"That's a good idea," Rebecca agreed, thinking that a good, hot bath would ease her aching muscles. "I could use a couple of hours to relax. Especially since Morgan has invited me to attend a concert with him this evening in New Orleans."

Della threw her guest an arch look. "He has?"

"Yes."

"Must be that charity thing he bought tickets to last month."

"He did say something about it being a benefit for some organization. I didn't quite catch the name."

"Could be a few things with Morgan. He has his pet charities," Della said with a slight smile, "as do we all. Now, would you like something for lunch?"

"Would it be possible to get some of your great iced tea and perhaps a sandwich?"

Della smiled again. "I think that can be arranged. You just go on upstairs and take that bath and I'll fix you something myself."

"Thanks," Rebecca said as she made her way indoors.

Della continued to peel her apples, wondering about her cousin's sudden keen interest in this tourist.

Well, it's about time that boy settled down and found himself a wife, she thought, sampling one thick wedge of apple, her mouth puckering from the sharp taste. Yes sir, he was sure enough falling for that pretty Yankee, just as much as she was falling for him. Anyone could see that fact plain. She couldn't wait to share the news with Jack and several other interested family members.

And if she wasn't mistaken, and Della reckoned she rarely was, there'd be another entry soon in the old family Bible.

In the back of her mind, Della could already see Belle Chanson transformed into a grand setting for a wedding. And, she thought with a deep grin, if she was lucky, perhaps a few of the actors from Rebecca's soap would be invited. Now that would really be exciting. Imagine if she could get one or more to reveal upcoming plot lines. That would purely be the frosting on the cake.

It was a good thing that she'd packed at least one evening dress, Rebecca thought as she hooked the black stocking to the lacy garter belt. She stood back and gave her reflection in the old-fashioned cheval glass a grin. Damned if she didn't look like an ad for an upscale lingerie catolog. These were more of her parting gifts from several of the actresses on her show. A complete underwear wardrobe updating, including bras and panties in several shades, along with stockings. It all would have been better suited for a trousseau, but Rebecca guessed that she shouldn't really complain.

She giggled as she recalled the card that had come with the items. "Here's to success—big ratings and even bigger men."

Rebecca stepped into her high-heeled black

shoes and slipped the black dress over her head, adjusting the fit. It was knit, with a round neckline and puffed sleeves. Her next move was to place the gold locket around her throat. It lay against the bodice of her dress, and Rebecca clutched the lovely piece of jewelry in her hand for a few moments, wondering if she was doing the right thing. Should she follow her heart's inclination and see where it would lead her? Or did she already know?

Oh Rachel, Rebecca wondered, what would you do? Would you be willing to take a risk now? Throw caution to the wind and take what you want? Or would you hold something back and wait to see what developed?

You wrote that you yearned for Matthew with all your heart and soul. God, I now know how deep that yearning must have been, for I feel it for Morgan. So strong that it frightens me.

What do I do?

Morgan thought the same thing. What exactly did he do?

He knew what he wanted to do—skip this concert and instead make love to Rebecca. Wipe away all traces of any other lover she'd ever known. Imprint himself on her and unleash her deepest, most erotic fantasies. Bring them to a boiling point and start again. Over and over, till they'd explored all the possibilities.

This was a primitive desire, something that

came from the deepest reaches of his psyche. It twisted and turned in his gut, feeding on itself till it grew higher and sharper. He would know no real peace until they shared themselves.

Morgan adjusted his black tie, checking himself in the mirror.

They'd had such a good time today. Rebecca had been a plucky rider, trying to keep up when he occasionally gave Shadow a run. He admired her courage in trying to make up time, and laughed with her when she almost toppled from the saddle when the Duchess refused to take a small jump. Morgan admitted he was showing off when he urged his mount to take a leap over a stone fence, sailing over the obstacle with little effort. He turned and saw Rebecca moving her horse toward a lower point in the fence. He should have told her that the Duchess wasn't much of a jumper, but the expression on her face was priceless as the horse and rider approached the jump and the mare decided that it wasn't for her. Rebecca clung to the horse's neck, avoiding an ignominious tumble to the ground below. She began to laugh, and he'd joined in, having made the jump back to her side, thankful that she hadn't been hurt, and happy that she could see the comedy of the incident.

His life had never seemed empty before, but after a few days in her company, Rebecca's presence added immeasurably to the quality of it. Without her, it would be dull and flat.

Was it too soon to ask her to marry him?

Maybe.

He had to consider what she wanted. What she felt.

Tonight, he was determined to discover that for himself.

Rebecca enjoyed the concert and the party afterward, held at a large, converted warehouse overlooking the river. Lights from ships going to and fro on the mighty Mississippi winked in the darkness; she stood at one set of floor-to-ceiling windows, watching a boat that bobbed up and down, speculating on what was happening below deck.

A friendly, ponytailed young waiter appeared beside her and offered to refill her glass. The white wine was chilled to perfection, and Rebecca accepted it, holding out her glass and thanking him politely.

She turned her head and caught a glimpse of Morgan, who'd been commandeered by their hostess soon after arriving. He nodded his head in her direction and Rebecca smiled in return. He looked so handsome in that white dinner jacket; the words suave and debonair were coined with him in mind, she thought.

Rebecca knew she wasn't alone in that belief, for she'd seen other women at this party, and at the concert, openly admiring him.

All throughout the concert they'd held hands, their fingers intertwined. Even when they parted to clap in appreciation of the performers' talents, they instantly resumed their former position as soon as possible, as if their skin had bonded.

Bonded.

Rebecca considered this word and all its implications. She had bonded mentally and emotionally with Morgan already. All that was left was to bond sexually. And that was for her the most challenging and daunting prospect.

Because, Rebecca admitted, she was in love with him. There was no doubt about it.

It was happening all over again.

"Sorry about that," Morgan whispered against her ear. "I couldn't get away any sooner."

Rebecca leaned back, the support of Morgan's tall frame a welcome buffer from the rest of the party. He slipped an arm about her waist, drawing her even closer. It felt so right to be here with him, as if it were meant to be.

"Would you like to leave?"

"Yes."

"What would you think about coming to my town house for a nightcap?" he suggested. "It's not far from here, and right now, I'd rather not share you with a roomful of patrons at a bar."

"I think that's an excellent idea," Rebecca responded, her voice husky. She was nervous, but it was what she wanted, to be alone with him.

"Then let's get the hell out of here." Morgan took her glass and placed it on a nearby table, hustling her quickly to the old freight elevator that had been repainted a whimsical robin's-egg blue.

In a matter of minutes they found themselves outside in the slightly muggy air. Morgan escorted Rebecca to his car and they were soon negotiating their way through the Vieux Carré.

Morgan pulled up in front of a house surrounded by iron grillework and a tall, iron-post gate. Rebecca could smell the scent of lilacs and honeysuckle as she walked with him through the wide gate and to the door. In the distance she heard a night bird calling plaintively to its mate.

Morgan punched in the security code and then slipped his key into the lock, opening the door. He flipped a switch, flooding the entrance hall with light from an overhead chandelier.

"Welcome to my home."

Morgan escorted her to the living room, which opened onto the back garden. While he opened the French doors, Rebecca gave the room a thorough glance. It was quiet and elegant, traditionally furnished, with a sense of style. Her eyes widened in surprise when she saw one large item in the corner, looking distinctly different from the rest.

"I don't believe it," she murmured, casting a look in Morgan's direction.

He stood there, a charming grin on his mouth. He had removed his white jacket, which lay on the back of the sofa. "I bought it on a whim," he explained. "When I saw it I couldn't resist, and I've never regretted it." He walked closer to her, pulling loose his black tie, then undoing several of the top buttons on his white dress shirt.

"It's a hoot," Rebecca declared with an engaging smile. "Does it work?"

"See for yourself," he said, pointing to the pewter cup that rested on top, filled with quarters.

Rebecca couldn't resist, feeding the money into the machine and watching as it came alive, colors swirling in their neon glory as she made several selections. Soon, music from the antique jukebox filled the room.

Morgan went to a cabinet and pulled out two snifters that looked distinctly like Waterford to Rebecca's eyes. "Brandy?"

She recognized the label as being one of the best and nodded her head in agreement. He was a man who obviously liked quality.

Morgan handed her the snifter. She took a drink, appreciating the taste, then set the snifter down on the coffee table. Rebecca held out her arms and invited him softly, "Dance with me."

Morgan swallowed a generous amount of his brandy, the warmth of the spirit adding fuel to the fire of his longing. He complied, enfolding Rebecca within his arms.

They began to move around the polished oak floor, swaying seductively to the beat of the music, her head on his chest, one arm curled about his neck, the other held close, trapped between their bodies.

Rebecca inhaled the scent of his warm body, the mixed smell of man and cologne, invigorating and powerful, like the man himself. She was being drawn deeper and deeper into the tunnel of love, her body clamoring to take the ride of a lifetime.

Unbidden, her fingers explored the soft texture of his dark hair, thick and curling at the nape of his neck. Slowly she brought her hand down and around, trailing her fingers about his neck, skimming lightly over the material of his shirt until she found the opening. Her curious fingers slid between the opening of his shirt to the skin below. There, the hair on his chest was abundantly crisp.

Morgan inhaled deeply, loving the feel of her hand on his skin. He waited to see what she would do next, and was rewarded when Rebecca undid several more of the buttons, pushing aside his shirt and exposing his chest.

He released her other hand and linked both of his arms about her waist, pulling her closer to the contours of his body, making her aware of the rising tide of need that tightened his flesh.

They remained that way for several more minutes, their movements slowing as they swayed in harmony.

"Stay here with me tonight," Morgan asked, his voice betraying the hunger inside him.

Rebecca answered unhesitatingly, "Yes."

Chapter Seventeen

The moment had come.

Morgan realized the importance of the question he'd asked Rebecca, and the significance of her response. It was fantasy and reality intertwined, his wildest hopes and his daring dreams.

He kissed her. This time he didn't hold back; Morgan delved deep, stirring emotions as his mouth stoked the fires in her body to a white-hot flame. His tongue teased and tutored, searching for a response.

Rebecca gave it unstintingly. Her head swam as each kiss grew more intense, more passionate. She felt the reckless energy rise within herself as she matched Morgan kiss for kiss. It was as if they were both starved for this type of communication.

Finally, gasping for breath, Rebecca let her head fall back. Morgan took the opportunity to taste her neck, kissing the column of her throat with abandon while Rebecca's hands slid up the solid wall of his chest, pushing aside his shirt. Tugging it free of the waistband of his trousers, she shoved it down his arms. It bunched and draped around his waist, catching at his wrists, locked there by the gold cuff links he wore.

Rebecca unfastened one, flinging the stud to the floor. She pulled his arm free, bringing his wrist to her lips, kissing the strong bones there before releasing it. Next she moved to the other arm, doing likewise to it.

Rebecca stared at the wide expanse of his bare chest before her. Her tongue flicked out to wet her lips.

Morgan captured her hand and brought it to his chest so that she could feel the thumping beat of his heart.

Rebecca spread her fingers wide, her palm flat against his skin, the heat from his body warming her hand. She stretched her hand out and rubbed his male nipple with the tip of her little finger, gently scoring it with her nail.

Morgan grew hotter and tighter with each of Rebecca's ministrations to his body. As no woman before, she excited him beyond all reckoning.

Her hands glided to the bones of his shoulders, kneading his muscles with a gentle touch. Her lips and tongue followed, deriving pleasure from the small shudders she could feel beneath his skin. It gave her an enormous sense of gratification that she could give Morgan some measure of the delight he'd given her. Both of her hands threaded through his hair, bringing his lips back again to hers.

Morgan pulled the fancy clasp that held her hair in place, letting it tumble about her shoulders. He tossed the ornament aside, fisting his hands into her scalp, forcing her lips closer to his, thirsty once again for the nectar they contained.

When they finally broke free, Rebecca moaned deep in her throat.

Morgan didn't want to take her here on the floor. At least not yet. Maybe later. He had to proceed slowly, gathering some control. Now was the time for comfort and caring, for showing her all that he thought lovemaking could be.

"Upstairs," he whispered rawly, taking her hand in his and locking their fingers together.

He touched one hand to the wall and the stairs were illuminated. A stained-glass window overlooked the landing above: it depicted the richness and color of a garden—Eden, perhaps—lush with sensual detail.

Morgan led her up the stairs, past the window, to one of the larger bedrooms. He opened the door, showing her inside. A tall, Art Deco lamp illuminated the room with a soft glow. It was very masculine, with an immense bed dominating the space inside.

Rebecca caught her breath at the painting of a horse that hung on the opposite wall. It was Rachel's gift to Matthew over 130 Christmases ago.

A sign? she wondered.

She took it as such, believing that in some small way, she and Morgan were the chance that Rachel and Matthew hadn't had.

"Take off your dress," Morgan requested in a raw, commanding tone laced with the soft-as-honey accents of his native state.

Rebecca took a deep breath and did what he asked, though instead of pulling the dress over her head quickly, she took her time, raising the material over her skin an inch or so at a time.

Morgan took a seat in the large, overstuffed wine velvet chair, watching Rebecca's slow, teasing response. She revealed a glimpse of thigh, then continued pulling the dress upward, revealing the black garter belt that held up her stockings. Inches more and he could see the French-cut panties of black silk.

His breath coming faster, Morgan regarded the look on Rebecca's face—she was enjoying this. Her lips curved in a secret smile.

Rebecca drew the dress upward the rest of the way, tossing it in his direction.

Morgan caught the garment, a delicious grin on his face as he brought the material to his nostrils and inhaled her scent before draping it over the arm of his chair.

Rebecca stood there, clad only in her underwear and high heels, waiting for the next move in their private, high-stakes game.

"Come here, 'Becca."

Moistening her lips, she tilted her chin up. Feeling strangely powerful and oddly free, she sauntered the short distance to his chair, standing in front of him. Rebecca could sense the reaction she was having on Morgan. It was there in the hungry depths of his eyes, evident in the rising and falling of his chest, and, she saw dropping her gaze downward, in the hard ridge of constrained flesh that his trousers couldn't hide.

Morgan tapped an empty spot next to him on the wide seat. "Put your leg there," he instructed in a voice barely above a ragged whisper.

Rebecca did so, and Morgan ran his hand along her well-toned calf, his fingers caressing her stocking-covered flesh. As he did so, he could feel his body tightening even more with a desperate ache.

Slowly, Morgan lifted her foot and slid off her shoe. It landed with a dull thump on the carpet. His wide palm held her foot while his other hand stroked up her leg, massaging as it went. He reached the top of her knee and slid higher, finding the strap that held the stocking to the small scrap of lace. With a flick, he loosened first one side and then the other. Carefully, Morgan rolled the black stocking down her leg, taking his time.

His reward was the rhythmic rise and fall of her breasts that threatened to fall out of their lace-and-silk prison as she tilted her head backward, her breath coming quicker. She was obviously as excited as he. Tremors shot through her body.

Morgan dropped the stocking on the floor. He followed the same procedure on her other leg, his lips following the path his hands had blazed.

He started to stand up and Rebecca stopped him, gently pushing him back down again to the depths of the chair.

"Let me," she said as she bent down, kneeling on the carpet before him. She removed his black slip-on shoe, sliding it off the long, narrow foot with ease. Rebecca then reached beneath the leg of his trousers, her fingers finding the top of the dress sock, peeling it downward until she had it removed completely. She couldn't resist a smile when she looked at his well-groomed foot.

His other leg was treated to the same attention even as her hands shook with the overwhelmingly sensual experience of playing the role of handmaiden.

Morgan got up and brought Rebecca with him. He kissed her again, sipping at her mouth, drawing all the sweetness she had into him. Tongues mated in a duel of desire while Morgan slipped his hands around her back, unhooking the fastening of her bra. He tugged it down her arms, freeing her breasts. His hands replaced the cups of silk as he lifted and caressed the soft flesh, teasing the nipples into hard peaks.

He bent his head and tasted first one, then the other.

Rebecca gasped with the pleasure she felt. She clasped his dark head to her bosom, content to let him suck. Each pull of his mouth triggered a sensation like a streak of lightning in her belly.

This was all so new to her. Though she'd been married and had slept with Ben, nothing had ever affected her like Morgan's erotic gestures. He took her to another place, where the only thing that mattered was what she felt. And right now she felt as if she were about to shatter into a thousand pieces.

It was then that Morgan lifted the locket from around her throat and Rebecca whimpered. "Be careful," she said, her hand upon his. "It's very valuable to me," she added, fearing that Morgan might, in his haste, somehow damage her prized keepsake.

"Trust me," he said, and she did. He slipped the locket into the pocket of his trousers for the moment.

Morgan continued his exploration of her body with one hand as the other snaked about her waist again, holding her tightly to him as he dipped his head and took her mouth. He found the waistband of her panties, pressing downward with his hand, his palm cupping the silk-covered mound. Satisfied, he slipped his index finger beneath the lacy band of the high-cut briefs.

He probed gently, feeling the quivering of her flesh as he did so. Lower, and lower still, until he discovered the nest of curls that was hidden beneath the scrap of material.

With care, Morgan stripped away Rebecca's panties, pushing them down her legs until she willingly stepped out of them. His hand returned to the spot, probing the blonde curls, delighted to discover the moist, warm heat waiting for him.

Rebecca moaned deeply.

At that, Morgan swung her up into his arms and carried her the short distance to the Renaissance bed, the carved headboard dominating the space. He laid her down on the spruce-green sheets and stepped back, quickly stripping off the remainder of his clothes.

Rebecca lay there, watching him through heavy-lidded eyes, fascinated by the play of lean muscles as he moved efficiently. She gasped in delight and wonder when she saw the visible proof that Morgan wanted her—his sex rose high and hard, ready and eager for the task. She quivered with anxious anticipation of Morgan's joining his splendid body to hers.

She welcomed him to the bed, holding out her arms in invitation.

Morgan slid onto the bed, drawing her close

to his lean body. They began to kiss again, the intense heat and passion flaring anew.

Heated moments later, as Morgan moved to enter her body, he heard her gasp.

"What's wrong?" he asked, afraid that somehow he'd inadvertently hurt her.

"It's just that it's been so very long for me," Rebeccca answered, her breath coming quicker. Damn, but this was embarrassing, she thought as they lay skin to skin, about to cross the threshold.

"How long?"

"Almost four years," she replied. Rebecca could see the widening of his eyes as he listened. She took a deep, calming breath and explained, "Since before my divorce."

He was astonished. "There's been no one since your husband?"

Rebecca quietly corrected him, the color rising in her cheeks. "There's been no one *but* my husband," she said, her voice husky.

"Oh my God!" Morgan exclaimed softly. "You mean to tell me that I'm only the second man you've been intimate with?"

Rebecca nodded, blushing again. She lifted her hand and touched his cheek lightly. "Does that bother you?"

"Bother me?" he repeated, humbled by the truth. A smile on his lips, Morgan kissed her tenderly. "I'm flattered, darling. The fact that you haven't slept with the entire male population of New York excites me, if you want to

329

know the truth," he admitted chauvinistically.

"Does it really? Excite you, I mean?" Rebecca asked.

Morgan grinned. "Can't you feel it?"

"Show me," she prompted.

And he did. With power and grace, Morgan took her to another level of existence, to a world where senses exploded and light fractured, where time stood still, then spun out of control. Rebecca was in uncharted territory and Morgan was her guide, showing her the wonderful realm of the imagination, the realm of love, with all its infinite possibilities.

As she lay there, suffering sweet exhaustion, her heart hammering against the wall of her chest, her eyes closed in dreamy contemplation of the event that had just taken place, Rebecca acknowledged that she had finally found what was missing from her life. All that she needed to make her life totally complete was waiting for her in this man's arms, in this man's bed.

She'd never known the wonder of rapture until Morgan had shown her. When he eventually spilled his seed, she cried out her happiness to the world, little caring if she shouted or screamed, so intensely happy and alive did she feel.

Morgan rested in her arms and Rebecca closed them about him, wanting to keep him as close to her as she could, for as long as she could.

Contented, she drifted off to sleep.

* * *

He wanted to surprise her.

Carefully, he'd made his way from the bed so as not to wake her and dressed as quickly as possible, eager to carry out his plan. At the doorway, Morgan turned and gazed at the sleeping woman.

Rebecca was incredible. Last night had been a revelation to Morgan, increasing his awareness of himself as a man, and as a man in love. He'd been moved by the sheer force of her innocence, blown away by the way she embraced life and lovemaking. He felt as if he'd scaled Mt. Olympus last night and been invited to feast with the gods.

Hers was the face that would launch a thousand words—and none of them capable of doing her justice. He would try to write down his thoughts and feelings sometime later, but he wondered if he could ever truly chronicle just how it was that she had changed his life.

A faint smile played over Morgan's lips as he recalled one of the songs that they'd danced to. Yes, with her he was born again. Better. Stronger. Wiser.

An ordinary diamond wouldn't do for her. When he picked out a ring, it would have to be as special as the lady herself. Unique and one-of-a-kind.

But he couldn't think about that now, he chided himself. That could wait. What couldn't wait was the treat he had in store for her, so he hurried from the room.

Rebecca awoke with a slow smile spreading on her face.

She felt wonderful, as if she'd shed one skin and discovered another. One that was fresher and cleaner. One that was attuned to all of life's mysteries.

All because of Morgan Devereaux.

Rebecca moved on the bed, the soft feel of the luxurious cotton sheets soothing her weary muscles. She felt pampered, privileged, and precious.

Opening her eyes, she expected to find Morgan there beside her.

His side of the bed was empty, with only an indentation on the dark pillowcase to indicate that he'd slept there; though, she amended, they had done very little real sleeping last night. After that first glorious lovemaking, they had dozed for a short time and then awakened refreshed and ready to try again. In Morgan's arms she found another part of herself, a woman who enjoyed the completely sensual side of her nature. She reveled in the passion she'd felt and explored with him.

Rebecca had given him her trust and been rewarded with the keys to the kingdom.

With that thought, sorrow gently assailed her. She and Ben had missed out on so much. The real tragedy would have been to have stayed married to him, thereby preventing both of them from reaching their full potential with other partners. God, she hoped that Ben was sharing something this exciting, this fabulous with Ally. He deserved it.

Morgan was, she reckoned, even without actual comparison, the most accomplished lover. He made her feel as if nothing was beyond her reach. As if mountains could be climbed and buildings leapt in a single bound.

Her spirit had soared.

So where was this superman?

Rebecca sat up, plumping the queen-size pillows behind her head and drawing the sheet up over her bare breasts. Doing so made her think of Morgan's hands fondling and caressing her flesh, of his mouth tasting and suckling.

And he hadn't stopped there. Throughout the night, Morgan had traversed her entire body, becoming familiar with all its secrets.

The huge bed felt so empty without him.

Rebecca felt so damned empty without him.

In such a short time, Morgan had infiltrated her life and taken root. She found it hard to imagine sleeping alone any longer.

Suddenly, that thought scared her. Being so self-reliant, she'd grown accustomed to thinking and acting for herself. Now, having fallen in love, there was someone else to consider.

Scarier still, suppose he didn't love her?

And what of the past? Rebecca still hadn't told him about the connection they shared.

Would what had happened between Rachel and Matthew affect them? How could it? Why would it?

She just didn't know, and that frightened her.

Right now, all she wanted to do was curl up in Morgan's strong arms, feel his heart beating as wildly as hers, kiss that adorable mouth, and surrender once more to the unbridled delights of his lovemaking.

Was that too much to ask?

Rebecca glanced at the square brass clock that sat on the night table. It was early yet.

Where could he have gone?

Rebecca heard the sound of a door closing downstairs. Was he going out or coming in?

She got out of bed and went to the bathroom that was part of the master suite, washing her face and brushing her teeth, making use of the wine silk robe that hung behind the door. Rebecca wrapped the belt about her waist and pulled it tight, smiling at the fact that it reached her toes.

She had her answer sooner than she expected when the door opened and in walked Morgan, an assortment of paper bags upon a tin tray. He was casually dressed in running shorts and a black T-shirt that sported the logo of a Broadway hit musical.

"Miss me?"

"You have to ask?" She made a move toward him as soon as he neared the bed, leaning over to encircle his neck with her arm, kissing him full on the mouth. "Now, does that answer your question, sir?"

Morgan playfully shrugged his broad shoulders as Rebecca climbed back into bed. "Barely," he replied, "but perhaps that's because you haven't had breakfast yet."

"So you're here to tempt me with food?"

"Quite right," he responded, sitting down on the bed and opening the bags, placing the contents on the painted roses that covered the tray. Hot cafe au lait, warm croissants, fresh fruit.

Rebecca drank from the large container of coffee, loving the flavor. She bit into the croissant, savoring the taste. "Oh, this is heaven," she sighed.

"Now, isn't that funny," he said, his drawling voice dripping honey. "My idea of heaven was last night."

Rebecca colored under Morgan's intense regard. "Yes," she agreed, "that was pretty good."

"Pretty good? How about spectacular?"

It was Rebecca's turn to shrug her slim shoulders. "Above average, I'll grant you that," she said, taking another bite out of her croissant, her eyes glinting with a hint of mischief, "but with some practice, you could be top-notch."

"I'm a firm believer in perfecting one's craft," Morgan said with a straight face, "so after our repast, I think that I should get back to the subject at hand. What do you think?"

"That's a splendid idea," she said. "Practice does make perfect, or so I've heard."

335

"You're going to find out soon enough," Morgan added with a sly grin.

"Then," she said, "I'd better make sure I'm fortified for the ordeal."

"Ordeal?" His black brows raised high at that remark.

"Experience?" she countered.

"Ah," Morgan sighed, "that's more like it. I should warn you that we Devereauxs love a challenge. We never give up without a fight."

"Really?" Rebecca could recall an instance where a Devereaux had given up, much to her ancestor's chagrin.

"Is something wrong?"

Rebecca blinked. "What?"

Morgan touched her hand. "You looked so far away just then."

I was, she thought. About a 130-odd years away. But Rebecca couldn't tell him that. Not now.

"Sorry. It was nothing." She smiled. "You were saying?"

"That I want you." Morgan's voice deepened. "Now." He stood up and placed the tray on the floor. Next, he stripped off his T-shirt and shorts, giving Rebecca proof that he did indeed want her then and there.

Rebecca, sitting cross-legged on the bed, undid the sash and let the silk flow down her arms and onto the tumbled sheet.

"I want you too," she said just as honestly as he had.

336

Morgan joined her and swept her into his arms, his mouth melting over Rebecca's in a soul-shattering kiss.

It was the crash of a cymbal, the bang of a drum, the wail of a woodwind, and the hum of a violin. For Rebecca and Morgan, the symphony had begun again.

Chapter Eighteen

"Oh my God!" Rebecca exclaimed.

"I agree," Morgan murmured, his arms tight about Rebecca as they lay in his bed, sated from another round of lovemaking.

She flashed him a withering look. "No, silly, I didn't mean it that way."

"You mean you weren't commenting on how we are together?" he teased.

"Not this time," she said, a frown wrinkling her brow.

"Then what?"

"Della."

"What has my cousin got to do with anything?"

Rebecca flushed. "I never came back last night," she pointed out.

"And you're afraid that Della will think something's happened to you, or worse, that you spent the night with me?"

"Well, yes," she said.

"You don't have to worry, sweetheart."

"I don't?"

Morgan kissed her swiftly. "No. Before I went out to get our breakfast, I called Della and told her not to worry, that you were safe with me."

Rebecca groaned, "Oh, no," and pulled the sheet tighter about her body. "What will she think?"

Morgan shrugged. "That you wanted to be with me."

"But . . ."

"But what?" he asked.

"We've only known each other a few days."

"So?"

"She's liable to think it's too soon for us."

"Then that would be her problem," he answered, unconcerned.

A sharp flash of an idea hit Morgan's brain. Did Rebecca regret the time they'd spent together?

"Or is that your problem?" he asked, concern threading through his voice. Morgan shifted in the bed, sitting up. "You don't feel that way, do you, 'Becca?"

"No," she reassured him, "I feel as though I've known you longer and better than I knew my ex-husband."

"Good," he answered. "Because I feel that I've

known you for years instead of mere days."
Morgan wanted to ask Rebecca about her ex-
husband, but now wasn't the time for past history. That could come later. He didn't detect
any bitterness in her voice, nor had she indicated any lingering problems, so that matter
could wait. After all, he figured they had a lifetime to get to know all there was to know about
each other.

"Don't worry about Della," he insisted. "She
isn't a judgmental person at all."

"That's good."

"So now that we've settled that, how would
you like to spend today?"

"Well, if I'd known we were going to stay in
the city, I would have brought a change of
clothes and you could have shown me your New
Orleans."

"That's easily fixed," Morgan assured her.

"How?"

"Darling, New Orleans has shops," he pointed
out. "I think that I can find you something. Just
write down your sizes and give me an hour or
so, and then we can explore the city."

Rebecca grabbed his robe and donned it
quickly, getting up. "My purse is downstairs,"
she said, going around the bed, only to be halted
by Morgan's hand grabbing her arm.

"Don't worry about the money right now. Let
me take care of that."

"I like to pay my own way, Morgan."

"Fine," he said. "I've no problem with that."

341

Gail Link

He understood and respected her independence. "I'll give you the bill and you can write me out a check later, okay?"

"Okay," she agreed.

They had a terrific time exploring the city.

Rebecca bought a cheap notebook and pen in a drugstore so that she could make notes for her storyline. While doing that, she explained to Morgan that she was planning on using his city as a backdrop for her new soap. She jotted down possible on-site locations for filming while they visited all the usual tourist spots and then some out-of-the-way places Morgan insisted on showing her.

Some of her favorite places were the antique and bric-a-brac shops along Magazine Street. Rebecca wandered into several, checking prices and getting ideas for the show. She collected business cards, and promised that someone from her show would be contacting them in the near future about purchasing several of the things she'd seen.

For Morgan, it was a chance to see New Orleans through Rebecca's eyes, and his beloved Crescent City sparkled and enthralled her, which filled him with pride.

On a tour of the houses in the Garden District, he noted that Rebecca paid close attention to one house in particular.

"Is there something about this house that you

find interesting?" he asked as they paused before a lovely home.

She paused on the sidewalk. It was the house that Rachel had lived in all those years ago. Rebecca recognized the address, and although she could tell that the house had been renovated, it was still, to her mind, Rachel's house. Morgan's question was the opening that she needed to tell him about the past.

But she couldn't stop in the middle of the banquette and explain the whole story to him. Not here. Not now.

She prevaricated instead. "Would you believe me if I said that there's a welcoming aura about this place?"

Morgan gave her a skeptical look.

"What can I say?" she asked, shrugging her shoulders.

"Would you like to see inside?"

Rebecca shot him a startled look. "Are you serious?" To get inside and see where her ancestor had lived? That would be more than she could hope for.

"Actually, I know the owners," Morgan stated matter-of-factly. "Tom and I went to college together," he explained. "We see each other occasionally, and I don't think Margery—that's his wife—would mind showing you about the place if she's home." Morgan squeezed the hand he held. "Want to try?"

"Yes, but . . ." She hesitated.

"What's wrong?"

"I'm not exactly dressed for a social call." She waved her hand, indicating the shorts that Morgan had purchased. They showed a lot of leg.

"You look fabulous," he insisted, "and Margery's not a snob. More than likely if she's home she'll be dressed the same way."

"Okay then."

They strolled through the gate and up the walkway, Morgan knocking on the door with its stained-glass insert.

A minute later a tall, T-shirt-and-shorts-clad redhead opened the door, a toddler on her hip. "Morgan," she said with a decidedly English accent.

"Hello, Margery. Forgive me for stopping by without notice," he said, "but I've got a friend who would like to see your house. We were just passing by . . . if you wouldn't mind?"

"Please," she said with a beckoning smile, "come right on in." She stepped back, allowing them entrance. "It'll be a relief to have some adults to talk to today."

Margery showed them into the parlor, where the sunlight streamed into the room through the bay windows. Trees in wooden tubs abounded, along with carnival masks in porcelain that adorned the white painted walls. The richly grained wood floor gleamed from obvious care.

Margery sat down on the rocker next to the fireplace, putting her baby on the floor with a pile of his wooden toys, while Morgan and Rebecca took a seat on the couch.

Morgan made the introductions, then commented, "Matthew's getting bigger each time I see him."

"Matthew?" Rebecca asked, her brows raising in curiosity.

"Matthew Thomas Shaunessey," said his proud mother, her eyes on the baby boy. "My daughter Katie's upstairs having her nap."

"We won't stay long," Morgan promised.

"No matter," Margery said with a smile. She rose from the rocker. "If you'll keep an eye on Matt," Margery requested, "then I could show Miss Fraser the rest of the house."

Rebecca insisted that Margery call her by her first name.

Margery gave the other woman a friendly smile. "Then come with me, Rebecca."

Later, walking back to Morgan's house, Rebecca was thoughtful, recalling her fascination with the old house. She'd spent almost an hour poking about the place with Margery as her guide. So much had changed there, but still Rebecca felt that if she closed her eyes, she could see the way it once was, as Rachel had described it in all its glory.

She'd enjoyed meeting Margery, but spending the time with Morgan had meant so much more to her. Holding hands like starry-eyed kids, finishing each other's sentences, sharing thoughts, created an even deeper bond between them.

And that brought out the fear that lurked in the back of her mind. How long could this relationship last? Would something come along to destroy what they had? Or was she reading too much into this affair?

"I want you to have dinner with me tonight," Morgan remarked as they walked back into his town house. "Just the two of us."

Rebecca gave him her answer. "I'd love that."

"It'll be something simple," he said with a smile. "Nothing like what *Tante* Isabeau made for us."

She shot him a startled look. "You're going to cook?"

"Yes," he responded. "Is that so surprising?"

Rebecca laughed.

He arched a black brow. "I take it that you don't?"

"That's what restaurants and microwaves are for," she commented.

"Well," Morgan admitted with a shrug, "my culinary skills run along the lines of the very elemental, but I can survive on that."

Rebecca gave him a long, assessing look. "Handsome. Talented. Charming. And you can cook." She raised her hand and brushed a stray lock of hair off his forehead. "My God, Morgan. Why hasn't some lucky woman snapped you up before this?"

"Because no one I'd met before was the woman I was waiting for," he said in a serious tone. "Until now." Morgan captured her hand

and brought it to his lips. "Until you."

Rebecca shivered from the intensity of the look he gave her.

Morgan's hands were busy unbuttoning the white camisole top he'd purchased earlier for her. In seconds, he had it undone and off her body, pitching it in the direction of the hall tree, where it miraculously hooked. He looked down, his eyes devouring her breasts in the plain white bra he'd chosen. He reached out and unhooked the front closure, disposing of that article of clothing just as rapidly.

Rebecca pushed up his T-shirt, her hands eager to caress his wide chest with its dark forest of hair. She wanted to feel the weight of it against her breasts, wanted to taste it on her tongue.

"I can't wait," he said in an anguished tone, his voice raspy with need.

"I know," she said, echoing his sentiments.

Morgan put his hands on her bottom, lifting her up. Rebecca curled her legs around his waist. His mouth made contact with hers, taking her past the limits of sanity.

Within less than a minute, they were on the floor of the living room, divesting themselves of their remaining clothes. This time it was Rebecca who called the shots as she rode to fulfillment atop Morgan's lean, driving body.

"Come over around eight," he told her, kissing her soundly.

347

Rebecca got out of the car, carrying her evening clothes and shoes in the plastic department store bag. She stood there and watched silently as Morgan drove his car toward his converted carriage house. She heard the excited bark of the black Lab as Jester greeted his master with affection.

These last several days had been magical, filled with love and laughter, passion and promise. In fact, they'd been so good Rebecca was afraid it was all happening too fast. Was she caught in a whirlwind that would toss her about and then drop her back to earth, broken? Or was this the real thing? A love to last a lifetime and beyond? Had she taken on too many of Rachel's memories to think straight? Was her heart clouded by the influence of what had happened before?

All these thoughts crowded into Rebecca's brain, each vying for prominence.

Belle Chanson had been a welcome haven when she needed it, she thought as she walked through the screen door, hoping that she wouldn't run into anyone just yet.

That hope was dashed when Della came into the hallway from another room, carrying a garden basket filled with fresh-cut blooms.

"Hello," Rebecca said.

Della gave her a knowing, understanding smile. "Good to see you," she responded. "I trust that you enjoyed your minisojourn in New Orleans?"

"Very much so, yes," Rebecca replied, moving toward the stairs.

"Will you be joining us for dinner this evening?"

"No, actually I won't," Rebecca said, pausing at the bottom step. "Morgan's invited me to supper at the Carriage House."

"I see," Della said with a twinkle in her eyes. She lifted one of the roses, a lovely ruby-red one, its petals like velvet, and handed it to Rebecca. "Perhaps I should deliver some of these to Morgan, for his table."

"It's exquisite," Rebecca pronounced, inhaling the delicate fragrance of the rose. "I've always been partial to roses."

"So have I," Della insisted. "Jack's the gardener in this family and he has so many beautiful varieties. You should have him show you his gardens while you're here." Della glanced at her watch. "Goodness, look at the time. I've got a million things to do." She hurried off toward the dining room while Rebecca climbed the stairs.

Entering the bedroom, Rebecca looked around. How familiar it all seemed. She dropped the bag onto the bed, slipping out of the white sneakers she wore, and padded to the bathroom, turning on the taps to fill up the tub. She needed a relaxing bath before she joined Morgan.

And that wasn't all she needed, Rebecca realized with a touch of sadness. She also needed a chance to think. Away from Morgan. Away from this place with its overwhelming influence.

She would have to cut short her trip.

She was paid up for another week's stay here, which would be forfeited when she left. Well, that couldn't be helped.

Rebecca glanced at her suitcase. She would pack when she finished her bath and leave as early as she could the next morning.

Her decision made, she undressed and headed for the bathroom.

Morgan put the long-stemmed red roses that Della had brought over into a vase. He placed it on the table, which he'd already set. The salad was tossed, waiting to be served. Della had also left a loaf of fresh-baked wheat bread and a crock of herbed butter. Chicken simmered in a primavera sauce, while the penne pasta waited to be cooked.

All he needed to make the evening complete was Rebecca. Now, and for the next 60 or 70 years.

But did she feel the same?

Jester poked his head into Morgan's hand, demanding some attention.

He fed the dog and walked into his office, checking the assorted messages left on his phone. The cover of the paperback edition of his last book had arrived today. He couldn't wait to share it with Rebecca.

There were so many things he wanted to share with her. Every aspect of his life. Just as he wanted to share hers. For the next several weeks he was determined to tape her soap because she'd told him the last of her work would be on during the next three weeks. He supposed that he'd have to get used to living in Manhattan for part of the year.

Jumping the gun, aren't you, Devereaux? he asked himself. You haven't even mentioned living together yet. Maybe she likes living by herself. Maybe she isn't as eager as you to have a roomie. She may just like her life the way it is, without complications, without entanglements.

They would have to talk about that. Now that he'd found her, he couldn't imagine living without her. Somehow they would work it out to their mutual satisfaction, he was sure of that. They had to.

Morgan, momentarily lost in thought, heard the knock on his back door along with Jester's excited bark. "Morgan?" the feminine voice called out.

He looked so damnably handsome, she thought, as he stood there with a welcoming smile on his face. The faded denim shirt went well with the dark blue jeans that hugged the long length of his legs.

Morgan dropped his gaze down the length of her body, remembering the outfit she wore from the first day he'd met her. Only now he knew what Rebecca looked like without it. He'd touched and tasted every square inch of her flesh.

"Come on in."

" 'Said the spider to the fly.' " she quoted.

"Hardly," Morgan said with a laugh, ushering her in. When she crossed the threshold, he took her in his arms and kissed her. It was a kiss of love and longing, of hope and hereafter.

Rebecca returned it, losing track of time and place. When they eventually separated, she felt like a fraud, for she was aware that tonight was their last time together, at least until she sorted out her feelings.

Jester padded over to her, and Rebecca gave the dog a friendly pat, bending down to ruffle his ears.

"I think you've made a conquest," Morgan said, glad that Rebecca responded well to his pet.

She stood up and the animal then went back to his dinner. Rebecca ignored the remark about the conquest. She had wanted to respond to Morgan, asking if it was only the dog she'd conquered. Instead, she chose not to say anything.

"Mmmm, something smells good," she said, her arm about his waist.

"I told you that I could manage a few simple meals." Morgan showed her into his kitchen, handing her a large glass of minty iced tea.

Rebecca sniffed appreciatively of the aroma that permeated the kitchen. "It's more than I can do," she said as she watched Morgan stir the chicken and sauce. He dipped a wooden spoon into the mixture, bringing it over to Rebecca for a sampling.

"Tastes as great as it smells," she confirmed.

"It'll be ready in a few minutes," he added, checking the boiling water. Dropping the pasta in, he set the timer and escorted Rebecca on a minitour of his house.

"This is where I live most of the time," he explained to her. "I find that it's much more conducive to my work." He showed her a smaller room that had a desk and computer, along with a phone. "That's for my secretary."

"You've got a secretary?"

"Just part-time. She helps with the calls, organizing my schedule and research. I'd be lost without her."

"That's exactly how I feel about Sandi, my secretary. She's more of a PA, actually. I made sure when I took this deal that she was part of it." She took a large sip of her iced tea. "What are you working on now?"

"The Civil War." Morgan opened the door to his office. Dusk was falling, so he put on a light. The room was surrounded by windows, giving a feeling of space and comfort. A large desk rested against the wall, with his laptop given a prominent spot. Oak file cabinets stood along either side of the desk, which was littered with papers and several books, one left open, with passages highlighted in yellow.

Rebecca was taken aback by the portrait that hung on the wall over Morgan's desk. She recognized the handsome face; it was a slightly more world-weary version of her lover.

"Looks a lot like me, doesn't it?" he asked.

"Uncannily so," she remarked.

"It's an ancestor of mine, one Matthew Justin Devereaux. He lived at Belle Chanson during the time of the War Between the States."

Rebecca wanted right then to tell Morgan that she knew all about Matthew Devereaux.

"There's an interesting story about him," he said, staring at the portrait. "He fought, believe it or not, for the Northern side."

Rebecca pretended surprise. "He did?" Oh, why hadn't she told him before? Now it was too late for explanations.

"Yes. It made him something of an outcast around here for quite a while, or so my grandfather told me. I hope to find out more about him when I get access next week to Matthew's private papers."

"His papers?" she asked, her voice barely above a whisper.

"My grandfather kept them in a safe-deposit box. He didn't want them to be lost, misplaced, or damaged. It was his way, he said, of preserving the past. He was very proud of his grandfather."

"What a valuable research source right in your own backyard, so to speak," Rebecca commented. Now she knew she had to leave, although she wondered what light those papers could shed, if anything, on how Matthew felt about Rachel.

Perhaps it was better that Morgan read Matthew Devereaux's account of the war, and possibly his love for an Irish girl lost to him, before he discovered their connection.

The faint ring of the timer signaled that dinner was ready, and they strolled back to the kitchen.

Later, replete with good food, Morgan dimmed the lights in the living room. An hour ago a cold front had swept through, dropping the temperature at least 20 degrees. Rain threatened as lightning streaked the sky in an awesome display and thunder rolled. The ceiling contained several large skylights which gave them a chance to watch nature's show in privacy.

"There's one more room I want to show you," Morgan said in a husky voice as they sat close to each other on his comfortable couch.

"The laundry room, right?" she joked, wishing that they had more time together.

"Not quite," he responded. "It's upstairs." Morgan directed Rebecca's attention to the spiral oak staircase that led to the loft above.

"So show me," she whispered, as eager as he for their eventual joining. She wanted the memory of this night imprinted on her brain and her body, so that when the lonely hours came, and come they would, she could have this at least for comfort.

He stood up, bringing her with him. Morgan kissed her, making her head swim with the power of his mouth. When he broke off the kiss, he murmured in a raw voice, "Come with me."

Taking her hand, he led her up the circular staircase.

There, a bed awaited them. Unlike the huge walnut Renaissance bed that dominated his bedroom in New Orleans, this was a simpler piece of furniture. It was golden oak, with Gothic designs. A quilt in shades of brown and cream was thrown over the bed; plump pillows covered in cream-colored cases were an invitation to relax and enjoy, which Rebecca had every intention of doing.

Rebecca swiftly shed her shirt, not caring that it would wrinkle, and unsnapped her jean skirt, letting it fall.

Morgan stopped what he was doing, his shirt undone, his jeans unzipped. She was beautiful, he thought. A golden goddess, Venus incarnate, come to show this mortal that paradise existed, that nirvana was indeed attainable.

He had proof of the divine power of love. It stood before him.

Rebecca licked her lips, feeling the heat of his gaze from several feet away. It scorched her flesh, sending a tremor through her body. Only this man had the ability to do that to her. Only Morgan could move her so that she craved him with a force previously unknown to her.

Trembling from the desire he brought out in her, Rebecca joined him, whispering, "Take me. Love me."

Morgan's response was to do just as she asked.

Rebecca eased her way from beneath his warm arm. Dawn was soon to break and she wanted to be on her way. It was tough enough to leave him. She wanted nothing so much as to crawl back in his bed and forget everything but this.

But she couldn't.

She stood there for a few moments, thinking how she loved him.

Good-bye, my love, she whispered silently. I hope that I can find the answers I need.

Gathering her clothes, Rebecca crept down the stairs, tears streaming down her cheeks. She dressed quickly, afraid that her resolve would weaken if she spent another minute in this house.

Jester, asleep on the rug, raised his head and looked at her.

Rebecca put her fingers to her mouth and said "Sssh" to the dog, praying he wouldn't bark and disturb Morgan.

The Lab seemed to understand, and he placed his head back on his paws, watching her as she crept along toward the back door.

Safely outside, Rebecca made a dash for the

main house, running across the dewy grass barefoot.

Less than an hour later, she drove her rented car down the long, oak-lined drive and out the gates, away from the spectres of the past.

Chapter Nineteen

"She's gone."

"What?" Morgan asked, his voice rising when he heard the news. "You're kidding, right?"

The other guests gathered for breakfast cast suspicious glances in the direction of Della and her cousin.

Realizing that they needed privacy, she ushered him through the etched glass doors to the smaller room, closing them behind her. "It's true, Morgan. I found a note that she left for me on the table in the hallway. Jack said he thought he heard a car early this morning. It must have been Rebecca leaving."

What the hell was happening? Morgan wondered, bewildered by the turn of events. This made no sense to him. They'd been so extremely happy last night. Everything had been perfect. What could have made her want to leave?

Della's voice took on a compassionate tone. "Rebecca left you a letter also."

Morgan looked sharply at his cousin. "Where?"

She produced the envelope from the pocket of her apron and handed it to him. "All I know is that Rebecca told me that she was sorry she had to go, but that something had come up all of a sudden."

Morgan's face wore an expression of stony pride, but Della could see the pain visible in his eyes. He loved this woman, that much was plain to her, and he was hurting from her defection.

"Do you want me to make you something to eat?" she asked in a vain attempt to take his mind from sad thoughts.

"No thanks, Della. I've lost my appetite."

He'd had one this morning, which was why he'd gotten dressed and come looking for Rebecca. He wanted to find out why she'd left so early, and suggest that they have a private breakfast in bed. The excuse of something coming up was too convenient and rang hollow to him.

"Morgan, you mustn't jump to conclusions," Della warned.

"What's to jump? Rebecca was here and now she's gone."

"It could be just as she said in her note to me—that she had to go."

Morgan stuck the envelope in the back pocket of his jeans. "I'll see you later, Della."

His long legs ate up the distance between the two houses until he was back in his own kitchen, pouring himself a large mug of strong black coffee, needing the stimulation of pure caffeine and chickory.

He took the mug and walked into his office. Morgan sat down at his desk and picked up a brass paper knife, slicing the envelope open. He paused before removing the contents, drinking a large amount of the coffee. Gingerly, he laid the envelope on the desk, staring at it.

Fear kept him from reading what it contained. His thoughts ran backward, processing images of them together for the last few days. Nothing seemed wrong. In fact, everything had been so right between them. Almost perfect. As if fate had designed this meeting, this loving.

He recalled every scintillating detail of their time together in bed. That too had been extraordinary. So complete and natural, as if they'd been lovers forever, with no awkwardness between them. No games. No pretenses. Just total honesty, and the pure passion that springs from unrestricted, unconditional love.

Morgan hadn't imagined that. No one could ever convince him otherwise.

Damn it!

Why?

Morgan picked up the envelope and took out a piece of stationery he recognized as belonging to the estate. It was ordered specially for Belle Chanson. A check floated to his lap. He glanced down at it, picking it up. It was made out for the exact amount of the clothes he'd purchased in New Orleans for her yesterday. Rebecca's Manhattan address and phone number were printed clearly on the check.

He put the check aside and read the letter.

Dear Morgan:

These past few days have been among the most special in my life. You've given me so much joy and happiness in such a short time that I can't begin to truly express my feelings, except to say that what we shared comes along, I dare say, once in a lifetime if one is lucky.

You're probably wondering why I didn't say this to your face instead of leaving you a letter.

I don't know. Maybe I'm a coward. What I do know is that I love you, Morgan. Very much. And that scares me, for reasons too numerous to mention.

So I'm asking you for time—time to think, to sort out all the things that are rattling about inside me.

Will you give me that time?

Please don't try to contact me. I won't be returning to New York.

There are some things that I wish I'd told you about when we first met. I didn't come to Belle Chanson just to research the area for my new show. Yes, that was a reason, just not the main one. Had I been honest with you from our first meeting, I might not be writing this letter to you now. I've never lied to you, Morgan, but I've omitted certain facts. Somehow, I think that you'll discover them on your own soon enough. Perhaps it might make a difference to you. I don't know.

Where do we go from here? I wish I had the answer to that.

Morgan fisted his hand, crushing the letter in the process.

Several hours later, Morgan entered his house in New Orleans, having visited the bank and picked up the contents of the large safe-deposit box.

While he'd wanted to book the first flight to New York and search for Rebecca, he knew that he had to respect her wishes, no matter what he thought of them. And to be truthful, he didn't exactly know what he thought about her request. She'd written that she wouldn't be in the city, so there was no point looking for her there.

Morgan debated calling Rebecca and leaving a message on her machine. But what would he say? I love you? Morgan quickly realized that he couldn't say he loved her on the phone and then calmly hang up. The words were too important to throw away on a machine. They had to be said face-to-face.

Maybe he should have said that to her while she was with him. He'd held back for fear of rushing her with the truth of his feelings. Now, in retrospect, perhaps he should have thrown caution to the wind and simply told her.

But if he merely sat around and wondered about why she'd left, he would go slowly mad. So work was his panacea.

After collecting the package, he could have turned his car around and returned to Belle Chanson. But he didn't want to see the pitying look in Della's eyes, nor did he want to see happy couples strolling the grounds, hand in hand, sneaking kisses. Besides, being here, in this house, where they'd first made love, would give him some sense of comfort. Memories were ghosts he could live with.

He walked into the living room, dumping the contents of the envelope onto the coffee table. Restless, he made his way to the jukebox and dropped in several quarters, perversely picking out the same songs she'd chosen.

Returning to the couch, Morgan sorted through the materials. There were a stack of letters, some splattered with mud, others with what appeared to be droplets of blood, tied with a velvet ribbon. The handwriting was feminine. There were two leather-bound journals with the initals *MJD* in bold, Gothic script stamped on the front. There were several old newspaper clippings, faded with age and delicate to the touch.

Next, he found a small velvet bag. He opened the drawstring and dumped the contents into his palm. What appeared to be a woman's handkerchief, with something wrapped in it, and a ring, obviously made for a woman. It was an exquisite piece of jewelry, fashioned, he assumed, for a betrothal ring. It was made of gold, with a large, rose-colored diamond in the center. A flawless stone, with delicate color. One of a kind.

Morgan unwrapped the hanky. It was embroidered, with a red rose and ivy trailing along one side as a border. A man's gold signet ring was contained inside. In delicate script were the entwined initals *M* and *R*.

Instantly, Morgan and Rebecca sprang to his mind.

Normally, Morgan eschewed jewelry, but this ring was something different. He slipped it on. It was a perfect fit, almost as if it were made for him.

He wondered which he should read first. The unknown female's letters, or his ancestor's journals?

Better the journals, he decided. They would keep him occupied and his mind off Rebecca.

Morgan opened the volume that had the number one written inside.

New Orleans—1860

I never knew that love would happen in an instant—that it was possible to fall as hard and as fast as I did. But it's true.

Several days ago I met a young Irish woman, new to our country, and since then, nothing has ever been the same for me. I cannot explain how, or why, it happened, but I love her.

These are uncertain times, with talk of war looming ever larger. The situation forces my hand. I cannot sit idly by and watch the country I love splinter into two distinct and separate countries, each with its own agenda, its own culture. I must do what I can to preserve our future.

But what of my future?

That question weighs heavy on my mind as I begin to dream about a life with Rachel.

"You're a superb horsewoman," Matthew Devereaux said, as they'd both taken their mounts and sailed over the broad jumps with ease.

Matthew and Rachel had made an appointment to ride, and a groom from Belle Chanson followed at a discreet distance. Ever since their first meeting, Matthew had wanted to spend as much time with the Irish woman as he could. He, the former carefree bachelor, was well and truly in love.

How had it happened? With one look, his world had stopped and then begun spinning anew. All due to a mere slip of a girl, for she was, in truth, more schoolgirl than woman. Young, gently reared, a virgin. Not the kind of woman he could tumble whenever he had the fancy. Rachel Gallagher was a lady. Foreign to passion's claim. Untutored in love's ways.

She was the kind of woman who deserved the wedding of a lifetime. Who deserved a perfect wedding night. As much as he wanted to make love to her, and that was an almost overwhelming feeling each time he was with her, Matthew understood that he wouldn't. To seduce her would be to violate Rachel's trust in him.

Oh, but how he imagined the way that night would be. It kept him from sleep some evenings, wishing that she shared his bed already, that they were husband and wife.

Yet that couldn't be. Not while this nation could be plunged headlong into war at any minute. Matthew hoped that cooler heads would prevail, but he doubted it.

And so he couldn't think about marrying Rachel until this issue was settled, once and for all.

"Is something amiss, Matthew?" Rachel asked, her delicate brogue sounding like music to him.

"Nothing," he prevaricated.

"You're certain?" Rachel patted her mare's neck, slanting a glance in Matthew's direction. "For if 'tis anything that I can help you with, I would do so gladly," she insisted.

He shook his head. "Shall we have our luncheon here in this meadow?" he inquired of her, shifting the conversation. "What do you think?"

"It looks most pleasant," she said, casting her gaze toward the river.

"Then let's do it," Matthew suggested, signaling for the groom to come. The boy carried the hamper that Angelique had fixed for them.

As soon as they were settled, Matthew insisted that the boy enjoy himself a little farther away, giving the lad the opportunity to fish.

The young groom needed no further encouragement and he headed his horse in the direction of the river while Matthew and Rachel sat down beneath a live oak, their meal spread out before them.

Sometime later, the warmth of the sun beating down upon them, Matthew, who lay supine on his share of the blanket, booted feet crossed at the ankles, inquired of Rachel, "What do you want?"

"What a strange question, Matthew." She looked down into his handsome face. "I want the same thing every woman does, I suppose. A home, a family, and the love of a good man." She sipped at her glass of wine. Between them, they'd consumed nearly half the bottle. "And what about yourself? Now what would you be wanting?"

Matthew raised his eyes. He'd shock her to the core of her soul if he told Rachel what he truly wanted. He could sum it up in one word. "*You.*"

But Matthew couldn't say that—and he wouldn't. He was older than she, wiser, more adept in the ways of the world.

"Well," she asked, a smile on her face, "will you tell me or should I guess?"

"Tell me," he whispered.

"I think you're a man who wants more of what he's had," she observed.

"Now what do you mean by that?" Matthew demanded, intrigued by her comment.

"Simply put," Rachel stated, "you've a life that allows you to sample all the best it has to offer. You like that, and you'd want that to continue. For yourself and for your family. You respect the tradition of your ancestors, though you are not shackled by it. You wish sons to carry on the Devereaux name and heritage. A wife who would fit in with your plans, one who would provide you with the children you want.

"There, have I summed it up correctly?"

Matthew smiled. "We want the same things then, Rachel, don't we?"

" 'Twould appear, sir, that we do."

Matthew checked his gold pocket watch. It was getting late, and he ought to take her home, for as much as he was enjoying the afternoon spent in her company, he couldn't take the chance of damaging Rachel's reputation. Someday he'd like to come back here, after they were married, and make love to her in the green grass, shaded by the trees.

He called to the groom, who arrived several minutes later, his catch proudly displayed for Matthew and Rachel to see.

So much has happened since that day.

I have broken it off with Dominique. From now on we will be friends only. In truth, since first seeing Rachel, I haven't even slept with Dominique.

And I have won Rachel's heart, for she is now my affianced bride. She came to Belle Chanson to help with Marguerite, and it filled me with joy to see the woman I love in residence at my family home. One day it shall be her home as well. She is so near to me—yet so far, for there are rules that govern our conduct. I would do nothing to impugn her honor, much as I am sorely tempted.

Matthew sighed as he read the coded communique that Achille handed him. It had arrived by way of a drummer, come to call on the plantation to sell his wares. A few items had been purchased, among them a box of fine Cuban cigars for Matthew. The message was inside the box.

He would have to leave again. Striking a match and lighting one of the slim cigars, he burnt the paper with his orders, watching as it turned to ash.

Achille stood there, accepting a cigar from the wooden box. He slipped it into the pocket of his shirt; he would save it and smoke it later, perhaps tonight, after making love to Angelique. "When do we leave?"

Matthew blew out a circle of smoke. "Early tomorrow morning. You know what to include for the journey."

Achille smiled and inclined his head. "It will be done," he said, leaving the room.

Matthew longed to tell Rachel just what he was doing. To share this part of his life with her, so that there would be no secrets between them. Except that he couldn't. It could mean her life should she discover what was really behind his so-called business trips. No one in his family knew, though he was certain that his father suspected something. That way, should anything untoward befall him, no one could reveal anything about him or the operation. Only Achille was privy to the truth.

Matthew inhaled the smoke, blowing it upward to the ceiling. His mother didn't even know that her own brother was a force in the Underground Railroad; in fact it was his uncle who had introduced Morgan to a certain man in the government who proposed this venture.

For Matthew, it was a chance to make a difference, no matter how slight. As a well-connected Southern gentleman of wealth, power, and breeding, a man who could speak three languages, he could gain entrance to places no Northern-born spy could. He'd proved that over and over again. He was determined to do as much damage as he could to the growing Southern spy network, to root out the people he considered traitors to the Union, and to help end the war he knew was coming.

Matthew stood at his window, looking outside. He wanted to spare as much of his state as he could from the harsh ravages of war. New Orleans and the Mississippi were of vital interest to the Union. He couldn't bear to think of this place under siege, with troops from both sides wreaking havoc on the countryside.

So he did what he could—what he had to do.

Tomorrow would see him on his way to Texas, there to meet up with a Texan loyal to the Union, one Travis Reitenauer, who would help him find a stolen shipment of gold that was going to be used to buy arms in Mexico for the Southern cause. Word had come from a reliable source that the transaction was to take place very soon.

Once more he would have to leave the woman he loved behind. Each time it became more and more difficult to ride away from Rachel, away from the life he wanted.

But Matthew told himself that if he didn't continue to pursue this course of action, he wouldn't have a life to come back to.

And he was cautious. He had a reason to be extra careful—Rachel. For no matter what,

Matthew was determined that he would come back to her.

Thinking about her made him restless. Perhaps he could accidentally run into her somewhere in the house. And, if he was lucky, she'd be alone.

Matthew was in luck, he found, when he discovered his beloved in the library. They would be quite alone.

He watched her from the doorway. She was perched on a sliding ladder, several rungs up, searching for a particular book. He could see the lace-trimmed white pantalets peeking from beneath the informal skirt she wore, along with the white stockings and flat slippers. Tonight, for dinner, Rachel would wear more formal clothes, including a hooped dress, but right now he enjoyed the way the material clung to her legs, the way it emphasized her slim figure.

She reached for a volume that was just a little bit beyond her grasp and almost tumbled from the ladder.

Matthew was there to prevent her from falling, his strong hands about her slender waist lifting her down, ever so slowly, from her perch.

Rachel gasped in surprise. "Matthew," she said in a breathy whisper.

"The very same, my love," he pronounced, kissing her tenderly.

Rachel had no hesitation about responding, winding her hands about his neck, pulling him closer.

Matthew longed to lock the library door and shut out the world. This was all the world he wanted right now: Rachel, here in his arms. One day he would make love to her here, amid the books. He would enjoy tutoring the tutor.

Matthew removed his mouth from hers reluctantly. "I must leave here tomorrow. An unexpected business trip," he explained.

"Must you?" she asked, resting her head against his broad chest.

"I'm afraid that I have to."

"I shall miss you dreadfully," Rachel said, one of her arms draped about his waist, clinging tightly, the other placed over his heart.

"Will you?"

"Of course," she responded, leaning her head back and gazing into his face, letting him read the truth of her statement in her honest eyes.

"God," he whispered on a groan, "I love you, *chérie*. So very much." Matthew gathered her tightly to his body, his arms secure about her, wishing he never had to let her go.

"Should you need anything while I'm gone, do not hesitate to ask my father. You know my parents consider you their daughter now as well as Marguerite."

"I shan't have need of anything," Rachel said. "Just so long as you come back to me."

"I will."

The next morning Matthew was up early, before the first rays of dawn lit the land. He saddled a fast horse, wishing he were riding Cimarron instead, but a horse such as that was too distinctive to use. It was better to ride a nondescript animal that wouldn't be noticed. An average brown with no distinguishing marks.

Matthew smiled. He had used his horse's moniker as his own code name though, relishing the irony in that choice.

He checked the saddlebag, hiding away the Colt pistol he carried on these assignments. A knife was tucked into his knee-high black boots, and a derringer rested in the pocket of his buckskin jacket. Achille also carried a concealed weapon in his clothes. Matthew didn't like surprises, and believed in being prepared for any eventuality. He checked the crude map and hid it in the inside pocket of his jacket.

"Another cup?" Achille asked, indicating the small pot that Angelique held.

Matthew nodded, and Angelique filled the cup that Achille held out, then passed along to Matthew.

While Matthew and Achille were drinking their coffee, Rachel had sneaked out of the big house along the gallery and down the outside stairs. Unable to go back to sleep when she'd awakened almost a half-hour ago, she'd gotten up and seen Matthew walk toward the stables, followed minutes later by Angelique and Achille.

She had to see him once more before he left, so she ran through the dew-covered grass in the direction of the stables. Dawn was barely breaking, the first streaks of light filtering across the night sky, when she reached the stable doors, open slightly.

Matthew turned as the door opened further.

"Rachel! What are you doing here?" he demanded, albeit in a gentle tone.

"I couldn't let you go without saying goodbye."

"We said that last night."

"By all the saints, I don't care," she stated. "Please," she begged, "give me a minute of your time."

Achille and Angelique took the hint. "I'll take the horses and wait for you outside," Achille said, Angelique following him out the door.

Both Matthew and Rachel threw the couple grateful looks.

"You shouldn't be here, Rachel," Matthew admonished her, his eyes drinking in the sight of her clad only in a thin robe of wool covering her nightgown, the hem of which peeked out from beneath the loose wrapper. Her feet were bare.

"Promise me you'll take care, my darling," she whispered. "I shall think of you often, and pray that God keeps you safe in his hands."

Matthew hastened to reassure her. "It's just a business trip, sweetheart. Nothing more."

"These are dangerous times, Matthew," Rachel cautioned. "Be wary. And," she said in her most insistent tone, "come home to me."

"Always," he promised. "No matter how

long—no matter what, I shall always find my way back to you, my love."

Matthew swept her up into his arms for a deep, delightful kiss. Their mouths melded, each drawing comfort and strength from the other until Achille's gentle, discreet cough interrupted them.

"Daylight's coming soon. We'd best be off."

Matthew sighed. Achille was right. He couldn't afford to tarry any longer, much as he longed to.

He released Rachel and walked out the door, mounting his horse.

As he rode down the lane, Matthew turned his head and saw her standing there by the stable door in the morning mist, watching him. She waved.

He faced front again. Damn this war.

Chapter Twenty

War has taken its destructive toll on the land. No matter how noble and just the causes, it still hurts to see the results. So many dead or wounded. Men, still little more than boys—on both sides—their lives forever altered, their country forever changed.

I pray to God what comes after is worth the sacrifice.

Matthew poured another shot of whiskey into his glass, tossing it back quickly, trying to put out of his mind the horrific images that crowded into it—he'd seen battlefield images that were a stark contrast to the bloated speeches of the politicians on either side of the conflict.

He sat in his hotel room in Washington, waiting for orders. He'd arrived several days ago after successfully completing another mission, tired and weary of the constant subterfuge with which he'd lived these past few years.

The only fresh and beautiful things in his life were the letters he'd received from his beloved Rachel.

Damn! But he wished that she were here with him. Her sweetness could drive away the dark thoughts, the angry frustrations, the bitter despair.

How many times had he read and reread her latest letter? Matthew had lost count. By now he had it memorized.

> *My dearest Matthew:*
> *I pray that this letter finds you in good health and safe. Your family and I wait patiently for the day when you return to us, and this interminable war is finally over, so that everyone is back where they belong.*

It went on further, telling him all the news of Belle Chanson and its people, the gossip of New Orleans, and Rachel's observations. Her calm assessment of events intrigued him. How he would have loved to have seen Rachel's practical and generous heart at work with some of the small-minded people he'd met in his travels.

Matthew sipped at his whiskey, thinking about the meeting that he'd had last evening at the White House. What would Rachel have made of Abraham Lincoln? Matthew had been impressed with the quiet dignity of the man, and with the compassion he'd seen in Lincoln's eyes. The burden of this war weighed heavily on the president, and Matthew judged Lincoln worthy of the task. With Lincoln's guidance, the end wouldn't be as acrimonious as some in the government had suggested. They'd had a chance to talk alone for almost half an hour, and Matthew had come away with a sense of hope.

All this he'd written in his journal. Someday he wanted Rachel to read it, so that she could see just what loving her had meant to him. In the midst of this hellish nightmare, she was a shining star.

Matthew picked up the book, glancing at the last words he'd entered.

There are many things worth fighting for: love, honor, country; but the greatest of these, I know now, for me, is love. I can put aside all else save that if I must.

I have one last mission. Then I am coming home to you, my love. That I promise.

Four months later—New York State

Matthew had meant to keep that promise.

Circumstances had prevented him. His final foray had gone wrong. Investigating a nest of copperheads—Northerners sympathetic to the Southern cause—Matthew thought he'd succeeded in his mission until a double agent betrayed him.

Ironically, he was turned over to the very man he'd been hunting, the head of a ring of Southern spies who'd managed to inflict damage to the Union via robberies, sabotage, and even murder. This group used whatever means they could to justify the end result.

Matthew sat in a room, waiting for his jailer to pass sentence. He had little hope he would be allowed to live. To this group, he was a traitor to the Southern cause. A spy. And so the penalty would most likely be death.

He moved and pain shot through his body. Bruises covered a good portion of his flesh. He'd been severely beaten to coerce information out of him. When he hadn't delivered what they expected, he was beaten further. One of his guards had even put a pistol to his head and cocked the hammer, laughing as he squeezed the trigger.

The gun had been empty.

"I hope I get to do you," the man sneered into Matthew's ear now. "You rotten nigger-loving Creole son of a bitch." The man smacked Matthew across the mouth.

"How very brave of you," Matthew taunted, blood dripping from the cut on his mouth, "to say that when my hands are tied. Do you think that you'd be quite so brave if I were free?"

"I don't care, Mr. Fancy-man. You're the gentleman. Me," he spat a stream of tobacco juice to the floor—"I'd as soon slit your throat. That way we wouldn't have to waste a bullet on you."

"Come now, Johnny," said the leader of the group. "Is that any way to talk to our distinguished guest?" He walked over to where Matthew sat, bound to the chair. The man pulled up another chair and sat down.

"I guess you know why I'm here," he addressed Matthew in his silkiest tone. His was the voice of an educated man, from Mississippi, Matthew guessed.

"Why don't you tell me?" Matthew replied.

"First of all, you're not who you say you are."

"I'm not?"

That got Matthew another cuff to the mouth from the man named Johnny.

The other man smiled. "We know who you are."

"Enlighten me," Matthew said, bracing himself for the blow that didn't come.

"We have our own sources, my dear fellow," he drawled. He pulled out a paper from his jacket pocket. It was a rough charcoal drawing of Matthew, with his name scrawled along the bottom. He held the drawing up to Matthew's face so that Matthew could see it. "Nice, don't you think? Although the artist didn't have time to flesh out the picture, it is you, isn't it, M. Devereaux?"

Matthew remained silent.

"No need to confirm it, though I must admit that your guise as a gamester from New Orleans wasn't far from the mark. Even to the last name. Dominic." He stood, pacing about the room. He turned and faced Matthew again. "Allow me to introduce myself, sir. Capt. Bradley Martin, at your service."

The man laughed. "But then I suspect that you already knew that, Capt. Devereaux. No matter. What I've come to tell you is that you are a problem that needs attending to."

Matthew sat quietly, not saying a word as the man resumed his seat.

"You are what I despise most, Mr. Devereaux. A traitor to your own country. By rights, you should have offered your talents in this game to Louisiana, to our cause; instead you betrayed the land of your birth for the foolish notion of the grand and great Union." Martin produced another item from his pocket. Matthew's new signet ring.

Matthew inhaled sharply, his nostrils flaring. He'd woken up after his last beating to discover the ring was missing. He'd assumed someone had stolen it for the gold.

Martin tossed the ring into the air, snapping it up in his hand. "A nice item of proof, wouldn't you say, to provide to the Yankees?"

"Give it back," Matthew said.

Martin and Johnny laughed. "Can't do that, I'm afraid," Martin said almost regretfully. "I imagine your family will want it as a memento of their gallant son who died fighting for his traitorous cause. And to make it even sweeter, we have your journal to add, along with several letters from your lady friend. You won't be needing them any longer."

Matthew sucked in his breath at the casual way the man described informing his family of his demise. Oh, God, he thought. Rachel. Rachel.

"Your death will serve as an example to those who betray their own," Martin said matter-of-factly. "Think of what pain it will cause your family. Do you have a wife, Devereaux? A sweetheart? Imagine her discovering the man she loves is dead. How long do you think it will be before she finds solace in the arms of another man? Can you picture her with another man—maybe even in your bed, him spreading her thighs, mounting her?"

Matthew tried to shake loose his bonds, fighting against his restrictions.

"Ah." Martin sighed. "It would seem as though I've hit a sore spot. Too bad. It'll happen. You can count on it. Another thing to thank the Yankees for. But where you're going, it'll give you something to think about."

"Going?" Matthew demanded. Was this man playing some kind of sick game?

"You're too valuable a commodity to simply

385

destroy as one would a rabid animal, Devereaux," Martin explained. "You may be of use to me in the future. As a negotiating tool."

"But you indicated . . ."

"That you would have to die? Yes, of course. And you will." Martin smiled again. "Only you won't, actually. Tonight you leave for a place where no one will find you unless we want them to. Your people in Washington will be duly informed that we had to execute you as a traitor. All very simple."

Matthew imagined the hell that Rachel and his family suffered through believing that he was dead. And there was no way that he could refute the proof that would be sent to them.

A calm, gentle breeze floated through his cell window. While others died on the battlefields or endured the horrors of prison camps in the States, he languished on the island of Bermuda. He knew the island had been one of the havens for Confederate blockade runners, and he was transported to this place by one such runner. His hosts, as they preferred to be called, were a Charleston man and his British-born wife, whose estate he was confined on. Faithful to the Confederate states, they gave shelter to the band of intrepid runners whenever they were in port.

Matthew had tried, and failed, to get them to accept his word that he would not try to flee the island if they let him out of his single-room abode. He had no actual contact with his "hosts;" all meals were delivered by a mute servant.

Months passed and his hopes of ever leaving the island dissipated further with each new day. He sank deeper into despair as he imagined how this was affecting his family, and most of all, his darling Rachel. Had she indeed forgotten about him?

No, his mind screamed. She wouldn't. She would still be there when he got home. Waiting. He had promised her that he would come back, no matter what, no matter how long it took. He'd meant what he said. And Matthew knew that he would use whatever means he must to achieve that.

Rachel.

The thought of her kept him sane, kept him functioning. He made it through each day with her image solidly in his heart. It was as if she were there, whispering to him to hold on, to believe that one day they would be reunited and nothing would ever part them again.

Isolated, Matthew had no real knowledge of how the war was progressing, whether or not it still raged, or how his country fared. His solitary confinement was a daily test of his own mettle. He could see the ocean, hear the sounds of birds, see the stars, but he wasn't allowed to feel the sun on his skin, to ride a horse, swim, or communicate. His only form of recreation was books. He read and reread whatever his hosts spared him. Arcane texts, or garden manuals, it really didn't make much difference to him. It was a way to pass the endless hours.

And so Matthew held on as best as he could until the day came when Capt. Bradley Martin reentered his life.

Matt heard the lock turning and sat up. He'd already been served his plain breakfast, and it was too soon for lunch. Was today the day someone would give him a chance to go outside the four walls of his prison?

A short man walked through the door and into the small space. "Hello, Devereaux," the man said.

Matthew recognized that voice. He could never forget the man who'd condemned him to this existence.

"Martin," Matthew acknowledged, his voice sounding dull and flat to his own ears.

"My God, man," Martin shuddered, "you smell like a pig."

"It would seem as though you've arrived before Saturday then," Matthew concluded, "and therefore before my weekly bath." He coughed. "How very ungentlemanly of me to stink," he finished in his most sarcastic tone.

"Still the same, eh, Devereaux? I would have thought this time here would have broken that stiff-necked Creole pride of yours."

Matthew stepped out of the shadows. The man who stood before Capt. Martin was gaunt and very pale, with long, unkempt hair and a scraggly beard. His clothes were threadbare.

Coolly, Martin explained his reason for being there. "If you'll recall, I said that you could prove valuable one day. Well, it would seem as though that day has come to pass. You're to be exchanged for another prisoner of war."

"So," Matthew asked wearily, "the war is still on?"

Martin answered, "Yes."

Matthew had kept crude track of time while incarcerated. "What year is it?" he asked, checking to make sure he was correct in his assumptions.

"1864."

Rachel.

Matthew wanted to hit Martin, beat him senseless for all the wasted years he'd missed with his beloved, but he knew he didn't have the strength for any form of combat. What muscles he had were lax. Hell, just standing this long was taxing his reserves. Tired, he sat down on his cot.

"Why now?" Matthew questioned.

"Because you're my ace in the hole, Devereaux."

"How do you figure that?"

"You're still remembered fondly in Washington, especially in certain high circles of power. I contacted a few people I know there, friends who are sympathetic to the cause of Southern independence, and they discovered how much weight the name of Matthew Devereaux still carries. Enough that certain parties were interested in discovering if you were still alive.

"Through these other people, I was able to determine that if I could produce you, I could have the prisoner that I want, no questions asked."

"This person must be very special," Matthew said.

"My brother, Devereaux," Martin replied. "He's all I have left and I don't intend to see him rot in a Yankee prison for the remainder of the war. You're his ticket to freedom."

It would soon be over. Matthew wanted to yell for joy. Home. Back to Belle Chanson, back to his family, and most importantly, back to Rachel. This time for good.

The officer who escorted the Southern prisoner was a volunteer, a man who knew Matthew Devereaux. He waited in the designated meeting place, an out-of-the-way small hotel in Richmond, to make the exchange.

Martin arrived almost an hour late, with a thinner, paler Matthew Devereaux, whose long hair had been cut short, and his beard shaved.

"Paul," Matthew said when he entered.

The Union officer's eyes widened, then narrowed in disgust at what had been done to his friend. "My God, Matt," he responded, forgetting his own prisoner. "We thought you were dead."

"Almost," Matthew managed to say before he began coughing, "but not quite."

Paul Davis grabbed a pitcher of water that stood on a crude low bureau, and a glass, and poured Matthew a drink. "Here, it's not much, but drink this," he said.

Paul Davis, a lawyer by trade and a soldier by choice, snapped out a question to Martin. "Now are you satisfied?" He helped Matthew to a chair. "Take your man and get out of here before I forget we made an agreement."

Martin, his brother beside him, said in a cold voice, "Oh, we'll be leaving all right, but you won't." He pulled out his pistol and aimed it at Matthew and Maj. Davis.

"What?" Davis demanded.

"You really didn't think that I was going to let Devereaux go scot-free, did you?" Bradley Martin laughed, a sharp, nasty sound. "Wrong. You're both going to enjoy the hospitality of the Confederate government for the remainder of this war."

This time Matthew did lunge for Martin, only to be stopped short by Davis, holding him back. "Don't be foolish, Matt. He's got a gun and he'll use it."

"Your friend is right, Devereaux. I will use it if I have to; however, you won't die, I can promise you that. You'll just wish you had."

"You son of a bitch!" Matthew snarled the words.

Martin checked his pocket watch, unconcerned. "Your escort should be here in the next few minutes."

Matthew silently cursed his luck. Just when he thought he would be on his way home, he'd come up against this bastard and his cruelty.

Rachel.

Forgive me.

I survived the hellhole known as Libby Prison in Richmond. Just barely. Unfortunately, Maj. Paul Davis wasn't so lucky. Pneumonia killed my brave friend within six months of our arriving there. His death will always weigh heavily on my conscience. If it wasn't for me, Paul wouldn't have been there. He deserved so much better out of life, as did the others who shared our plight.

By the time I was freed at the end of the war, I was little more than a ghost of my former self. I was so sick, being actually more dead than alive, that I was placed in a hospital for complete rest and care.

Whenever he awoke, Matthew noted that the same nurse seemed to be at his side. If he needed anything, she was there with a ready smile and a gentle touch. She washed him, fed him, dressed him, read to him, and even held his hand. Her hair was blonde, and occasionally Matthew confused her with Rachel, thinking his beloved was there with him.

One day, almost four months after he'd entered the hospital, Matthew came fully alert and remained that way for most of the day. His appetite was returning, and he'd gained back about 15 pounds on his excessively lean frame. The nurse was there with some mending in her hands when he opened his eyes.

"Who are you?" he asked.

"My name is Julia, Capt. Devereaux." Her accent was soft and very Southern.

"You're always here."

She gave a slight laugh. "It just seems like it," she said.

"No," he argued. "I think that you've been my guardian angel."

Julia put down her mending. For the first time, Matthew noticed the wedding ring on her finger. "Aren't you confusing me with the woman whose name you constantly called out: Rachel?"

"I spoke her name?"

"Repeatedly, Capt. Devereaux."

Matthew looked at her. "I think"—he smiled—"that you can call me by my Christian name, Matthew. It isn't as if you don't know me rather well by now."

A charming blush rose in her cheeks. She had blonde hair like Rachel, and her eyes, he noted, were blue. But neither were the exact shade of Rachel's. She was older than Rachel, too, he guessed. In her late twenties, he supposed.

"Shall I fetch you something to eat?"

"I am rather hungry," he answered.

"Good," she replied. "It's a sign that you're doing better. The doctor will be pleased." She rose from her chair. "I will return shortly," she promised, leaving him alone.

When she did, Matthew overheard a man in the next bed discussing something with the man beside him.

"Could you repeat what you just said?" Matthew asked.

The other former soldier looked at Matthew. "I said it's a pity that ol' Abe is dead."

Lincoln was dead? No. It must be some other person the wounded soldier was referring to. "Which Abe are you referring to?"

"Hell, man, there's only one that was president. Why, Lincoln, of course."

When Julia returned she found Matthew lying in bed, his cheeks wet with tears. "What's wrong?"

"I just found out that President Lincoln is dead."

"I'm sorry," she said sympathetically.

"He was a good man," Matthew said.

"I think so," she agreed, placing her tray on the table beside his bed. "He didn't deserve to die like he did."

"How?"

"He was assassinated."

Matthew's eyes closed in pain and she touched his hand in a gesture of comfort.

"Did they get the killer?"

"Yes." Julia fixed the pillows behind Matthew's head so that he could sit up straighter. She laid a napkin across his bony chest. "It would have been better for us had he lived. Without Lincoln, I fear what the victors may do to us."

Was she aware that he was a Union soldier, or had she assumed that because of his speech, he was a Confederate officer?

He looked down at his thin frame. "I doubt that this *victor* is going to be doing much of anything for a while."

Julia dipped the spoon into the soup, carefully feeding it to Matthew. "If you're wondering if I know that you're a Union soldier, Capt. Devereaux—Matthew—I do. It doesn't make any difference to me," she explained softly. "I'm a nurse. You're my patient."

"Thank you."

"No thanks are needed, Captain."

"What does your husband think about your angel-of-mercy work?" he asked, swallowing another spoonful of the soup.

Julia's eyes darkened with sadness. "I'm a widow."

"I'm sorry."

"He was a good man who died fighting for what he believed in."

"As did far too many good men on both sides," Matthew added.

"That's true," she agreed.

"Are you from this area?"

"Yes. I'm a native Virginian," she responded proudly. "My family on both sides have been here since before the Revolutionary War."

"So have mine, in Louisiana," Matthew informed her, then added, "well, almost as long."

"Then you have family there? Is Rachel your wife?"

Matthew smiled. "I hope to make her my wife when I return. It's been so long, and they were all told that I had been ex—killed years ago."

"Then imagine how thrilled they will be to see you come home. I wish that some miracle could bring my Blake back to me alive." She wiped his mouth. "I think it'll soon be time to trim that beard."

"I'd rather be clean-shaven, if you don't mind."

"I can arrange that," she promised. "Now, let's finish this, shall we?"

Matthew got stronger each day. When Julia volunteered to write to his family for him, he declined her offer. He didn't want them finding out from a letter, and thinking that perhaps it was someone playing a cruel joke on them. No, better to wait and then telegraph later when he was able to travel. He did, however, have her write to Paul's family for him, telling them how brave their son was, and that he died a hero. Small consolation, Matthew knew, but it was the best that he could do.

Julia was his constant companion, and became his trusted friend. They shared memories of the lives they had lived before the war. She helped him adjust once more to life, to getting up and about. They walked, with Matthew regaining his health gradually, until finally the doctors at the hospital pronounced him fit enough to leave.

When he heard the news, he wanted to share it with Julia first.

"Have you seen Mrs. Baker?" Matthew asked the doctor.

"She didn't come in today," the older man replied, making notes on Matthew's case in his notebook. "Under the weather, I think."

Matthew got Julia's address from one of the other nurses. After getting dressed, he decided to walk there since it was only a few blocks away.

He found it easily.

She seemed surprised to see him at her front door. "Matthew, what are you doing here?"

"I've got good news. May I come in?"

Julia noticed her neighbor watching the scene from her window across the street. "Please," she said and ushered him inside.

She was nervous, he could tell. It was in the way she moved, the way she sat so stiffly in her chair.

Matthew began to feel awkward. "The doctor told me that I could go home this week. Isn't that wonderful?"

Her voice was soft, barely above a whisper. "Yes."

"I was hoping you'd be there to share my good fortune, and when you weren't, I just had to come and tell you."

"I knew."

"You did?"

She nodded her head. "Dr. Mason told me yesterday. You must be so happy."

"Of course I am," he acknowledged. "Finally I can go back to the life I was supposed to have, and put all of this behind me."

Julia smiled at him. "I wish you a safe journey, Matthew."

"Would you consider coming along? You don't have any family left here, and I would love for you to meet mine. Stay at Belle Chanson for as long as you like."

"I can't," she said.

"Why not?"

Julia answered him simply. "Because I love you."

Matthew was dumbstruck. He hadn't even realized.

"So you see, it really wouldn't be a very good idea for me to accompany you, to be there when you have your reunion with your fiancee."

"I didn't know."

"I'm glad of that, Matthew, for I wouldn't want to have your pity."

"My God, Julia," he said, "you would never have that. Believe me."

Julia rose, her hands stiff at her sides. "I think it would be better if you left now."

"Yes, I think you're right." Matthew didn't want to draw out her pain. He felt the guilt weigh heavily on his shoulders. He cared for her as a friend, but his heart was promised to Rachel. Were it not for her, he might have been able to love someone as kind and gentle as Julia, but he couldn't. Not in the way Julia deserved. Not in the way he loved Rachel.

He stood at her door, and before he left, he leaned over and kissed her cheek. "Forgive me," he murmured.

She gave him a bittersweet smile. "There is nothing to forgive, Matthew." Julia touched his hand. "Be happy."

As Matthew walked back toward the hospital, he believed he would be, at long last. After all, he was going home.

Chapter Twenty-one

Belle Chanson.

He was finally back where he belonged.

Matthew halted his horse outside the gates of his house, taking a deep breath. He'd sent his family a telegram, using his uncle's name, informing them that a surprise was coming. No hint that it was their long-lost son.

He'd arrived in New Orleans late last night, but instead of going to his house in the city, he took a hotel room, preferring to remain as anonymous as possible. Then this morning, he rented a horse from a local stable and set out for home.

And he was here now.

Matthew wasn't sure what he would find when he got back. So many of the places he'd passed had been damaged. So much had changed. Including him.

What would his family think? More importantly, what would Rachel think? She must be living with his family, for he had taken a walk early this morning to the Garden District, going to her home there. It was empty, with no sign of occupation. He stopped and inquired of a neighbor and was told that the Gallaghers had left the city several years before.

So that must mean that Rachel had chosen to wait for him with his family.

Suddenly, a familiar voice called out, "M. Matthew, is that really you?"

Jerome, one of the gardeners, shielded his eyes from the harsh glare of the hot sun, staring at the tall, mounted rider as though he were seeing a ghost.

"*Oui*, Jerome."

"But . . ." the astounded man replied, unable to believe his eyes.

"I know," Matthew smiled, "I'm supposed to be dead." He dismounted, holding out his hand, clasping the gardener's. "See, I'm real."

The old man broke down, tears coming freely. "It's a miracle."

"My family?" Matthew asked. "They are all here?"

"*Oui*, monsieur."

Matthew inhaled the fragrance of the wild roses that grew around the gates. "I guess I'd better go. I've kept them waiting for far too long," he said, remounting his horse.

He wanted to set the horse into a gallop, eating up the distance from the gates to the main house, but he forced himself to take it in an easy canter. As he went down the path, he noticed a huge marble stone beneath one of the largest oaks. Matthew directed the horse over to it and saw that the monument had his own name on it.

It was incredibly disconcerting to see one's own memorial. It was like a splash of cold water in one's face, forcing an individual to recognize his own mortality.

He would see it removed first thing tomorrow morning. He had his life back; he had his second chance.

Matthew heard the excited screams that came from a young, female voice. "Mama. Papa. Come quick." He looked up and saw a coltish figure waving on the gallery before she vanished. She emerged a few minutes later bursting out the front door of the plantation house, her feet flying over the dirt, yelling at the top of her lungs, "Matthew. Matthew."

Matthew jumped down from his mount and ran the rest of the way to meet his little sister. "Marguerite," he said through his tears. He swung her around, kissing her and holding her tight.

Marguerite cried, unable to let her beloved older brother go, clinging to him with all the strength she had.

They stood that way for several minutes, until Matthew glanced up and saw his parents standing on the steps of the veranda, looks of disbelief and shock on their faces.

Frances Devereaux, tears clouding her eyes, grabbed hold of her husband's hand. "Eduoard. Is it really he? Oh my God! Is it really our boy?"

Eduoard, his own eyes misting considerably, could only nod his head, for his throat was too constricted to talk.

Matthew took hold of Marguerite's hand and pulled her along with him as he hastily made his way to his parents.

"Mama," he said, holding out his arms.

Frances leapt into her son's embrace, shuddering from the impact of feeling Matthew's arms around her. It wasn't a dream. It was real. Achingly real. Her son was alive and here. The unexpected answer to unvoiced prayers.

When his mother was finally able to let him go, Matthew clasped his father into a mutual embrace, each man reluctant to break the reconnected bond. "Papa," Matthew said, choking back the tears.

"When we received that telegram from your uncle in Philadelphia, I never thought it would mean that you were alive. He only said it would be a surprise. A surprise?"

Matthew admitted, "I sent the telegram. I didn't want you to find out that I was alive in such an impersonal way."

"How?" his mother asked, touching him once

again as if to make sure she wasn't hallucinating.

"Why?" his father demanded.

Before he could answer their questions, Matthew had one of his own. "Where's Rachel?"

Marguerite started to say, "She's mar—"

Frances shushed her daughter. "Marguerite, go to the kitchen and get your brother something to eat. Now."

Marguerite pouted, and her mother gave her a warning glance.

Matthew sensed that something was very wrong. "Marguerite, I would like something cool to drink, if you would, *ma chère*."

Marguerite happily dashed off to do his bidding.

Matthew faced his parents, saw the look they exchanged. He repeated his question. "Where's Rachel?"

Frances ached for the pain her son would soon face. She wet her lips and decided to be honest. "Matthew, Rachel's married."

Matthew's hands fisted automatically. He inhaled sharply. "No," he said adamantly.

Eduoard stepped in. "It is true, son. We were told you were dead. Rachel refused to believe it, at first, as did we all. She never gave up hoping that you would come back to us. She waited and waited." Eduoard cleared his throat. "We encouraged her to put the past aside and go on with her life when we saw how much the man obviously cared for her. She was young, and

405

had her whole life before her. There was nothing to be had from waiting forever." He swallowed. "Or so we thought."

Matthew stood as still as if he were carved from the same marble as his monument. He couldn't believe what he'd heard.

"Rachel loved you so much," his mother asserted. "I think," she voiced her opinion, "that she still does."

"He's a good man, Matthew," Eduoard put in.

"You know him?"

"He was a Union officer, part of the army stationed here, responsible for New Orleans. In fact, it was Capt. Fraser who told us of your death."

Matthew demanded, "Where is she now?"

"Rachel moved away," Frances said.

"Where?" Matthew demanded again, his voice strangely flat.

"Rachel went to her husband's farm in Vermont."

So far away, Matthew thought. But not far enough.

Frances read correctly the determined look in her son's eyes. "It's over, Matthew. Let it go."

"It'll never be over between us, Mama."

"You have to let it be," she urged him. "Rachel has a child." Frances saw Matthew's eyes widen slightly in shock. "You cannot destroy the happiness she's managed to make for herself."

"What about the happiness we planned on

having? What about the children we wanted?"

"Perhaps it wasn't meant to be."

Matthew kept hearing that line repeat itself in his brain as he and Cimarron galloped across the land. He rode his horse to the point of exhaustion for both the animal and himself. He finally stopped after they jumped the last wooden fence, getting off his lathered horse, cursing against fate.

Rachel.

He thought about seeking her out in Vermont. About walking up to her front door and demanding that she see him. About telling her husband that he had a prior claim. That Rachel belonged to him and with him, now and forever.

No power on earth could stop him.

Except himself.

Matthew recognized what exchanging wedding vows would mean to a woman like Rachel, what having that man's child would mean. It would be a bond she couldn't break. Maybe another woman could toss one or both aside when her former love stepped unexpectedly back into her life. But not Rachel. His mother had tried to tell him that.

And no matter how much he wanted to deny what his mother had said, Matthew knew she was right. Rachel wouldn't have taken her promise to love, honor, and cherish lightly. Even if she didn't love this man as much as she had him, she would keep her vows.

Matthew could damn his own honor to hell, but he couldn't destroy Rachel's. He loved her too much for that. So much so, in fact, that he would condemn himself to a life without her, without the greatest love of his life.

"*Rachel!*"

Matthew screamed her name in agony.

Someday.

Somehow.

If not now, then another time, he vowed. My soul will never know peace until we are finally together. You must know that, Rachel. Wait for me.

It was late and Frances Devereaux was unable to sleep. So much had happened today. After dinner she had gone to the little chapel she'd had built recently and made her prayers of thanksgiving. She also prayed for guidance for her son, for she feared Matthew would rashly set out on a path that would lead to ruin for all concerned. She begged God to spare her son any more pain, and to give him direction.

As a mother, she wanted to spare Matthew further pain. She wanted only what was best for him. That should have been Rachel.

She slipped out of bed, careful not to wake Eduoard. Donning her robe and slippers, Frances carefully opened and closed the door. Some instinct led her to Matthew's room.

Frances eased the door open and saw the

empty bed. The sheer bed curtains were pushed back, and fluttered in the breeze. The gallery doors were open. A glowing light and the smell of fine cigar smoke indicated where Matthew was.

"Matthew."

At the sound of his mother's voice he spun around. "I thought you were asleep."

Frances joined him on the gallery. "I tried, but it was impossible."

They stood in companionable silence for a few minutes until Frances made the observation, "If I go to sleep, I'm afraid I'll wake up and find that this has all been a dream."

Matthew smiled and brushed the knuckles of one hand across his mother's cheek. "It's no dream, Mama. You can go back to bed and when you wake in the morning, I shall still be here," he assured her.

"And what about the day after that?"

He raised a black brow in puzzlement. "What do you mean?"

"Rachel."

He ground out the rest of his cigar under the toe of his boot. Matthew placed both hands on the railing and leaned over, staring out into the night. "It's over," he said, his voice grim.

"Are you sure?"

Matthew gripped the railing tighter, his head bowed. "She's chosen a life without me, and I must accept that."

"And have you?" Frances knew her son, knew

409

the depth of his love for this woman.

"Yes." Matthew stood up, relinquishing his hold. "I have no other choice. As much as I may want to go there and bring her back here, it won't work. It would be different if Rachel came to me. Then, nothing and no one could ever force me to give her up." He sighed deeply. "But she won't come. And I can't ask her."

"I think that's very wise of you, darling. You've both been given a second chance at a new life. You mustn't spend your life wondering about 'what ifs.'"

Frances yawned. "Oh my, I do believe I can sleep now."

Matthew kissed his mother's cheek. "*Bon soir*, Mama," he said.

"Good night, my darling," she responded, making her way back through the open doors, leaving him alone.

Matthew stood there for almost a half hour more.

Finally, exhausted, he walked back into his bedroom. Earlier his mother had given him his belongings from the *garçonnière*, including the torn rosary she'd found lying at the memorial site, and the signet ring Rachel was given by Capt. Fraser when he informed her of Matthew's death. Matthew picked up the ring from the night table and slipped it on, curling his hand into a tight fist.

He could never truly say good-bye to Rachel. Never.

I waited to write to her, for what could I say? Rachel, I want you? Rachel, leave your husband and son and come back to me? Rachel, I intended to keep my promise? Rachel, why the hell couldn't you have waited a little longer?

So I did the only honorable thing I could do. Not what I really wanted to do, certainly not what my heart wanted, but the expedient thing.

Matthew eased back into his former life, finding it had been jumbled and tossed until only a few things remained the same. Many of the families he knew had lost sons, husbands, fathers in the war. His own cousin, Alain, had been killed at Shiloh. Men he'd hunted with, ridden with, played cards with, drunk with, filled the cemeteries. So much change had been wrought—and at what a price.

Months passed, and Matthew worked diligently from sunup to sundown, trying to keep his mind away from bitter thoughts and useless dreams. He even managed to pass some hours without thinking of Rachel.

However, tonight she was once more on his mind. Just yesterday his mother had received a letter from her, announcing the birth of her second child. And today a package he'd ordered almost four years ago had arrived from England. It had been delayed because of the war and the subsequent blockade of most Southern ports.

The irony was another twist of the knife in his heart. It was the real engagement ring he had meant to give Rachel. A rose-colored diamond, in a setting of pink gold. A one-of-a-kind ring for a one-of-a-kind woman. He was even going to have their wedding rings inscribed alike: *Toujours*. Always.

Matthew drank the rest of the whiskey in his glass before pouring himself another generous measure. His mother had arranged a dinner party this evening, with several suitable females present. Matthew knew just what her game was, for this was not the first time. They were there for his inspection, so that he might consider one of them for the possible position of his wife. Even his father had been dropping broad hints that Matthew needed to think about the future, about maintaining the Devereaux name.

He thought about the girls who had come tonight, and shuddered. One was a giggly, insipid schoolgirl; another was a flirt; the third was simply boring. None could hold a candle to Rachel.

He always came back to Rachel.

"Matthew."

"Good evening, Mother."

"So it's Mother now, is it?" Frances inquired, coming into the library where her son had taken refuge.

"Have they gone?"

"Yes."

"Good."

"Matthew, you've got to make an effort or you will never find a wife."

He shot his mother a cool glance. "I'm not looking for one."

"You should be."

"I thank you for your concern, *Mother*, but I can find my own bride, when *I'm* ready."

"And when will that be?"

He raised a brow. "I didn't know there was any rush."

Frances Devereaux decided to be honest with him. "She wouldn't want you to be alone, you know."

Matthew turned his back on his mother.

"You can ignore me if you will, but you can't ignore the truth."

"Which is?"

"That Rachel will never be your wife."

"I know that," he said wearily, downing the whiskey.

"You won't find a wife in that bottle, either."

"So now I'm a drunk?"

"No," Frances responded, "you're not. You could always hold your liquor quite well, Matthew," she pointed out, regarding the half-empty bottle with dismay. "It just seems as though you're holding a lot more of it lately."

"So what if I am?"

"This isn't like you, darling." Frances walked closer to him. "It's been years since I've heard you laugh, Matthew. I recall that you had a beautiful, rich laugh." She paused, as if temporarily lost in memories. "Life must go on. Your father and I want to see you happy again. We'd love to have children running about this house again. That'll never happen if you don't let go of the past, or try to love again. It doesn't have to be the way you loved Rachel." Frances laid her hand on his stiffly held shoulder. "I never could have loved another man as I love your father. I understand that kind of love, really I do."

"Then leave it be."

"I wish I could," she replied. "But I can't ignore the fact that you're hurting."

"Parading a gaggle of simpering sweet things before me won't stop the hurt."

"I never thought it would stop it," Frances said, "just maybe dull it a little."

"You can invite all the unattached females in New Orleans and every parish in Louisiana, for all I care, Mama, but it won't change the fact that I love Rachel."

Frances's patience had worn thin. "Fine," she snapped. "Feel sorry for yourself. Continue to drift through life if you wish, drinking more and more. I wash my hands." She turned and walked away from him, but before she left the room, Frances delivered another sobering thought to her son. "Rachel wouldn't have wanted you to waste your life, Matthew. The man she fell in love with wouldn't have let that happen."

Matthew heard the door close and he poured

himself another large whiskey. But as he raised the glass to his lips, he stared into the bottom. His hand shook, splashing the contents of the tumbler onto the cuff of his shirt.

He slammed the glass onto the table.

His mother was right. He was wasting his life. Rachel had made a new life for herself without him and he must do the same. Matthew had the welfare of the family and Belle Chanson to think about. He would be 33 on his next birthday. High time he had a wife and family of his own. It wouldn't be the wife of his heart, or the family he longed to create from that love.

Very well then. So be it.

Matthew sat down at a nearby desk and pulled out a sheet of paper from the drawer. Dipping his pen in the silver inkwell, he took the first step.

So began my correspondence with Julia Baker.

We exchanged letters for almost a year before I decided to ask her to marry me. I had been totally honest with Julia, for I respected her too much to be otherwise. She knew that I had loved another woman, that I was merely fond of her, and that I wanted a wife and children.

I invited her to come to Belle Chanson for a visit.

She did, and never left. We were married in a quiet ceremony with only my family in attendance, as we both wished.

Julia has given me so much, enriching my life beyond all expectation. Even now she carries my child within her. I am a contented man. Yet I cannot deny that there are times when I look at her and I wish she was Rachel. That when we make love, I pretend it is Rachel I hold in my arms, Rachel I possess, Rachel who will bear my child.

That is my secret, and one that I will never yield except to this journal. For within these pages I must keep faith with myself.

And that candor makes me acknowledge that as happy as I am, as wonderful as my life is, I still dream of being reunited with my beloved Rachel. If not in this lifetime, then perhaps in another, for I love her beyond all barriers that exist between us and that love.

Wait for me, my love, and never forget.

Chapter Twenty-two

Morgan closed the journal, astounded by the story he'd read there.

It was a chronicle of a man's life: of hope and despair, of love and loss, of heaven and hell.

And what touched Morgan the most was his ancestor's overwhelming belief in the power of love—that nothing could defeat what he thought possible—that someday he and his Rachel would be united.

Rachel Gallagher Fraser.

Rebecca Gallagher Fraser.

Morgan's thoughts spun wildly through his brain. Coincidence?

Somehow, he thought not.

Could that be what Rebecca was referring to in her ambiguous note? Did she know about the love affair? Was that really why she'd come to Louisiana? To visit the actual place where it happened?

Morgan rose from the couch, raking a hand through his hair. He felt the pain of Matthew's loss of the woman he loved as keenly as he felt his own. His great-great-grandfather's words had touched him on so many levels.

Could it be true?

Was Rebecca related to Rachel?

A sobering thought struck Morgan then. Were he and Rebecca doomed to repeat the mistakes of the past? Was that why she'd left?

Morgan examined the ring he'd slipped on earlier. His index finger traced the intertwined initials. He remembered Matthew's description of Rachel—she'd had blonde hair and blue eyes, like Rebecca. She wrote, like Rebecca. Both he and Matthew had fallen in love at first sight. Then there was the portrait of Matthew that hung in his office. It could have been a portrait of an older Morgan.

Night had fallen, and when Morgan looked at the clock, it read 10:35 P.M. His stomach rumbled, and he realized that he hadn't had anything to eat all day. He supposed he could fix himself a can of soup. That was a far cry from what his original dinner plans had been. Tonight he had planned to ask Rebecca to marry him. He'd made up his mind when he awoke that morning before he discovered that she'd left. Morgan knew it was impulsive, but he didn't care. It had felt so right. He wanted Rebecca as his wife. He wanted to be her husband. He wanted that connection—he wanted forever with her.

Rebecca was his chance of a lifetime and he didn't want her to slip from his grasp.

But she had.

In less than a week she had altered his world. So few days to have made such a dramatic difference in his life.

But she had.

It was crazy.

It was love. Pure and simple. A love stronger than anything. A love he couldn't afford to lose.

He glanced at the bundle of letters tied in the violet ribbon. Rachel's letters to Matthew.

Morgan flipped a switch on his stereo, flooding the room with the plaintive sounds of a sax as it wailed its song. It was a local jazz station, playing just what he wanted to hear—music with a blues flavor. Music that expressed the tormenting ache of loneliness that almost overwhelmed him.

Memories crowded in on him. If he closed his eyes he could see them there, on the floor, loving with abandon. He could hear her laughter, smell the tantalizing perfume she wore.

It was complete seduction—body, mind, and soul—beyond the point of no return.

Morgan sat back down. Food could wait. Carefully, he picked up the bundle of letters and untied the velvet ribbon. His hunger forgotten, he began to read.

Rebecca entered her house in Vermont, a deep chill settling over her. She'd been unable to book a nonstop flight back home, so she'd had to make a stopover in Chicago for several hours.

The chill wasn't confined to Rebecca's skin—it went deeper, directly to her heart.

Weary, Rebecca set her suitcase down on the kitchen floor and glanced around the empty room.

Had it been only a few days that she'd been gone? God, it seemed like a lifetime.

She was exhausted, both physically and emotionally, worn out from coming face-to-face with a force so unique and all-consuming, something she both welcomed and feared—love.

She missed him.

Rebecca dutifully checked her phone messages. A call from her parents; another from Nicole; one from her agent telling her that the network loved the proposal that she'd faxed and that the project had a green light; the last one was from Ben, telling her that he and Ally had decided to get married in June. She listened to Ben's voice, brimming with happiness, and a touch of wistfulness.

No messages from Morgan.

Had she really expected there to be one? After

all, she'd just left this morning.

Maybe he'd called her New York number?

Rebecca dialed it, checking her messages there. No luck. Just the same old same old.

Her note was specific enough—do not try to get in touch with me. She had made it very plain that she wanted Morgan to leave her alone. Obviously he was going take her at her word.

Rebecca realized how quixotic that sounded, and she didn't care. She stared at the phone for several minutes, expecting to hear it ring. Wanting to hear it ring. Needing to hear it ring.

And of course it didn't ring.

She could call him.

Feeling like a fool, Rebecca grabbed her case and marched down the hall and up the stairs to her bedroom. Throwing the case on the bed, she opened it, removing the contents. She paused when she encountered Rachel's nightgown. She laid that aside for the moment.

When she was finished with the rest, Rebecca checked the empty case again. She went through her makeup bag. Her great-great-grandmother's locket wasn't there. Panic began to set in. She'd lost it.

Rebecca tried to recall when she had last worn the gold locket.

Her hand flew to her mouth. Morgan had removed it before they made love, sticking it into the pocket of his trousers. It was probably still there.

She'd lost both the locket and her heart to

Morgan Devereaux. Without thought, without care, without shame.

Well, it was too late to worry about either now. What's done is done, she determined.

Rebecca quickly stripped off her clothes, tossing them aside, and donned her great-great-grandmother's nightdress. It felt smooth and soft against her skin, making her think of Morgan's hands caressing her flesh, soothing and stroking with his magical touch.

Oh God, she wanted him. Right now. So much so that it hurt.

She looked at her empty bed; Rachel's quilt was folded at the foot. How much nicer it would be if only Morgan were there waiting for her, his arms opened wide to gather her against his hair-roughened chest.

Had she made the right decision? Granted, she'd thought so at the time, believing that it was better to put some distance between them. She figured that she would be able to put things into perspective.

Yeah. Right.

Rebecca slipped into the bed, stretching her hand out across the unoccupied space beside her. Unable to bear looking at the empty spot, she snapped out the light.

She missed him.

Morgan had fallen asleep on his couch, having read all of Rachel Gallagher's letters to Matthew. They were poignant, honest, and stirring.

He could feel the palpable emotion that ran through each one of them. She had loved Matthew Devereaux as much as he had loved her.

When he awoke, he was stiff and in need of a shower. He knew why he hadn't climbed the stairs last evening and spent what remained of the night in his own bed. It would have seemed almost sacrilegious to have slept there without Rebecca beside him.

But it was morning now and the ghosts of the night were gone—or so Morgan thought as he stepped into his bathroom. As he opened the glass door of the shower, preparing to step in, his mind replayed its own visual recording—he and Rebecca in there two days ago. Steam had fogged the glass as he gently rubbed the soap all over her body, concentrating on lathering her breasts and belly, exploring as he went along. Echoes of her moans floated through his mind as he brought her to a shattering climax, then joined her, her hands clinging to his back, her nails grasping his slick wet flesh as they soared beyond the confines of an earthly place.

Morgan stepped in and lowered the temperature of the water jolting his already aroused body. He let the water sluice over his skin and laid his head back against the cool green tile.

She filled his thoughts. Rebecca—I can't let you go. Not now, not ever, he vowed. As Rachel was for Matthew, so you are for me—the love of my life. Morgan was willing to buck fate—or anything else he had to—to be with her.

Shaved and showered, he walked back into his bedroom, noticing the trousers he'd worn that night casually draped over the chair. He'd forgotten to put them away, and when he went to pick them up, Morgan felt the weight of something in the pocket.

Examining the contents, he found the locket Rebecca had been wearing the first time they'd made love.

He examined it more closely, walking over to the window to check the design on the front.

Morgan gasped when he saw it was the same as the signet ring he wore. An entwined *M* and *R*. Snapping open the lock, he inhaled a deep breath of surprise when he saw the miniature portraits inside. It was Matthew and Rachel, he assumed. They were dead ringers for he and Rebecca.

So she had known. She must have, he concluded, staring at the pictures.

But why then had she fled?

An idea had begun to grow within his mind. Morgan supposed that it was farfetched, but he couldn't shake it. It was preposterous but it persisted anyway.

Were they the chance for Matthew and Rachel to finally be happy, to eventually fulfill the love they should have had all those years ago?

Morgan recalled the words he'd read in his great-great-grandfather's journal. Matthew had promised Rachel he would return for her, to her. No matter what. No matter how. Was he the instrument of Matthew keeping that promise? Was Rebecca Rachel's chance to be reunited with her former love?

Morgan snapped the lid of the locket shut.

He walked over to the night table and picked up the phone there, rapidly punching out a phone number.

"Hello. I'd like to speak to Lt. Tommy Shaunessey, if you wouldn't mind. Yes, I'll hold, and please tell him it's Morgan Devereaux calling."

Morgan smiled. He waited until he heard the familiar voice come over the line. "Tommy. Good to talk to you. Yes, we will have to get together sometime soon. Uh-huh," Morgan said. "Dinner would be nice, but it'll have to wait. I need your help, if you can," he explained, "to locate someone, off the record."

Fax machines were a wonder, and a convenient blessing, Morgan thought later as he fed the information into the machine in his office. He had told Tommy he had an address in Manhattan for Rebecca, and asked him to also check Stowe, Vermont, for any listings there, since that was where Rachel Gallagher moved when she married Barrett Fraser. It was a long shot, but Morgan thought it worth the risk.

Jester raised his head from his paws and watched Morgan as his master picked up the phone.

Morgan was taking another risk, betting heavily on the power of love. It could all blow up in his face, but he knew he couldn't afford not to try.

Satisfied that the exclusive jewelry shop had what he wanted, he placed his order and asked for special consideration to rush the request.

The owner, whose family had done business with the Devereaux family for generations, assured Morgan that he would have what he wanted without delay.

Morgan swiveled in his seat, calling Jester to him. He ruffled the dog's fur, looking down at his pet. "I think it's time you had a partner, boy. Another dog for company, preferably female. What do you say?"

Jester barked in agreement, as if he really understood what Morgan was saying.

Morgan laughed. "Of course, we're going to have to add on to this place, because it isn't going to be big enough for our expanding family, Jester. Or," Morgan considered, "maybe it's time for another house altogether. We'll see," he said, a wide smile on his face.

He heard the back door open and close. Morgan took a guess at who was there and he was proved right.

"Hello, Della."

She stood there, a concerned look on her face. "How are you?"

"Do you believe in fate?"

"What has that got to do with how you are?" she asked, puzzled by Morgan's question, especially since he chose to ignore hers.

"Just answer me."

"I suppose so," she responded, shrugging her shoulders. "Why?" This was an unexpected turn of events. She'd come here expecting to find him morose and withdrawn; instead, he seemed to have discovered some inner wellspring of happiness.

Morgan picked up the locket from the top of his desk and snapped open the lid, handing it to Della. "Look at this," he commanded in a soft voice.

She picked up the piece, staring at the images inside, gasping in surprise. "It's you and Rebecca," she said, her gaze returning to Morgan. "When was this done?"

He raised a brow. "I'd hazard a guess and say over a hundred and thirty years ago."

Morgan didn't have long to wait for Della's reply. "What are you talking about? Is this some kind of joke?"

He shook his head. "No. It's Matthew Devereaux and the woman he had intended to marry, Rachel Gallagher."

"Oh my," Della responded, blinking in surprise. "I could have sworn . . ."

"That it was me and Rebecca," he said, removing the locket from her hands. He stared at it before snapping the lid shut. "I know. When I saw it, I was, to put it mildly, flabbergasted."

"Where did you get it?"

"Rebecca left it in my house in New Orleans. I discovered it there this morning."

"This is a little too weird," Della observed.

"It's a long story and someday I'll fill you in on all the details, but right now I have a favor to ask of you."

"Sure."

"Watch Jester for me. I'm going out of town for a few days."

"How long?"

Morgan leaned back in his chair, an enigmatic smile on his face. "For as long as it takes," he replied, "to win a lady's heart."

Rebecca needed someone to talk to, having spent the day after she returned to Vermont in a creative frazzle, unable to work, unable to concentrate. She called Nicole late that night, asking her friend to come over the next morning.

Nicole arrived early that day, bearing breakfast: some fresh bagels, cream cheese, and homemade preserves. As they devoured the toasted bagels, Nicole listened to her friend's story—all of it, including the abbreviated version of the splendor Rebecca found in Morgan's arms.

"So what are you going to do?" Nicole asked, sipping her coffee, her gaze focused on her friend.

"Go back to him," Rebecca replied. "I told Morgan that I needed time to think, to get some kind of perspective." She gave a roll of her eyes. "My God," Rebecca said, "I haven't been able to think of anything else. He's in my mind, my heart, my soul."

"Sounds like love to me," Nicole said with a happy smile, taking another bite out of her bagel.

"But it scares me," Rebecca stated.

Nicole sighed. "Honey, it scares most of us sometime in our lives. That's life." She refilled her coffee mug. Rebecca might not be anyone's idea of Susie Homemaker, but she sure could make one helluva good cup of coffee. "What scares you," Nicole observed, "is that this man got under your skin. Morgan got in."

Rebecca flashed her friend a wary look.

"Didn't he?"

Rebecca nodded. "Yes. Like no one ever has. But what if we're doomed to repeat what happened to Matthew and Rachel?"

Nicole put her cup down and addressed Rebecca in a sober fashion. "Have you ever considered the possibility that you and Morgan are the chance they never had? That you and he are the heirs to a love that never died?"

"Have you ever considered writing, Nicole? I might have a staff position for you," Rebecca said.

"No, I let the people with talent take care of that," she said with a light laugh. "Seriously, you should think about it. If you love him as much as I think you do, you can't afford to let a once—or in this case twice—in a lifetime feeling pass you by."

Rebecca did consider her friend's words all that day. Nicole was right. She was letting fear of the unknown, fear of losing, stop her from reaching out with both hands to embrace the best thing that had ever happened to her—Morgan Devereaux.

Hadn't she felt as though her heart had been torn from her chest and left in New Orleans? What beat now inside her was merely a mechanical device that kept her body stable. She existed. Loving Morgan had heightened her senses, sharpened her perspective, taught her that love was indeed the greatest risk, capable of providing the greatest rewards.

She loved him.

And she was damn well going to show him.

Rebecca went to her phone and dialed her travel agent. "Yes, hello," she said into the receiver, "I know that I had to cut short my trip. It couldn't be helped. But I want to go back as soon as you can get me a flight to New Orleans."

She waited, tapping her foot on the floor. "Nothing till tomorrow afternoon?" Rebecca sighed. "Oh well, guess that will have to do," she said. "I'll take it. You've got my credit card number, so just put it on the plastic. Thanks."

It was all arranged. Tomorrow she was going back to Belle Chanson—back to Morgan, where she belonged. The rest of the details they could work out later.

Her decision made, she could take the remainder of the day and start the paperback she'd picked up in the airport bookshop, another one of Morgan's.

Morgan eased the rental car along the lane, hoping he was right. Tommy had come through for him, finding the Fraser home in Stowe. Maybe he should have called, but he didn't want to take a chance that such a call could possibly make Rebecca bolt once more, this time to someplace where he couldn't locate her. Morgan prayed he was right, and that she'd come here thinking he wouldn't find her.

This was the house. Lights were on inside, so he knew that someone was home. Slowly he turned into the drive, but he didn't go all the way up. Parking the rental car, he got out and walked the rest of the way on foot. In the outside pocket of his jacket he carried the locket; in the inside pocket he had Matthew's ring for Rachel. He'd removed both from his carry-on flight bag after landing in Burlington.

Morgan stood before the door, smelling the scent of wood burning. He lifted his head and saw smoke rising from a chimney. There was a slight chill in the evening air. A fire on such a night would be nice, especially if one had the woman one loved in one's arms, he theorized.

Oh well, Morgan supposed if he wanted to put it to the test he'd better get inside.

Rebecca thought she heard knocking. With a touch of the remote to her CD player, she softened the volume, listening intently. There, she heard it again, stronger this time. Someone was at her kitchen door.

She got off the sofa and made her way to the kitchen, throwing on the outside floodlights. "Who's there?" she asked cautiously.

"A man who loves you," was the reply.

Morgan.

Stunned, Rebecca unlocked the door, pulling it open. "Morgan," she repeated, this time aloud in a shocked tone.

He walked in and without further ado, swept Rebecca up into his arms and kissed her, slamming the door shut behind him with his foot.

Firelight played off his bare frame as Morgan sat up.

Rebecca lay on the quilt, which had been hastily removed from the sofa and tossed onto the floor by her earlier. Morgan had carried her into this room, and they couldn't wait. Clothes had been torn off in a frenzy as mouths clung and devoured, as hands roamed and discovered. Now, replete for the moment, Rebecca savored the joy of loving Morgan.

"You left something behind when you abruptly departed," he said, getting up to pick up his jacket. It lay in a heap on the plush sofa, buried under her terry robe. Nearby, her nightgown was strewn over the coffee table, hiding the paperback copy of his novel. His white sweater lay next to it.

Rebecca admired the symmetry of his lean

body, blushing when she saw the faint marks her nails had made on his back.

He turned, the dark blue wool jacket in his hands, and watched as her eyes took full inventory of his body. He grinned. It pleased Morgan that Rebecca took as much pleasure in his body as he did in hers.

He walked back to her, bending down and holding out the locket. Carefully, he eased it over her head, letting it fall between her breasts.

It was then that Rebecca saw the signet ring on his finger. "Matthew's ring," she said.

Morgan nodded.

"So you know."

"Everything," he replied.

Then Morgan removed an object from the inside pocket. Slowly, he unwrapped the woman's handkerchief, revealing a gorgeous ring. The firelight made the rose diamond glow even brighter. He held it up, watching Rebecca's eyes widen. Letting the jacket fall, Morgan picked up her left hand and slid the ring onto her third finger. It fit perfectly, as he knew it would.

"Will you marry me?"

Rebecca wet her lips, tears flooding her eyes. There was only one logical answer to his question. "Yes."

Morgan sealed the promise of their union with a swift kiss.

Rebecca stared at the ring. It was the most beautiful thing she'd ever seen. "Thank you," she whispered.

"You're welcome, my love," Morgan said, gathering her into the security of his arms.

"I can't believe that you came for me," Rebecca said, her tears of joy soaking his skin.

Morgan ran one hand into her hair, gently tugging her head back so that he could look into her eyes, letting Rebecca see the truth in his heart. "I promised you I would, didn't I?"

Epilogue:
NO COWARD SOUL

"Are you ready yet, *chèrie*?" Morgan called from the bedroom.

"Just a minute," Rebecca replied, gazing out over the gallery railing. She took a deep breath, catching the mixed scents of the plantation. In the paddock she could see several horses prancing, including a big red one that reminded her of one from long ago. Jester barked a fatherly warning to one of his pups as his doggie mate enjoyed the warmth of the day while she nursed the rest of her litter.

Picnic tables had been set up outside, loaded with food and drink. Many of their guests had already arrived. Some had come by car, others by plane. She and Morgan had moved into the main house with Jack and Della so that Nicole and Mike, and Ben and Ally, could use their house. Belle Chanson glowed with life, as if the clock had been turned back over a century. No paying guests were allowed this week, for the rooms were needed for friends and family.

Rebecca and Morgan were celebrating their first wedding anniversary. Her hand gently touched her stomach. She had a gift of her own for Morgan, confirmed today. A new life was growing inside her, a mixing of their blood, a combining of their heritage.

They had so much to celebrate. Her new day-time drama was number one, knocking her old soap to number two. She'd added another Emmy to the collection housed in her New York apartment. Morgan had two books on the *New York Times'* best-seller lists: his newest had just made the hardback list—it was the Civil War book he'd written, loosely based on Matthew and Rebecca's story; and his latest in softcover was number one on the paperback list.

Morgan came up behind Rebecca, slipping his arms around her waist, nuzzling the bare nape of her neck. "God, one lifetime with you will never be enough for me. I love you more each day."

Rebecca leaned her head back, her right hand caressing the side of his face. On her left hand gleamed the gold wedding band. They'd had their ceremony right here on the grounds of Belle Chanson. Della had done her usual superb job in seeing to all the details, and Rebecca had a day she would remember as long as she lived. The perfect touch was the inscription Morgan had put into both of their plain gold bands: *Toujours*. Always.

And that was right, Rebecca knew. She and Morgan were meant for each other; it had always been so. Theirs was a love time could not erase, nor fate defy. Strong. Indomitable. For always.

I love hearing from my readers. Please write to me at:

P.O. Box 717
Concordville, PA, 19331 (SASE, please!)

I hope you enjoyed *There Never Was A Time*. Writers like challenges, and that's what this book was for me. Reincarnation is an interesting concept—especially when one thinks of it in connection with love. A love that breaks all boundaries, including time, to be fulfilled.

Thanks for sharing your time with me.

An Angel's Touch

Forever Angels

TRANA MAE SIMMONS

Tess Foster is convinced she has someone watching over her. The thoroughly modern woman has everything: a brilliant career, a rich fiance, and a glamorous life. But when her boyfriend demands she sign a prenuptial agreement, Tess thinks she's lost her happiness forever. Then her guardian angel sneezes and sends the woman of the nineties back to another era: the 1890s.

At first, Tess can't believe her senses. After all, no real man can be as handsome as the cowboy who rescues her from the Oklahoma wilderness. And Tess has never tasted sweeter ecstasy than she finds in Stone Chisum's kisses. But before she will surrender to a marriage made in heaven, Tess has to make sure that her bumbling guardian angel doesn't sneeze again—and ruin her second chance at love.

_52021-4 $4.99 US/$5.99 CAN

Dorchester Publishing Co., Inc.
65 Commerce Road
Stamford, CT 06902

Please add $1.75 for shipping and handling for the first book and $.50 for each book thereafter. NY, NYC, PA and CT residents, please add appropriate sales tax. No cash, stamps, or C.O.D.s. All orders shipped within 6 weeks via postal service book rate. Canadian orders require $2.00 extra postage and must be paid in U.S. dollars through a U.S. banking facility.

Name _____
Address _____
City _____ State _____ Zip _____
I have enclosed $_____in payment for the checked book(s).
Payment <u>must</u> accompany all orders.☐ Please send a free catalog.

Timeswept passion...timeless love

A LOVE BEYOND TIME

FLORA SPEER

When he is accidentally thrust back to the eighth century by a computer genius's time-travel program, Mike Bailey falls from the sky and lands near Charlemagne's camp. Knocked senseless by the crash, he can't remember his name, address, or occupation, but no shock can make his body forget how to respond when he awakens to the sight of an enchanting angel on earth.

Headstrong and innocent, Danise is already eighteen and almost considered an old maid by the Frankish nobles who court her. Yet the stubborn beauty would prefer to spend the rest of her life cloistered in a nunnery rather than marry for any reason besides love. Unexpectedly mesmerized by the stranger she discovers unconscious in the forest, Danise is quickly arroused by an all-consuming passion—and a desire that will conquer time itself.

_51948-8 $4.99 US/$5.99 CAN

A Time to Love Again by Flora Speer. When India Baldwin goes to work one Saturday to update her computer skills, she has no idea she will end up backdating herself! But one slip on the keyboard and the lovely young widow is transported back to the time of Charlemagne. Before she knows it, India finds herself merrily munching on boar and quaffing ale, holding her own during a dangerous journey, and yearning for the nights when a warrior's masterful touch leaves her wondering if she ever wants to return to her own time.

_51900-3 $4.99 US/$5.99 CAN

Time Remembered by Elizabeth Crane. Among the ruins of an antebellum mansion, young architect Jody Farnell discovers the diary of a man from another century and a voodoo doll whose ancient spell whisks her back one hundred years to his time. Micah Deveroux yearns for someone he can love above all others, and he thinks he has found that woman until Jody mysteriously appears in his own bedroom. Enchanted by Jody, betrothed to another, Micah fears he has lost his one chance at happiness—unless the same black magic that has brought Jody into his life can work its charms again.

_51904-6 $4.99 US/$5.99 CAN

Dorchester Publishing Co., Inc.
65 Commerce Road
Stamford, CT 06902

Please add $1.75 for shipping and handling for the first book and $.50 for each book thereafter. NY, NYC, PA and CT residents, please add appropriate sales tax. No cash, stamps, or C.O.D.s. All orders shipped within 6 weeks via postal service book rate. Canadian orders require $2.00 extra postage and must be paid in U.S. dollars through a U.S. banking facility.

Name_____

Address_____

City _____ State _____ Zip_____

I have enclosed $_____in payment for the checked book(s).

Payment <u>must</u> accompany all orders.☐ Please send a free catalog.

Timeswept passion...timeless love.

TIME'S HEALING HEART

MARTI JONES

No man has ever swept Madeline St. Thomas off her feet, and after she buries herself in her career, she loses hope of finding one. But when a freak accident propels her to the Old South, Maddie is rescued by a stranger with the face of an angel and the body of an Adonis—a stranger whose burning touch and smoldering kisses awaken forgotten longings in her heart.

Devon Crowe has had enough of women. His dead wife betrayed him, his fiancee despises him, and Maddie drives him to distraction with her claims of coming from another era. But the more Devon tries to convince himself that Maddie is aptly named, the more he believes her preposterous story. And when she makes him a proposal no lady would make, he doesn't know whether he should wrap her in a straitjacket—or lose himself in desires that promise to last forever.

_51954-2 $4.99 US/$5.99 CAN

TIMESWEPT
PASSION...
TIMELESS
LOVE

The RELUCTANT VIKING

SANDRA HILL

"Picture yourself floating out of your body—floating...floating...floating..." The hypnotic voice on the self-motivation tape is supposed to help Ruby Jordan solve her problems, not create new ones. Instead, she is lulled from a life full of a demanding business, a neglected home, and a failing marriage—to an era of hard-bodied warriors and fair maidens, fierce fighting and fiercer wooing. But the world ten centuries in the past doesn't prove to be all mead and mirth. Even as Ruby tries to update medieval times, she has to deal with a Norseman whose view of women is stuck in the Dark Ages. And what is worse, brawny Thork has her husband's face, habits, and desire to avoid Ruby. Determined not to lose the same man twice, Ruby plans a bold seduction that will conquer the reluctant Viking—and make him an eager captive of her love.

_51983-6 $4.99 US/$5.99 CAN

Timeswept passion...timeless love.

TESS MALLORY

It is just a necklace, a gift from her grandfather. How can Victoria Hamilton believe that the heirloom will help her travel through time—until she finds herself in the sights of the most desirable Rebel soldier she can ever imagine? But even though Lt. Jake Cameron saves Torri from death on a Civil War battlefield, the clever beauty can't convince him that she isn't a spy sent to stop his mission. In the face of cruel reality, Torri and Jake dare not trust each other. Yet in the tender mercies of their hearts, they have no choice but to surrender to the overwhelming power of love.

_51976-3 $4.99 US/$5.99 CAN